F[illegible]MER

Duncan Campbell

Foehammer first edition

Published by Duncan Campbell 2014

v.150103

Cover design by Mike Coles.
ISBN 978-0-9931515-1-4

Dedication:

To Jaz, Geordie, Big Paul, Youth and Raven—and all those who have served.

Deadification:

Dear George and Tony. Don't think we didn't notice, and don't think we'll ever forget.

Prologue: What Lies Beneath

She is nearly at the divide, and the gray canopy is becoming clearer and brighter with every push. Soon she will be able to open her mouth and let out the pain in her chest. Bubbles rise around her, then the ceiling bursts open to a boundless blue sky and she is home. Two paddles take her to the rim where she reaches for the hardened crust. The edge breaks and powders. Extending her claws, she tries again, only to find the slab crumbling and falling into the sea. It is too early for this. The ground should be rock not slush. It is too warm.

At the third attempt she hauls herself onto the watery ice floe and starts to shake the chilling moisture from her fur. Once dry, she sets off across the snow and then suddenly stops. Lifting her head and opening her nostrils to the breeze, she turns inland and moves toward something in the ice.

There is old meat nearby. She starts to savor the scent of ripe carrion only to discover that it's hiding under something else. Something unknown.

As she moves closer a vibration disturbs her body. It is wrong. Sniffing hard, she is hit by a powerful insect stench and her muscles react. She finds herself turning and running with all her available strength. While she flees, she makes strong place memories. She remembers that with the food there is danger, something large and strong that wins fights and never loses.

Behind her, a jointed crab-like limb is protruding from a shadow in the melting ice. Fused onto the outside of this appendage, and trembling in the spiraling eddies of chilled air, are the sucked-clean bones of a human arm and hand.

The wind begins to strengthen and, as the ice-flecked gusts whip and whirl the snow from around its base, the long skeletal claw begins to move.

June

Chapter 1

The White House, Washington DC

There were three corpses on the left of the overview screen. Not just corpses. Corpses of corpses. Captain Ramez had watched his team neutralize them with brutal efficiency, but something about the way the slack-limbed guards had slumped to the floor had left him sad and empty. They'd once been men of training and discipline like him. But they'd been changed. There was no doubt about that. Their reaction times had been nonexistent. They'd hardly begun to raise their weapons to their dull, flaking faces when his men had taken them down.

After briefly inspecting the bodies, his squad had moved on and crossed the T-junction at the end of the corridor. They were only a few yards from the nanoscanner that marked the entrance to the Situation Room, and that was where the comms usually started to weaken.

As they approached the big tube, his hands clenched into fists and his determination pushed his remorse aside. His guys were *not* going to vanish in there. He was going to stay with them all the way. He'd doubled their radio strength and given them ear plugs to protect them from the trance effect. They were better prepared than any of the military units and were briefed to take it just a stage at a time. His department was going to solve the mystery of what had happened inside the White House and they were going to be recognized as the unsung heroes they were.

Jackson was leading the others in a slow crouch toward the emerald glow at the end of the machine. There was no need for any instruction. There were no faults in their movement or spacing and their actions were smooth and precise.

Soon they were all through, and the view from the leaders' cams showed him a long table dotted with papers and water jugs. He was beginning to get a sense of the size and layout of the room when the feeds rippled and the first icy fingers of anxiety started to squeeze at his stomach. Seconds later the images flickered and vanished and he was faced with a bank of black screens.

He cursed slowly and softly under his breath. The booster relays had been a long shot. Not even fixed cable could get a feed out of there. There was technology better than theirs built into the walls and the controls were out of their reach.

With a long sigh of frustration, he put his knuckle to his mouth and started to chew it.

The timer was already up to sixteen minutes and nothing had come back. No sound, no images and, even more importantly, none of his men.

He glanced over his shoulder at the rest of the team. He'd go in with them. Course he would. He wasn't the kind of commander to wait outside. Besides, he wanted to know. He was desperate to get a peek in there.

Seventeen minutes elapsed. Three more to go until the arranged backup. What could have happened to them in that time? Their ears were blocked and they were as sharp as scalpels. So where were they?

He took his hand from his mouth and caught a whiff of nasty-smelling saliva. He'd read somewhere that meant bad breath. Had the guys pulled back from him when he'd done the final briefing in the van? He was trying to recall the reactions of his men when the counter clicked over to nineteen and he was snapped back into the moment. One minute to go and he was thinking about his dental hygiene. Displacement thoughts. It happens. The mind wants to run away sometimes.

Moving gently from foot to foot, he started to get his legs warmed up. Deep down he knew that red team weren't going to appear in the next sixty seconds. He was going to have to go in there. He'd told himself he wanted the opportunity to get a look, but his body seemed reluctant. Cold sweat was sticking his shirt to his chest and his belly had tightened into a ball.

He was still searching for excuses to back out when his arm acted without him. He felt his hand go into the air and then sensed near-silent movement as his team lowered their visors. Twenty minutes was showing on the clock. He would take point. They would be alert and they would stay far apart. Didn't matter if it took all day. This would be the slowest, most cautious mission in the history of the force.

They were inside the West Wing, moving down a broad corridor lined with plaster columns. He had two behind him and three on the opposite side. They passed the bodies then moved across the T-junction and stopped in front of the scanner. Murphy and Blake were nearest and were signaling to go through. He raised his thumb. No harm letting them if they really wanted to.

Shivers wriggled up his spine as he stepped into the long, hexagonal tube. Something about the smooth plastic interior of the machine gave him the creeps, but in five long strides he was through the curtain of green light and onto the exit ramp.

His men were waiting for him, crouched against the inside wall with their weapons primed. This was it. This was the Situation Room, and this was where their knowledge started to thin.

All eyes were on him. He gave the ultra-slow signal and let the leaders get ahead. He'd keep the group thin. Worst-case he'd lose his point man, but the others would have plenty of time to react.

As they approached a pair of wooden doors at the end of the room, he noticed a scattering of dark circles on the carpet. Bloodstains. Now perhaps they should think about pulling back. In five minutes they could be out in the fresh air packing up the van.

He said nothing, and moments later they reached the end of the table and hunkered down on either side of the big mahogany slabs.

The polished timber concealed the staircase to a bunker, and they moved through slowly, covering every possible angle of attack before picking up the pace.

Next they came to the squeeze space, but it wasn't a problem. Turning sideways, they slipped through one by one and moved up to the reception room.

As they trod toward the gray metal doors, a distant whining noise started to drill into his head. It was strange because his ears were sealed. *Any sound would have to come through the radio system, and the feedback reducer would ... clean ... the ...* He struggled for a moment, smiling at his own attempts to remember some silly technical word that was no longer important. Anyway, the whistling wasn't only in his ears, it was in his skull and stomach too. All the hollow spaces inside him were vibrating.

As the piercing tone got louder, his shoulders dropped and his breathing deepened. He was certain that there was something safe and strong close by. He was going to meet the person in charge and they were going to give him all the answers he needed.

As they reached the doorway, the feeling of imminent reassurance got stronger. He couldn't remember where he'd met the guy before, but he knew that he was going to be able to make everything alright.

Stepping across the wide steel threshold, they found themselves in some kind of lounge area.

He watched his lead men moving in short, slow steps in front of him and smiled. There was something funny about the way their arms were swinging loosely at their sides. He'd always encouraged that, a bit of humor in the team. It was good for morale.

They passed sofas arranged around a vending machine and then trudged toward a thick yellow door that dominated the far wall. Murphy and Blake let their rifles fall from their hands and part of his brain hurt for a moment. There was something wrong about the way they did it.

His fingers opened and he dropped his. That was better. Leaving the bulky weapon lying on the carpet was strangely satisfying.

When he looked up, the two leaders had gone. They must have slipped through the big blast door to see what was on the other side. Lucky them. A glance over his shoulder confirmed that the rest of the guys had come in behind him. They were smiling too. Miller had lifted his visor and his eyes were dreamy and happy. What a great idea.

A flick of the catches released his own helmet, and he tugged it off along with his ear defenders.

A second sound came from the room in front of them. It was raw and oscillating and made him think of people with their mouths open. He wondered what it was while he dragged himself forward. *Come on, come on. Let's get in there so I can see this.*

He stepped through the steel doorway into some kind of long, wide hall. He knew there was a lot to see, but he didn't want to look up yet. The controller was just in front of him, and the thought made him shy. His boots were heavy but he managed to drag his way toward the figure and stop at its long, bony feet.

Now he would look up. Now he *had to* look up.

Above him there was a curved face made of some kind of ancient honeycomb. He longed to touch it. He wanted to feel the gnarly texture under his fingertips, but he knew he couldn't.

The big, domed head came toward him, and as the mouth moved closer to his nose he was able to make out ridging and chipping on the wet gray fangs. The points of the incisors grew larger until they were circles swelling in his vision. Then he felt pressure on his eyeballs. The gel of his corneas was pierced and the teeth pressed deeper into his skull. As he stood trembling he heard the high, wavering tone again. It was a scream. He could hear a man screaming. He suddenly recognized the timbre and pattern of the noise. *That's my scream,* he thought.

Chapter 2

Adrian "Cryboy" Eastman, New York, mid-June

Someone had started a new thread. A twitch of his finger broke a beam on his controller and paused his game of *Growth*. The words "Invasion Foothold" were blinking in the air in front of him. He already knew the gist of the contents and was aware that it would irritate him, but he opened the page anyway.

While he read, he reached out and tapped the candy wrappers that were strewn along the coffee table. He'd tossed down a protein bar with three mouthfuls left and still had a precise memory of where it had landed. He found it and took a bite while he finished the idiot's opening thesis.

The situation in the White House was due to invading aliens setting up camp and preparing to take over the rest of the planet.

He let out a snort of disgust. It was a rehashing of several older conspiracy theories and was full of gaps. There hadn't been any sightings of spacecraft, it didn't really explain the guards turning into half-deads, and it didn't give any intelligent ideas about what extraterrestrials would be doing in there. Worst of all, it completely ignored the Arctic path, and good theories didn't leave out bits of evidence just because they didn't fit. Someone needed to explain the weird video footage of the animals crawling across the ice and the strange events in Alaska and Russia.

He swallowed a mouthful of the banana-flavored snack and felt his hands tighten with irritation. Some of his fellow hackers were idiots. It was a shame, but he had to admit it.

While he chewed, he began to compile his own assessment. Three previously unknown creatures had been filmed traveling down from the North Pole in late May, with small clusters of sick people appearing along the way. The worst outbreaks had been at Fort Wainwright and the Kotelny naval base, both of which had been closed and locked down. Even weirder was the subsequent disturbance in the White House. Again, the majority of staff had become ill and the area put under quarantine. The shambling wrecks in all three places hadn't died, but they hadn't responded to any sort of treatment either. More importantly, no one else at any of the sites had since been infected.

He finished the bar and squeezed the wrapper tight in his fist. Why was nobody else interested in the anomalies? Snapnews and the other major channels never discussed how a virus could only be infectious for such a short time, or how it could be localized in three such diverse locations.

No, his theory made much more sense. There had to be a secret lab in one of the polar camps. Both the US and Russian military had teams up there to support the last oil extraction projects and someone must have got infected with a bio weapon. That was much more logical. But how did it get into the West Wing? And what was happening in there? Were they threatening the president or begging for a cure?

He tossed the wrapper onto the table. *Soon we'll find out. You can't keep data locked up. It leaks. It seeps out here and there and when it does we'll find it. We'll find it because we know how to look.*

He closed off the discussion thread and refocused on his game. Nine hours in and his carefully nurtured organism was beginning its first encounter with invading bacteria. He watched with increasing pleasure as the acidic defenses he'd built into the cell walls started to eat away at their attackers. *That's it. Defend. Defend then grow. Grow and you'll become invincible.*

It was nearly an hour later, and his amoeba had almost covered the entire virtual lakebed, when he sensed something and paused the action. There was an unusual, high-pitched hum that stood out from the collage of city sounds that his mind was compulsively monitoring.

Driven by a sudden intense curiosity, he stood and moved to the room-length window.

Pressing his face close to the huge pane, he scanned left to right. He ignored the regular shapes and looked for anything new and different among the lines of colored lights that blinked and shimmered along the rows of skyscrapers.

In the far distance, hedged in the canyon between two lines of buildings, a tiny rectangular shape came into view.

He grinned and started to step from foot to foot. It was a biplane. He loved biplanes. They could reach a really high angle of attack before they stalled. There would be beautiful spiral vortexes forming in the air around the wing tips.

The plane grew larger, rising and falling in unseen thermals as the single small propeller pulled it toward him. As it approached, he got a growing sense that this was some kind of a stunt or a joke intended for him. It had to be. It was coming right in his direction.

Fifty yards out it banked and turned toward the window. His rocking quickened and he slapped his hips with his palms. At forty yards he made out a figure with shiny black eyes and green fur strapped into the cockpit. It was a teddy bear just like his. This was definitely for his benefit. But who'd sent it and why?

The side of the plane caught a flash of light from a nearby building and he read the words *Cryboy Two* on the fuselage. It had his name on it! He stopped moving and stood transfixed, his hands opening and closing into fists as he watched.

Whoever had sent the thing was really smart. It was slowing with each turn, which meant it had to be powered by some kind of mechanical source, perhaps a super-strength elastic or clockwork mechanism. There'd be no emissions, so it would be undetectable by the authorities. It was also small and moving erratically, so analysis would pass it off as a large bird.

The aircraft made tiny adjustments until it was flying straight toward him, and then the wing-mounted machine guns released a puff of white smoke. *That's a warning,* he thought. Seconds later the weapons kicked into life and bullets sprayed the window.

He stood unflinching as the pellets struck, bursting on impact to leave splodges of green liquid on the glass.

He knew that the paint would contain substances only visible through the laminates. He was certain that it could only be seen from the inside of the apartment. Only by him. Another really clever touch, and exactly the sort of thing he'd think up. So who was showing off a new toy? His mind raced through the possibilities and kept coming back to the big West Coast hacking crews. They had the brain power and a ton of good reasons to want him on their team.

The plane fired its final projectiles and came straight at his head. As the balsa structure hit the frame and smashed into splinters, he flooded with two simultaneous emotions: immense joy at the spectacle the small aircraft had brought him and sadness that its existence was over.

Looking down, he saw the fuselage burst into flames and realized that all evidence of the machine was vanishing. There'd soon be nothing left but woodchips and ash.

That was slick. The coolest real-world stunt he'd ever seen.

There was a number written on the window. The spots were dribbling and fading, but the symbols were already etched onto his memory. It was an old-fashioned system: a bunch of numbers and dots. An IP address.

He leaped to a network machine and tapped the case. The reference produced a traditional opennet site—raw, unshielded and unproxied. In the root directory there was a neat little *read me* file. He opened it and started to process its contents. He liked the way they'd structured the data, and he liked the fact that they'd left everything unencrypted.

The first sections were a bit wild. They were claiming that all this had happened before and that there were historical documents that described people turning black-eyed and brain dead. There were links to scans of ancient scrolls, and when he'd checked them with consistency algorithms, he started reading. They were fascinating. Even more interesting was that in with the academic papers were bang up-to-date military and NSA files, stuff that normally would have taken months to crack.

There was a chat room set up, seeded and waiting with blinking expectancy. He began to post messages and the answers came straight back.

He talked to them all night, gripped by the strange project that this Dr. Weaver and his backers were setting up, and delighted that they recognized how much he had to offer.

Chapter 3

Sean "Jester" Solberg, ungated Chicago, late June

A cigar tube. He'd finally got it. It was like sitting inside a cigar tube. He tapped his cigarettes into the hubcap in front of him and enjoyed the satisfaction of being able to put a description to Jack's bar. The sheer ingenuity of the young immigrant who'd turned an industrial relic into a working hostelry was impressive. Jack had taken an angle grinder to the old tanker truck, and the ancient vehicle was now essentially a tunnel with living quarters at one end and a bar made of shopping carts at the other.

The counter was made of old road signs. A set of green highway exit markers ran from the doorway to the central partition and ended with a red octagonal *Stop* sign.

Jack didn't seem to have noticed the significance of this but every time Jester reached for more liquor and cigarettes the word shouted up at him, and he was able to silently mouth the word *no*. It wasn't exactly stand-up comedy, but it kept him amused. These days he took his entertainment where he could find it.

He smoked and drank silently. The smell of simmering rice added a starchy tang to the scent of smoldering tobacco, and the quiet was only broken by the occasional clank of metal pots and the rumble of plastic wheels on wooden slats.

Without taking his eyes from the TV screens, he reached for his shot glass and knocked back a mouthful of liquor. A man with a barbeque-sauce suntan was being interviewed in front of a Manhattan office building while the words *Canmore promises transparency* scrolled under his smirking face.

Jester swallowed and let out a long sigh. Senator Canmore was the man whose financial scandals were supposedly behind him. The guy whose best friends ran most of the banking sector and who happened to own the country's biggest security hardware company. There he was trying to convince people that if he was made head of the Interim Authorities he'd open up his business affairs to public scrutiny. But it didn't seem likely. Seemed like once he had the power he might just end up accidentally steering all the investigative committees in new and completely fruitless directions.

He started to stub out his cigarettes, grinding the tips hard into the makeshift ashtray before refilling his glass. With his eyes still glued to the TVs he coaxed out another pair of Marlboros and guided them to his lips. The program cut to a break, and while he sparked his lighter to life he felt a flash of irritation. There was that commercial again. The vaccine for the virus that didn't exist. It wasn't cheap either. But then if you were scared shitless, maybe the thirty-six monthly payments didn't seem so bad. If the suckers took a glance at the business pages they might notice that Canmore had an eighty percent stake in the company pushing out the cure.

He sucked in the flame and shook his head. *Fuck your virus. It's a bio weapon. No doubt about it. Some dick went to show it off in the White House and the thing got out. So how about a bit of honesty now?*

He was blowing smoke up toward the central manhole when a small compact Cambodian man appeared from the residential end of the tanker and approached the barrier. Using the side of a cart as a step, he nimbly cleared the divider and landed in front of the counter. He stood for a moment wiping his hands on the side of his pants and then stepped up to a carrier bag that sat on the end of the bar. "Okay. Now I look," he said in heavily accented English. Lifting the faded plastic, he pulled a book from the top of the pile then glanced up with a frown. "Green eggs?" he asked quizzically. "This cooking?"

Jester shook his head. He knew that Jack wasn't exactly the sharpest knife in the drawer, but he wondered how a picture of a crazy-faced cat in a hat could look anything like a recipe book. "No. Beginners. Kids," he said, pointing to the living quarters. "I was thinking … for Daniel."

"Oh. Thank you." Jack turned to seek out his son. "Daniel?" He held up the book. "This one for you."

The sound of plastic wheels accelerated and then suddenly stopped, and Jester stretched up to see a boy in mismatched pajamas sitting on a tricycle. The child studied the cover of the gift for a few seconds then looked away and started to turn his vehicle with big swings of his legs.

Jack turned the book reverently in his hand. "Where you get this?" he asked.

Jester jerked his head behind him. "The projects back of Mill Town. Still some good stuff there."

The barman put the battered volume on a shelf inside the partition and was teasing out the next title when a murmur of hushed voices reached them and they turned to stare at the doorway. A few moments later the bar's steps squeaked and a large silhouette loomed at the curtain. When a hand slid between the strips Jack started to walk toward the door and Jester turned and set his gaze deliberately on the TV screens in front of him.

Customers usually came in noisily, big groups of Cambodians or Haitians chatting and joking, before spending the whole evening nursing a single homemade beverage. This was different. These voices were too quiet and tight to be anything but trouble.

The floor creaked, and the visitors came in one by one. They were big men, moving slowly, and they'd stopped talking as soon as they'd got inside.

He tapped ash into the hubcap and then pushed it forward until a distorted image of the top of the room appeared on its surface. Three figures in hooded sportswear were standing surveying the bar.

Jack greeted the newcomers with a tip of the head. "Evening."

"Yo! You speaky English, Mister?" one of them asked.

Jester reached for his glass and tipped some guaro into his mouth. They weren't immigrants. They were from the city. And that was their spokesman. Cocky and loud.

"I can. Enough, yes," Jack replied. "What drink you like?"

The front man turned and asked his pals what they wanted. The rear couple shrugged and scanned the inside of the tanker. Jester saw them peer at the rickety shelves and then turn and look in his direction. They stared at him for a good few seconds before turning back to their companion. "Dunno. Coke, I guess."

So they were young. Dumb fucks. So used to bars with scanners they didn't realize they could get liquor.

"Three Cokes," the leader said aggressively.

Jack explained that he only had homemade cola, and they took it reluctantly.

After tasting it they snorted and then sniggered, but dutifully handed over a couple of bucks.

Jester was pleased to see his friend ignore the cash box and slip the money into a back pocket.

For the next few minutes Jack moved backward and forward giving the surfaces a dab with a piece of rag. He kept glancing back over his shoulder, and it was clear he was thinking about little Daniel, who was still playing somewhere behind the divider.

He wants to get him out of the way, and I don't blame him. This is going to turn bad. These guys are gathering points for a gang site. Jester flicked a glance at the group. *Yep, button camera. Fella in the middle's got his chest puffed out to get a good picture.*

Then it started.

The small guy stood and pointed a micro-pistol at Jack's head, and the man on the left swung himself over the counter.

Jack shrank back and blurted out a single word in his native tongue.

The jumper landed and grabbed him by the shirt, pulling the Cambodian onto his tiptoes and drawing back his fist.

"The green," he demanded. "All of it."

Jack shifted his gaze from the gun to his attacker while reaching vainly for a length of steel on the shelf behind him.

Jester grasped the neck of his beer, and when the big man gave Jack a shake, he threw it. The robber's fist had started to move when the bottle hit him on his forehead. He staggered backward and was still reeling when Jack's hand clasped metal and the wheel brace came arcing through the air. The man lifted his arm, and the rod hit him above the ear with a thud.

"Hey!" the leader shouted, waving his gun.

Jester cocked his head and smiled apologetically. *Yes. Two of us causing trouble now. And I was right. You were never going to use that thing.* Palming his shot glass, he swung from his stool and started strolling down the bar.

The guy tracked him with the gun, and Jester flashed his eyebrows as he approached. *That's it, dicksplash. Keep that ever so slightly shaking arm locked right this way. I wouldn't go for the chest though. I'd go for the head and empty the clip. Even then it ain't gonna save ya. Whatever you do I'll still rip out your heart and eat it. Just give me an excuse.*

The gunman scowled. "Yo! Clown. Where the fuck you going?"

That'll do. A whiplash snap. A sparkle of light and the glass hit the man in the left eye.

Jester was almost at the end of the bar. In the corner of his vision he saw the big robber reach the counter and brace himself to jump back over. The leader was moving the gun between him and Jack in fast sweeps when there was a creaking sound and his friend landed on the floor behind him, accompanied by the sound of smashing glasses.

Jester stopped and deepened his smile.

The young man found his voice again, shifting his weight from foot to foot while he dabbed at his face. "What the fuck you want, freak?" he demanded.

Jester's hand went to his mouth and very deliberately extracted a cigarette. He squinted at it for a moment and then lifted it to his ear and held it like a dart.

The leader's eyes narrowed and he started to squeeze the trigger on the little gun. "Fuck you!"

Jester threw and the man fired. The pistol went off with a sharp pop, but Jester was out of its path. His body had followed the trajectory of his throwing arm and was already hurtling toward his attacker.

The bullet hit the back wall and spun off, leaving the tanker's lining ringing like a steel drum.

The cigarette hit the man between the eyebrows and Jester's shoulder smashed into his chest. He let out a sound—half-curse, half-grunt—and then tried to lower his weapon. Jester had his wrist in both hands and squatted. A sharp jerk sent the man over his hip. He hit the floor with a crack and Jester kept him moving, rolling him toward the entrance and then extending a leg that sent him down the steps.

Jester tossed his attacker's pistol to Jack, who trained it on the two remaining men, and their attitude quickly changed. After spitting out a few expletives and dramatic threats, they slipped backward through the makeshift wall and joined their leader outside.

Jester moved to the curtain and watched them help their companion to his feet and set off up the road.

When they'd vanished over the brow of the hill, he turned and reassured Jack that they'd gone. The shocked bar owner let out a sigh of relief and started a tirade of profuse thanks.

Jester stopped him with a wave of his hand. He didn't want any gratitude. He hadn't liked them and would have chased them off anyway. They were the worst sort: bullies with weapons picking on a single unarmed opponent.

When he was sure that Jack had calmed down, he decided to go and watch the men cross gate. The nearest checkpoint was only ten minutes away and unauthorized access was difficult to pull off. Once they'd gone through, it was unlikely they'd come back.

He stopped just before the brow of the hill and squinted into the distance. The young men were just up ahead, striding toward the outer fence. As they neared the gate he heard some cries and shouts and spotted a fourth in front of them, crouching with a stick wedged in the gap.

Jester stopped and reached for his cigarettes. As the group approached the entrance they shot quick looks back up the road, but he stayed perfectly still and their nervous glances never found him.

When the last of the gang had passed through, the heavy springs slammed the door shut with a clunk. He watched them swagger between the tank traps toward the first checkpoint, flicked a flame to his Marlboros and took a long suck.

The whole event had been pretty unusual. The police usually kept a close eye on people crossing gate but things seemed to be loosening up. Maybe it was true, maybe Canmore had convinced the Interim Authorities to ignore anything that was going on outside the city zones.

He turned and set off back to Jack's. When he'd reassured the young bartender that everything was safe he'd start for home. There was a lot to think over and the solitude of his hammock would provide the best environment for reflection.

Just over an hour later, he found himself approaching the corner of the old foundry. Leaving the road, he picked his way through the broken masonry and rusting car parts down toward the warehouses. The scent of wood smoke gradually strengthened and he spotted yellow flames flickering through the glassless windows of a crumpled truck.

It was dinner time in Mill Town, and the Algerians were cooking something up. Probably a skinny rat on a bed of dispenser scraps. They'd share it with the Angolans and the Gambians next door. The dust-bowl people liked to eat together. It didn't matter what little bounty leaked from the city; whatever they found, they shared.

The slow melodic loop of an African chant started behind him as he moved down the hill and, not for the first time, he found himself amazed at how cheerful they were. He had to remind himself that this was their big chance, their fresh new start. It was better than watching their croplands desiccate and blow away on the desert breeze. Better than watching the last dribble of diarrhea drain the life out of their newborns as their womenfolk clutched them close and wept.

His mind drifted to his African missions, and the heat and smell of death came back to him. They didn't know it, but he'd seen the disaster that had driven them there. He'd been dug in outside their settlements overseeing the destruction of what he'd been told were terrorist training grounds. The politicians had claimed that he was making the US safer, but that hadn't turned out to be true. It seemed they should've spent some more bucks on stopping the whole continent from drying up and blasting away on the wind.

He reached the muddy ditch that ran in front of his building and jumped onto the hood of an old pickup. Rocking on his heels, he took a final look at the camp before beginning his climb.

Ten million of them turning up for supper had certainly caught the feds by surprise. The coastguard's exclusion force had kept them out for almost two days before they'd started slipping through. He didn't blame them for trying though. He'd have hijacked a bathtub to get out of there.

The six foot leap to the bottom of the cast-iron fire escape proved easy, and he started to climb, the railings flaking and crumbling in his hands as he swung up the flights of rusting metal.

At the top he sauntered through a graveyard of scattered car parts toward a shabby wooden structure. Here, hidden between the ancient air-conditioning outlets, there were some packing cases and a stretch of tarpaulin tied between two posts. With a well-practiced ease he threw himself into his makeshift hammock, settled his head and reached for his cigarettes.

As he smoked, he watched the searchlights on the city walls send caterpillars of pale-blue light crawling along the horizon and let his mind return to the events at the gate. Things were changing in there. First the administration had vanished and then a weird virus had broken out. For a while he'd watched from a distance but now the ripples had made it all the way to Chicago. It looked like their well-ordered society might be starting to fall apart and this gave him a lot to think about.

When he'd sucked his Marlboros to their filters, he flicked them into the breeze, crossed his hands across his chest and lay back to watch the clouds build and disperse in the dark plum sky. The wind brought sprinkles of warm rain to his face and then, much later, to his slow-closing eyelids.

Chapter 4

Dr. Julian Weaver, New York, late June

The guards nodded and then stepped back to let him slip into the bright open-plan office. He was quickly through the scanners and soon marching past the big cubist sculptures toward the back of the reception area. The feeling was good. The sensation of striding into the luxury building and being waved through security was something he could really get used to. Here he was important and respected. He was an expert hired to root out whatever was buried away in the West Wing, and it was clear that his ultra-wealthy employers had made sure that everyone treated him with respect.

As usual it didn't last. While he rose through the building the rush started to fade and cold tight doubt crept back into the pit of his stomach. The power he'd been given had come pretty speedily and he was certain it could be switched off even faster if he didn't prove useful. With the thought of a rapid firing growing in his mind, he straightened his back and started to run through his confidence-boosting mantra. *I am strong and in control. My posture is commanding, my breathing deep and regular.*

There was a moment of sinking deceleration, then a slice of light widened into a view of workstations receding to the far wall.

He made straight for his office, giving his analysts a brief wave before slipping inside. With his forearms resting on his desk, he sucked deep breaths into his abdomen until the knots of tension loosened and his shoulders lowered.

Blinking his eyes into focus, he started to stare at the racks of monitors that ran down the walls. It was all so new and different. He had a room the size of a tennis court and more processing power than a government department. It was ten times bigger than the cupboard he had at Columbia or the shared space he'd been given back in Oxford.

While he gazed at the banks of technology, he started to run through his goals for the day. The key concepts were self-assurance and authority. He was going to take command of the people around him and show them that their confidence was not misplaced.

In his first few weeks there'd been frequent mention of a leadership partnership. That perhaps a retired general would work alongside him to cast an eye over his mission plans. Luckily this chatter had faded away. He wanted to believe that as his government and business employers had got to know him they'd realized that he was more than up to the job, but he wasn't so naïve not to realize that there'd probably been other factors. One of the internal memos, that probably wasn't meant to have made its way into the central archive, noted that an ex-military man wouldn't be "clean" like he was. He knew exactly what they'd meant. He was a minor academic with no political ties or influence. An experienced army man would have contacts all over the Pentagon and a strong will of his own. They wanted to keep things quiet, and they wanted people who did what they were told.

It had taken some getting used to, but now he was going to make the most of it. Wonderful sums of money were moving into his bank account and he had the opportunity to be part of something really amazing. He needed to rise to the occasion and excel. He would deal with problems the way they did. He would stay solid and unwavering. He would speak in short sentences and then crack cynical jokes to prove that he wasn't daunted by what was going on or the importance of the missions.

Although his central screen was showing him a complex chart of his outstanding activities, he ignored it and pulled a tatty sheet of notepaper from under the ink blotter. Here he had scribbled his own *to-do* list in pencil, and he found the ability to doodle on the page and rub things out far more comforting than wrestling with the AI's vaguely patronizing interface.

This stage of his project was all about finding the right people and he had five ticks against the team he needed. The next row showed a tally on how many of these individuals had been successfully recruited, and this column contained only a single affirmative. His first hire had been his technology specialist, the gangly Mr. Eastman, who operated under the strange nickname *Cryboy*. The AI had advised him to recruit someone with this young man's abilities as early as possible. They'd predicted that he'd be able to quickly find the others, and they'd been right. The kid pretty much kept his own hours, but when you gave him a challenge, he took to it. The missions were dependent on resisting the creatures' trance effect and it had taken Cryboy less than a day to find someone who seemed to be able to protect themselves and others from hypnotism. Although this shaman character spent most of his time living with tribes in Africa, Cryboy'd also found out when he was going to be coming home.

Straight after that he'd tracked down a military patient who was immune to all forms of hypnosis. The problem was, after his release from hospital, this individual had disappeared. Vanished. They'd almost given up looking when they'd found some footage of him on a Chicago gang site. The crew were claiming that they'd killed him, but Cryboy had been certain that the corpse shot was a fake.

Since then, this pale and uncommunicative hacker had got really serious. He'd infiltrated or commissioned a bewildering host of drones, ships and satellites to scan for this Jester character and was confident they'd eventually find him.

The women had been easier. There was a Russian lady working in Switzerland who had the brute strength they needed and a girl in outer Vegas who the computers were convinced would keep the men working as a team. Because she was chipped, Cryboy had been able to hack into the Federal systems and pull off her personal data. The AIs now knew almost everything about her, but Weaver's own sense of decency had kept his browsing at a summary level. One thing was clear in his mind and made him uncomfortable though. Compared with the others, she seemed very young and very ordinary.

He looked back down at his list. In the next twenty-four hours they had to finalize the plans for recruitment. The simulations had made it clear that the requests had to be creative and attention-grabbing while demonstrating the resources that they had at their disposal. The result was three complex stunts and a fourth case of straightforward wording.

All of it made him feel uneasy. It was clear from the biographies that the men were difficult characters. If the first invitation didn't raise their curiosity then he'd have to visit them himself and resort to what would basically be begging, and that wasn't an option that he relished.

There was a flash of light from a terminal and he turned to see a series of heads revolving above his desk. This machine was monitoring the reactions to the Washington crisis and was the only one he'd allowed to project throw-images. The spinning torsos were part of a promotion for the reality program *Seduction Three.* The premise of the show was to take five engaged couples to a beach resort where a team of gigolos and temptresses tried to lure them into acts of infidelity.

He could guess what the voiceover was saying. People were meant to bet on who was most likely to succumb to physical temptation, and each of the couples was being given a harsh personality assessment designed to draw an emotional reaction. He understood why it worked but kept himself from getting drawn in by applying the same self-control he'd used in his youth to keep his gaze from the victims of car crashes at the side of the road.

He reached out and scrolled to the bottom of the page. All the main video articles were covering either the *Seduction* show or an ongoing celebrity divorce. There was nothing at all about the White House situation, and it had been like this for more than a week. The guards with the brain disease had been a temporary amusement. When it turned out that they didn't growl or chase people, the country had lost interest. The missing president and West Wing staff had drawn even less attention. After a few days of speculation about a virus, the story had gradually faded into text-only updates.

Filled with a restless frustrated energy, he stood and strode to the office's big window. Far below him, lines of city runners were crawling down the street, their tiny boxy shapes occasionally broken by the bulk of a limousine or electric truck. On the sidewalks, the people were a mass of distant milling blobs, and he found himself glaring at them with growing anger. *Your leader and his administration disappear and soldiers with a form of living death shamble around the West Wing. Does that not interest you, America? Are you not going to do something about that?*

A ping from his micro made him jump and spin around. He moved quickly back to his desk and let his logistics directors know he was ready. There was a morning of meetings ahead. For a few hours his mind would be filled with robot weapon assessments, and then they'd review the plans for the invitations and the delivery stunts would be set in motion. They had one shot to lure the potential team members to the office, and then he had one go at persuading them to sneak into the White House to capture a strange-sounding creature. Getting them to believe that such a weird entity really existed was going to be tough. He wasn't sure how he was going to convince them, and, even worse, he wasn't even sure that after several weeks of intense data analysis, he'd managed to convince himself.

July

Chapter 5

Helga, Zermatt, Switzerland, early July

The church hall was buzzing with a sense of repressed excitement. Somewhere behind the thick drapes, instruments were being tuned and children were conversing in hushed urgent voices. Helga allowed herself a small smile of pleasure as she absorbed the scene, then joined the line for the ticket desk. While she waited, her mind drifted to her recent exchanges with Svetlana back home and anxiety started to bubble in the pit of her stomach.

Things were going wrong again. A virus in some remote military base had made a load of soldiers sick, and there were rumors that the authorities were refusing them any medical treatment. Their families hadn't been allowed to contact them and the area had been locked down. It had been enough to trigger more antigovernment protests and during the unrest criminal gangs were stepping up their activities. Opportunists were making grabs for power and the money men were getting ready for war. The people had fought so long and hard to redistribute the nation's wealth, and it looked like it was all going to get stolen away again. There'd be more deaths and more displacement, and the youngsters would be the worst hit; they always were.

She turned to watch the kids rushing excitedly around her and was glad they were safe and healthy. Those involved in the production were dashing out to greet their parents, and she started to imagine what it must be like to put them to bed. Their faces would look so calm and peaceful when they closed their eyes and drifted off to sleep. She bet their mums and dads left them and went to watch TV, but how could they do that? Who cared about the politicians and the soccer? She wouldn't go. She'd stay all night, watching their feathery eyelashes fluttering while their chests rose and fell. The moms didn't know what they'd got, or how lucky they were.

The scene around her softened as her eyes watered and glazed. *But maybe that's me too: the lucky one; the survivor.*

The group in front of her peeled away and she found herself looking at Frau Schneider from the school board. The small lady in the tweed suit greeted her formally and politely, and Helga started to fumble in her purse. The old bag was being nice to her now, but she was one of the ones who said nasty things about the immigrant assistants. They were the workers who needed more checks and more registration.

She found her ticket and held it out. After a short pause, she looked down and was horrified to discover that the older woman was staring at her forearms. Helga tucked her purse under her arm and pulled down the sleeve of her cardigan. It was enough that she was large and foreign. She didn't want to be examined like an exhibit in a freak show.

As if suddenly keen to end the transaction, Frau Schneider snapped up her head, pushed her thin lips up at the corners and pointed to the front of the seating area. Helga returned the smile with as much warmth as she could and moved down the aisle toward the first row.

She found her name-card and then stood and studied the chair it was resting on. It was only a single tubular frame, and she prayed that it would hold her. The last thing she wanted was to be humiliated in front of the town's educational establishment.

Lowering herself onto her seat, she checked for any creaking or bending and then relaxed her thigh muscles and settled her full weight.

For the next few minutes she sat trying to make herself as small as possible, with her knees pressed together and her purse placed precisely on her lap. She felt out of place and was still trying to figure out why she was there. The production was being staged by one of the arts academies for secondary pupils, and the places were usually reserved for parents and teachers. She'd received a mystery ticket written in Cyrillic, and there weren't many in the town who were able to do that.

The lights dimmed, a curtain twitched at the back of the set, and a young conductor, who she recognized as the music teacher from the high school, walked proudly onto the stage and introduced the performance as "highlights from Prokofiev's *Cinderella.*" Seconds later the orchestra started up, and eight children danced neatly into twin spots of light.

She leaned forward and rested her elbows on her legs. The boys and girls couldn't have been much more than eleven or twelve, but they were moving incredibly gracefully, and the music was charming! They were only teenagers, but the violinists were playing with real passion.

The king's messenger arrived at Cinderella's house with the invitation, and Helga watched with delight as the young man jumped and spun toward the waiting ballerinas. After he'd handed the card to the wicked stepmother, something unusual happened. Instead of exiting through the wings, he moved to the front of the stage and started to climb down. She was struggling to work out what was going on when the lad stopped right in front of her, bowed, and held out a second envelope. It had her full name handwritten on the front, and she took it quickly and pressed it down on her lap, shooting apologetic glances down each side of the row.

The messenger danced to the end of the aisle, crouched and produced three colorful bouquets of flowers from under a seat. He handed one to her and the others to two of the senior teachers from the school. There was a ripple of applause and the conductor brought the first act to a close.

The house lights flickered on, and while the audience moved noisily to the back of the hall, she sniffed her roses and then cautiously lifted the envelope and levered it open.

After reading the strange message several times, she folded it carefully and thrust it into her purse. Her heart was beating hard and blood had risen to her cheeks. It was a joke. It had to be. Someone was teasing her about her size, and she winced with the familiar sting of humiliation.

She stood and went to the rear of the building to join the line for coffee and juice. While she was waiting, she couldn't help pulling out the card and reading it again. This time she saw things more clearly. It wasn't a prank at all. The handwriting was the same as her ticket and there was an embedded microlink to help her send a quick reply. This Weaver man knew about her physical abilities and seemed to be genuinely asking her for help. He even mentioned "a considerable fee."

As they shuffled forward, she wondered if the pay would be enough to sponsor places for the refugee children. Her class went off to summer camp at the end of the week so she wouldn't have to arrange any cover. But what were they going to ask her to do? No violence she hoped. She'd had quite enough of that. No, perhaps they needed her strength for something.

She slipped the invitation away and then nodded a greeting at one of the local dance instructors. Things had changed. Faraway events had reached her and she'd have to decide if she could refind her taste for adventure.

Chapter 6

Jodie Goodwin, Las Vegas, Nevada, early July

There was an airship landing on the RockSands hotel. When the traffic slowed, Jodie looked up and watched its silver envelope sink closer to the ridge of rooftops. She sighed and pushed her hair behind her ear. It would undoubtedly contain a bunch of wealthy folk coming in for dinner and a show, and she couldn't help wishing she could join them. She'd be on the shooting range trying to get a load of pill-pumped old-timers to develop some accuracy. Two hours of shouting into half-deaf ears for less than fifty bucks wasn't her idea of a perfect evening.

She drew to a halt by the entrance to a mall and glanced out of the window at a pretty young girl who was standing talking into her reader. She'd pulled off the month's prissy but sexy look with an expensive-looking cream blouse tucked into a tight beige skirt. Jodie felt a brief stab of jealousy that only increased when she lifted her gaze to the young woman's hair. It had clearly just been set, and hung in tight glossy curls that wouldn't have lasted two minutes out in the desert wind. These folk didn't get their styling blown to shreds or get grit in their eyes.

A further small pulse of envy hit her when she looked down at the shoes. They were real leather and matched the ankle bracelets and the stitching on the skirt. The chip reader was by the same designer, so it was all coordinated. The young power shopper had probably just spent ten thousand bucks without blinking.

Jodie tried to push out her resentment with a long exhalation. There were haves and there were have-nots. She'd had more money than most when she was winning competitions in her teens. Her best friend Hannah had spent her youth flipping burgers, when all she'd had to do was turn up and take down targets with a rifle. It didn't always last though. You took the rough with the smooth.

A blur of movement pulled her attention back to the road, and she inched on the power and started the long slow crawl to the west gate.

As she drove, she reflected on the afternoon's shopping. She'd been ruthlessly self-controlled and had only bought a triple pack of underwear and a single deep-red lipstick. Both had been on sale and pretty good value, but she knew she was going to have to keep justifying them to herself. On the plus front, a lot of men had checked her out, the best being the tall guy with soulful eyes who'd found some good excuses to make conversation in the coffee shop. He'd been on vacation though, and she'd quickly decided that commuting to Seattle was never going to work.

She flashed her lights at the watchtower; the signal flicked to green and the heavy portcullis started to rise. A short burst from the runner's engine and she was in the pen looking up at the observation deck. As usual they were slow to react, and she felt the familiar flash of frustration that dealing with the access authorities gave her. *You lot could be quicker, yeah? You know I'm here.*

Eventually a slice of bright light appeared, then widened, and the giant steel barrier rolled open.

As she coasted forward, the chip in her arm vibrated then let out the long beep that warned she was crossing gate. She tried not to let it irritate her and concentrated on swerving around the first of the battered tank traps.

The heat hit her like an oven blast. She flicked on the fan and the motor whirred into life, sending a tepid breeze onto her face as she scanned the perimeter fence. Small clumps of tumbleweed were rolling from pole to pole, and strips of white plastic clung flapping to the posts, but it was clear. It was always clear. She'd never understood why every city had had to be walled and gated. Yes, the East Coast had been overrun with immigrants, but they'd never made it far inland. Why would they? Why would you swap desert for desert? In reality, Vegas was already protected. It was an island in a sea of baking dirt. They should pull the walls down. Then those who couldn't afford to live gated wouldn't feel like second-class citizens. It might help spread the cash around a little better too.

As she gazed into the distant haze, the chain-link gate slid back and she found herself looking out along the western road, its dark cambered surface dusted with shifting pools of thin white sand.

She parked in the shade of the shooting range's eastern wall and went straight up to her apartment. Although her reader was blinking "Pollution Hazard," she decided to take the risk and go running. She needed to burn off some calories before dinner and, even if the air wasn't as clean as the purified stuff that was pumped around the cities, she had a sneaking suspicion that the government exaggerated the danger of living out of gate.

After a quick change, she was back outside, walking quickly and swinging her arms to loosen her muscles.

At the burnt-out frames on the edge of the old town she broke into a slow jog. The buildings thinned and the view of the dunes quickly broadened, each pounding step taking her further from the faded billboards and deeper into the clusters of speckled cactus. As her feet slapped the tarmac, her mind drifted and she began to consider whether she had the cash to upgrade Hank's insurance. He was getting slower every day and, although he'd come out west to help her, she wasn't so sure that it wasn't quickly going to become the other way around. She'd just formed a picture of her nursing an elderly man when an image of her mother came to her and she was stabbed by a pang of guilt. She had to call her. It had been nearly a week since they'd spoken and her dear mom was having a tough time with her health. There should be someone visiting her every day and sitting with her. It would be nice if her brothers did it, but deep down she knew it was no good leaving it to the boys. It was her duty. She should be there.

She was half a mile into the pure wilderness when the sound of a gasoline engine made her slow and look behind her. The sleek oval lozenge of an interstate airship was hanging low on the horizon, and below it a car was visible: a small dark rectangle moving toward her with bursting stars of sunlight flashing on its windshield.

She tensed. Gas engines were mostly used by bums and crims. Did they know she was out there on her own? Her fingers found the weapon taped inside her pocket while a pulse of adrenaline set her hands tingling.

A few strides later she cast another glance over her shoulder, now puzzled as well as anxious. The car wasn't one of the bashed-up pickups that the drifters rode. It was a vintage classic, one of the big vehicles that the old-style presidents used to get driven around in.

She stopped and stood facing it, moving her feet off the crumbling tarmac and onto the sand so that she was ready to run. Her mind had slipped into overdrive and she could feel her heart thumping loud in her ears as she went over her escape options. There was a rough track nearby that would take her down into the desert, but it offered no real cover. Her best bet would be zigzagging through the cactus to the closest sandbank.

Keeping the small gun tucked out of sight, she studied the oncoming vehicle and frowned. It was totally weird, but the license plate read, *Jodie One*. She tracked the driver's window with the short barrel while she tried to figure out why her name might be on the front. It must be some kind of stunt. The style of the limo and its arrival had a hint of organized crime about it. But she'd never had any dealings with them. Or had she trained some of their guys without knowing it?

Hazy through the reflections on the glass, she identified a single male at the wheel dressed in a dark suit and chauffeur's hat. The other seats were empty. Was someone about to pop up and level a weapon at her? The idea of a robbery with a driver in uniform seemed very odd.

The car drew to a halt a few yards away. The door swung open and a pair of black leather shoes and sharp-creased trouser legs lowered onto the tarmac. There was a faint crunch as the soles took the man's weight and then his head and shoulders appeared. His cap sat on cropped blond hair and the lightly tanned skin around his bright blue eyes was worn into gentle wrinkles.

"Miss Goodwin?" he asked in a soft deep voice.

She swallowed, nodded and wiped her forehead. Sweat had formed on her brow and was trickling between her breasts and down her stomach. This wasn't an abduction or a stick up. This was just weird.

He took a step forward and offered a hand. She looked at it for a while and then slipped her fingers off the little gun and reached out to shake hands. Who the hell was he? And how had he arrived at exactly the right time to catch her jogging? Was this a competition? A casino sweeping for new members?

"Chris," he said by way of introduction, and her voice was suddenly out in the hot air working without her permission.

"Pleased to meet you, Chris," she said sharply. "I'm Jodie, as you know. What can I do for you? I was exercising." She cringed inside. What was she trying to achieve with those words? *I'm a tough girl; you don't impress me with your fancy old cars. Busy lady, you know. Run my own business and don't take crap from men.*

He dipped his chin. "Yes, I apologize for the interruption. I shall be as brief as possible." As he spoke she noticed that his eyes were smiling. So it was a prank, definitely a joke or promotional stunt.

He held out a small envelope and she took it, detecting a firmness of card under the paper. It felt legal, and for a moment she wondered if it was a summons on the range.

"Okay," he said with a shrug. "That's me done. I'm not meant to talk to you. Just deliver the invitation." He pointed at the card as he slipped back into the car. "I'm working for them at the moment though—Weaver and the others." He held her gaze with real intent, his voice calm and reassuring. "They're okay."

She stood and watched him drop into the driver's seat while the thick parchment sucked the sweat off her skin. The gasoline engine roared and then throbbed, and the car began to move backward down the crumbling highway. He kept a perfectly straight line along the center of the road then spun through a hundred and eighty degrees with a sharp squeal of brakes and continued without losing speed.

Far on the horizon the airship floated silently toward her, dropping in the sky until the fuselage met the heat haze from the tarmac. The vehicle drove into the body of the ship and disappeared. A ramp was lifted and the craft gained height, rotating as it climbed. The propellers sped to a silver blur and it started to move east across the desert.

She studied its departure for a few moments, then tore open the envelope and pulled out a single piece of manila card. The writing sparkled and shimmered in the sunlight as she read.

Dear Ms. Goodwin

We hope this message finds you in good health. Please allow me to introduce myself. I am Doctor Julian Weaver and I'm writing to ask that you come to a meeting I'm arranging in New York. Please excuse the stunt with the fancy car. Our AI advisors insisted that a show of wealth would both grab your attention and convince you of our sincerity—I'm not so sure—so my apologies if it seemed a little over the top. Let me explain why I am contacting you. I am assembling a team to help resolve the situation inside the Quarantine Ring in Washington and we would more than appreciate the contribution of your considerable skill with firearms to the group. We are holding a kick-off meeting in New York on Monday the 12th and would very much like you to attend. We will provide airship transportation to this event and a substantial fee for participation in the mission.

If you are able to come, please send electronic confirmation <u>here</u> as soon as you can.

For collection, please be at this location at 6.00 p.m. on Sunday the 11th for an overnight voyage. Bring hand luggage and your weaponry of choice.

Best regards,

Dr. J. Weaver

PS Feel free to check me out on the university website here.

She read it a couple more times then slipped it into her sweatshirt and started jogging again, slowly picking up speed until she was back to her full pace. Her mind was buzzing as she ran. She quickly decided that the phrase "situation inside the Quarantine Ring" was referring to the half-deads, but the rest of it left her puzzled. What exactly was she going to be asked to do? And who was this Dr. Weaver?

At her usual marker, she slowed to a stop, bent and rested her hands on her knees. Sweat dripped onto the sandy tarmac as she sucked in big gulps of air and wrestled with the other questions swimming in her head. Why her? Why go to so much effort to get her attention? Yes she could shoot but so could plenty of others.

She turned for home and pushed her legs as hard as they would go.

As she neared the range she caught sight of an elderly man standing in the entrance with an automatic in the crook of his arm. Seeing her daddy sent a glow of comfort rising through her that was quickly snapped clear by pain. It wasn't him. It was Hank, her business partner. She could still see an echo of her father though, like a light flickering inside his best friend.

"I saw a ship," he said, pointing into the desert. "Right where you go running. Just a couple of minutes ago."

She nodded then told him she'd seen it too and walked past with a shrug. Part of her wanted to tell him the full story but she kept quiet. She'd think it over first; maybe do a bit of research.

He hung in the doorway while she checked the messages on the admin terminal. There were more cancellations than enquiries. The hotels were getting increasingly reluctant to take any of their precious guests ungated for shooting lessons, and it was having a clear effect on revenue.

Things were going to have to change. She'd have to start entering competitions again. Even the small prizes would make a difference. Hank would have to run things while she was away. Or she could go and work on one of the ranges in town. Yes, that would mean going from boss to employee, but maybe it was time to take a little dent in pride.

When she looked back up, he was still studying her from the other side of the room, and she guessed he was trying to find a way of talking about her personal safety without seeming overbearing.

"There's reports of more bums camping out by the old trailer park," he said eventually. "Seems the cops aren't chasing them off anymore."

She nodded slowly, knowing that he was building up to the touching and intensely irritating idea of escorting her when she went out. "Yeah, some of the old-timers have been talking about it," she replied casually. "Should only be temporary though. It's just a glitch while they're setting up the new administration base."

He shook his head. "Not if Canmore gets his way. He's got folks pretty heated about wasting resources out of gate."

Her eyes drifted back to the screen while she analyzed his response. She wasn't going to get drawn into his doom and gloom political debate. People were only listening to Canmore because they were scared. More than eighty percent of the population now lived gated, so he knew he had a vote winner on his hands. None of them had any patience or respect for the folk who couldn't afford to move into the cities, and he knew it. As soon as they cured the virus, the president would take control again, and everything would settle down. In the meantime her safety was not an issue. She lived and worked in a secure building that was packed with weapons and ammunition. There were other people she knew who were far more vulnerable. "It's not around here that concerns me," she told him eventually. "It's what might be going on in Texas."

"Your mom?" His eyebrows lifted into arches. "She'll be okay. There's plenty of good folk around her and a security guy up at the junction."

Yeah, the old fella with the limp who was asleep whenever she drove past. No, he was only saying that to try and reassure her. If this got any worse somebody was going to have to move in with mom.

After another long pause, he came out and made the suggestion. "I should come with you when you go jogging."

"Yeah right." She let her head fall to the side and squinted at him. "I don't think, just 'cause there's some weird news reports from Washington and the occasional low-flying blimp, I need a chaperone when I'm exercising."

"I'd stay well back. You wouldn't know I'm there," he told her earnestly.

"I know I wouldn't. 'Cause you won't be there, 'cause I ain't gonna tell you when I'm going."

He considered this for a moment then nodded and grinned. "You're a cold-hearted mare."

"Yep."

Pleased that she'd put him off without offending him, she lowered her gaze to the desk and ran her eyes down the evening's schedule. It was all senior citizens on a bargain basement rate, and the thought of a whole shift trying to get them to slacken off their aggression was seriously depressing. "You wanna do the old-timer's slot tonight?" she asked hopefully. "I promised them an hour with semiautomatics."

"Nope."

"No." She looked up to find a smile on his weather-worn features. "Didn't think you would."

Chapter 7

Jester, ungated Chicago, early July

These city cars are a bit small. I'm gonna have to write neat. Jester stared at the paintwork and visualized the words of the poem appearing on the crumpled steel. Happy that he could see the layout, he picked up the torch, lit the oxyacetylene and started to tune the gases. When he had a hissing orange spout, he thrust his face forward and sucked in the fumes. The toasty gasoline smell took him straight back to the times he'd spent squatting in the open air carving out phrases and verses. Burning the words smoothed out the noises in his head. Paper wouldn't do. Ink and paint wouldn't do. It had to be scorched. Etching balanced his inside with the outside. For a few moments it produced some quiet and calm.

He dialed in enough oxygen to turn the jet an intense blue-white then stuffed a couple of Marlboros into his mouth and swung the flames onto the tips. When his lungs were full of smoke, he leaned close to the dirty metal and started, murmuring the first six words softly as he blistered valleys into the metal. *I rose from the chill ground.*

By the time he'd finished, his legs had cramped and his face was damp with drops of thin warm rain. He stood and stretched, then limped to the cylinders and choked off the gases. Yawning, he dropped the torch onto the gravel and crossed the rooftop in slow shuffling steps.

When he reached his living quarters he flopped into his hammock and shook a couple of cigarettes into his mouth. He was drawing his first deep inhalation when an unusual pop echoed up from the street below. It was the unmistakable sound of a mortar. He opened one eye and looked up into the thick clouds. *Who the fuck is firing a mortar in Mill Town? And more importantly,* what *have they fired and where's it going to land?* If it was a shell then he had no more than a couple of seconds. There was no point running because he didn't know where it was going to hit. And besides, maybe it was his time.

With this last thought echoing in his mind, he blew out a thick jet of smoke and scanned the sky.

A small blob appeared. A fast-spinning parachute falling bright against the evening's passing clouds. The canopy was blown closer as it fell, and he could see that it was going to land slap in the middle of the roof. He gave a nod of admiration to the team down below. Whoever had fired it had got the trajectory and the prevailing wind exactly right.

The shape below the dome became clearer and he was able to make out a head and four limbs extending from a torso. It was some kind of a dummy or giant doll.

He sat up and swung his legs out of the hammock. This wasn't an accident or coincidence. This was meant for him.

The manikin landed twenty yards away and the chute settled and disengaged.

He sucked hard on his cigarettes and watched the toy figure move toward him with a whir of motors. It was dressed in a fool's costume, complete with coxcomb and curly bell-tipped slippers just like his.

He felt a buzz of energy, as if suddenly reminded of an old joke, then pushed himself onto the ground and started to saunter toward it. This was the best stunt he could remember. It had to be Thumper and the guys from the ward. They were the only ones who knew him well enough and had the military expertise. They'd really *planned* this, worked together to get it slick.

The doll bent, and its stripy pants slipped down to reveal a pink plastic backside. A shutter drew back in the center of the buttocks and a cylinder poked out. There was a comic farting sound that made him grin, and then the tube dropped onto the floor. It lay still for a few seconds before opening with a click to reveal a piece of thick parchment.

Still smirking, he picked up the paper and held it to his face. He read it quickly and then started to scratch his chin. Who the hell were this Weaver guy and his team? His eyes crept back to the toy on the roof. They were people who could arrange a damn cool stunt, that was certain. They were also smart. They knew what he looked like, they'd nailed his sense of humor and they'd somehow found where he lived.

He spat out his filters and strolled back to his hammock. There was plenty to chew over. Things had suddenly got interesting, and for the first time in years, he was feeling like he might actually be alive.

Chapter 8

Curtis Ferguson, approaching New York, early July

Dr. Jim Barnes saw the bulkhead curtains bulge and gave his friend a quick warning. "She's coming."

Curtis Ferguson put down his sheet of datafilm, turned to the window and started to take small sips of his drink.

The stewardess arrived at their seats and flicked her eyes across each of them before holding out a long ivory-handled machete. "Dr. Barnes. The captain says I can return this now."

Barnes looked down and managed to suppress his smile. There was something ridiculous about his friend's weapon and the way they'd smuggled it through customs that was going to amuse him for a long time. "Ah yes!" he exclaimed. "The ceremonial artifact."

Her eyes followed it as he took it from her and laid it across his knees. "Kinda looks like a big knife to me," she commented.

"It does a bit, yeah," he replied, squinting at the leather scabbard with what he hoped was a thoughtful expression.

"So …" The attendant pushed a few loose hairs behind her ear. "… anything else I can get you before we begin our descent?"

"No, all good, thanks."

She looked past him and her eyes burned into the back of Curtis's shaved head then followed the movement of his arm as he raised his juice to his lips. "He … drinks … from … a … cup?" she mouthed dramatically.

Barnes felt the corners of his mouth twitch. "Yes," he whispered in a conspiratorial tone. "They have cups in the forest, just not plastic."

"Oh, Right. Well. Buzz me if you need anything." Her fingers drummed the back of the seat and she turned and set off for the galley.

"Here ya go, Tarzan." Barnes passed across the machete and watched Curtis lift his hip and slide it through his pocket.

Carrying a short sword was only one of his friend's little eccentricities. He also refused to be chipped or to use any modern communication devices. Barnes had spent almost a half a day registering him as a visiting tribal leader, which meant that for the duration of his stay, his childhood pal was officially some sort of anthropological specimen.

When his friend had settled back in his seat, Barnes brought the topic around to the video footage he'd just shown him. "So what do you make of the Washington half-deads?" he asked.

"It's unusual," Curtis replied. "But I really can't say any more than that."

"Fair enough. Thing to think about is that there's two phenomena going on here. Yes, there's the sick guards, and that's interesting 'cause if it's a virus, and if it's happened before, then that explains all the animated corpse myths in folklore. The second thing is the reaction. In Russia, there have been riots and protests, even though the only footage they have is from a remote military base."

"And here?" his companion asked.

"Well, there hasn't been much of a response at all. The Washington crisis doesn't always get top billing on the news. There's a celebrity divorce getting more airtime."

"Yeah …" Curtis replied. "… and do you know, that doesn't really surprise me."

Barnes heard the dry, slightly superior cynicism in his fellow traveler's voice and was reminded of what he called "the academic's tone." It had probably been picked up from his scholarly parents, and it seemed to make an appearance whenever the state of Western society was being discussed.

"Well," he continued, "you can expect to get a ton of questions about it this afternoon. I'll try to keep us on tribal belief systems, but the postgrads are really fired up about it." He regained eye contact with his friend and leveled his index finger at him. "Reminds me. You ever made any enemies in the crim underworld?"

Curtis frowned. "Nope."

"No. Didn't think so. Tell you why I ask though. This geek security guy rang up on Monday and shot a load of dumb questions at me. When I asked why he was calling, he said the whole uni system had been hacked. Seems our visitors had checked out *shamanism and hypnotic protection* and then got out of there. Our tech guys put up a new wall that same day." He leaned closer to his friend. "Here's where it gets interesting. Very next night, the guys hack back in, right through all the new stuff. Pretty wild yeah? This time they only go to my personal data and …"

"And …?"

"And they only opened one thing."

"Yeah?"

"Yeah. File with your name on it."

Curtis jerked his head back and frowned. "Shit."

"Yes indeed. Somebody knows all about you, and they know you're coming to town today."

His friend pulled a face then lifted his hand to his chin and started to scrape the skin on his throat. After a few moments he gave a few slow nods and turned to look out of the window. Barnes leaned over to follow his gaze, and together they watched the bar-graph-squares of New York rise up toward them through a blanket of shimmering heat.

Chapter 9

The Ferguson residence, Manhattan, early July

Professor Ferguson was standing in her husband's study, waiting for him to acknowledge her statement about dinner, when he finished typing and met her eye. While they were looking at each other across the room, she heard the front door close and realized that her son was back. A sensation of expanding warmth rose through her chest. Her boy was home again and there was no feeling like it.

An instant later, a tall young man appeared in the doorway and greeted them with a nod and a casual "Hi."

She quickly moved to him and, after lifting herself onto tiptoes and planting a kiss on his cheek, stood with her hand on his shoulder. His jacket fell open, and when she saw the smooth muscles on his bare chest, a background ache swelled into a flood of full-scale guilt. He'd grown strong, but was that due to her nurturing or because of the lack of it? She had to admit that they'd neglected him. Their need to get published and win funding had always seemed so important. They'd moved too often and he'd skipped too much school. She tried to honestly assess how often he'd got a bedtime story and found herself filling with the frustration of good intentions that had always been pushed aside. He and Ella had never had enough attention. She was certain of that. That had been the price that she and her husband had paid for their academic reputations.

She refocused on his face, and the soft smile that sat deep in his eyes melted some of her remorse. On the other hand he'd always been so easy. He'd eaten everything and anything and had only been ill that one time. He never complained and never asked for money. He didn't seem to own anything and didn't seem to want to. The other moms found him too good to be true.

Still wondering how he had become so incredibly self-sufficient, she gave his lapel a final dust and asked him how his day had been.

"Okay." He gave his usual slow half-nod. "A handful of postgrads. Small outbreaks of intelligent conversation."

"Good. So it's useful for them?" she asked. "To get your perspective on tribal customs? Do they listen to you?

"They do, yes. The only thing that slows it down is the language. They use the most complex jargon for the simplest of things."

She nodded, a vague suspicious that he was using his insider's position to mock the academic method, making her keen to change the subject. "A letter came for you this morning," she told him. "Hand delivered."

"Right," he said absent-mindedly and glided out of the room.

"We'll be eating in about forty minutes," she shouted after him. "It's my lamb stew."

Although she was supposed to be on her way to her study to finish a paper for the Columbia Social Sciences Conference, she was drawn to the kitchen, where she stood in the doorway watching him scoop handfuls of nuts and seeds from the snack jar. "It looks very fancy," she commented.

He grunted something and then raised his eyebrows and she continued.

"The letter. It's all done in ink on expensive stationery. I'll go and get it."

She set off for the hall dresser and came back brandishing the manila envelope. While he was levering open the paper with his finger, she moved to his side and stood waiting expectantly.

He pulled out a piece of card embossed with flowing gold letters and she read with him.

"'The situation inside the Quarantine Ring?' Do they mean the virus?" she asked when they'd both finished.

He looked up at the sky framed high in the kitchen window and smiled. "Yes, but I don't think it is a virus."

"No? So what is it?"

"I don't know exactly. I think there's something very unusual happening and the half-deads are just a small part of it."

Dr. Ferguson appeared in the doorway. "So you're into all this supernatural hokum too, are you?" he asked.

She was aware of the sudden tension in the room. Her husband had come in all guns blazing, seeming to relish the chance to challenge his son intellectually, but Curtis didn't take the bait. After taking a deep breath, he turned to look at his father and replied in soft, matter-of-fact tones.

"I was just telling Mom, I've seen a whole bunch of footage on the half-deads and it seems real. I've also got a strong sense that there's something even stranger going on."

Dr. Ferguson raised his eyebrows. "Go on."

"Okay," Curtis paused, "but wait a sec ..."

She saw him drop his shoulders and realized that he'd just taken control. By stepping back from the confrontation, he was going to give his father the space to hang himself. Her husband was intelligent—well known for it—but her son was wise. He was wise beyond his years and had been since his teens. The father would quote the studies and the statistics and the son would simply shake his head and say that he *knew* something different. The one seemed to be a reaction to the other. Maybe it was always like that. Maybe that was how families worked.

Curtis narrowed his eyes and then continued. "Tell me what *you* think is going on first."

"There is a virus, we know that," her husband said. "We also know that this administration isn't being honest about it. It's clearly a bio weapon that's breached containment. They'll fix everyone up and destroy the evidence. Then they'll deny they're developing such things."

"No." Curtis shook his head and looked up at the window. "It's not the government. It's something else." He lifted the card and met his father's eyes. "These guys have asked me to help. They want me because I might be one of the few people who can explain what's going on."

Her husband shook his head, and she reached out and squeezed her son's shoulder.

"You're not going are you?" she asked. "What if it's a trap, or a weird cult or something?"

"It's not. This feels right. They've picked me out and tracked me down for a reason. The signs are good."

She analyzed his words. *This feels right*. That was him all over. Feeling. Intuitive. "Really? You think it's safe?" she asked, struggling to keep the emotion out of her voice.

While he stood nodding, she gave her husband a look that invited him to step in, but he didn't. She could hear him justifying his silence later. The boy left home years ago. We can't control him when he's in Africa, so why should we do it when he's staying with us? He had a point, but then knowing you should let go didn't always make it any easier.

She suddenly remembered the e-link on the card and realized that the only way this Dr. Weaver was going to get the response he wanted would be if she sent the confirmation herself. "So would you like me to reply for you?" she asked.

"Yes thanks."

She scanned the link with her reader and started to tap out a short message. While she wrote, she considered whether her son would be in any danger. Probably not. If they tried any tricks they'd be in for a hell of a surprise. He had a sixth sense beyond anything she'd ever encountered. He read people to their core in seconds and had the calm self-confidence of someone three times his age. In addition there were not many New Yorkers who were quite so fit or who carried a twenty-inch knife down their pants.

When she'd sent the notification, father and son gave each other a strange nod of recognition and left the room one after the other. She stood in the empty kitchen with the invitation still clasped in her hand and found herself feeling drained and hollow. Her son was going to a meeting. He'd been asked to do some specialist work and it was nearer to home than any of his other trips, so why should this affect her?

She contemplated the question until she was broken from her trance by a few light taps on the window. It had started to rain. As the spots landed on the glass, her head flooded with a procession of images. She saw warm droplets falling on the city's parks and sports fields, running off the dusty sidewalks and slipping into the giant storm drains that wormed beneath the metropolis. The torrents soon met others, and the newly braided streams bubbled together into the vast deep ocean.

She knew that she had to let her son go, but she didn't feel any joy at the thought. In fact, as she turned and walked to her study, her eyes filled with unexpected tears, and she felt only grief. Grief and loss.

Chapter 10

Seventh Grade

Curtis Ferguson is kneeling with the other boys, watching his shadow shorten and sharpen on the hard-baked earth. They have all knelt motionless since before dawn; a silent obedient line of young males waiting to become men.

The chief appears and walks behind them with his machete swinging at his side. When he reaches the end of the row he stops and slowly turns. The testing is about to begin.

Curtis keeps his head bowed and his eyes lowered. The pain from the stones pressing into his knees has numbed and his body has gradually become a statue of itself, only the slow rise and fall of his chest betraying his frail humanity.

The headman's legs appear as a dark blur in his peripheral vision. *He's only two boys away*. He hears the blade swish and then the feet of the headman arrive in front of him. *Now it's my turn*.

The chief swipes twice, but Curtis does not flinch or cry out. A couple of hot feathers have flicked across his forehead. He feels no pain, though he sees two crimson jets land on the cracked ground. *I didn't flinch or cry out*. His stomach suddenly twists and his testicles send a venomous kick into his lower belly. *I didn't flinch or cry out*. His tester moves out of sight just as his brow begins to sting and burn. *I didn't flinch or cry out. I've passed. I've become a man*. His blood is in his eyes. It presses thick and sticky against his eyelids and runs around his chin, where it dries tight against his skin.

He is looking down, watching the glow of the rising sun creep across the savanna. His head and shoulders are clearly visible in the line of boys. The chief is nearing the end of the row, and just beyond him Curtis can make out the top of the village wall and the huddles of people clustered there. The whole tribe is watching.

I'll soon hunt with the men. I'll cut and shape my own spear and be allowed to fix a killing point. I won't have to collect the water or milk the stinking cattle with the children and the girls anymore. I could soon be face to face with a pack of hyenas or in the hunters' line chasing a roaming lion from the fields. Pride swells in his chest. *Ella will be so pissed. She won't get any respect unless she gets married.*

His cuts have become a searing tear across his skull but the sensations are contained and blanketed by his pride. He allows himself a smile. *I've become a man.*

Thousands of miles westward, his classmates in Manhattan are drifting off to sleep in their soft warm beds. When they wake they will begin their first semester in seventh grade.

The Meeting

Chapter 11

Jodie

The pop of gunfire was echoing along the back of the range as Jodie walked slowly and purposefully to the rear door. With her shotgun case tucked tight under her arm, she pulled open the heavy slab and stepped out into the evening's oven-dry heat. It was odd that she was creeping out of her own place of business, but she really couldn't face the conversation with Hank. She'd convinced him to take her lessons, and left a note, and this meant that she didn't have to explain what she was doing. It felt cowardly, but it made leaving so much easier.

Once she'd cleared the building, she set off at a brisk pace, sweat forming instantly on her brow and down her back as she strode toward the broken highway. She might be back soon. There was no way she'd hang around for long. Maybe this Weaver character was a weirdo who set these things up as a joke. She'd wait ten minutes max. No sign of a blimp and she'd come straight back. Hank would never know.

But the airship was there; a blinding white bulb, unmarked by any name or logo, that was coming in to land as she cleared the billboard on the edge of the parking lot. It was bigger than the last one, and her chest tightened as she approached it. *Shit, this is real. That's a top spec interstate, and it's going to take me to New York.*

There was a young man standing on the bottom of the steps with an arm hooked around the rail. He raised his hand in greeting and she smiled then slowed and cupped a palm onto a revolver. *Take it easy now, girl. Use your instincts and bide your time.*

She stopped near the landing gear and gave the youth a nod. He was clean-shaven and dressed in traditional livery, and when he saw that she wasn't going to come any closer, he jumped down and walked over to shake her hand.

When they'd introduced themselves, she squinted at the big craft behind him. "So what can you tell me about this?" she asked.

He glanced over his shoulder. "Burman IS class. Hired by a Doctor Weaver to take you to New York."

"How many on board?

"Captain, first officer, an engineer and me. I do the cooking."

"Good ship? Safe?"

"Apart from my cooking, yes. Best I've worked on. Brand new."

"What do you know about Weaver?"

"He's paying us. Not met him." The kid seemed to sense that she wanted something more and added a final comment. "All our customers have to pass security and credit checks though."

She pursed her lips and then tapped the weapons at her hip and asked him if she could keep them on. He agreed, and she realized that she couldn't stall her decision any longer. She had to either turn and leave, or start going with the flow.

A few minutes later, she was standing at the rail watching the desert road shrink to a ribbon on the sand below. As the roof of the range and Hank's apartment block came into view, she found herself blinking back tears. *Maybe I should've told him.* She pressed the back of her fist to her eyes and shook her head. *No. I don't have to share everything. He works for me. He's not my keeper.*

The early morning light found her back on the airship's walkway, peering into the cold wet air while the giant craft dropped through layers of cotton-candy mist. The absurd luxury of her cabin had not smoothed out her night. The sensation of gliding through the air combined with a constant anxiety about what was going to happen in New York had kept her rolling from one side of the enormous bed to the other. She had risen and dressed early and, after picking samples from the range of dishes laid out in the banqueting room, had taken her coffee outside.

It was incredibly exciting to be doing something new and dramatic, but she kept wondering if there'd been some kind of mistake. All she could do was shoot targets. Even more disconcerting was the possible tradeoff between risk and reward. A voice in her head kept telling her that there had to be some danger involved or they wouldn't be spending so much cash. Her plan was to take it a step at a time and find out as much as she could. There had to be a way of getting decent money without jeopardizing her safety.

The cloud cleared, and she found herself standing wide-eyed with her cup held at her mouth and her breath tight in her chest. Spreading to the haze on the far horizon was the white-rippled ocean and the proud columned squares of New York.

She'd been to a couple of competitions in the city when she was a teenager, but on both occasions she'd arrived by plane and she had no recollection of being anywhere near the window. Since then, the emissions laws had driven most air traffic into blimps, and the view from the gallery was far more dramatic and awe-inspiring than she'd ever have imagined.

The final fifteen minutes were even more spectacular. The ship cut a sharp scything diagonal through the traffic of local craft, until they were floating over a landing stage on a slim, elegant skyscraper. The ship's cables snaked onto magnetic moorings and they hauled themselves onto the top of the building.

She took her bag and shotgun case, and with nervousness and expectation buzzing in her stomach, shook the steward's hand.

There was a thickset security guard in a suit and tie waiting on the edge of the platform who led her across a roof terrace toward a long wall of glass.

They stopped a few yards from the doorway and she followed his gaze into the room beyond.

"There's a Dr. Weaver in there, maam," he announced with a tip of the head. "He's expecting you."

Is this a joke? She caught a glimpse of a broad-shouldered figure standing over a table of food and wondered if it was a wrestler in a dress. Jodie paused at the threshold and watched the person reach down and daintily pick up a piece of bacon with a pair of serving tongs. *No, it's a woman. She has breasts and a soft complexion.*

The lady turned and beamed at her, and she smiled in return and stepped inside.

A man in a plaid shirt immediately looked up and started to stride toward her. "Miss Goodwin?"

She pushed her pack higher on her shoulder and shook his hand. His face was mahogany tanned, with pale skin hiding in the crow's feet around his eyes.

"I'm Jools." He ran his fingers through his short dark hair. "Julian Weaver. Welcome." He stood back and placed his hands on his hips. "Really. Thanks for coming. I'm very glad you're here." He gestured toward the rear wall. "Grab yourself a drink."

As he started to move away from her, she lifted her hand and asked him if he could explain the day's agenda. He very politely refused, and told her that everything would become much clearer when all the others had arrived. She hid her frustration behind a tight smile and gave him a nod.

Further down the table there was a thin young man with a short blond Mohawk sitting tracing tight circles on the polished surface with his index finger. As she stood watching him, the giant lady moved past her and lowered herself carefully into one of the seats. Jodie stole a sideways glance and found herself staring at the thick purple veins that laced up her bulging arms.

Forcing herself to pull her gaze away, she moved to the back of the room and fixed herself a drink.

When she'd spent as long as she could standing stirring her coffee, she sat and tried in vain to make eye contact with one of her companions. She failed, and as each second dragged by, her sense of unease increased.

After spending several minutes studying a handful of cards, Dr. Weaver moved up and stood eyeing the room's internal door. "We're waiting for two more," he told her in a secretive voice. "One en route from Chicago, the other expected on foot. Won't be long now."

She nodded hesitantly and then looked across at the skinny youth on the far side of the table. He needed a good meal and a lesson in basic manners, and the longer he sat gazing into space the more uncomfortable she felt. She began to wonder if they were going to have to work together, and the thought filled her with nothing but dread.

She was discreetly assessing the large woman on her left when Weaver turned to look across the roof terrace. Following his gaze, she saw a big man in a strange costume step off the landing platform. He came toward them in a slow rolling gait, puffing out his cheeks as he waddled from side to side. As he got closer she realized that he was dressed like a medieval fool, in a black and red suit and a hat with drooping, bell-tipped prongs. He was thickset: just over six feet tall and about two sixty pounds. Clearly he'd once been a well-muscled athlete, but he had gone to fat around his waist, and his shoulders were sad and slumped.

The next moment he was poking his head through the opening in the glass, scanning the room with a dumb grin plastered across his face.

Weaver walked over with his hand held outstretched. "Mr. Solberg."

The man leaned forward while he pumped his greeter's arm.

"This is sex addicts anonymous, yeah?" he said in an exaggerated, conspiratorial tone. "You don't need to say anything. I can see it in your eyes. You've got it baaaaad."

Weaver lowered his gaze and then looked back up. "Yes … well, no. I mean, obviously not. But you are Mr. Solberg aren't you?"

"Yes. Me Solberg," the man confirmed. "Call me Jester, though. Been called Jester for a good few years now."

"I'm Julian Weaver. I sent the invite."

The man grinned and took a couple of steps forward. The light in the room revealed a long silvery scar that ran from ear to nose on his left cheek.

"That you, was it?" he asked. "Nice job. Mortar expert. Mini-me with special delivery buttocks. Got my attention."

Weaver smiled. "Yes, well. Thanks for coming."

She took small self-conscious sips of coffee and found herself positioning and repositioning her pencil while Weaver busied himself at the front of the room and the "Jester" man sat back in his chair grinning.

The silence was broken by a sudden movement at the door, and she glanced over her shoulder to see a handsome black boy with finely chiseled cheekbones and deep brown eyes move slowly into the room and stand surveying them.

Weaver looked up and then strode rapidly toward him. "Mr. Ferguson?"

The young man nodded and his expensive-looking suit flapped open to reveal a bare muscular chest. "Yes."

Weaver shot out his hand and they shook. "You are very welcome. Thank you for coming."

Jodie watched as the young man pulled out a chair and slipped his body onto it in one fluid movement. As soon as he was seated, he leaned forward and rested his elbows on the table. Then, suddenly, his big dark eyes were fixed straight on her. She quickly looked down, embarrassed by the power and intensity of his gaze.

While she sat thinking about the latest arrival, Weaver went to the head of the table and started to address the room. "Ladies and gentlemen, I am very pleased and greatly relieved to see you all here."

She glanced up and rolled her shoulders. *Now concentrate, girl. He's going to explain who you're working for and what you'll have to do to earn this "considerable fee."*

He scanned their faces before continuing. "Of course, I'm sure you've come with lots of questions, but let me first introduce myself. I am Dr. Julian Weaver, lecturer in Religious History here at Columbia. I also have a secondary role as the caretaker of a set of ancient records, and it's this very unusual collection of documents that puts me in front of you today." He raised his hand. "First, I think it best if I begin with my part of the story. About three weeks ago I received a visit in my office. No phone call, no appointment, just a couple of very powerful men inviting me to take a ride in a limo. So, I take the trip, wondering for the first five minutes if I owe anybody any money and if I'm about to become part of a concrete bridge." He paused and smiled at his own joke. "Anyway, one of the men was a representative from the US military and the other the billionaire financier Mr. Martin Sophos. It seems that he and some of his business partners had been looking for a solution to the White House crisis. They'd hired a bunch of analysts and one of them had found an article I'd written about zombie folklore in *The Journal of Comparative Beliefs*. It seemed there was a very high correlation between some of my descriptions and what had been happening in the West Wing. I have to admit that I'd also been thinking the same thing myself but was a little reluctant to take my thoughts seriously. Well, these guys did. They immediately offered me a role, and, as I was doing a supervisory semester, this was very attractive."

He stopped and held up his palm. "I digress. I'll try to stick to the facts. I took the job and we started profiling the people we'd need to carry out the missions. I'll introduce you all in a minute, but just to convince those of you who are skeptical about our financial resources, the men behind all this have made themselves available and would like to meet you."

He flicked his hand over his micro and then stood watching the internal door.

Three men, all short and barrel-chested, came in and moved toward her in a blur of business suits and mirror-polished shoes. She was reaching out her hand to the first when there was a thud behind her. The Russian lady had knocked over her chair and was bending over to pick it up. When she straightened herself, her face was flushing bright scarlet, and Jodie pulled her eyes away and pretended not to have noticed. *Such a shame,* she thought. *She tries so hard to be graceful.*

The first man had changed course when they'd lost eye contact and was down the table shaking the young black man's hand and patting his shoulder. The two others were in front of her with their arms outstretched: a Mr. Glover and a Mr. Gillkin. They talked quickly and enthusiastically while she nodded and pushed her hair behind her ear. She could make out the individual words, and they were all very positive and encouraging, but the exact meaning of what they were saying kept eluding her.

After a while, they drifted away, and Mr. Sophos had her hand in his, his skin hard and dry like the leather of an old car seat. He released her and stood back, nodding and expressing his pleasure and high expectations, all the time his bright animal-like eyes scanning the room, absorbing the scene and somehow making her feel irrelevant.

The next thing she knew, everybody was saying goodbye. She shook the three hands again and watched the broad shoulders and neat clipped hairlines leave the room. *Okay, so those guys are the money. They're pleased to meet us. Happy that we're all here. Good for them.* She moved back to her chair and sat down. Coffee and adrenaline were pumping her blood fast around her body, fueling a brain-numbing headache and distorting her sense of time. Her hands found her pencil and began to twist it. *But what do they want us to do? Right now this just feels like some kind of freak show.*

When everybody had settled, Weaver pointed at the door. "Those guys were honest with me so I'll be honest with you. Since the outbreak there's been a lot of unrest in the markets. They've seen their stock depreciate and a lot of their projects put on hold. This means they're feeling a lot of pain while others are benefiting from the situation. The promotion of certain false vaccines and the need to increase security measures is helping push up the stock of some of their rivals."

"You're talking about Canmore?" The Jester man had leaned back in his chair and was scrutinizing Weaver through narrowed eyes.

"Yes. But we'll come to that later. First I think I should introduce you all." He picked up the cue cards and tapped them against his palm. "So, starting with the ladies. May I tell you about our guest from Europe? Helga. Thank you for joining us."

A deep smooth voice with a heavy Russian accent filled the room. "Dr. Weaver, you are very welcome."

Their host's eyebrows rose. "This lady has some very interesting abilities that I'd like to share with you all. Do you mind Helga?"

The big lady shook her head. "Not at all. Speak what you know."

Weaver looked down at the card. "Helga Oscova, born in Protvino, just south of Moscow. A keen athlete and javelin champion in her teens, she was then drafted into the Russian military and fast-tracked into the Smetna Program ... We think perhaps without your full consent."

Helga widened her eyes and gave him a knowing look. "It was military, Dr. Weaver," she shrugged. "You know military."

"Quite so. The Smetna process is reported to have involved the prescription of hyperstrength steroids to selected personnel. Helga completed this training and was then deployed on classified military operations. She received an honorable discharge six years ago and then moved to Switzerland." He glanced up. "It's only your membership of the local gym that enabled us to find you, Helga. That, and reports from the weight training community of you not only breaking records but actually lifting the machines themselves."

"I still keep fit." She rubbed a hand across her shoulder. "I have to lift. My body needs that."

"Yes indeed." Weaver looked down and let out a short sigh. "It's a beautiful thing: a lady with a strong body." He made a small bow in her direction. "Anyway, we are honored to have you here today." Helga smiled from under her fringe while he shifted his gaze around the table. "Now, continuing with the ladies. Miss Goodwin."

Jodie smiled and tightened her grip on her pencil. *So what's he going to say about me? What does he know?* She pushed her hair behind her ears while he scanned the information.

"Born in Austin, Texas. Won the state rifle competition aged eight and continued shooting throughout her teens. Awarded medals in long rifle, standard rifle and sporting clay. Five times consecutive winner of the world quick draw competition and holds an honors degree in catering from Dallas Community College."

"Yep." She flashed a smile at the others, keen to add some balance to her description. "I like to cook too."

He smiled and raised his eyebrows. "Ms Goodwin, thanks for coming."

She gave a few nods of acceptance. *You're welcome. But you're going to give us details of a job and hand out some big payments, so let's get to that.* With some relief she saw his gaze move down the table to the boy-like figure hunched in his chair.

"And so to one of our earliest recruits: Mr. Adrian Eastman. Also happy to go by the name Cryboy. A highly skilled computer scientist and software engineer, he's involved in pioneering work on laser defense systems and he's been extremely useful to us as … well … as a hacker. His skills have helped us track down a couple of you who otherwise would have been impossible to find. Cryboy, thank you for your work to date."

She watched the thin young man rock in his chair and his role and personality made perfect sense. *Yeah, figures. He's an IT geek. That's why he looks like he's never seen the sun.*

"So to Mr. Solberg … Jester." Weaver looked up at the large figure in the strange suit and lowered his eyebrows. "We have no history of you prior to your military records."

The big man pulled a face. "Not that interesting. It was mostly ballet and needlework kept me busy as a kid."

"Yes, quite." Weaver scanned his card and then looked back up. "Ex US Army. Quickly recruited into Special Ops. Served in Africa and the Middle East. Martial arts expert and special weapons trainer. In 2021 was treated for stress disorders in an experimental military hospital and then discharged on health grounds. These illnesses and how they were treated are particularly significant." He held out his right palm. "And we'll come to that later. Following discharge, Jester moved to ungated Chicago, acquired his current name and chose to dress in the manner you see."

"Excuse me." Jodie pointed at the man's suit. "You mean … that's not a costume? You wear that all the time?"

Jester smiled. "There are many here among us who feel that life is but a joke." He bowed and the top of his hat flopped forward, the bells hitting the table with a crack and a jangle.

"Oh, right." She pressed her fist to her mouth, suddenly aware that she'd been impolite. *Seems to me we've got a room full of nutjobs here.*

Weaver cleared his throat. "Yes, well. Let's move on." He turned to Jester's right. "Finally, Mr. Curtis Ferguson. The son of two very distinguished social scientists. Spent his youth studying some of the earth's most remote tribes. Currently living something of a nomadic existence, but evidently a very sought after lecturer in anthropology. And, I might say, very difficult to track down."

He flashed a smile at Cryboy, and then there was a knock on the door. "Refreshments have arrived," he said cheerfully. "Shall we take a recess?"

With one hand holding her hat on her head, Jodie stood on the roof terrace and watched Jester stick a couple of cigarettes in his mouth and set a flame to them. "You smoke two at a time?" she asked.

"Mostly, yeah." He held out his arm and examined the tips. "There's never enough cancer in one."

She nodded hesitantly. *Christ. That guy's a total basket of fruit.*

After a sip of coffee, she turned and started to discreetly study Curtis. The sunlight had revealed scars on his forehead that looked like a letter V, and she wondered if he'd marked himself with the initial of his nickname and then rejected the idea. Weaver had said he'd come from an academic background so it seemed unlikely that he'd done anything so radical. But then if he was so intelligent and well brought up, why did he have such a dangerous vibe about him?

A movement snapped her out of her thoughts and she looked up to find him in front of her with his hand out. "I didn't get a chance to introduce myself. I'm Curtis."

They shook and, although the skin on his palms was calloused, his grip was gentle.

For a while she stood and watched him drink his water, shifting her weight from side to side until finally catching his gaze. "So what do you make of all this?" she asked. "What do you think they want us to do?"

He fixed her with his deep brown eyes and somehow smiled without moving his features. "I'm waiting to find out more. I'm curious though. Very curious. What do *you* think?"

"Well, it looks like there's a team being put together. They're going to ask us to deal with the half-deads."

He nodded, and when it was clear that he had nothing else to say, she took a mouthful of coffee and turned to look across the skyline. *It's nice that he had the manners to come and introduce himself, but after that? Well, he's not much of a talker is he?*

Chapter 12

Helga

Helga walked slowly across the rooftop with a feeling of intense anticipation buzzing in her stomach. She kept her steps short and controlled, trying to overlap her legs and place her feet lightly the way the fashion models did. The Curtis boy stayed back with her, matching her pace and rhythm while the others moved ahead.

As Jester pushed his broad, fat-thickened shoulders through the gap in the glass wall, she found herself assessing him with a trained military eye. She'd been surprised at the revelation that he'd once been a professional soldier. Even more so when it had become clear that he'd been part of an elite. He didn't have that mindset anymore. Now he gave off a very strange energy—angry and sad at the same time. Like an alcoholic.

They reached the doorway and the young black man ushered her inside. He was a very different case. An absolute charmer, but perhaps not as innocent as he seemed. He had secrets too. Somewhere behind his smile and his soft, dark eyes, he was hiding things.

She reached her chair and then slowly lowered her weight and looked up. Weaver was standing watching her and began to speak as soon as she'd settled.

"So, I should perhaps explain why *I'm* here today," he announced. "As I said, my involvement is connected to my position at Columbia. Early last year I was handed some historical documents by my predecessor. These papers are a collection of dramatic stories and warnings about a very unusual threat to mankind." He touched his thumb to his chin. "Until a few months ago I took the value of the stories to be one of sociological curiosity, but I have since seen some very convincing evidence that suggests that they may have more than novelty value. So, let me show you something that very few people have seen."

Helga picked up her pencil and tapped the eraser against her lips. They were getting to the important bits. He had old records that talked about people turning into half-deads. This would perhaps explain why an academic had invited them to what sounded like a military mission.

He waved his hand across his controller and a stretch of gray-white land appeared on the wall behind him. “These are military satellite images from the Arctic,” he told them. “You are, of course, aware that it’s considerably smaller than it used to be. The ice floes have been melting for some time, and in April this resulted in the release of three … entities that we believe are the cause of all our problems.”

The image zoomed in until a dark shape appeared on the ice and began to move across the snow.

As they watched, the camera angle lowered and it became clear that they were looking at some kind of large bony animal. After about twenty seconds the picture twisted then refocused and she felt her stomach tighten. *What the hell is that? It’s disgusting.*

A strange almost featureless face had filled the wall. There was a mouth—a dark lipless oval with fangs at each corner—but where there should have been eyes and a nose there was only a curved helmet of gridded bone.

Is that real? It looks like some kind of giant insect. She looked at Weaver, who was standing with his knuckles pressed to his lips, and wondered if he was playing some kind of trick on them. She watched him rub his chin and knew that he wasn’t acting. The thing worried him. He was eaten up with stress.

After a few moments of stunned silence he turned back to face them. “We believe that this is one of the creatures causing the half-dead infestation. There are a couple of lower quality clips of similar animals leaving the same area at the same time so it seems reasonable to assume that these things have caused the three infestations.”

Jodie looked up with her eyes half-closed and Helga turned to watch her. *Yes, interrupt him. Ask him for more details.*

The younger woman pointed at the wall. “Sorry, Dr. Weaver, but before you go into the history, what are you saying that thing *is*? Is it supposed to be real?”

“Well, we don’t really know. The—”

“Is it a ninja alien from another dimension, Joolsey?” Jester asked with mock sincerity.

“Well.” Weaver clasped his hands behind his back. “I think our answer is no to that.”

“So what do you think they are?” Jester asked.

Helga found herself nodding. *First silly, then serious questions. His brain’s dancing in there, flipping around like a frog.*

"Personally I'm still keeping an open mind," Weaver told them. "But biological analysis suggests that they're a type of arthropod."

She had started to write the word on her pad when Jodie looked up. "What's that?" she asked.

Weaver looked at her sympathetically. "It's the group of animals that includes insects and crabs."

Jodie stared at their host through narrowed eyes. "So, if they're animals, what are they doing in there? I mean … what do they want?"

Weaver nodded. "Well, that's a million dollar question, Ms. Goodwin. But it's possible that in human terms they don't really want anything at all. I think before we examine the question of motivation, we should look at the story to date. Let me show you our theory."

He broke one of the beams on his micro and the image on the wall morphed into a world map. There were two dotted routes descending from the North Pole, and he started to give accounts from each area.

Helga knew a lot of this already and it was starting to make more sense. There'd been small outbreaks of half-deads in remote parts of Siberia that ended in the military base on Kotelny. The footage of these creatures leaving the Arctic in late April explained this perfectly. But the governments had kept it pretty quiet. These pictures hadn't even appeared on the opennet and it made her realize that Weaver probably wasn't exaggerating the money and hacking power he had at his disposal.

When he'd finished his explanation, Jodie slowly lifted her chin and met his gaze. "What you've shown us explains the outbreaks up north but what about the problems inside the White House?" she asked.

He held up his index finger to acknowledge her point. "How one of these things got to Washington remains one of the biggest unknowns. But, as we have footage of three animals and three outbreaks, there seems to be a logical fit."

Jodie leaned forward. "And these old documents. What do they say about these creatures?"

"Well, there are references to tall 'demons' that cause the appearance of half-deads. There are also warnings that these entities need to be dealt with quickly and that they have a hypnotic effect on people."

He paused to take a sip of water and Helga studied his face. She wanted to know how old the papers were and where they were from, but decided to keep quiet and let the Americans talk. They were quicker and more confident than her.

"We have the images," Weaver continued. "We have a bunch of pattern matching, and we have the half-deads. So this is a fairly strong hypothesis, even if it takes a while to absorb.

"Sorry," Jodie asked, "but if these things are real then why hasn't the military gone in and solved the problem?

Helga allowed her mind to wander to her recent messenger chats with her friend Svetlana. *The Russian soldiers did go in. They sent special forces to Kotelny. Some never came out. Some came out with the disease: walking but already dead.* She tuned back into the accounts. *Yes, that's what he's saying. Same thing in Washington.*

Weaver lifted his shoulders and smiled uncomfortably. "The military are now preparing a strategy based entirely on the use of robots and UGVs—that's unmanned ground vehicles to you and me. Currently they're adapting and rebuilding bomb disposal units that are small enough to get through the squeeze space and fast enough to capture a large animal. The Quarantine Ring is a holding situation while they build and test the new technology. We've discovered a big problem with their timescale though. Whatever is in there has secured a habitat and arranged a supply of food, and that suggests only one thing. It seems likely that they will want to reproduce as soon as possible."

"Reproduce?" Jodie scowled. "You're saying that thing might be about to have babies?"

Helga sucked a breath between her teeth. She understood the American girl's alarm. The idea was disgusting.

"Yes I am," he confirmed. "And we need to stop them before they do."

Jester nodded knowingly. "And you're going to ask us to sneak in and deal with them?"

"Yes, that's what I'm coming to. But first, how about a spot of lunch?" Weaver glanced at his reader. "Restart at one?"

Helga sighed and shook her head as she rose from her seat. *Okay, I'm hungry, but he could have got to the point. They talk too much over here. If this was Russia, we'd be getting on with the job by now.*

Chapter 13

Cryboy

Cryboy wedged his can of soda under his arm and tore open the wrapper on his protein bar. When he'd pushed out exactly an inch he used the action of moving it to his mouth as an excuse to lift his gaze to Jodie. He'd wanted to spend the meeting studying the Ferguson kid but had found that it was always her who caught his attention. She was even better-looking in the flesh, and every time she'd leaned forward she'd showed off a nice smooth section of cleavage. Even now he found himself strangely mesmerized by the movement of her mouth as she chewed.

"So what do you think? Are these guys for real?"

He'd been studying the glossy sheen of her lips but now that the words were hanging in the air he realized that she'd addressed the comment in his direction. A jolt of electricity ran down his arms and his throat tightened. He took a deep breath and forced his mind to analyze exactly what she wanted. She was asking him to verify things. His response should be simple. He needed to show her that he was thorough and demonstrate that he had all the facts at his fingertips. "They're telling the truth," he said in a voice that was deliberately loud and slow. "I checked them out. All the data he's presented. All the dates and events. All correct. Accurate."

"Yeah?" she asked. "Even that creepy video clip and the stuff about the giant crabs?"

"That's a theory," he said. "It's our working hypothesis."

"Sounds a bit wild to me." She turned to Jester. "Do you believe this? Had you heard any of this before?"

A flash of rage pulsed through Cryboy's chest. *Don't talk to him. He's homeless. No chips. No gated access. He's a nothing.*

"Do I believe it?" Jester shrugged. "No, I don't believe anything, miss. I don't even believe we're here right now."

Cryboy allowed himself a smile. *See. Talks bullshit.*

"You should be asking him." Jester tipped his head at the black kid. "He's the anthropologist. They're supposed to know about supernatural creepies."

She turned to Curtis and repeated the question.

Curtis shook his head. "Nothing about the three creatures. No."

"But what do you make of it?" Jodie asked. "The animals with mind control powers and all that?"

He shrugged. "I don't make anything of it yet. I'm curious."

She sighed noisily. "Right, well. I'm a bit more than curious. I'm actually having trouble taking all this in. I'm not at all sure about these 'arthurpods.'"

Cryboy flinched and the correct word flew out of his mouth before he could stop himself. *Let's get the basics right. If you people learn something you might succeed. You might succeed and you might stay alive.*

He took the last bite of his snack and then stuffed the wrapper into his tracksuit pocket. *We use the term arthropod because our expert systems have conducted systematic analysis. We use it because it fits.*

He opened his cola and tuned in to the conversation that was continuing around him. The Ferguson kid had noticed that Jester wasn't chipped and the two of them were congratulating each other. How dumb was that? It just meant they couldn't move around a gated city and were forced to live like outcasts. It seemed the girl found their stubbornness pretty idiotic too, 'cause she was quick to ask them how they survived without being able to get into a mall or a store. Jester gave her some smart alec reply about having two arms and a brain and she went quiet.

Cryboy took a big mouthful of soda and sneaked another peek at her. She was standing looking at her sandwich but he was fairly sure that he could interpret her body language. *She's confused now. Didn't know there were any US citizens unregistered. She thinks everybody's got one state chip. Doesn't know I've got four and a scrambler. That'll impress her. When she knows that, she'll start to figure out how powerful I really am.*

There was a clap from behind him and he turned to see Weaver standing beckoning from the meeting room.

He walked slowly across the roof and tapped the last drop of liquid onto his tongue. According to the agenda, Weaver was going to ask them to carry out missions. He was going to make it sound easier than it was. He was happy to use the simulation's high probability stats instead of taking a median.

As he lowered the can, the skin around his eyes started to twitch and he felt drops of water slide down his nose. *We're doing this too sloppy. Most of these people are going to get killed and then we'll have to start again. They should have given this to me to organize. I know how to get the best out of the gun platforms. I would have brought in the firepower they're going to need.*

Chapter 14

Jodie

Weaver was standing at the head of the table with a mug held across his stomach. He told them that he was going to try to cover all the further points as quickly as possible, and Jodie flashed him a smile of encouragement. He seemed like a nice guy but she wasn't sure she'd made her mind up about him. Although he was generally pleasant and polite, he had an odd habit of rushing through the big points and then going agonizingly slowly through the little details.

When he'd first shown them the videos, she'd assumed that the whole giant insect theory was some kind of hoax, but, as it had become clear how much money had been spent on getting them all together, a seed of doubt had started to grow in her mind. Maybe the rumors that the news networks didn't have any real journalists were true. If so, then it was just possible that he knew more about what was going on than anyone else did.

He certainly increased his pace, and for the next few minutes she found herself struggling to keep up. He told them that he'd been searching for people who'd be able to resist the hypnosis and then announced that he believed both the Jester character and the Curtis boy had this almost unique trait. In the case of the young black kid, it was due to his mastery of some shamanistic technique and he was the most important because he could also protect someone else. This meant that the team that was going to go down to neutralize the arthropods could only consist of three people.

She was gazing around the table wondering who the third member was going to be when she realized that Weaver had stopped and was looking at her. "So who's number three?" she asked curiously.

He swallowed and gave an uncomfortable half-smile. "Well … we were hoping the third member would be you."

Shit. Why me? I don't want to do it.

"Don't worry. You don't need to decide now," he said quickly. "We've got plenty more to talk about."

She nodded and wiped her tongue across her teeth. His announcement had left her feeling light-headed, and for a while she found it even more difficult to concentrate.

Weaver went on to describe how sophisticated software had selected them and how they were each contributing a specialist skill. But it wasn't going to be just them. It seemed their backers were also making a contribution to the team and there was a lady who came highly recommended from Mr. Sophos who sounded like a fantastic organizer and a real high achiever. After announcing that he was going to let this person introduce herself, Weaver tapped his controller and an attractive woman in her mid-thirties came in. Her blond hair was pulled back into a pony tail, and her short, compact body was clad in a tailored, chalk-stripe trouser suit. She walked to the head of the table with the earnest manner of a museum curator and greeted them with a smile and a nod.

Her name was Maddie Barker and she'd already been working on the project for a couple of weeks. As she explained her background, she referred to their host as "Jools" and smiled at him in a slightly sickly way that gave Jodie the impression that she was keen to stress how well she knew him and associate her own importance with his.

Maddie described her role as one of general planner and coordinator and said that she was coming along to keep everything running smoothly.

Jodie could see that this made sense and was pleased to hear that Maddie was also a trained security operative, which meant that she'd also be bringing more firepower to the team.

When she'd finished her short speech, the lady turned to Weaver and he thanked her.

"So," he said sharply, "you can probably now guess why I invited you all here. I'm going to ask you to go and catch the arthropods, and I'd like—"

"Hang on a second, Joolsey." The Jester character was rocking in his chair with his hands across his lap. "You just said arthropod*s*.

Plural. So are you asking us to do all three? The invitation only mentioned Washington."

"Ah, right. Yeah. That was to simplify things. The truth is we're not entirely sure. There is currently a possibility that if you are successful there might be advantages in tackling Fort Wainwright and the Russian site too." Weaver lifted his hands. "But let's take it a step at a time. I suggest we take another short break and I'll press you for a commitment on your return."

"Yeah, well, something else you missed out …" Jester had cocked his head and was holding his index finger in the air. "The invitations mentioned a considerable fee. So how much are we going to get paid?"

"Well, our plan at the moment is to talk to everybody individually and work out personal deals."

"Ball park." Jester said. "Are we talking thousands or millions here?"

"Well. Certainly in the low millions."

"For each job?"

"Yes."

"Nice. Sounds like you guys are serious."

"We are."

"Okay. And you mentioned a military man in the car and seem to know a lot about what the army are up to. So what's the *official* status of all this?"

"We get unofficial guidance and information," Weaver said with a wry smile. "They are making sure that our efforts are complimentary to theirs."

Jester nodded and then stood and started to saunter toward the rooftop.

Jodie started to follow, then paused at the back of the room to fix herself a drink. She was still feeling queasy and needed a few moments to gather her thoughts. The setup didn't feel right at all. The other team members were all a bit odd, and the job sounded like something that should be tackled by professionals.

As she moved out into the bright sunlight she tried to focus on the positives. There wasn't anything that sounded particularly complicated, and assuming they were all protected from the hypnosis, the three of them ought to be able to tackle one of those creatures. If the jobs only took a few hours each, she could be a multi-millionaire before the end of the week. Perhaps it was the opportunity she'd been waiting for.

Swirling currents of wind tugged at their clothes as they stood in a loose circle. Jester lit a pair of cigarettes, rolled his eyes at her and then turned to stare at the cloud that lay smudged across the horizon. She sipped her drink as she watched him. It was slowly beginning to dawn on her that the men were all socially inept in totally different ways. The computer kid was the usual geek who avoided eye contact at all costs. The Jester character was either nuts or, even worse, acting nuts. The closest there was to normal was the polite black kid with the huge scar on his forehead who was supposed to be some kind of witch doctor. If the job wasn't quite so dangerous and the money so promising the whole situation would have been hilarious.

"Well," she said, looking around the group, "I think we're supposed to be deciding if we're going to do this or not."

None of them moved. Jester took occasional drags on his Marlboros and the others sipped their drinks or stared thoughtfully into the mid-distance. Frustration started to bubble up inside her and she was just opening her mouth to criticize their attitude when Helga lifted her head.

"I will do this," she said in her thick Russian accent.

Cryboy flicked up his eyes and nodded. "I'm already in."

Jodie looked at her other companions. If Weaver was right, they were the most important ones because they could resist the hypnosis effect. Curtis was still staring into the far distance but Jester looked up and smiled at her. "What about you?" he asked.

She found herself nodding. "Yes, I'll do it." That was a shock. She had no idea she was going to come out and say that so quickly and was still analyzing her response when Curtis swung his eyes to hers and smiled.

"Yeah, me too."

"Well then …" Jester grinned and flashed his eyes. "I suppose I'd better come along and look after you jokers."

Weaver was looking at them expectantly when they slipped back inside, and she told him the news straight away.

He raised his eyebrows. "You're in? All of you?"

"Yep." She could see the relief in his eyes and it only added to the doubt that was lurking deep inside her. What exactly was she agreeing to? And why was he so tense?

He smiled and lifted his hands. "Oh, that really is good news. I have to say the chances of success are much higher with the full team."

Jester cocked his head. "So what *are* the *chances of success,* Joolsey?" he asked. "And what exactly are we going to be doing?"

"Well." Weaver took a deep breath. "We're expecting the same sort of setup at each location. Once inside, there will be some half-dead guards to deal with. After that we start to hit some unknowns. We don't know exactly what there is at bunker level, but once you're down there you need to locate the arthropod creature and overcome it. When you've knocked them out, radio for the backup team and they'll send down a UGV with one of the lead containers."

"Then what?" Jester asked.

"Then the box is buried and the job's done."

Jodie lifted her head and squinted at Weaver. He was rushing when they should be taking each detail step by step. "So what's the timescale for all this?" she asked.

"Well …" He glanced across the terrace. "We need you to get going pretty soon. Straight away in fact."

"Now?"

"Yep," Weaver nodded. "We have a jump jet on the lower roof. You'll be in Washington in just over an hour."

The big empty office seemed to be poised expectantly around her as Jodie sat and stared at her reader. They were due to leave in ten minutes, and although she was flooding with extremes of excitement and apprehension, her overall feeling was an irritating restlessness from the huge quantities of caffeine she'd taken. She desperately wanted to find a sane calm voice to tell her whether she was doing the right thing, but she knew deep down that the only person who could judge the decision was her.

She kept her finger hovering above the screen. It wasn't the time to think about herself. She'd already committed to taking the next step and what she had to do now was make peace with the most important person in her life.

A swipe reactivated the device. She'd left it in privacy mode since the previous evening and was going to claim that it was one of the job's security requirements. It was a little white lie that would keep her mom from calling her every few hours.

The second bending of the truth would have to be a bit bigger. She'd have to change the missions into something fairly harmless sounding.

Choosing a voice-only connection, she initiated the call. The line opened to an echo and the air tightened in her chest. *They're an hour behind. She'll be in the kitchen cleaning up after lunch.*

The line rang again. *She'll be looking under her rubber gloves. Putting the dish towel down and drying her hands before she picks up.* Emotion tightened her throat and water swelled in her eyes.

A third ring. *Oh god, I'm not going to be able to do this*. She swallowed hard. Fourth ring and a click.

Her mom's voice: frail, faint and distant. "Hello?"

"Mom? Hi, it's me."

"Oh hi, honey. How are you? Where are you?"

"I'm good. How are *you*? What ya doing?"

"Oh, I'm okay. Can't complain. Knees are a bit sore."

"No?" She squeezed her eyes shut. *She shouldn't be suffering with her joints. She's got the medication for that.* "I thought that had cleared."

"Well. They're not bad like before. Just at night."

"Are you taking the anti-inflammatories?"

"Yeah. It's nothing. It'll go." Her voice brightened. "How are you? Hank says you're away."

Christ, she's spoken to Hank already. They're thick as thieves those two. "Yeah I'm working. They flew me out to New York. First class interstate. Bankers with more money than sense."

"Wow, New York. So what is it? Firearms training? An exhibition?"

"Yeah, training. Super-wealthy clients." She looked up from her arm and stared at an expanse of tinted sky. "These guys are paying big money, Mom. More than the range takes in a year. It's a real break. Enough to go gated."

"Oh. Well that's good, hon." The line fell quiet. "Are you sure they're genuine? How do you know you're going to get all this cash? I mean … why are they paying so much?"

"Mom. They're legit. I've checked it all out."

"Oh." Silence. "So what's the catch? There's no such thing as easy money, you know."

"No catch, Mom." She pulled the frustration out of her voice. "It's a good job. Lucky break … These things do happen, yeah?" *Be nice to her, be nice to her.*

"So what exactly do they want? Is it dangerous?"

Her breaths started to shorten and catch. *Can't lie to her. Can't lie to Mom.* The waiting tears broke loose and dripped hot down her cheeks. *Got to hold myself together.* "Sorry, Mom. Dropout on the line. Listen. I've got to run back into this session. Just sneaked out."

"Oh. Okay."

Hurt her already; she hates short conversations. "I'll try to call you," she said, poising her finger over the terminate button.

"When you can. Don't trouble over me."

"Okay, Mom." A half-cough cleared her throat. "Love you."

She clicked the line closed and stood frozen. The tears flowed freely and there was release, tension seeping from every muscle and sinew. *I can't get hurt. Can't get injured. Mom can never know. No cops turning up at the house. I can't do that to her. The grief and worry would break her.*

She turned and started to walk back to the meeting room. *She can never get that visit. I have to stay unharmed. I have to do this and I have to survive.*

Washington

Chapter 15

Cryboy

Cryboy kept his gaze fixed on the wisps of air that were rolling over the aircraft's wing tips and dabbed his nose with the back of his sleeve. As the jet started to creep forward he felt a tingle in his arms and legs. In just a few seconds they'd start to feel the Gs. It was the most exciting part of any flight and his body was buzzing with anticipation.

When he was sure his nostrils were totally clean, he pressed his palms against his tracksuit pants and started to reflect on the day's meeting. They'd all signed up and that was good. If they were going to use a small squad of humans, the one thing that the sims had agreed on was that it needed the full team. What was weird though was how little interest his companions had showed in the archive. Weaver had told them that there were lots of collaborating accounts about these creatures from different regions and cultures, so why weren't they more interested in that? This was a unifying theory that held the key to the world's supernatural myths. He'd have been all over that in an instant.

The engine jumped a pitch, and as his body was pressed back into his seat, a second anomaly occurred to him. Weaver had mentioned the guard animals but not the crawlers. So when was he going to warn them? Perhaps he wasn't. None of the AIs believed the accounts and most of the human analysts seemed doubtful. But it kept coming back to the same issue. If they'd been more curious then Weaver wouldn't have been able to miss so much out. Skipping things was wrong. There was a sequence to the way he'd investigated the theory, and he'd expected the newer recruits to follow the same obvious route. But they hadn't.

He watched the aircraft's panels flex and ripple against the flow and considered why it might be that his new teammates didn't seem to think straight. He started by listing them in terms of their mental capabilities. The voodoo man, Mr. Curtis Ferguson, had the highest IQ by far. Cryboy'd hacked what school records he could find and they were fairly impressive for someone who'd only attended about a quarter of each year. The problem with Curtis was what he got up to when he was living with his shaman friends. According to his lectures there was a distinct possibility that he'd fried his brain with psychoactives, and maybe that was why he seemed happy to take everything in his stride.

The roar of the turbines deepened to a stomach-shaking throb and suddenly they were lifting up into the New York sky. As the plane tipped and started hurtling forward, he moved down the list. Sean "Jester" Solberg had virtually no records at all. His high-school assessment simply stated "Incomplete Session," which was education board code meaning that the student had got up and left without finishing the test.

Next was the girl. She asked questions but then moved onto new topics. She didn't have any logic and there'd been absolutely no root cause analysis in her lines of thought. But then she was female and they worked differently.

Images of wombs and ovaries formed in his head and then morphed into sharp pictures of her long legs and the smooth dual curves of her cleavage. For a moment he was lost in a collage of erotic thoughts then he became aware that his palms were sweating and pressed them tighter against his legs. *Stop this.* He looked back through the porthole and sent his mind to a safe comfortable place. He considered how the stress patterns in the wings could be simulated by AI and how the engineers plotted where they needed to bend and by how much.

After a few minutes contemplating tolerance algorithms, his gaze moved across the aisle and he was reminded of the final candidate. They hadn't managed to get any educational records for her but he'd already decided that the big Russian lady was okay. She didn't talk much but when she did she was logical. She was shy like him; probably because English wasn't her first language.

He turned back to the swirls of vapor rolling over the flaps and his eyes slowly glazed. *So will they do what's necessary to succeed? They need to gel and become one unit. People can do that. It's called storming, norming and performing. Not seen it. Read about it. Still don't get why they're not asking more questions? Was it Weaver? Did he make it sound easy? He looked relaxed, acted calm. Didn't tell them everything. The half-deads are easy to kill so they think it's all going to be that simple. It's misdirection. Like a magic trick.*

A rush of air snorted out of his nose and his head twitched. He put the side of his finger under his left nostril and dabbed away a trickle of mucus. *We'll need to find replacements. They're looking but not hard enough. I've told them that. Most of this lot won't survive. I should be okay though. I've got teddy here.* He squeezed the toy on his lap. *Must keep it close at all times. Fifteen minute battery life. Should be enough for anything.*

Chapter 16

Jodie

Once they were buckled in and the big engines had started to roar, Jodie had filled with an exciting sense of purpose and determination. Boarding a state-of-the-art jet on a skyscraper rooftop and then settling back in the sterile luxury of the cabin and listening to the calm softness of the pilot's voice had been extremely reassuring. She was now part of a team, and the sensation of rising gracefully above New York and then zipping across the sky was undeniably exciting.

Her large female companion was also the source of considerable confidence. They had chatted while waiting to board the plane and she'd decided that, although a little timid, the Russian lady was absolutely charming and definitely worth bonding with. Her immense strength was also strangely comforting. While attempting to adjust her safety belt, the big woman had somehow ripped the strap from its housing and then shamefacedly held up the broken bolt before slipping the remains under her seat. They'd shared a stifled giggle over the incident and Jodie was now enjoying having a female friend who seemed to be able to break steel with her bare hands.

The vast grid of streets and buildings below them soon disappeared behind a layer of cloud, and she pulled out the keyboard on her reader. Just before starting her first sentence she realized that her fellow traveler wasn't chipped and perhaps didn't have any way of communicating with the outside world. She caught her eye and offered to send a message for her. The other lady said that she did have a cell phone but had decided that it was easier and simpler not to say anything to anyone. Jodie was instantly curious and couldn't help taking the opportunity to find out more about her personal life. She asked if she had a husband or a partner she needed to contact and Helga looked down at her lap and shook her head.

It seemed they had quite a lot in common. "No, me neither," Jodie told her and then looked down and started to type.

After a few moments the ridiculousness of what she was writing made her pause and turn back. "I was just about to message my business partner," she told her companion. "So I wrote: *Going to Washington with a soldier clown and a voodoo boy to capture a giant crab*. Then I thought, 'Nah, I can't write that!'" She chuckled and shook her head. "So I said: *Hope you got the note. Just a short trip. Back at the weekend*."

Helga's mouth curled upward and she started to nod. "That is good thinking. Good to be positive. Good to believe that you will return."

Jodie lowered her gaze and tried to stop the smile sliding from her face. From what Weaver had said, her new friend had been on military missions before. She'd probably sat on planes chatting to people who hadn't been on the return journey.

The rush from the takeoff drained out of her and she suddenly felt small and alone. It was clear that she was inexperienced and out of her depth and being propelled toward a situation that she didn't fully understand.

The flight was surprisingly quick, and it was much sooner than she'd have liked when the plane bumped onto the tarmac outside Washington and they were ushered into the first of a trio of waiting trucks. They immediately set off toward the city center and Maddie gave them a lightning-speed tour of the bunks, comms booths and kitchen facilities that lined their new transportation.

As Jodie had come to expect, everything was state of the art, and even more impressive was the fact that there were two almost identical vehicles following close behind them. Both carried duplicate sets of the equipment for the mission and a couple of large lead boxes that were designed to imprison the animal. It seemed that their employers were very keen to ensure that all their gear had *redundancy.* Jodie quickly grasped that this meant having backup versions of everything, but she couldn't help thinking that the only thing that wasn't going to be easy to replace in the event of a disaster was herself and her teammates.

After the exploration of the vehicle's fixtures and fittings, they were taken back into the central aisle and kitted out with protective nanosuits, lightweight body armor and robust-looking communicators.

She had just settled at the table and was still trying to get comfortable in her Arti Silk vest when Curtis slipped into the seat opposite her. His jacket flapped open as he eased himself along the bench and she caught a flash of taut muscle before lowering her eyes to her mug.

He was in good shape—you couldn't help noticing that—but he also had a really weird dress sense. He'd refused any kind of specialist clothing and was still in his dark suit. Although it was cashmere and clearly very expensive, it was crumpled and he did nothing to look after it. He wore it without a shirt and with leather baseball boots that he took off at every opportunity. Everything he owned was made of natural materials, which she found weird and made her wonder if he was some sort of reverse vegan. Even more puzzling was the fact that he'd been described as some kind of magician. He was supposed to protect her from hypnotism but nobody had really explained how he was going to do it. It didn't make much sense but seemed to be what the mission depended on.

When she next looked up, the young black kid was watching her, and she took the opportunity to ask him if he knew what they were going to find in the White House bunker.

"Nope," he said flatly.

"Oh," she replied. "It sounded from your intro that you knew something about what we're going to be dealing with."

"No. I don't know what these things might be."

"Right." She looked down at the tabletop. "I was hoping somebody did."

A flash of fear and frustration tightened her jaw. *Seems like they expect us to capture some kind of dangerous animal without really knowing what we're up against. I'm not sure they've really got this all figured out.*

After sitting in silence for a few moments she looked up and caught his eye again, this time keeping her voice deliberately soft and calm. "But don't you think this is a bit rushed?" she asked. "That maybe we should have a bit more time to get ready?"

He rubbed his chin. "It's fast-moving, yes. But I don't think we *could* do much training because we don't really know what's in there."

She gave a few hesitant nods then let her gaze drift back to the lines of headlights moving up the street.

On the plane she'd made a plan to swap places with Helga. It made a lot more sense for the big woman with military training to go down with the men and catch the creature. Her only problem was how to broach the subject. Although they'd spent the flight bonding, they were still a long way from the point where she could bring the idea up. She wasn't even sure there was an acceptable way of suggesting that somebody else did the dangerous job while you waited around as backup.

Every jolt and roll of the big truck was making her aware of the time ticking away, and to stem her rising panic she tried to convince herself that what they were doing was normal and safe. Maybe this was how these things worked. People with money snapped their fingers and stuff got done. Maybe they were going to be completely safe. How would she know? She'd never been part of anything like this before.

"Okay guys."

She was snapped from her daze by Maddie's voice and turned to see her place a micro on the table and slip onto the end of the bench. Jester, Cryboy and Helga were standing behind her, and soon the whole team was seated at the small table.

"We'll be at the gates in about fifteen minutes," their organizer announced. "I'll go over the basic plan and then Dr. Weaver will come back online to check we're ready. He reckons you folk might have some more questions for him."

Jodie pushed her hair behind her ear. *Yeah, I got questions. Too many questions. It's all moving so fast now.*

There was a beep, and a throw-image stabilized in the air above the table.

"There we go. The West Wing." Maddie pointed at a diagonal line that led into a group of glowing rectangles. "We're going in through the service entrance and then we'll split into two. Jester, Curtis and Jodie will take the central hallway to the Situation Room and then make their way down to the bunker. Once they've neutralized whatever creatures are down there acting as guards, they'll have to locate the target and—"

Jester's head shot up. "Hang on a sec," he said suspiciously. "Creatures acting as guards? What are you talking about?"

Maddie froze. "Didn't Dr. Weaver mention that one of our spy units was eaten by some sort of vicious dog?"

"Nope." He stuck out his lower lip. "Don't think so."

"Did he read you the descriptions of the crawlers?"

Jester shook his head and their organizer looked down at her computer.

"Well, he'll be dialing in any minute now. I'm sure he'll tell you then." Her eyes tracked the back of her hand as she smoothed it across the tabletop. "As I was saying, you need to find the target as quickly as you can. We don't know if there are young yet, but if there are, you'll have to deal with them too. You need to neutralize the creature, but make sure you don't kill it. Once you're certain it's unconscious, call for us. Helga and a load shifter will bring in the coffin. We load it onto the truck and get out quick."

Jodie suddenly found herself speaking, her voice much louder and faster than she would've liked. "Sorry?" she asked. "You said we need to neutralize the target but not kill it?"

"That's right."

"Why's that?"

Maddie frowned. "You didn't talk about the consequences of killing one of these things?"

"No." Jodie felt irritation reddening her cheeks. "He mentioned trapping them and then putting them in a box, but he never said we couldn't kill them."

"He didn't? Well, I'll leave that to him too."

"Basically though ..." Jester rested his forearms on the table. "We go in. Put it in a box and bring it out."

"Yes," Maddie confirmed.

"Good," he commented. "Simple plan. I like that."

He had just settled in his seat when there was a crackle of static, and three coin-sized, colored lights appeared in front of them. The dots converged and became recognizable as Weaver and then his voice filled the truck. "Hi, everyone. Can you all hear me okay?"

Jodie examined the projection with her teeth clenched. The young academic was all charm and manners but he seemed to have a brilliant gift for forgetting inconvenient facts.

When nobody answered his question, Maddie leaned forward and greeted him cheerfully. "Hi, Dr. Weaver. Yes we can. Good you called. I think we've got plenty of questions for you."

"Okay," he nodded. "Go ahead."

Jodie glanced at the others and then dove in. "Maddie was just saying we had to neutralize these things but not kill them."

"Ah … right." Weaver started to scratch his nose.

"So?" she asked. "Can we shoot them?"

"Yes … well … we think you probably can, because we don't think it'll do them much harm. If the first shot *does* appear to have inflicted real damage then I have to ask you to stop."

Jester lifted his face, a gleeful light dancing in his pupils. "You're saying we *can* shoot them as long as it doesn't do them any harm?"

"Well, it's somewhat paradoxical but—"

"Paradoxical! That's fuckin superb, pal." Jester had raised his arms in some kind of celebratory gesture. "I've heard some bizarre briefings in my time but to hear that we can engage the enemy as long as it doesn't seem to do them any harm. That's … that's … I don't know." He dropped back against his seat. "That's made my day."

"Yes," Weaver replied. "I'm aware of how it sounds."

A synthesized female voice spoke from somewhere behind him. "*ETA eight minutes.*"

"Let me give you some detail. There's a theory that these creatures contain some very horrific … entities. So if they're blown to bits or cut in half then these things will escape and create another kind of infestation."

"Right. And so what *are* these things?" Jester asked.

"Well, that's also quite difficult to describe. It's possibly a type of gas or a type of energy that is toxic to humans."

Jodie leaned forward in her seat. "But we don't know this for sure?" she asked.

"We don't, no. But it's a scenario we're trying to avoid."

Jester leaned forward and pursed his lips. "So we've got to keep these things alive and just get them in the box?"

"Yes, exactly …"

"*ETA seven minutes …*"

Jodie sighed and pushed her hair behind her ear. Everything seemed to be getting more complicated when it should have been getting simpler. "This is a lot of information to take in all at once," she commented, scanning her teammates for support. "Can't we take a couple of days to run through all this? Maybe do some training together."

"Well, we're already a bit behind schedule. As I said, we're very concerned about these creatures breeding."

"But … how?" she asked. You said there's only one of them in there."

"Well it's very possible that they're parthenogenic—that they can produce an ovum that develops without fertilization."

"Okay," Jester replied. "All very interesting. So here's another thing, Joolsey. Maddie just mentioned some animals that are acting as guards down there."

"Yes." Weaver cleared his throat. "Thank you, this is true. I did mention the dogs but I think I forgot to talk about the crawlers."

Jodie stared hard at Weaver's face. "Crawlers?" she asked.

"Yes. The scrolls call them that … crawlers, climbers, sometimes Upir or Ekiminu … lots of names."

"Yeah right. But what are they?"

"Well, we don't really know …"

"ETA six minutes …"

"A kind of jumping animal with a nasty bite."

"So can we shoot them?" she asked. "Kill them, I mean?"

"Yes." Weaver's voice cut out and his face flickered and then turned green. "Hello? Can you hear me?"

She nodded. "Yes."

"Sorry, you're obviously approaching the White House firewall. What was I saying? The accounts say they're difficult to kill but there are no warnings about doing so." He squinted into the camera. "Any other questions?"

"Well …" She racked her brain but found so many interwoven lines of thought she couldn't pick out a single issue. "Can we talk to you again if we think of anything?"

"Yes …" His features broke into vertical stripes and then his mouth moved without sound. "… But you need to …" There were a few pops and crackles and then his face faded and the line fell silent.

She looked around and tried to gauge the reactions of her teammates. Helga met her gaze and widened her eyes but the others seemed lost in thought. Acutely aware that they were only minutes from the White House, she used the energy from her rising panic to form a basic survival plan.

It was clear that despite Weaver's sense of urgency they actually needed to take the mission a step at a time. Once they were inside the West Wing she'd talk to her comrades and persuade them to approach the first stage as a reconnaissance trip. She was confident that when she'd explained her feelings the two men would agree to taking things slowly. They could scout around for a while and then get out and report what they'd seen to Weaver.

She was still finalizing her strategy when the big vehicle slowed at the perimeter and Maddie went to the cab to oversee their security clearance.

It would have been nice to hit some sort of unexpected hitch or delay, but, much sooner than she would have liked, they started up again and their organizer came back and asked them to assemble by the rear doors.

They moved up together, and while Jodie checked and rechecked her shotgun, she found herself glancing resentfully at Curtis. He'd refused to use a rifle, and Weaver must have known about this because there was a range of primitive tools in the truck's armory. The young black kid had chosen a couple of wooden spears and she eyed them suspiciously as she tightened her gun belt. *So he only uses manual weapons. How dumb is that? What use are those going to be against guys with automatics? The half-deads sound slow but there could be a lot of them.*

She was still fretting about the limited firepower in the team when there was a squeeze of brakes and they stopped. The big vehicle settled with a hiss of air and she felt her throat tighten. This was it. They were about to try and creep into the White House, and she needed to make sure that everyone moved as slowly and cautiously as possible.

Chapter 17

Helga

The whole setting felt more like a magical grotto than the start of a mission. As Helga peered out of the rear doors she was amazed by how calm and beautiful everything was. The pure white façade of the West Wing was glowing serenely in the beams of multiple spotlights, while falling flares scratched bright trails in the sky above the roof.

On the steps below her, Cryboy was holding out some sort of metal disk, and when a line of green bulbs lit up on the rear, he mumbled something to Maddie and the two of them crouched and jogged to the first section of lawn.

Their organizer seemed twitchy and Helga wasn't surprised. If what they'd been told was true, there was a distinct possibility that some of the confused half-dead guards would start shooting, and she had a suspicion that Maddie didn't have any real combat experience.

They were beckoned forward, and when the others had filed out, Helga braced her weapon and followed. She moved up and had just squatted behind a low hedge when she heard the pop and crack of fireworks. It was the diversion. Weaver had hired mercenaries to create a demonstration at the eastern fence and they were making as much noise as possible.

Even though they were harmless, the whistles and bangs were close enough to the sound of real battle to unnerve her, and she found a gap in the leaves and eyed the windows on the first floor. The inside seemed empty but they still needed to get moving. They had no cover where they were and wouldn't last twenty seconds in a firefight.

Craning her neck, she saw Cryboy move to the veranda and connect his micro to the stonework. He squinted at the device and then turned and nodded and they set off again, creeping forward to a covered walkway that ran down the side of the building.

Their route took them to a service entrance that was hanging open with its security scanner flashing green. The rest of them stopped, but the Jester character went inside and strolled up a dimly lit corridor to a pair of fire doors where he crouched and put his ear to the crack.

While he was listening, Maddie took a bag off her shoulder and pulled out a fan-shaped machine. She took a couple of slow steps toward him then placed the object gently on the floor and came back.

Helga guessed that the device must have been part of some prearranged entrance strategy but was interested to see that the ex-soldier chose to ignore it and started to push the panels open with the barrel of his rifle.

The action set her pulse pumping loudly in her ears. She'd had all kinds of doubts about Weaver's crazy plan but now it was for real. The Jester character was right outside the West Wing's main corridor and it looked like he was going in.

Chapter 18

Jodie

Just breathing seemed to be a challenge. Jodie was trying to get as much air in and out of her lungs as possible while she watched Jester lean into a brightly lit hallway. *Christ. He's going to get seen. We're going to get caught any second.*

After peering inside, he straightened himself and then turned and looked right at her. *Shit. He wants me now.* His eyes moved over her shoulder and she turned to find Curtis hunkered down behind her.

"I think it's our turn up front," he said, smiling shyly and tipping his head.

She stared at his face and tried to absorb his words. He was right. This was it. It was time for the three of them to go inside, and the moment had come far too quickly.

When they reached him, Jester was standing grinning with his arms folded on his rifle. He held his finger to his lips, pointed to his right and announced in a loud whisper that there was a large group of half-dead guards about two hundred yards away.

Pins and needles flushed through Jodie's legs and she found herself looking enviously at the others behind them. *I should swap places with someone. They've got me figured all wrong.*

Jester jabbed his finger in the direction of the soldiers. "Simple plan. We move up close, take them out quick, and then wait to see what kind of reaction we get. You both okay with that?"

She felt her jaw lock tight. *Shit. Got to get myself out of this.* When she met his gaze, the words just tumbled out. "I can't shoot men," she told him. "I can't kill people. Even if they're sick."

"Well," he nodded slowly. "You're part of the firepower, honey."

"I know." *Fuck. Take me home. Just take me home.*

"Tell you what ..." His eyes rested on the machine on the floor. "We're creeping up behind this thing anyway. Wait till you can smell the half-deads and then decide. I'll take that lot out on my own if I have to."

She nodded. *Okay, let's get it over with.*

After studying her for a few more seconds, he turned to Curtis and stuck out his lower lip. "So what about you? You going to be okay in there? I mean, how are you going to cope when the bullets start flying around?"

"Easiest way to deal with bullets is not to be there when they arrive," the black kid said calmly.

Jester squinted at him and then shook his head. "Jeez, you might be more nuts than I am."

Curtis lifted his eyebrows and held the other man's stare. For a while the two of them seemed to be locked in some sort of point-scoring contest, and to break the tension she tipped her head at the device on the floor and asked what it was.

Jester pulled his gaze away and looked down. "Laserwall," he told her. "Projects a picture of the view minus us."

She was studying the strange machine when he bent and pressed a button on its casing. It immediately sprang to life and motored up to the doors. He pushed them open and the thing slipped nimbly through the gap. A few seconds later a hiss cut the silence, and a dark blur, like a smudge of pencil, rose to the ceiling. When the hallway was completely sealed, a sudden burst of light turned the particles into specks of color.

"Well," Jester said, jerking his chin at the projection. "The light show's working. Let's hit the dance floor." A shimmer of bells cut the air and suddenly he was in the passage with his rifle tight to his cheek. He stood staring down the barrel for a few seconds and then turned to her and nodded.

The air in her chest was glued solid as she pushed herself forward. *Oh Shit, this is it.*

The broad corridor was lit by glass chandeliers and lined with small desks and elegant chairs. At the far end, a group of straight-backed soldiers was standing motionless with their rifles held across their chests.

She inched up the barrel of her gun while struggling to convince herself that they couldn't see her. It was weird, but it did seem that the little contraption had made them invisible.

The cloaking device crawled steadily along the gilt-edged carpet and they followed. Curtis came up behind her, moving silently on the balls of his feet with a spear on his right shoulder.

After just a few steps her boot connected with something and sent it skidding across the floor. She checked that the guards hadn't moved then looked down and discovered clusters of shell cases. A glance to her right revealed arcs of bullet holes in the wooden paneling and heat flashed to her face. *Oh Christ! What the hell do I think I'm doing? The last people in here were professionals and they got beat. I'm not a killer. I can't even flush a spider down the plughole.*

She wiped her hands on her shorts. *This isn't going to work. I'm going to freeze up, I know it.*

They kept on. The men's features became clearer and she was able to see that their faces were mottled with flakes of hanging skin. A whiff of something bitter drifted into her nostrils and she pressed her finger tighter against the trigger. *Okay we're close now. Let's get this done.*

After a couple more steps the stench of rotten meat and stale pee flooded her throat and made her retch. The fan of light rippled and flickered and she swiveled her gaze to the back of Jester's neck. *The machine's running out. Why isn't he shooting?*

Patches of shadow grew in the air, then the soldiers' heads turned and their lifeless black eyes locked onto her. Their arms lifted and a bristle of gun barrels leveled at her head.

Shit. Her heart stopped. *He's not going to fight. It's just me.* She fired twice and blew holes in the chests of the nearest two.

Jester's rifle came alive at his shoulder. Time broke into a frenzy of cracks and flashes and the half-deads crumpled sideways.

She kept firing, and when the last of the corpses had hit the floor, Jester turned and gave her a nod.

"Good work."

She let the air out of her lungs and lowered her gun. *Oh boy. This is real now. We're doing it. We've started a raid on the White House and I've just killed some people.*

She knelt and pressed cartridges out of her belt with trembling hands. Male voices were shouting in her head and she tried to remind herself that the soldiers had already been dead. She repeated again and again that she'd actually put them out of their misery, then made a determined effort to carry on. While she was doing things she could keep the doubt and fear away. Stopping and thinking was not an option; she had to keep moving.

"Well. Good work guys," she said, standing and pumping the barrel. "Let's keep going, yeah?"

"Agreed," Jester replied, surveying her curiously before turning and sauntering toward the T-junction ahead of them.

She trod after him and for a while her surroundings whizzed by in a blur.

A strange white tube called a "nanoscanner" took them straight to the Situation Room and then they were moving alongside a long table strewn with pads and water jugs. A pair of steel doors loomed in front of her and she found herself looking down a flight of steps at a narrow landing.

It was the entrance to the bunker.

She would have liked to have stopped and got her bearings, but the strangely costumed ex-soldier set off down the staircase without a pause and they followed.

There were a trio of big gun platforms parked haphazardly on the walkway below, and when they'd woven between them, they were confronted by a section of blank wall with a narrow gap in it.

"What's this?" she whispered.

"Squeeze space," Jester told her quietly. "Stops any wannabe Caesars grabbing a joystick and crossing the Rubicon."

She wasn't sure what he meant, but Maddie had said something about a barrier to prevent attacks from battlefield robots and it seemed they'd reached it.

Turning sideways, they were able to pass through, and on the other side they found a short stretch of corridor leading to a pair of gray metal doors.

Without consulting her or asking if she was ready, Jester pulled the nearest panel toward him and peered around it.

"Back up," he said suddenly, pushing his palm at her.

She flattened against the wall. "What?"

“Sentinels. High-spec ones.” He dropped to a crouch and leaned against the doorframe. “They’re bad news. I’ve lost buddies to these things.”

With her heart beating fast and a cold sweat forming down her back, she watched him pull a magazine from his vest and toss it into the room. There was a distant thud and he shook his head. “They’re not online. Must have lost signal and closed down.”

“So what do we do?” she asked.

“If they switch on, the main danger’s an ID error. But don’t worry, you won’t know anything about it. Just means we’ll be able to send you home in a couple of condoms.” He looked back, and then continued in a softer tone. “No, seriously. All we can do is keep an eye on them.”

He started to inch into the room and she felt her shoulders tense. *Fuck. Now we’re fighting machines as well.*

A path of dirty footprints led down the middle of the carpet and disappeared under a big yellow blast door. Standing on either side of the trail were a pair of metal pyramids, each about four feet high and coated in dull green paint.

She eyed them suspiciously, careful to stay behind Jester as she followed him inside.

They crept forward a couple of yards but the machines didn’t move. The numerous hatches on the battered casings stayed firmly closed, and when she was absolutely certain there was no immediate danger, she stepped out from behind her companion and started to scan the rest of the space.

There were seating areas on either side of her. On the right, a trio of pale-blue sofas formed an enclosure around a coffee table, and the paneling on their left was lined with a row of leather armchairs. The place seemed safe and fairly uninteresting, and she found her eyes were quickly drawn back to the big yellow slab that dominated the far wall. The longer she studied it the more it seemed to exude a quiet menace, like some kind of dam struggling to hold back a sinister force.

Curtis slipped in behind them and had only taken a few steps when his eyes narrowed and he leveled a finger at the door. “Don’t touch that,” he said firmly.

“Why?” she asked, surprised by the sudden authority in his voice.

“I need to find out what’s through there.”

"How are you going to do that?"

He held up his palm. "Just give me some time."

As he turned and went to the back of the room it dawned on her that he was going to try the magic he claimed he could do, and that gave her some hope. Whatever happened, the results would be useful. If he couldn't do anything, they'd have a good excuse to back up and rethink the plan. If he did claim to see something then they could get straight out and report it to Weaver.

Curtis moved behind a leather armchair and sat cross-legged on the floor. When he'd settled himself, he pulled a leather pouch from his jacket and started tapping a thick powder onto the carpet. Coaxing the dark granules into a mound, he slid a single match into the center and it started to smolder. Wisps of gray smoke rose into the air and when they'd thickened into a single plume he leaned forward and sucked the fumes up into his nose. After several long noisy inhalations he started humming and the room filled with a deep continuous tone.

She perched herself on the arm of a sofa and caught Jester's attention. "I guess this might take a while," she said in a loud whisper.

Her teammate looked up with a couple of cigarettes in his mouth, rolled his eyes and nodded.

The sounds Curtis was making slowly became the words of a chant, then reached a crescendo and stopped. He was so still and serene it looked like he'd fallen asleep, and she was left wondering what they were meant to do while they waited. She checked her weapons a few times and tried to run through some breathing exercises but found that her concentration was soon broken and her eyes were eventually drawn back to the giant yellow slab.

Jester had finished his cigarettes and was grinding the stubs into the carpet when a muffled clunk came from behind the far wall. She looked up and saw the circular handle on the big door begin to turn. *Shit.* She slipped off the sofa and raised her gun. *This has got to be bad news.*

Jester dropped behind an armchair with his rifle at his shoulder, and then turned to her and frowned.

The wheel stopped turning and there was a hiss of pressurized air.

The next thing she knew, a high-pitched tone pierced her ears and the big panel started to swing open.

Chapter 19

Jester

A wall of freezing, meat-scented air wafted across the room and four black-eyed soldiers stepped into the doorway. They were met by a blizzard of rounds and crumpled sideways. Their slow-folding corpses had just settled when a second squad marched into view. Jester picked off the front two with double taps to the forehead, but the rear pair managed to lower themselves behind the gun platforms and started returning fire.

He was inching sideways for a better aim when he noticed that Jodie's shotgun had fallen quiet. His eyes flicked to where he'd last seen her but she wasn't there. She was in the center of the room shuffling toward the yellow door with her weapon lying behind her on the floor.

He dropped his rifle and sprang forward. Launching himself into the air, he grappled her to the ground and rolled them both toward a sofa. Bullets ripped into the carpet near their feet but he got them behind the big divan and the firing stopped.

He slipped off her and inched his head up. As the top of his hat rose above the seat back, rounds started tearing into the armrest and he dropped himself flat.

He felt something pressing against his arm and looked down to see Jodie trying to crawl away. "Oh fuck." His eyes darted around the room and came to rest on her hips. With a sharp tug he unclipped her ammunition belt and looped it around her ankles, resting a foot on the strap.

A hail of automatic fire whistled over his head and he peered across the room. "Shit. Rifle." He pulled the communicator from his vest. "Maddie, this is Jester. Do you read me?" A heavy-caliber burst raked the wall and showered him with plaster chippings. He lowered his head. "Maddie, need support here. Trapped in the basement. Curtis's out, Jodie's out. Need backup or an exit."

He listened for a moment and then squeezed the button again. "Maddie, we need an exit here."

A cluster of bullets shredded the cushioning and ricocheted off the brickwork behind him.

He dropped the radio, pulled his Glock from a pocket on his thigh and peered over the top of the sofa.

The space behind the gun platforms was packed with black-eyed soldiers.

Cursing softly, he dropped a couple with holes in their foreheads then slipped down and found the communicator again. “Maddie? I really think you should be getting us out. Whole bunch of half-deads here with good cover. We need to pull back.”

A spray of slugs ripped through the armrest and hit his body armor. He looked over to his rifle on the far side of the room and shook his head with frustration.

An instant later he was back up placing shots into the heads of his attackers. The leaders slumped to the ground but more appeared behind them. “Jesus!” he shouted. “Don’t you guys ever stop? Haven’t you got *graves* to go to?”

There was only a small group of half-deads left standing, and with almost comic slowness, one swung up an arm and released a grenade.

Jester watched it roll and then snapped out his leg and chipped it toward the entrance doors. It settled on the threshold and he flattened himself alongside Jodie and covered his ears. There was a flash and an ear-splitting bang and he was thrown against the wall. He hit the blocks face-first and then landed on his side while a rain of burning fabric fell onto his crumpled body.

He groaned and lifted his head. Gingerly dabbing the shards of metal jutting from his neck, he pushed himself up onto all fours.

“Oh boy,” he said, thrusting his chin at the doorway. “Now look what you’ve done! We’re never going to get this cleared up before Mom gets home.”

He started to crawl back toward Jodie, moving jerkily with his right arm swinging limply at his side.

When he was behind the couch he sat back and reached for the communicator with his left hand.

“Maddie, my dear. Here’s the situation. Big bunch of half-deads got good cover. We’re behind a chair but the half-inch of plywood and flowery polyester ain’t giving much protection. Very low on ammo. I’m out and the lady’s got about twenty rounds left. After that I got nothing but body odor, flatulence and a sharp sense of humor.” He looked at the mouthpiece. “You copying any of this? You there?”

He tossed the device over his shoulder and reached for one of Jodie’s revolvers. He was slipping his finger into the trigger guard when an alarm started to ring and the ceiling sprinklers spurted into life.

"Okay. Great." He glanced up and started to nod. "Now it's raining." His gaze moved to the buckled doors. "And we're trapped."

A pair of bullets hit his armor and knocked him sideways. He rolled onto his stomach and started to return fire, pumping shots until the pistol clicked empty.

He found the second revolver and was taking aim through a hole in the frame when a crash shook the doors behind him and his attackers stopped firing. He turned and saw a second force bend the threshold. On the third impact, the crosspiece snapped and the panels swung open to reveal Helga standing with an assault rifle under each arm. She gave him a quick glance then trained both weapons on the half-deads and released a torrent of bullets. The remaining guards shuddered and folded to the ground. She kept firing until both weapons clicked empty then stepped back out of sight and Maddie's voice filled the room.

"Is that it?" she asked. "Are you safe now?"

Jester nodded and cleared his throat. "Yes, thank you very much. Very kind of you to pop in."

"We can't come any closer because of the hypnosis," she told him.

"Okay …" He pushed himself up onto his knees. "Well, so long as it's not personal."

Maddie pushed her voice louder. "But we need you to bring the others out."

"Yep. No probs." He slid his left arm under Jodie, flipped her onto his shoulder and stood. As he jerked himself upright, a movement caught his eye and he turned to see Curtis standing staring at the fan of corpses in front of the yellow door.

"The controller's gone," the young black man said quietly. "There were shadows behind it, animals I think. They've moved back inside."

"Okay, right." Jester nodded slowly. "Well … we're getting out of here anyway." He hitched Jodie higher and started for the exit. "You know how it is. Union regulations. Mandatory coffee break every three hours."

Chapter 20

Helga

Helga took a tentative sip of tea and watched the rain trickling down the window of the truck. She heard the sound of locker doors being closed and turned to see Maddie's head appear as she stood and slid a rifle into its rack. Although she was moving around with a casual good humor, Helga knew that their organizer wasn't too happy. The mission definitely hadn't gone the way she would've liked and she was very clearly a results-driven kind of lady. On the other hand, she wasn't so perfect herself. It didn't look like she functioned well under pressure and that was a concern. If Helga herself hadn't started to look for the bunker, they would probably still be standing outside the West Wing wondering what had happened to the others. Maddie had never stopped reminding her that they couldn't go downstairs because of the hypnosis, but in the end she'd ignored her. Why have a backup team at all if they couldn't risk a quick reconnaissance trip? Sometimes you had to trust your instincts and take risks to save your comrades.

Even when they'd picked up radio signal on the steps the American had forgotten to press the talk button on the communicator. A beginner's mistake. She'd panicked as soon as she'd heard Jester's voice with shots in the background.

The run through the building had certainly been an eye-opener. There'd been more bodies than Helga had expected and the sick guards had been worse than she'd thought. She could still taste the rotting stench of death and it was something that would stay with her for a long time.

But at least she knew for certain that there really was a half-dead disease. She'd tried to believe what everybody had said, but it was one of those things that only became real when you saw it with your own eyes.

Even more significant was the fact that the trance effect was real too, and it was clearly going to be a big problem.

She was lost in thought, following the passage of one particular drop down the glass, when a movement opposite her caught her attention. Jodie had pushed herself up in her seat and was pulling her blanket tighter around her.

Helga subtly lifted her gaze and tried to read the other woman's thoughts. When they'd arrived, the Jester character had been fighting on his own. The other two had been asleep and that wasn't good. The Weaver man had made the missions sound easy but it wasn't looking that way at all.

A twinge above her knee made her shift her weight and hesitantly stretch out her right leg. Everything was fine for a moment and then a pain like a hot needle shot through her thigh. A small tear in the quads—nothing serious. Her glutes would ache like hell but she'd put up with worse. The door had been heavy, but she'd dealt with it. And more importantly her heart was okay.

Curtis appeared in the central aisle, and she gave him a sideways glance as he slipped into the seat opposite.

He reckoned he was some kind of healer and had been trying to fix up Jester. Now she was sure he was going to apologize to Jodie. He hadn't done anything down there, just sat in the corner like he was asleep.

The black kid rested his hand gently on the young lady's shoulder and asked her how she was feeling. She replied politely but Helga could see that she was still stunned and confused by what had happened. Eventually, the American girl asked him why he hadn't been able to protect her, but he didn't have much of an answer. Their conversation gradually faded to nothing and Helga took another sip of tea, lowering her gaze to the inside of her mug before either of them caught her watching.

She was still staring at the slow-moving traffic when Maddie came and sat with them.

"So. Mission debrief," their organizer said, placing her elbows ceremoniously on the table and unrolling her micro. "Here's what I got so far: Security systems were overcome, half-dead resistance was dealt with and then the team moved to the lower floors. That's a good start but I think we need a bit more than that." She looked up at Jester and Curtis. "Can you tell me about what happened in the bunker?"

Jester touched the Band-Aids on his neck and then rolled his eyes while the black kid sat gazing thoughtfully into the mid-distance. In the end it was Jodie who spoke first.

"We went down into some kind of reinforced room," she said softly. "A bunch of half-deads came in and then there was a terrible whistling noise … Sorry, but I don't know anything after that."

Maddie nodded and then turned to Curtis. "So what happened? Can you tell us about your attempts to protect Jodie?"

"Yes," he replied calmly. "I went to explore what was around us and found a lot of strange forces very close. What happened then was unique. Everything went dark and veiled shapes pressed in from all sides. I was still looking for Jodie, groping around in a kind of fog, when all the shadows pulled back and disappeared."

Helga saw Maddie look down at the back of her hands and understood her frustration. It wasn't at all clear what the boy was trying to say.

"The shadows pulled back?" Maddie was frowning and there was clear irritation in her voice. "What are 'the shadows'? There was a lot of *what* very close?"

Curtis ran his hand slowly across the tabletop, a look of pain and sadness growing on his features.

"A lot of entities that I hadn't seen before," he said slowly. "They appeared like shadows because I didn't know what they were … I couldn't *conceive* them. Does that help?"

"Well …" Maddie nodded slowly. "Yeah … sort of." Her fingers strummed through the controller's lasers. "Problem is … during all that time, Jodie was in a trance. You need to protect her, see. That's kind of critical."

Curtis kept his eyes focused somewhere in the mid-distance and gave a small nod.

Jodie looked down at her gun belt and Helga felt a pang of sympathy for her. She'd never even been in a firefight before and now she had to worry about getting hypnotized as well as shot.

After a few moments the young American girl looked back at their organizer.

"So what now?" Jodie asked. "Seems like it was a lot tougher than we thought and the hypnotic protection stuff isn't working. Perhaps we should go back and talk to Weaver …" She let out a long breath and lowered her eyes. "I mean … I'm not sure I want to carry on."

Maddie rolled up her micro and held the tube neatly in both hands. "Well, the official plan is to keep moving. We're going back to the airfield and then up to Alaska for a briefing."

"Alaska?" Jodie had spurted out the word in surprise and everyone around the table except the computer geek had sat up and was frowning quizzically.

Maddie lifted her gaze and sucked in a deep breath. "Yes. But of course you are free to leave if you so desire. We can arrange to have you dropped off somewhere en route."

"Hang on a moment." The Jester man had leaned forward and was unusually serious. "This sounds like it might be something to do with the 'vague' possibility that we might be wanted for the Russian job too. Sounds to me like this bit was prearranged."

Their organizer lowered her head until she was looking at her hands. "As I understand it, our destination is a safe place to discuss our next possible course of action. As I said, although we'd like you to stay, you're all free to do as you choose."

"Well, I'm happy to go." The big man shrugged. "As long as you've got me some thermal underwear." He glanced curiously at the American girl. "I'm not sure about poor old Jodie here though."

Maddie met Jodie's gaze and raised her eyebrows. "I understand your position and I think maybe you should go and have a private chat with Julian."

Jodie did so straight away. Helga watched her walk to the comms module and understood her pain. The diversion to Alaska was going to take her a long way from home, and it was clear that the missions were going to be a lot more dangerous than she'd expected. The explanation from Curtis hadn't been very reassuring and hadn't even made much sense. If he was a fake then that young lady was going to be in serious trouble.

Chapter 21

Weaver

Shit, they failed. Weaver stared at the tabletop and allowed his vision to blur. He knew that he should talk to them, but his fingers seemed to have got stuck a few inches from the dial beam and he didn't have the energy to push them that little bit further. Instead, he curled his hand into a fist and started rapping the desk with his knuckles. The girl had got hypnotized. The Curtis boy had just sat there with his eyes closed and she'd gone under. The reports had said that he'd be able to protect people, but maybe they were wrong. And if he couldn't, then they were really screwed.

He slipped forward until his forehead was resting on the desk. *If she goes into the nest then it's game over. Nobody comes out alive.* An icy chill gripped his stomach. *Christ, that can't happen. I can't have her young life on my conscience.*

He sighed, feeling his breath blowing back on his cheeks as tiny drops of moisture sprouted on the wood. *It's not just me though. I'm not the only one responsible. I didn't start this. I'm just a cog in the wheel.*

A glance at the clock confirmed the time. *Nine minutes before they leave the truck. There's not long enough to talk to them properly. I should wait till they've landed. Yes. I'll grab some sleep while they're in the air. Give them a chance to rest.*

He had drifted into a doze when a buzz from his terminal made him squint at the screen. There was a call coming in from the lead vehicle and the video feed showed the Goodwin girl sitting on the bench biting her lip.

He straightened himself and flicked the line open. "Jodie, hi. Julian here." He'd tried to sound relaxed and confident but the result was just creepy, a late-night radio DJ greeting a phone-in caller.

"Hi, Dr. Weaver," she said softly. "Can you talk?"

"Yes, of course. First though, I have to say I'm glad you're okay. I've seen the reports and I'm sorry it was so rough for you down there."

"Yeah," she pushed her fingers into her hair and started combing it. "There were a lot of half-deads. I wasn't so sure about the killing but … they are completely sick, yeah? There's no cure?"

"They are effectively walking corpses—yes, we can confirm that. No higher cognitive functioning at all. Just a kind of muscle memory."

"And the hypnotism," she continued, "it's real. One minute I was shooting and then I was gone."

He found himself nodding. *Yes I know. Total cock-up. But the boy himself didn't go under, so maybe he has got some powers.* "Yes. I'm sorry about that. Just a glitch, I hope. I mean, he is confident he can do it." A knot tightened in his stomach. *She's going to quit. Course she is. They nearly got shot to bits and no one can guarantee she won't get hypnotized.*

"Yeah." She slid her hand down her cheek. "I'm wondering if it might be easier with someone else. Maybe someone who's resistant to the hypnosis."

"Well … we really see you as part of the team."

"I don't know." She shook her head. "I'm not sure if this is really—"

"Hang on," he interrupted. "This is a difficult time, I know. But there's a possibility that we're going to ask you to investigate another site, and this will give Curtis a second chance at protecting you. Here's what I suggest. Go along to Alaska but stay at the back. We'll get the others to keep an eye on you, and if you look like you're getting hypnotized they'll pull you straight out." He lifted his hands in a pacifying gesture. "Every site could be different. We just need you to go in and see what the lie of the land is."

"Yeah." She was frowning. "That's another thing. We were just sitting talking and then Maddie announces that you want to take us to Alaska. I mean, what's that all about?"

"Okay." He nodded vigorously, doing everything he could to show that he understood. "Yes, I did know that might be a possibility but probably didn't make it clear enough. However, I really must urge you to go. It's an ideal location for whatever we need you guys to do next, and I promise we'll do our best to make you comfortable."

She pulled a face and he suddenly remembered a paragraph of text from her file. "Here's something else we can do. While you're working as part of the team you're entitled to certain privileges. Our records show that your mother is living alone in ungated Texas. Would you like me to send some guards down to watch her street?"

She asked him to explain further, and when he told her he could send a group of security guys, her eyes glazed and she swallowed hard. "This is a benefit I get for being in the team …?"

"Yes." He lifted his hands again, palms facing the camera. "And you don't have to do anything. Just go along. Stay at the back. Maybe take down a few half-deads."

She went quiet and he sat and pondered his own feelings. It was low. It was cheap. But it wasn't entirely dishonest. He would organize the private police. It wasn't blackmail if you were offering something good, was it?

"Yes. Do it please." She was on her feet nodding at the screen. "Straight away. But the men have got to stay out of sight. No connection with me."

He flashed a thumbs-up, a corny gesture that he immediately hated himself for. My god, he was becoming some kind of politician. "Done," he said confidently.

She gave him a wave and stepped out of the booth.

He pushed back his chair and squeezed his eyes closed. It was clear that the doubters in the team needed some persuasion from some of his more secretive backers, and that wasn't totally unexpected. They knew what was going on and had promised to make themselves available. For the moment he'd kept Jodie on board, but he wasn't sure she liked him. He wasn't sure any of them liked him, and he wasn't entirely sure he liked himself.

Chapter 22

Jodie

She didn't need to decide yet. As the truck crawled through the Washington suburbs, Jodie tried to get used to the idea of going to Alaska but found she couldn't think straight about anything at all. It would've been good to talk it over with someone, but she was pretty much on her own. Maddie was having a long hushed conversation on her micro, Cryboy had disappeared into the vehicle's comms booth and her other companions were dozing or looking out of the window.

They had skirted the airfield's chain-link fence and were slowing at the gates when Maddie came over and rested a hand on her shoulder. Their organizer announced that they were going to meet some government people at the airport who would try to give them more information and explain why the trip to Alaska was so important.

Jodie nodded. She was too tired to put up much of a fight and part of her was now curious. She wanted to find out who these people were and what they were going to ask them to do.

Maddie moved on to tell the rest of the team and they were soon through the compound's security checkpoints and coasting into an enormous empty hangar. They were led across an echoey concrete floor toward a large rectangular box, a little bigger than a shipping container, where they paused and were given a short briefing. Maddie told them that there were important members of the Interim Authorities waiting for them inside, and they filed in one by one.

It was some kind of secrecy room made of smoked plastic and suspended on metal cables. Seated at the other end were four figures, three male and one female. Two of the men were in military uniforms and the third was rather overweight and looked as if he'd been poured into a gray suit several sizes too small. The woman was a striking-looking redhead, immaculately dressed in a fitted blazer and crisp white blouse. She was the first to rise from her seat and come and shake their hands, introducing herself as Senator O'Keefe but telling them to call her Mary.

Jodie immediately warmed to her and remembered seeing her on Snapnews taking on the big corporations about polluting out of gate.

The senator went on to introduce her companions as General Hernandez and Captain McDermott from the army and a Mr. Winchester representing the NSA.

"I recognize that you've had an extremely stressful day already," O'Keefe said, glancing at each of them, but seemingly holding her gaze mostly on Jodie. "I appreciate that it's late, and we will try to be as brief as possible. Firstly, let me say that although the results of your operation this evening were mixed, I congratulate you on your bravery."

Jodie was about to say something when Mr. Winchester interjected. "None of us knows anything about what you did today," he said flatly.

The senator opened her mouth, but this time Jester interrupted.

"Just before this chat gets any cozier," he said, sticking a pair of Marlboros into his mouth. "I think we'd all like to know your connection with Weaver and Sophos."

"Well—" the senator began and was interrupted again.

"Mr. Weaver is an academic conducting research," Mr. Winchester continued. "We approve of this." He glanced at his companions and held up his palm. "Our understanding is that Mr. Sophos is a businessman funding academic research. We also approve of this."

Jester had flicked open his lighter and was about to hold it to his face when General Hernandez spoke for the first time. "I'm afraid this whole area is a no smoking zone. Corporal Solberg."

Jester sucked fumes deep into his lungs and nodded, blowing out a huge ball of smoke as he replied. "Good," he said with a smirk, "I approve of that."

"I think I can be a little bit more forthcoming than our NSA representative here," the senator said, raising her eyebrows. "For my part, I'd like you to know that that there are still some politicians determined to represent the people. Some of us very actively want to restore a democratically elected government and we appreciate your help in this. You may not know, but Senator Canmore is trying to get a motion passed on Friday morning that would give him complete legislative power. Clearing this up gives us our best opportunity of preventing that. We'd like to be able to identify the president and vice president as either dead or alive, and we'd like the global situation to be fully resolved. So our plea is very simple. We are here to ask, if not beg you, to continue what you started and consider undertaking a mission in Russian territory."

"In an unknown polar location," Mr. Winchester said quietly.

Jodie found her voice. "But why?" she asked. "I mean, we've already tried and failed. It's definitely a job that should be left to you guys."

The senator and the military men nodded. "We are active," the general said. "I don't know how well you've been briefed, but we are preparing for a fully mechanized assault on both the White House and Fort Wainwright bunkers. Our AIs are less confident of a successful outcome than those of our hardware supplier, and we all share reservations about the businessman heading that company."

"Brutetek," Jester said, nodding and sucking on his cigarettes. "Brutetek have some kind of preferred supplier deal on the robots. It had never dawned on me till now." He seemed to find this tremendously significant and amusing, and Jodie's exhausted mind was struggling to click all the pieces together when the senator clarified it for her.

"Yes, that means that one of my colleagues has considerable influence over the missions, and we see this as a conflict of interests."

"You bet," Jester replied, blowing smoke at the ceiling. "It leaves Canmore calling the shots, and maybe he's not even too motivated to make them successful."

The officials exchanged looks and Jodie made certain that she asked the next question.

"So tell us about Russia?" she asked. "What do we have to do?"

General Hernandez stood and then flinched as if suddenly remembering something. He turned and offered his chair to the group, keeping his eyes mostly only on her and Helga. "I'm sorry, I beg your pardon. Would any of you like a seat?"

Jodie shook her head. "No we're fine. Russia," she repeated. "What we have to do?"

"Well, essentially the same as today," he told her.

"And what about Dr. Weaver?" she asked. "Does he know about all this?"

"He does now, yes. This was always a possibility, but the final decision was only made when we got the results of today's attempt. You might not be feeling too pleased right now, but you actually did pretty well. Two thirds of your team weren't hypnotized and you got out in one piece. That's a hell of a lot better than the specialist teams that were sent in. As for Dr. Weaver, you will still be working for him on this next one too. He's going to hire some of our assets and this will help you gain entry to the Arctic facility."

"So why are we doing the Russian's dirty work for them?" Jester asked.

Mr. Winchester lifted his head. "Unfortunately we can't—"

The major held up his hand. "I can only talk hypothetically, but imagine that we didn't want these creatures getting into the hands of anyone who might want to use them as a weapon on a civilian population. Also imagine a situation where our friends prevaricate for too long and this leads to further political unrest. Or imagine that their technology was twelve months or so behind that of Brutetek and they turned to Brutetek for help."

"Oh I see," Jester said, raising his eyebrows.

Jodie turned to her teammates to try to gauge their reactions. Cryboy was looking down and the Ferguson kid seemed to be in some kind of daze, but both Jester and Helga gave her a shrug and a nod. When none of them said anything else, the conversation continued as if they had agreed.

The general explained that they would be flown to a "secure location" in Alaska where the captain would link up with them and brief them in more detail. They were told that the meeting had never happened, although it was possible that some of them had bumped into each other accidentally in the airport's refreshment area. Hands were shaken again and the proceedings were quickly brought to a close.

Out in the hangar the two groups set off in opposite directions, the government representatives making their way toward a line of distant vehicles while Jodie and her companions left the building and started to cross the tarmac.

As they walked past the shrouded shapes of various small aircraft, Jodie realized that she was bone-tired and had a splitting headache. If their aim had been to exhaust and overwhelm her that day, they had undoubtedly succeeded. She'd been up since before dawn and undertaken an incredibly stressful armed raid as well as a bunch of long and confusing meetings.

She managed to keep a plan clear in her mind and it was the only thing holding her together. At the next site she would do the bare minimum but that would have to be it. Two attempted missions would give her sufficient cash to really change things. She'd have enough to move gated, and then she'd be able to really start her life and look after the people she cared for.

When she looked up, she saw Cryboy a few yards ahead of her, walking dreamily with his teddy bear in one hand and his micro in the other. Curiosity and a vague sense of loneliness urged her to catch up with him, and when she reached his side she flicked her head at the strange short-winged aircraft in front of them and asked him what it was.

"That's a stealth scramjet," he said, flicking her a sideways glance.

"What's a scramjet?" she asked.

"It's a supersonic combustion ramjet. This one's a Mach three hydrogen craft."

"Right," she replied, trying to sound excited. "But is it comfortable? You know, nice to fly in?"

He shook his head. "Don't know. I've never been in it."

Moments later he started to climb, and his voice floated back to her, soft and dreamy. "But it will be beautiful." He paused to fix his gaze on some invisible point on the fuselage. "The shock waves at that speed are incredible. There's amazing wave propagation. Exquisite cones and ellipses spreading out from behind the wings. It's like geometrical art. Beauty created by man cutting through nature."

"Right." She stared at the back of his head in amazement. *What the hell is this skinny freak talking about?* "Thanks. That's interesting."

He nodded, and as he stepped into the cabin she felt a snap of annoyance. Why were the men in the group so difficult to bond with? Each of the three was difficult and inept in their own way and it was making life more challenging than it needed to be. The whole thing would be so much easier if they could all just talk a bit more.

Her irritation only increased when she got inside the aircraft. The cabin was uncomfortably narrow and the portholes were thick glass ovals not much bigger than a human head. On each seat there was a foil tube that looked like a survival bag, and when she saw Helga trying to wriggle her legs into one, it became clear that they were meant to wear them during the flight.

Maddie was moving around the aisle trying to hurry everyone into position, and when she saw Jodie eyeing the metallic sacks suspiciously she rested a hand on her shoulder and explained that they were pressurized gel gloves designed to help passengers cope with the g-forces. Jodie asked how they'd move around and was told that the aircon would pump out a mild painkiller and sedative which meant they'd sleep most of the time.

It all sounded depressingly practical and antisocial, and Jodie didn't try to hide her frustration when she flopped down and started unzipping her boots. After dropping them noisily onto the floor, she started to fasten herself into the padded sleeve and felt it tighten against her muscles. After a little wriggling and bouncing she got herself fully enclosed then locked her harness in place and sat staring glumly at the seat back in front of her.

When they were all buckled in, Maddie stood on tiptoes in the aisle and told them in a schoolmistress's tone that unfastening the harnesses would automatically slow the plane. Looking directly at Jester, she went on to warn them that even a whiff of smoke in the cabin would reduce the engine power and then described a rapid deceleration out of Mach three as something akin to being turned inside out and trampled on by elephants. She finished her cheerful safety briefing by letting them know that they'd be in Alaska in a couple of hours and then went to climb into her seat.

Jodie exchanged a few words with Helga and checked that she was happy about the trip northwards but was soon pressed backward by an acceleration that was so horrifically relentless it was difficult to speak. The sensation of being sucked into her chair never ceased, but she gradually became sleepier and sleepier until she was lost in a world of noisy fretful dreams.

Chapter 23

An Awakening

He's lifted into a sitting position and a rough-grained ladle is held to his lips. The healer's leathered face looms large in his vision then he spies his mother stooped somewhere behind him. Her brow is creased and her eyes heavy and dark. He pulls open his mouth and sucks some of the liquid. The water is warm and smells of wood smoke. His throat instantly spasms and he falls back onto the thin bed roll. His limbs throb and ache, like a spiny fish is in his veins pumping venom into his muscles with every bulging breath.

The pain fades and his corporeal sensations evaporate and drift up into the steam from his bedside bowl. He rises from his body and vaults onto the hut's crossbeam where a banded gecko swivels its turreted eyes and studies him with intense indifference.

Looking down, he sees two women sitting cross-legged on the floor tending a restless child. As he studies the young man's features he begins to float again, pulled up through the thatched roof until he hovers at a vague height above the village. From there, he sees things that the boy hasn't yet found: paths and half-clearings in the jungle where the stumps and columns of previous settlements are poking through the regrowth.

Soon he begins to move; traveling effortlessly above the forest in spaces disconnected from time. He dips and rises over the canopy on thermals of earth-scented air, and then bounces through the lattice of leaves to sink back onto the ocean bed that is his physical shell.

His body is warm; the skin on his back is damp and his belly aches for food. He opens his eyes and his mother's features fill his vision. He smiles and she smiles back. Her tears drip onto his face then dry to leave tight moraines of salt.

He has become a traveler between worlds and is never sick again.

Bear Creek, Alaska

Tuesday, July 13

Chapter 24

Jodie

Jodie stretched out against the crisp linen sheets and arched her back. As she reached over and sleepily rubbed her aching muscles sudden flashes of memory filled her senses. She felt the heat and recoil of a weapon pressed to her shoulder and her ears buzzed with the harsh bark of an assault rifle. *My god, we fought our way through the White House.* An image of the lounge with the yellow blast door came to her and then her memories faded. *But what happened? We were in the bunker and then there was a noise in my head, like something climbed in and shoved my brain out. Then it's blank. Nothing. That can't happen again. I've got to keep further back this time. I have to stay out of trouble.*

With a loud yawn she pushed herself upright and sat gazing at her room with bleary eyes. They'd arrived at an airfield in a snowy wooded valley sometime in the early morning and been rushed out of the biting wind into waiting jeeps. A short drive had brought them to a scattering of cabins and she'd been surprised at how warm and cozy the rooms were. Once underneath the big comfortable duvet she had quickly slipped back into a doze. It was hunger and a need to pee that had dragged her awake and was driving her actions.

Thirty minutes later she was sitting on the edge of the bed pulling her robe tighter against her shower-warm skin and staring hesitantly at her reader. She pressed it on; the plastic molded to her wrist and the screen sprang to life with three filtered messages blinking in the corner. *Now, what's the best order for these?* Her mind ran through the contents, predicting the emotional hit of each while her finger hovered above the flashing envelopes. *Most difficult first. Best for last.*

She tapped open her mother's.

```
Hi, Hope all going well and theyr not working you 2
hard. Drier here now so hands r a bit better. I'm
sure ur 2 busy 2 call. Mom.
```

She let out a sigh. *How's she managed to squeeze so much guilt into just a few words?* Stretching her neck, she examined the wooden beams above her and tried to order her feelings. *Maybe it's just me. Maybe I'm overlaying the emotions. But "I'm sure you're too busy?" How does she want me to feel about that?* With another noisy exhalation she looked back at her reader and tapped open the second.

```
U OK? Don't feel bad about running out on a senior
citizen. Sold the range. Gave your shoes to thrift.
Hank.
```

Her mouth lifted into a smile. *At least his guilt-tripping is obvious. Probably thinks I've been swept off on a romantic trip. He likes that. Protective but not possessive. Daddy's generation. One of the best.*

With a final dab at the screen, she opened her closest friend's.

```
Got your msg. Glad ur okay. All very secretive.
Don't believe it's work. Alien abduction or hung
like a horse billionaire? Guess u'll call when he's
hospitalized 4 exhaustion. All well here. Mia got 3
gold merits last week! Call me girl! H xxx
```

After double-checking that all her tracking and location functions were still disabled, she sent a duplicated note saying that she was fine but working long hours, then switched the device off.

Loneliness hit her as soon as the display went blank. She swallowed and breathed out slowly, her shoulders sagging as the impact of the messages sank in. They had all hurt. She wanted to talk to the people closest to her but knew that she couldn't. The calls would get too long and emotional. She couldn't really explain what she was doing and was certain they would try to talk her into leaving. It was better to forget about home and concentrate on the tasks ahead. She had to finish the jobs and then get back with the cash. Once she had some serious credit she'd be able to fix everything.

The hum of voices and the sound of clinking cutlery reached her as soon as she entered the main house. The thought that the rest of the team were eating and drinking without her gave her a brief flash of paranoia and she quickened her pace. After moving through a cloakroom thick with hanging coats, she found herself in a huge kitchen warmed by a long cooking fire. Helga and Curtis were seated around a wooden dining table being attended by two middle-aged ladies in aprons who smiled warmly at her as she walked in and greeted her with a few friendly words in what sounded like mid-western accents.

Curtis turned and watched her as she crossed the stone floor toward them. "Hi, Jodie," he said casually. "Sleep well?"

She stopped and pushed her elbows behind her. His tone was so relaxed and friendly she thought maybe he was being ironic. Uncertain how to react, she decided that the safest option was to be equally easy-going.

"Yes, thank you," she replied, allowing a long yawn to push her mouth open before pulling out a chair and sitting with her back to the fire. "Very well."

She ordered an espresso and some bacon and pancakes and felt him studying her from the other side of the table while she began to quiz Helga on how she felt about working in her own country. The big Russian lady was almost infuriatingly calm about things, and she seemed more than happy both to undertake a mission in her homeland and to risk going back into a bunker again. It seemed that the unrest caused by the quarantined army base was spreading across the region, and this meant that normal families were finding themselves caught in battles between armed gangs.

Jodie was surprised by this. Snapnews only reported celebrity and sporting news from Russia, and her large friend's passion when she talked about how she used to help orphan and refugee children was deeply moving.

A steaming cup of coffee was placed in front of her and she blew on it. After a couple of sips she allowed her gaze to drift back to Curtis and found he was still watching her from the other side of the table. "So … how you feeling about tonight?" she asked.

"Good …" he replied. "Ready."

"But do you know what we're going to have to do?" she continued. "You know …" *Christ I'm going to have to spell this out.* "… what went wrong in Washington?"

"Yes, I have to find you and protect you," he told her. "Then I need to scout the shadow shapes and discover as much as I can about what we're facing."

"And … you're confident that you can do all this?" she asked. "I mean, it is kinda important."

He nodded calmly. "I can do it. Yes."

"Okay. So, when you say you have to find me, is there anything I can do to help?"

He smoothed his hands across the tabletop a couple of times. "Well yes, there is one thing I've been wanting to find out."

"Go on."

"I hope you don't mind me asking, but did you lose someone, someone very close to you just when you were … around your early teens? Around puberty?"

She looked down, staring hard at the tiny bubbles moving on the surface of her drink while she processed the question. *How does he know that?* With her eyes fixed on the steaming liquid in front of her, she inched up her head and opened her mouth. *It still hurts. It'll always hurt.*

"Yeah, my dad. I lost my dad when I was twelve."

"I'm very sorry about that," he said softly.

"That's okay." She fixed her gaze on the inside of the cup. *Didn't want to tell him that. I never talk about that.*

"Does that help?" she asked.

"Yes it does. Thank you."

"Do you need to know any more?"

"Well, yeah, if you don't mind, just one more thing."

"Go on."

"Before you became a woman—when you were a girl—did you do a lot of boy's stuff? Obviously the shooting, but cars and climbing and all that?"

She felt a twist of discomfort somewhere low in her stomach. It was like he was trying to look inside her.

"Yeah, I was a regular tomboy," she told him.

He nodded, his index finger held in the air. "Final question. Your father. He liked you to be feminine? To be girly?"

She swallowed hard. *Holy shit! He's inside my head now.*

"Yes he did."

He sat gently nodding while she placed her cup carefully back on its saucer.

"Is that okay?" she asked. "Is that enough? I mean …"

There were footsteps from the corridor, and Maddie came bursting into the kitchen with her micro and a roll of data sheets under her arm. She greeted them with a nod and a tight smile.

"Time for our mission briefing, guys," she said, placing the items carefully at the head of the table then glancing back into the main house, "Cryboy's gone to get Jester and we'll start as soon as they're here."

Chapter 25

Jester

Tap, tap, tap. Tap, tap, tap. The soft knocking had woven into his dream. Tap, tap, tap. He was at a long banquet table on top of a puffy white cloud. Alice was sitting in her school dress at the other end. Her eyes were smooth black and her glossy red lips were curved into a sickly grin. There were smudges of lipstick, or perhaps blood, on her teeth. She held the head of the Cheshire Cat in her right hand and rapped it three times on the table. Tap, tap, tap. The severed arteries left splodges of gore on the lacy cloth.

The table exploded and Alice shot into the air. He shot up after her, the wind tearing at his face as he was propelled upward by an irresistible force. Around him were familiar objects from the inside of a Humvee: a small red fire extinguisher, strips of webbing and a length of pink tubing covered in black hairs. After staring at the strange cylinder for a while, he realized that it was his buddy Frank's arm; the blue tattooed letters clear on the back of the hand, his simple plastic wristwatch intact on the sun-tanned wrist.

Tap, tap, tap. His cheeks were sucked into long saddle-bag wrinkles then he felt his bones being wrenched backward through his body. Tap, tap, tap. The acceleration slackened and he was suddenly weightless. He hung high in the thin atmosphere for a moment and then started to fall. His descent got quicker; cold air rushed past him and he became aware of a distant curving earth fast approaching.

Tap, tap, tap. His eyes flashed open. He was lying sideways on his bed. There was a layer of sweat clinging to his body and someone was knocking pathetically outside his room. With a snort of frustration, he tugged his foot free from the twisted sheets.

"Yeah?" he asked, slipping off the mattress and landing painfully on his knees. There didn't seem to be any kind of answer so he started to crawl across the floor. "Who is it?" After a few slides, he got himself up into a crouch, staggered to the door and pulled it open.

Cryboy was standing with his arm raised and his head bowed.

"What?" Jester snapped.

"Meeting," the hacker told him softly. "Planning meeting in the main house."

"Now?"

"Yes."

"Okay. Wait." Jester turned and moved toward the bathroom in heavy sideways lurches while his fingers teased open the crotch of his suit.

His short spurt of orange piss filled the air with the stench of ammonia and yeast. He cleared his throat, spat into the sink, then opened the mirrored cabinet and squinted at the shelves. A brown vial caught his attention. He popped the lid and palmed a small pyramid of pills into his hand. After slapping them into his mouth he replaced the container and continued his search. His probing eyes found a second taller beaker which he quickly opened and drained.

Moving back to his bed he plucked his Glock from the nightstand and dropped it into his thigh pocket. The remains of the previous night's vodka stood on the table and he found himself absent-mindedly lifting the bottle and sloshing the last few inches into his mug. After a long gulp he sighed and looked around the room. Mostly it was long stretches of bare pine boards and simple bland furniture, but there was a single item that he'd noticed the night before and hadn't yet investigated. Tucked against the far wall there was a beautiful gold-colored guitar with a scratch plate decorated with a pattern of interlocking leaves.

He walked slowly toward the ancient instrument and examined it for a while before reaching out and running his fingers across its strings. When he heard the faint chord, he grinned and then turned on his heels and walked briskly across the room. As he strode through the doorway he slapped Cryboy hard on the back.

"Come on then," he said cheerily. "Let's not keep 'em waiting, eh?"

Chapter 26

Helga

The place was usually used for banqueting, Helga was pretty sure about that. Someone had cleared out most of the furniture and laid the long table with pads and water jugs, but the paintings of winter folk scenes and the thick velvet curtains revealed the room's roots.

While they'd waited, Jodie had made polite and intelligent small talk, but it had been difficult to sustain a conversation with her. The American girl was nice but the situation didn't seem real and Helga had found herself unusually self-conscious about her level of English. It hadn't helped that although they were both gazing into space pretending to be lost in their own thoughts, Maddie and Curtis were obviously listening to what they were saying, and she was pleased when the chat faded away and silence finally prevailed.

She had passed a good few minutes running over the events of the last twenty-four hours and wondering what was to come when the computer boy arrived with the Jester character sauntering casually behind him. The big man was still wearing the same shabby fool's costume and sucking on two cigarettes at a time and this was vaguely surprising. On the first day she'd thought that the heavy smoking and his weird clothing had been an affectation, some pathetic attempt to show off and look tough, but he seemed to be keeping it up quite effortlessly, and this changed things. Now she wasn't sure who or what he was and she wanted to find out more. He needed to take the brunt of the combat duties and if he wasn't up to it then they were all going to be at risk.

When the two men had sat down and Jester had cracked a few strange jokes, Maddie began the meeting. She tapped something on her micro and told them that Captain McDermott would be joining them to provide some background information.

Sure enough, less than a minute later the military man entered, greeted them all with a cheery "Good afternoon" and took a place at the table. He was dressed in smart dark jeans and a thick navy sweater and started by removing any misconceptions that they might have had that they were at a military base. He told them that while there was an army facility very close by, their accommodation was subcontracted and so they were legally guests of a catering company in Delaware.

The helicopters and pilots they were going to be using were privately contracted by Dr. Weaver in New York, and, as the captain himself was on his day off and chatting to them informally, there was actually no military involvement in their mission at all.

He said all this in a friendly, almost jokey, manner, and Helga was pleased that, unlike a lot of Americans, he spoke clearly and without too much slang.

McDermott paused to see if there were any questions, and then went on to give them a brief background history of the events that had taken place in the Arctic. Most of this she already knew and had been covered by Dr. Weaver. He mentioned unknown entities appearing on the ice and talked about the infestations at Fort Wainwright, Washington and the naval base at Kotelny. He didn't stop to question how odd it was that one of the creatures had managed to get all the way to the White House without being seen, and he didn't offer any theories about what the things were or why nobody had ever heard of them before. He was a professional covering facts on a simple, need-to-know basis.

The trip to Kotelny didn't seem to worry him either. He told them that the place was surrounded by a hastily erected electric fence and a ring of tanks and surveillance trucks but seemed confident that they would get in undetected. They would fly to the island in stealth helicopters under the cover of a snowstorm and be left inside the protected zone with a single lead box and a mechanical load shifter to help them move it.

It was at this point that the charming young captain looked at her directly and told her that her strength might be required with some of the moving if the machine encountered any problems. She acknowledged his comment with a nod and then found herself looking down at the tabletop. It was good to be significant to the plan, good to know that she could help.

Still addressing his comments to her, the captain produced a small packet and slid it across the table. She reached inside and found several pairs of strong latex gloves. Apologizing many times and always being scrupulously polite, the young officer asked her if she would mind wearing them for the rest of the mission. While she pushed her fingers into them, he explained that the AIs had warned that her biometric data was likely to be on file with the Russian military and that she should be extremely careful not to leave any traces. This was going to involve some hardship as the others would have snowsuits and would need to take them off to avoid overheating once they were inside. In the case of an emergency evacuation she couldn't risk leaving any of her DNA and would have to cover the distance to the building in standard clothing.

McDermott leaned forward and kept his eyes on her. "Obviously we will give you a hat and a few extra layers, but we are in the middle of some very freaky weather at the moment. After an insanely warm spring we're back into winter. Predicted temperatures with wind chill are around minus thirty tonight so you'll need to get inside as quickly as possible. Are you okay with that?"

Before even allowing herself to absorb the full implications of what he was saying, she nodded. It would just be a couple of minutes. She could handle the cold.

The captain then produced a couple of rubberized devices the size of a cigarette packet and handed them around. They were civilian mountain climbing beacons and could be used to summon the helicopters. Maddie and Cryboy both had secure communications via their chips but he warned that they couldn't be relied on. Finally, he raised his hands and gave them all a knowing look.

"That's me done. Finished. I'll hand you over to Maddie now." He cracked a slightly cheesy smile. "I have to say that it's weird seeing a bunch of civilians conducting research so close to a Russian military base, and obviously I have no idea what you're doing there. Breaking into the building would be considered a hostile act, so I strongly advise against that … but, whatever you do, best of luck."

Their organizer thanked McDermott and then waited until he'd closed the door before continuing. A tap on her micro produced a detailed throw-image and they all leaned forward to study it. A red circle appeared in one of the laser-framed boxes and Maddie told them that "the target" was believed to be deep in the bowels of the building.

Next they came to the operational plan, and just like Washington's it was almost laughably simplistic. Their organizer concentrated mostly on the route and layout of the rooms, and Helga started to feel increasingly frustrated. What they needed to be talking about was what had gone wrong on the previous mission and how they were going to fix it.

It was only when every detail of their arrival and passage through the building had been outlined that Maddie lifted her gaze from the hologram and glanced around the table.

"Now, I know everything wasn't too smooth in Washington," she said in a voice that was clearly meant to sound friendly and caring.

“So let’s learn from our mistakes. This time we need to stay closer together and keep things tighter.”

Finally they were going to get a chance to discuss how they should support each other. Helga had a lot to say but she bit her tongue and waited. These guys spoke so quickly and confidently it was best to let them go first.

Maddie looked at Jodie, then at Jester and Curtis.

“My suggestion is that you guys go slower and watch closely for signs of the hypnosis. If you meet any serious resistance just pull back and I’ll call in the copters.” She shifted her gaze to Curtis. “And you need to make sure you’ve done your protection thing before you go down to the lower levels,” she told him matter-of-factly.

There was nothing but silence. Curtis gazed thoughtfully into space while the Jester character pulled a series of silly faces and rummaged for his cigarettes. In the end, the girl was the only one to show any reaction. A frown started to deepen on Jodie’s forehead and she looked first at Curtis and then at Maddie with an open mouth.

Helga was sure she was going to question the reliability of the hypnosis protection, and when she did there’d be an opportunity to suggest better ways of working.

But nothing came. Jodie stared into the mid-distance for a while, and then slowly lowered her gaze.

Maddie cracked an uncomfortable smile and started to scan the group. “We need to do this one guys,” she said softly. “There’s no slack in the plan now. It’s this or nothing.”

Still no one moved, and Helga knew she had to speak. The team needed more energy. They needed to communicate better and believe in themselves. Russian and then English phrases started tumbling around in her mind and she straightened herself in her seat. The action caused her sleeves to ride up and the fat veins on her arms were exposed to view. She tugged at the material until as much flesh as possible was covered and then let the words out.

“We can do it,” she told them, lifting her chin. “We are going over to my country. My homeland. We can do it there.”

It was okay. Her heart was hammering in her chest but everything was alright. It was better to let it out than hold things in, and nothing terrible had happened; the room still seemed calm and normal. She sucked in some air then risked a glance at her comrades. Four of them were looking at her with positive, maybe even admiring, expressions, but the computer boy was hunched over and moving uncomfortably in his seat.

"I'm not so sure about that," he said, addressing his words to the tabletop. "We were outgunned in the White House. If we want to improve our chances we need to stay stealthy for longer and we need more firepower." His index finger began to trace perfect circles on the polished wooden surface. "It would help if Curtis carried some real weapons and if other team members stopped wearing dumb costumes and tried to camouflage themselves."

Most of that was true. He was too quiet and needed to make eye contact occasionally, but the hacker had a sharp mind. It was a good analysis and Helga was suddenly excited that they were going to have a detailed conversation about their tactics.

Jester slowly pushed himself back in his seat and cocked his head. His body language was unnervingly strained and deliberate and the energy in the room quickly changed. His eyes swiveled to the younger man and he surveyed him like a bull preparing to charge.

"So *I* need to change things, do I?" he said, his voice horribly soft and contained. "I'm no good like this?"

It was a challenge. A trap. Helga could almost taste the cold metallic taste of violence in the room, and her heartbeat was wildly loud in her ears. The geek mustn't reply. If he did he'd be attacked.

She pushed herself higher in her chair, flexing her legs ready to stand. She was the differentiator. She was the only one with the strength to restrain the Jester man, but even so, as she watched him, she had doubts. It was not just his size, there was something that he was holding inside that made her afraid.

Cryboy shook his head and she wished she could reach out and stop him.

"Military clothing would slow the half-dead's reaction time," he said quietly, his fingers moving in faster and faster circles. "They have limited cognitive function but your costume draws attention. You should change it to increase the probability of success."

The muscles around Jester's jaw swelled into cords as he leaned close to his teammate's ear. How had they been let sit next to each other? That should never have been allowed to happen.

"Perhaps you'd like to grab a gun and come down with us yourself to *increase the probability of success*," he said through clenched teeth.

"But you're carrying out the missions in fancy dress. There's nothing wrong with you. You could easily put military fatigues on." Cryboy's finger stopped moving and pressed hard against the table. She could see his nail whitening as the blood was pushed out of it.

"You're dressed up in a dumb suit. It's like you're pretending to be a weirdo."

"There's nothing wrong with me!" Jester's chair crashed to the floor as he jerked to his feet. "There's nothing wrong with me!' he snarled. "What the fuck do you know? Do you have any fucking idea what this body has been through?" He jammed a pair of fingers at his heart. "Do you? Huh? You! Stuck on a computer like some soft-assed commander in a bunker. I've lost three buddies while I was standing talking to them. Boom! They're gone. That ever happened to you? You seen the vehicle in front blown into the sky? Your pals come out in flames? You been spiked with antibio? Eaten your lunch on a mountain of DU? Been gassed, nuked and mortared? Huh? You seen two of your best men gunned to pulp by your own drones? Gone to get help in a *special* clinic where you get forty thousand volts for breakfast? No!" He sucked in a deep breath and his voice lowered to a growl. "You had months of freaky radiation treatment that fucks your whole physiology? You got an immune system that works in reverse? No!" He thrust his head forward, veins bulging on his neck. "I lost everyone I ever loved. Had my baby stolen while I was serving my country. I live in a fucking trash can. My neighbors eat rats. My ear drums are plastic. I got shrapnel in eight places in my back. You saying I'm fakin' this shit? What are you saying?" Drawing in a deep breath, he wiped the spit from his mouth. "What are you saying?"

Cryboy was a curve of pale-blue tracksuit, his forehead flat on the table and his hands covering his ears. Jester was staring silently at the back of the boy's head but his words were still spinning in Helga's mind. There was too much death there. Too much loss and too much grief. Most tangible though was his pain. It was his hurt that made her slowly rise from her seat and start moving toward him. Time had slowed, and with all the others stunned to silence, she found herself passing the chairs one by one. There would be no more suffering. She had the strength to fix things.

As she got nearer, she looked up and met Jester's gaze. He was frowning and his eyes kept narrowing as she approached.

Now she could do something. Now she could heal the room. Opening her arms she slowly wrapped them around his shoulders and took in the whole of him. He was big. A little taller than her and broad but he let her envelop him. He didn't help but he didn't resist. They stood perfectly still and she knew that the others were watching. She began to squeeze a little harder and he allowed his arms and chest to flex. He folded within her grip and she kept her eyes closed and concentrated. She had to press. She had to push love inside him while being careful not to employ her full strength.

After a few moments he started shuddering and she released him. She stepped back to discover that he was grinning ear to ear and shaking with laughter. He looked at her with joy in his eyes and then glanced at Jodie and Curtis.

"The thing about being hugged by Helga," he said, shaking his head, "is don't fight it. Don't fight it. Go with it!" He met her gaze again, an expression of half-remembered pleasure growing on his face. "Damn you smell good," he told her. "I'd forgotten how good a woman could smell."

She lowered her head, feeling the heat rush to her face as her cheeks flushed. When she looked back up, he had set off toward the door and was pushing a couple of cigarettes into his mouth. As he passed Cryboy he reached out and trailed his arm across his back. The computer boy flinched but the gesture was a good one. It was conciliatory. The anger had gone.

"Okay." As soon as Jester was through the door, Maddie glanced around the group and started to roll up her micro. "Well thanks everyone, I think we've covered the main points. Let's finish the briefing in the copter."

Helga watched their organizer rush out of the room with a feeling of total disbelief. A bit of shouting seemed to have scared her off. Didn't she know that men needed to let off steam? Didn't she realize that they might have to fight among themselves before they'd be any good at fighting anything else? It was pathetic.

First Curtis and then the computer kid silently slipped out of the room, and Helga was left alone with Jodie.

The young American was fairly shocked about the Jester character's outburst, but was quick to understand that he had plenty of reasons to be angry. Apart from his history and past experiences, they were tired and were being messed around, perhaps not deliberately, but as a consequence of being caught in a situation much bigger and more complex than they had first thought.

At least Jodie was prepared to talk about things, and for a while they sat at the big table and shared their fears and concerns. The girl seemed to have finally pieced together what had happened in the White House and was very clear in giving her thanks. That was nice to hear, but even better was the fact that they made a kind of unofficial pact to look after each other on the next mission. It didn't matter if Maddie stuck to some dumb plan to keep the two teams apart; if Helga sensed the girl in real trouble again, then of course she'd go and help out. She'd signed up for the missions and that meant taking risks to aid her comrades.

But Jodie seemed to want more. Even after they'd made the promise, she continued to ask questions about their respective roles. She did so subtly and vaguely but got so uncomfortable that Helga could guess what was on her mind. She obviously wanted to know if she'd consider swapping places, and that was a different matter altogether. Dr. Weaver had been very specific about who was in each team, and it was clear that some of the best AIs in the world had spent a long time making the decisions. Switching roles could easily mess things up. They still weren't certain what there was down in the basements, and until they knew what was causing the hypnosis it was best to stick with the plan. But for now that could be left unsaid. The girl hadn't asked directly so no answer was needed.

They were still discussing the various strengths and weaknesses of the other team members when Jodie's reader beeped and she read out a message from Maddie telling them to assemble at the front entrance. It seemed a storm front was moving over Kotelny and their next mission was about to begin.

The big helicopter was spookily quiet. She could feel the rhythmic shudder of the rotors, but the sound of the engine was impressively contained. It was obviously fast too. There was a real sense of hurtling through the sky, even though there were no portholes in the long cabin.

The mood in the team was still somber. There were a couple of crew with them, two men in flight suits and helmets at the end of each bench, but they'd spoken only in short instructional bursts at the start of the flight and the group had quickly fallen silent. Helga was left alone with her thoughts and found herself carefully assessing her teammates.

The skinny figure next to her had been brave to stand up to Jester but he wasn't going to be much use in a fight. He had a gift with computers but after that he was just baggage. He had no weapons and was actually sitting holding the teddy bear that he liked to carry. There was something odd about his soft toy. He didn't seem to cuddle it or use it for comfort and he didn't even seem to be embarrassed about being seen with it. But then he wasn't somebody who ever seemed to consider the opinion of others. He was like Luca, the autistic boy at the school; maybe not as bad but definitely on the spectrum. He certainly wasn't interested in becoming a team player and this made him a risk.

She knew enough about combat operations to know that teamwork was a vital factor. There was no place for loners.

Jodie suddenly shifted on the bench and Helga pretended to scratch her cheek so that she could study the American girl's expression. She was staring into space with big sad eyes and Helga wasn't surprised. *She knows this is our last chance. Here it will all get decided. This is when we find out if this boy can actually protect her or not.*

Her gaze drifted and she found herself thinking about the Jester man. He was a special case too, a loose cannon who did what he wanted, when he wanted. Negative thoughts were beginning to form in her mind when an image of him lying on the floor of the bunker came to her, and she was reminded of how calm he'd been when outgunned and low on ammo. *He kept the girl out of trouble in Washington and that was vital. He has to do more of that. He's got that survival thing and now he's got to share it. He needs to spread it over them like a blanket.*

She sensed the copter slowing and lowering. Then the lighting dimmed and they were plunged into near darkness. A couple of luminous strips appeared on the floor and the doors opened.

Icy air chilled her face. They had goggles and she'd been given padded armor and a hat but she knew she was feeling it more than her teammates, who were snug in thick suits with fur-lined hoods.

She made her way carefully to the exit and stood holding a couple of straps, but there was nothing to see. White speckled white under a roof of gray. She tried to pick out the base or some kind of landmark, but her eyes found only rippling drifts and swirling flakes.

They didn't land but were held low and told to jump. Maddie and Jester went first and then it was her turn. She sank up to her knees and gasped. It was even colder on the ground, and the wind instantly ripped the warm air from her clothes.

Their chopper rose and vanished, and behind it she saw an even bigger helicopter lowering the load shifter. Ropes unlooped and then the cargo craft shot straight up into the clouds and they were alone.

She'd hoped some of the insane gusts had been downdraft but it was no different when they'd gone. It was just the six of them and a machine, and that was when everything went terribly wrong.

Chapter 27

Weaver

Dr. Weaver sat at his desk and stared at the remains of his sandwich. He was still groggy from the sleeping pill, and the coffees weren't cutting through it. He'd got about four hours and doubted they'd got much more, some on the flight and some at Bear Creek, but probably not enough to keep them sharp. And they had a job to do. He didn't deserve the luxury of rest. He didn't deserve anything because he'd been avoiding them and that made him a coward. He'd only managed to convince Jodie to go to Alaska because she'd called him. He should have told them about Bear Creek himself but he was hiding. He was hiding in his safe, secure office while they risked their lives, and that made him truly pathetic.

After rubbing his palms into his eye sockets he swung his gaze to the terminals in front of him and checked for updates. There was still nothing from McDermott. He'd been warned that stealth conditions would slow down communication but it didn't make waiting any easier. His guys were up there doing something incredibly dangerous and he knew nothing about what was going on.

There was no point dwelling on it though. He had to keep active. The only way he could really help was by keeping an eye on the big picture. He was the overview guy. The strategist.

He pulled his eyes from the internal feed and forced himself to concentrate on the news search. The global report was filling up with a string of stories about black-eyed corpses in some Russian fishing port called Dikson. It might be a new outbreak of half-deads; it might not. It was a shitty-sounding place with a stupid name and he said it aloud to try to cheer himself up. "Dick. Son. Son of dick." No. Not even a smile. It just made him even more ridiculous.

Even though the item seemed unconvincing, he forwarded the link to one of his analysts for further investigation.

His mind drifted back to the current mission and he was hit by a twinge of paranoia. Maybe McDermott wasn't going to update him because he'd been forgotten. After all, what was he going to do? He was thousands of miles away drinking coffee. He was the academic pretending that he understood a bunch of old documents when they didn't really say anything very clearly at all.

He shook his head and then swiveled to his master AI. The top screen was full of orange when it should have been green. The software was unhappy about a lot of things. At the very highest level it was unhappy about the White House. Not the politics of course, it didn't have much opinion about that. No, it didn't like the infestation there. It hated it, he could tell. It couldn't explain it, and that made it cross. He was sure that if it could stamp its feet and smash its fists on the table it would. But it couldn't. So it kept rerunning loops and changing little boxes from yellow to orange. Fort Wainwright and Kotelny were fine. It loved the fact that they were the same distance from where the creatures were first sighted and that the outbreaks had been reported on the same day, almost to the hour.

"Tough," he said out loud to the terminal. *You may be running loops of pure logic but you have to live in the real world. No one knows how the arthropod got to Washington, but you seem pretty sure it's in there so suck it up. Shit happens. Deal with it.*

He moved on to the most important estimates. The Ferguson kid's ability to protect others from hypnosis had been downgraded in certainty and so had Jodie's ability to get the three of them working as a team. The overall prediction of success was wavering between thirty and forty percent.

He hoped McDermott had told them to pull out if they encountered any problems. He'd said that himself, hadn't he? He'd told them at least twice. He'd told Jodie again the last time he'd spoken to her. He was sure of that.

An indicator flashed in one of the throw-images and he found himself reading the news update. A juggernaut class blimp had crashed in Nerchinsk. So what? It was taking fish and whale blubber to Mongolia. Big deal. The AIs did this. They trawled every piece of data that was out there and spat it up at regular intervals. The tags showed this as relevant because the airship had started out near the Arctic Circle and this type of craft had never crashed before. Well, big deal.

He turned and refilled his coffee. The pot was almost cold but he didn't care. He couldn't be bothered to ask for fresh. He was too tired. Groggy.

The tepid liquid sloshed around in his mouth and he grimaced. It was no good being at his desk. He should go and lie down again. He couldn't sleep but he could doze. That was something. Better than pretending he could help by staring at endless reports and predictions.

As he stood, another blinking light caught his eye. Yet another news flash from Asia. The cargo craft that had crashed in Nerchinsk had black-eyed corpses in it. Even more chilling was its place of origin. The damn thing had taken off from a fishing port in northern Russia, a crappy sounding town by the name of Dikson.

Oh shit. He started to rub his forehead. It sounded like they had another infestation on their hands.

Kotelny, Siberia

Chapter 28

Helga

Maddie clearly needed to be in two places at once. She was standing pointing where they should go while staring worriedly at the unmoving machine behind them.

Four of them pressed forward in a ragged line. Jester had taken the lead and the American girl was hunched up behind him with her arms tight against her chest. The Ferguson kid was third, walking straight and erect with his eyes vague and dreamy. When had he last spoken? Helga couldn't remember.

She guessed their route was taking them to the building, but the problem wasn't in front of them, it was back at the landing site. The UGV wasn't following and Cryboy had gone to look at it.

They were spread thin, and although their organizer wanted to be leading, she chose to go and find out what was happening with the machine. Already they were confused and disoriented. All this had happened in less than a couple of minutes and the snow around Helga's shins was slowing her, the snow in the air blinding her and the whistling howling gale pulling the warmth from her bones. She thought about going back to help with the robot but carried on instead. She was the only one without a snowsuit, and because her teeth were already chattering and her shoulders shuddering, she knew she had to get inside.

She doubled her efforts, striding forward in a determined attempt to catch up with the leaders. A tall metal structure loomed on her right and she found herself relieved to see something man-made. The shadow of a wall appeared and then she came across the Americans huddled around a door. It was a gray steel thing, just normal-sized with a small security scanner plastered with ice crystals. Of course it was locked, and Jester raised his eyebrows and rolled his eyes at her when she got close. This was where the mistake became clear. The computer geek was supposed to get them inside and he was far out of sight, presumably fixing the uncooperative robot.

"You okay, Helga?" the big man asked her.

She knew she wasn't. Her lips and toes were tingling and she was shaking so much her jaw was rattling. She shrugged and he kept his eye on her while he slung up his rifle.

"I can shoot it open," he said. "It's armored though. Might need a few grenades."

She shook her head. They needed to stay stealthy and they needed to preserve ammunition. Anything more than a couple of shots would get noticed; the sound would carry downwind. It was way too risky.

"She can't wait out here!" Jodie shouted, flicking glances between her and the landing site.

"Got to," he replied. "We give them three minutes and we try to keep her warm. Best we can do." He slipped his weapon behind him and moved up as if to hug her.

Part of her found that funny. It wasn't long ago that she was embracing him. Now he was repaying the favor and that was very sweet. Somewhere deep inside she smiled; she liked secret meetings with boys around the back of buildings. Nobody looking, a beautiful Christmas scene keeping their love from prying eyes.

Part of her was alarmed. She shouldn't be happy and she shouldn't be fantasizing. Mental confusion was a warning sign.

"Make like penguins, guys," Jester told the others. "Penguins!" he shouted.

They moved in close and she found herself at the center of a protective ring.

"Jump," he commanded, his face close to hers. "Up and down."

She started to move, bouncing as high as she could and then slowing. Tired. Sleepy.

"Do not stop!" he yelled. "Do you hear me? Move, Helga. Jump. We'll jump with you. MOVE!"

They all jumped. All four of them hopping up and down in time. It was hard to breathe and she couldn't feel her feet or hands, but it was also hilarious. Ridiculous. She wanted to smile but she couldn't feel the muscles on her face.

She didn't know how long they did their little dance, some deranged sports team celebrating a forgotten goal, but new voices joined them and she turned to see Maddie, Cryboy and the machine just a few feet away.

The geek examined the security panel and shook his head.

"Come on!" Jester shouted at them.

"No power," Maddie replied.

The big man left the ring and went to talk to her. "And they didn't know this?" Helga heard him shout.

Their organizer couldn't have looked more uncomfortable. And she was cold too, ghostly pale and shivering uncontrollably. Jester cursed loud and long. Shouting obscenities at the wind, and then coming straight back to her.

"Helga," he said right into her ear, "just a thought. Just a chance."

She nodded.

"Could you get it open? Kick it down?"

She did. It took nearly twenty strikes and some shoulder barges, but she got it bent and held on just two rods. While she was gasping for breath, with her hands on her knees, the geek took something from the machine and moved past her. They huddled around again and she saw the flash and spark of some sort of cutting tool. Jester gave the final shove and then they were stumbling inside.

The big man gave her no rest. She had to keep moving, swinging her arms and jogging until the pain came. A bag of nuts and raisins was thrust into her hands and someone managed to heat some water. They stood close together and drank, and Cryboy turned the tool into some sort of heater and soon it felt normal. A camping trip. Hikers in an abandoned cottage.

An angry discussion broke out near her but she ignored it and started to look around. She was definitely back in Russia. The walkie-talkies that sat on chargers on the ledge of the high barred window were the brand that she'd used in the army. There was a smell of stale smoke and body odor, and by the time she'd finished inspecting the single blank-screened computer and the scattering of cheap furniture, she concluded that she could've been standing in her old regiment's briefing room.

When she tuned back in, Jester was still pouring rage and fury at Maddie. He cursed the planning and he questioned again and again whether they'd come in the right door. It seemed they had, and eventually her companions stripped off their snowsuits and got ready to move on through the internal door.

The machine they had to leave outside. The machine was three inches wider than the doorway. As she lifted her rifle and limped after her teammates, Helga knew what this meant. This meant that if they did capture the arthropod then somebody was going to have to drag the box in and out on their own. That someone would have to be her.

Chapter 29

Cryboy

It wasn't his fault. He'd got the measurements exactly right. Some logistics clerk in an office somewhere had thought it wouldn't make any difference to switch robots. Most of the idiot nation he lived in paid no attention at all to detail. And now he was cold. He was never meant to have got cold. He was never even meant to be uncomfortable. Society had machines to do all the grunt stuff. It seemed to him that humans were now the weak link in the chain.

Cryboy watched Maddie drop the kit bag against the wall in front of the staircase door with a growing sense of frustration and anger. He'd been waiting for her to come and ask his advice but she'd happily led them through the building without referring to him. Why didn't she want his analysis? Weaver had told her to consult him during the missions but she seemed to have forgotten that.

There was a lot he could have told her. The dim lighting and warm pipes meant that at least two of the base's systems were still working. In the very first corridor they'd found the bodies of three half-dead guards who'd been shot in the head. He could have told her when that happened too. He'd hacked the report and knew the precise details of the last Russian mission.

The other thing she should have been doing was giving the team more background info. It was only due to his expertise that they knew which bunker contained the creature and how to get down to it, but instead of stopping and briefing them she was pushing ahead with the plan and seemed to be in a hurry to get the strike team into the depths of the building. This was going to lead to problems. There was no point having somebody of his capabilities along if they weren't going to listen to him.

He could feel his hands bunching into fists as she gave Jester the final part of his briefing. It was amazing how casually the ex-army man reacted to the information. When she described the route to the blast tunnels, he did nothing more than glance at the door and nod. Even worse, when she pointed to the big kit bag and reminded him that he had forgotten to take it in Washington, the thug in the clown suit just gave the gear a quick look then winked at her. Why would he do that? She was right. They were running out of ammunition when they'd rescued them in the White House. Every stage had been carefully worked out. The details were important.

Cryboy's frustration was not eased when Maddie turned to talk to the young black kid. She did nothing to get him to explain what he was going to do, just asked him to protect the girl and then stood back and watched while he drew a circle on her forehead that he called "the third eye."

Hadn't he tried to shield her before and failed? It was clearly a trick. That would be okay if the threat was psychological but it wasn't. The hypnosis was real. The soldiers that had gone under hadn't believed in it.

His tear ducts flooded and eyes started to sting. They really had a problem here. He needed to talk to Weaver. Maddie was too fast and too sloppy and the Curtis kid was a fake. They needed a plan B.

Chapter 30

Jodie

The shadows from the overhead bulb sharpened and she heard a faint click. Curtis had closed the door and once again the three of them were on their own. They were moving downward at a steady pace, it was dark and there were pieces of grit crunching under her boots. Apart from her own breath rasping loudly in her ears, the only sound was the faint snow-sleigh jangle from the bells on Jester's hat and shoes. She knew Curtis was coming down behind her, but he trod silently and without any sensation of movement.

Once again they were in a mad hurry. Maddie had somehow known the layout of the base and had rushed them to the top of the steps without giving them time to look around or get their bearings. They'd passed some dead guards and a few empty offices, and then been told that they had to go down a couple of levels. That was it. No discussion and no questions. Even worse was the fact that her companions didn't seem to mind. After spending the first half of the day screaming his lungs off, Jester had suddenly become remarkably calm and jokey. The Ferguson kid had only said a few words when drawing on her forehead and generally seemed happy in his own little dream world.

They'd gone down a long spiral staircase and were perhaps a hundred feet underground when she turned a corner and saw a pale-blue radiance up ahead. She reached the bottom and discovered that the light was coming through a doorway that led into some kind of cavernous space.

Jester had already gone through and was standing in a large oval chamber gazing up at a row of glowing glass blocks in the ceiling.

She stepped in to join him and found herself in a big empty room. In the middle of the floor there was an open trapdoor, like a giant manhole cover. As her eyes adjusted, she was able to make out a mass of muddy footprints leading around it to a pair of elevator doors on the far side.

She stood taking in the scene while Curtis trod past her and then moved quickly to the shaft and crouched at its edge.

She watched him peer down into the darkness with a growing sense of unease. It looked like he was sussing out the next stage of their journey and the thought was totally unappealing. She didn't want to go exploring any deeper. She wanted to close the hatch and go back to the surface.

While she was still deciding whether to leave the relative safety of the threshold, Jester strolled off to investigate a dark patch on the wall, and she realized that what she'd assumed were shadows were in fact big openings the size of storm drains.

After poking his head inside, he turned back to her with raised eyebrows.

"Blast tunnels," he said matter-of-factly.

She looked at him blankly and he moved his head in an explanatory circle. "They absorb the energy of an explosion. Make the place bombproof."

She nodded and then turned to see Curtis step away from the edge of the shaft and stab his finger behind him. "Lots of very unusual stuff down there," he told them.

Jester asked if it might be the animals Weaver had mentioned.

"If I can get into a trance then I might be able to find out," the young shaman replied, looking over at her. "And if I can locate Jodie I can also give her more protection."

She gave him a nod of acknowledgment and he trod to the back of the room and laid down his weapons.

For the next few minutes she watched him carry out the routine with the mound of powder that he'd gone through in the White House. There was soon a thin wisp of smoke rising into the air, and when it thickened to a gray column he leaned forward and started sucking it into his nostrils.

A silence descended on the chamber and she left the steps and walked over to join her remaining companion.

Jester was squatting against the wall, staring into his cigarette packet, when she reached him. She stared at Curtis for a while and then glanced down.

"What's he doing when he sits like that?" she asked.

The big man looked up with a couple of unlit Marlboros bouncing in his mouth. "He puts himself into a trance."

"So?"

"So then he's supposed to be able to access another world."

"Another world?" she repeated, struggling to keep the frustration out of her voice. "You mean drugs? Is it like drugs?"

There was a click, and a puff of burning tobacco rose toward her. "Is it like drugs? I have absolutely no idea, Jodie," he shook his head. "Is life like drugs? Is drugs like life? Is his *other world* somewhere up his left nostril? Fucked if I know."

She looked down and wondered why he was being so grouchy. As soon as they'd got to the bottom of the stairs he'd gone all sad and tired and that wasn't good. She needed her teammates to be on their best form.

"You okay?" she asked.

"Me? Yeah. Why do you ask?"

"Because you seem … you know … low."

"That's 'cause I'm sitting down and you're standing up." She caught a glimpse of yellow teeth as he twisted his neck and grinned up at her. "Nah, to be honest I don't like this place," he pushed himself to his feet and stood with his hands on his hips. "They only built it to dissipate the energy of an attack. You get out of that elevator then you get into the other one. It's empty. It's bare. It's devoid. It is a *void.* A place to avoid." He shook his head and started to walk away. "Shit's happened since we got in here and I'm bored."

She watched him stroll to the edge of the hole and peer down. His body locked rigid, and then a thin white slug slid out of his mouth and dropped into the darkness. *Oh that's gross. Did he really need to go over there just to spit?*

He wiped his lips and swiveled his head in her direction. "Have you *smelled* it down there?" he asked with wide eyes. "That's one hell of a strange stink." He took a couple of loud sniffs. "You know … I don't think we should hang around for psychic trance man to do his stuff. I'm not really much of a waiter."

Oh Christ. She set off toward him. *He's one of those guys: can't cope with the quiet times, always poking around for action.* She stopped and put her hands on her hips. "So?"

"So, I want to see what's down there," he told her.

The first faint signs of panic started to bubble in her stomach. "No I don't think so." She jerked her head at Curtis. "I think we should stick together."

He held up his index finger and lowered his voice to a whisper. "How about we go take a quick look? Just a peek. Ten minutes max."

She squinted down the hole and the sight of the concrete steps fading into darkness filled her with a cold sinking dread. When she looked back, he was watching her with an expression of high expectation.

"Nah," she said, shaking her head. "Much better we stay here till Curtis's ready."

He pursed his lips and set off downward. "Well I'm going."

Her discomfort became a fist beating inside her chest. How could he do this to her? "Oh come on!" she pleaded. "Don't leave me on my own."

He stopped and shrugged. "Come with me then."

She was aware of her fingers tapping her gun belt while she stood considering the offer. She didn't want to stay on her own with a man who was effectively asleep, but she didn't want to go down to the next level either. Perhaps her best bet was to find somewhere safe between the two of them. "Okay then," she said, giving him a nod, "just a quick look."

"An excellent decision." He set off again and she followed; doubt and fear churning her stomach as she took the first step downward. *Not sure this is such a good idea.*

The first thing she noticed was the stench. It made her think of sick animals, and the more she tried to swallow it away the more stubbornly it clung to her mouth and tongue. Even worse was the fact that Jester hadn't waited for her and was already out of sight somewhere below.

His behavior was confusing. He was selfish, sarcastic and bitter, but at the same time his constant desire to keep exploring meant that she never had to be near the front. She wanted to dislike him, but written deep in her mind was the fact that when things had gone wrong in Washington he'd saved her life.

After a short while she gave up trying to get nearer and resigned herself to her situation. She had to assume that while he was alive nothing dangerous could attack from the front and with Curtis and the others behind her she was in a position of relative safety. Although there was some logic to what she was telling herself, her body didn't seem to believe it. With every step she felt her heart pumping faster in her chest and her shoulders and arms tightening with tension.

After a long silent descent she felt something crunch under her boot and stopped. A flick of the flashlight revealed curls of shattered glass and empty shell cases lying around her feet. She scanned the ceiling and discovered a row of broken light-fittings. Even more disturbing were the impact holes and scuff marks from ricocheted bullets. It was clear there'd been heavy fighting down there and that was exactly the last thing she wanted to find.

While she was surveying the damage, a whiff of cigarette smoke reached her from below and she set off again, this time moving more quickly, brushing her shoulder against the outer wall to steady herself while she dropped from step to step.

The animal stink that filled the stairwell strengthened with each passing moment. First, the skin around her eyes started to prickle, and then a tickly itching broke out in her nostrils. She carried on, her desire to join her companion moving her noisily downward until she walked into a cloud of rising smoke. Her beam swung onto the pattern of Jester's suit and she found him sitting looking out into a large space.

"Hi there," he said in a gentle whisper.

"Hi," she replied.

"I'd like you to do me a favor, my love," he continued in soft sweet tones. "How about you switch that flashlight off and put it down near your feet?"

She stood perfectly still with the beam trained on the floor. Was he nuts? Why would they switch their only light off?

"We'll be safer without it," he said patiently. "It makes you a target and everything outside the beam seems darker. Better to get used to what light there is."

She did as she'd been instructed. The surrounding blackness seemed to leap out at her as soon as she'd clicked it off, but after just a few moments she was able to make out a couple of metallic squares on the wall ahead of them.

There was a crack and she flinched. A green glow enveloped Jester's hands, then a stretch of floor emerged beneath his feet and a long rectangular room formed around them. He held the light stick like a knife thrower and flicked it through the air. It skidded across a stretch of linoleum and came to a stop against the bottom of a cement wall. Two pairs of elevator doors shimmered in the faint light and dark rectangles at either side hinted at corridors leading off to the left and right.

"Just another big empty room," she commented.

"Yeah, but there are passages going off at the back there."

She swallowed and wiped her hand across her mouth. "And the smell?"

"Oh you noticed that? Well, it's not me if that's what you're thinking."

"No. I'm thinking Curtis was right," she told him. "He said there were dangerous things down here and I'm thinking we should go back up."

"Curious though," he said, rubbing his chin. "That smell. It's not *natural* is it? Even if there are hints of animal in it." He looked back over his shoulder. "Your shotgun all loaded?"

She checked her weapon and looked back up to discover that he was walking away from her. "Let's just have a peek down here," he said casually.

She watched him stroll away with growing horror. *Oh shit. I just want to get back up the steps.* Before she knew it, he'd reached the left-hand passage and was peering around the corner. *Shit! Shit! Shit!* With a massive effort of will, she pushed herself forward and followed.

When she reached him, he was hunkered down staring at the floor. For a few moments he was perfectly still, then he lowered his hand and brought up a grenade pin. He opened his fingers and it landed with a light tinkle. *Okay,* she thought, *I'm having so much fun finding bits of explosives, but how about we get out of here?*

Shuffling forward, he squinted deeper into the darkness and she followed his gaze. There was a mass of dark streaks just ahead and she was wondering what they were when an image dropped into place in her mind. *Bloodstains. Oh crap. Something's been dragged bleeding down there.*

A crack cut the air and a second light stick glowed in his hand. He flicked it down the hallway where it skidded and spun to a stop between two hulking silhouettes.

Her heart jumped. The weak green light was illuminating furry legs rising into shaggy-edged ovals. The shapes suddenly moved and two pairs of red-ringed eyes appeared. *That's it! Fuck this. Let's go.* A quiver of tension ran up the limbs and the bulky outlines started lolloping forward.

She pressed her shotgun to her shoulder. "Shit."

"Yes." He snapped up his rifle. "Shit indeed."

The sprinting animals were halfway toward them.

"Both targets," he shouted. "Now!"

His weapon exploded into life, firing triple bursts of rounds left then right. She blasted twice and reloaded. The shots sent chunks of fur and skin exploding into the air and the creatures stumbled and stopped. Their upper bodies folded and the red eyes flickered and vanished.

She let out a noisy breath. *Don't know what the fuck they were, but we've scrubbed them.*

"So what do you think—?" The beasts' shoulders twitched and the air throbbed with a low growl. The red eyes rekindled and they charged again.

Jester held down his trigger and sprayed another stream of rounds. "Get out!" he screamed. "Get up the steps."

She fired twice and saw their attackers crumple and skid to a halt a few yards away.

Jester's gun clicked empty. He changed magazines in three fluid movements then threw himself sideways and body slammed her. "Get the fuck out! Now!"

After a couple of wobbly steps she steadied herself and looked back. Just a few yards away there was a creature poised to pounce, but Jester was helpless. His first round had jammed and he was trying to clear it. She aimed and fired in a single motion, blasting both barrels between its eyes. *Gotcha! Now stay down.*

She assumed that with the targets out of action they were going to take their chance to leave, but as she was retreating to the staircase, Jester's rifle barked into action and he started to walk back into the corridor. The next instant, he'd vanished behind the wall and the air froze in her chest. The rifle fire stopped, there was a heavy thud and she heard growling and scuffling. *Oh shit!* She took a step forward and called his name.

His voice came back strained and muffled. "Don't shoot! You'll hit me. Just get out."

As she swayed on her feet, a dark shape slipped out of the end of the hallway. There was a rush of movement, she fired, and something hit her in the belly. She rolled as she fell. Her elbow hit the floor with a shock of pain and her shotgun jolted from her grasp.

Two huge claws tore at her vest and a scream rose inside her. *It's on me!* Wet fangs shone just inches from her face. Her fingers found the handle of a revolver and pulled it out. She aimed and pulled the trigger. Its head whacked her arm and the shot hit the ceiling. She smashed downward with the butt. *Get off, you fucker.* Talons snatched at her chest and pinned her flat on the ground. Dripping jaws snapped at her neck and a hot blast of rotten meat blew onto her face. *Shit! It's going to rip my throat out!* She hammered at the head and heard her own shrieks echoing off the walls.

The beast shuddered and let out a squeal. Its grip weakened and it rolled over with a long pole quivering in its side. Curtis was suddenly standing by her shoulder. He grabbed the end of his spear and thrust it deeper. An angry growl shook the air followed by the clatter of wood on stone. Light flickered on steel and his machete swung through the air. The growl cut off. There was a thud, and a spurt of warm liquid landed on her arm.

The next thing she knew he was crouching at her side.

"You okay?" he asked, pressing his thumb into the holes in her vest. "Did it bite you?"

"No, I don't think so," she said breathlessly. "It was on the armor. It didn't get through."

"Good," he replied. "You're lucky."

A terrible thought flashed into her mind and she jabbed her finger at the corridor behind her. "Jester. I think the first one got Jester."

He pulled her to her feet. "Okay, let's go see. But we've gotta move quick."

"Why?" she asked.

"'Cause there's more of them," he bent and tossed the creature's head against the wall. "Get yourself ready and stay sharp."

She snatched up her weapon and her hat. *More of them? No way. We've got to get out of here.*

When she looked up, he was at the corner of the passageway staring into the darkness. She stopped a few feet behind him and strained her ears. The muted sound of snarling drifted toward them but the growls were strangely soft and subdued. Seemingly unconcerned, Curtis crept slowly into the corridor with his spear raised and she followed.

After a few yards he stopped and pointed the tip of his weapon at the body of a huge dog-like animal that was stretched out in a pool of black blood. Jester was kneeling behind it with its head held across his thighs and a big serrated knife tight in his right fist. He looked up at them, his mouth and chin smeared with lumps of gore, and growled.

She flinched, but when she turned to Curtis she saw a smile flickering in his eyes.

"Well done," the young black kid said, giving his teammate a nod.

Jester spat out a mouthful of fur and blood. "Why thank you, young sir."

She peered curiously at Jester, and then asked him if he was okay.

He raised his eyebrows in response and she turned to study the creature's sprawling body. "And it's definitely dead?"

"Yep." He nodded and blew bits of fur from his lower lip. "I think I got lucky." He wiped his hand across his mouth, smudging gunk across his cheeks. "It was already full of lead, and then it kinda jumped onto my knife."

Curtis squinted at the creature's chest. "You punctured its heart?"

"Yeah," Jester confirmed. "*Lots* of blood."

She stood open-mouthed and studied the gutted shape in front of her. What the hell were those things? And why did her companions have to be so weird? Jester had nearly got ripped to bits but seemed to be enjoying himself. First he'd chosen to fight on his own, and then he'd found some sick pleasure in sitting with an animal he'd just butchered. He'd been chewing at the creature's neck when they'd found him. So had his combat experience really unbalanced him? She'd assumed that his joking and posturing had been an act, but he did seem to genuinely crave danger and violence.

A thump snapped her from her thoughts. Jester had dropped the creature's head on the ground and was standing wiping his knife on his thigh. He slipped the weapon into a sheath on his calf and then met her gaze with a grin.

She ignored him and asked Curtis what the creatures were.

"We'll talk about that later," he replied, holding up his hand and glancing down the passageway behind them. "We've got to check—" His eyes widened and he snapped his spear to his shoulder.

Jester snatched up his rifle and clicked off a grenade. A flash lit up the main room, and the bang rocked her on her heels. She caught a glimpse of animals crossing the floor, and then a roll of hot air hit her and yelping filled her ears. Jester's weapon barked into life, muzzle flames flashing and empty cases spinning to the ground as he poured a torrent of rounds at the approaching attackers. The nerve-shredding baying widened until it was all around them. Then three long dark shapes came racing into the corridor.

She tracked and blasted into the head of the first. It fell and was skidding on its stomach when a spear sank into its side. Snarling jaws turned and snapped at the air, then Curtis lunged and brought down his machete. The growl choked to a gurgle and its head dropped from its neck.

The second creature charged Jester's legs, chunks flying as his rounds found their mark. She hit it between its ears with an explosion of blood and splintered bone. The punctured head swiveled, burning eyes fixed her and it tensed to pounce. She was pumping cartridges into her gun when the long body left the ground. It seemed to hang in front of her, and then she snapped back the stock and blasted both barrels into its throat. It dropped to the floor with a heavy thud, its paws slapping onto her boots just as Curtis lunged and brought his spear down. Her ears throbbed with a nerve-jangling yelp; she felt its death throes, then a slice from her teammate's machete brought silence.

Rifle fire started again. Jester was keeping the third animal away from his legs with clusters of head shots. He started to walk backward, and as the creature twisted to hook its fangs into him, he fired a burst into its skull. Its head dropped and he took another step back and flicked his eyes at them. "Can you believe this?" he said, looking down at the flattened creature. "It gets back up again."

An angry snarl vibrated the air and the animal was suddenly up, lunging and snapping. Jester jumped back and hammered its head onto the floor with another stream of bullets. "All great family entertainment …" he commented. "But you can't afford to get trapped or run out of ammo."

Curtis strode forward and hacked off the creature's head.

"Thank you, kind sir," Jester said, giving his comrade a short bow. "Most obliged."

Curtis scanned around them. His eyes probed the shadows at the end of the smoky corridor, and then met theirs. "That's it," he said calmly. "That's all of them."

She took a wobbly step backward, bent and put her fist to her mouth. She coughed and a spout of vomit splattered onto the floor by her feet. She ought to care. Being sick in front of these men should matter, but it didn't. What mattered was life and death. The creatures were dead and they were alive.

When she looked back up, Jester was watching her with soft, thoughtful eyes. "Yep. Touch of travel sickness," he commented reflectively. "No shame in that. Can catch up with you at any time." He glanced around while reaching for his cigarettes. "Or perhaps it's the color scheme? The neutral tones on the wall clashing with this nasty gray floor? Makes me want to puke too."

Curtis was at her side, his arm resting across her back. "Okay." He squeezed her shoulder. "It's alright now. We're finished here. All safe."

She nodded, and then puked again.

Chapter 31

Weaver

A frail elderly lady was asking him questions. She wanted to know what had happened to her daughter. Where had he sent her? What had he done to her? A big general in an immaculately pressed uniform was demanding that he do more. A charismatic businessman wanted results. There were smiles and pats on the arm, but underneath an unnerving steely resolve. He saw six people trudging through thick snow, then a helicopter, mangled and smoking on a ridge of icy rock.

Weaver snapped his eyes open and sat up on the bed. It was no use trying to rest. The babble of voices was only getting worse in the darkness of the guest apartment. He needed to get back up to his desk. At least there he felt like he was doing something.

Yawning loudly, he looked down at his reader and checked that he hadn't missed anything. There was still nothing from McDermott and that was a real worry. Could they have crashed? They'd flown out into a storm. It was possible.

He stood and started tucking in his shirt. His clothes were creased and he was unshaven but he decided to go straight to the top floor. Who cared if a few people saw him looking crumpled?

As he walked the long corridor he tried to order his thoughts. Things had got complicated and he needed to make sense of the new developments. For weeks they'd had sightings of three creatures and three sites showing signs of infestation. How one of the things got to the White House was a mystery but the rest had fitted pretty well. Now there was a fourth outbreak, the arthropod theory seemed suspect and it looked like there was going to be a lot more work to do. His employers and their political friends were finalizing their decision about Mongolia but it was pretty clear what they were going to say. There was no point in sending his guys to Russia if they were going to let another creature get into the hands of the Mongolians or the Chinese. If the point was to restore order to the markets and make sure that no one ever tried to use these animals as a weapon, then all four had to disappear without anyone ever knowing they'd existed.

He turned the corner and went straight to the central shaft. There was an elevator waiting, and while he made his journey up to the control center he pondered why his backers were so keen to get a team that had already failed to try again. The most obvious answer was that they didn't have much to lose. Sure Sophos and Glover were putting money in, but it was only a fraction of what they'd gain if they got their business ventures moving again. O'Keefe and Hernandez had made certain that they had plausible deniability. If anything went terribly wrong the only people who would be in trouble were the six brave souls risking their lives. Everyone else would just slip back to business as usual. It had taken a while to figure it out but now he knew he was moving in a world of serious political operators. They had their hearts in the right place and they were working for a just cause, but they always made sure that the potential gain was very large and the risk kept as low as possible.

The office was quiet and there were only a handful of staff at their terminals. He made straight for his personal space and started his research. He was tired and he had a headache, but he had a duty to do as much as possible. There was nothing operational he could help with but his backers had discreetly mentioned that he might want to keep an eye on Canmore. Cryboy's hacking software was slowly piecing bits of data together, and it seemed that the senator had had some ridiculously ambitious plans.

Top of the list was Canmore's fairly unsubtle plot to take over the government of the United States. He'd realized that there was no statute covering the disappearance of a president and vice president and was ruthlessly exploiting it. If they were both found to be dead then there would be an election and a democratic government could be restored, but with their situation unknown, Canmore was pushing through some unique emergency legislation of his own. It shouldn't have been possible but it really did look like Friday's vote would be all he needed. Once the Interim Authorities became just "The Authorities," he would have almost absolute power.

There was some opposition, and O'Keefe was at the head of that, but a surprising number of senators and congressmen were keeping quiet. Enormous campaign donations from one of Canmore's lobbying organizations seemed to be smoothing things over nicely and they were just one of the activities that Cryboy's AI bots were monitoring.

Weaver began scrolling through the spyware updates. Sure enough, there seemed to be plenty of evidence of discreet payments to Canmore's growing army of supporters. Nothing that would stand up in court, but hundreds of transfers that had bounced through shell companies and ended up in a politician's consultancy account. Even more interesting was the discovery of a *Project Dublin* that Canmore was dedicating most of his time to. Cryboy's careful "soft probing" technique hadn't got inside any of the content yet but it involved both Brutetek and his life sciences company and seemed to depend on winning Friday's vote.

Well, it looked like they were right. There was indeed good reason to watch the scheming senator, but it left Weaver feeling like something of a spy and only added to his growing concerns.

He took out a piece of paper and started to write. The words came thick and fast, and even without a title he knew what he was creating. It was effectively a list of things he shouldn't be worrying about. He shouldn't worry that they might not be able to bribe the Mongolians to let them get into the temple. He shouldn't worry that the team wouldn't agree to go. He shouldn't worry that he was going to be fired. He shouldn't worry that Jodie was going to quit. He shouldn't worry about what Canmore was up to or the consequences of him winning the vote on Friday. He shouldn't worry that Curtis wasn't able to protect Jodie from the hypnosis. He shouldn't—

A ping. A lovely short message from McDermott at Bear Creek. Sent from a personal account but clear enough: "*Package safely delivered.*" Good. So they were in. They'd started the mission on Kotelny, so that was one less thing to worry over.

Now he needed to be Zen about things. They were probably getting on fine. The Ferguson kid had protected Jodie and they'd wrapped that thing in a steel net in less than ten minutes. The creature goes in the box and then they're straight back into the copters. In and out in less than half an hour. Easy.

Yes, a lot of the documents mentioned dramatic-sounding guard animals, but that could have been put in to scare off any sightseers. No, the next message would be announcing their success. If there was a time delay then his guys might be out already. They could be sitting in front of a big fire sipping cups of cocoa. Yes, that was the image to keep. His team—the ones he'd help motivate and persuade—safe, happy and warm.

Chapter 32

Jodie

Her teammates sat her on the steps and started working around her. Jester went back up to the blast room to collect their gear while Curtis started to inspect the corpses. She watched him moving around the room tossing animal heads against the wall and tried to pull the pieces of her mind back into focus.

Too much of what Weaver had described was coming true. There really were mutant animals running around in the bunkers, and the proof was lying in front of her eyes. When she'd first listened to him she hadn't actually believed what he was saying, but it now seemed more likely that there really was some kind of crab creature, and the implications were serious. She'd checked her bank account several times since they'd arrived in Russia and she'd already been paid for the kick-off meeting and their attempt in Washington. If they could complete this job then she'd get an even bigger sum and might never need to work again. But there was an obvious catch. She had to stay alive and uninjured and it looked like that was going to be much harder than anyone had thought.

Her companions were a key part of the equation. They were both obviously incredibly brave but there was a lot she still didn't know about them. Curtis had turned out to be surprisingly quick and effective but she didn't really understand how he was supposed to do his magic. Jester managed to maintain his relaxed jokey manner even under the most extreme circumstances, but the total disregard he had for his own safety was a potential cause for concern. The most significant fact about the men though was that they seemed determined to carry on, and she wasn't sure she had the courage to quit on them.

A sharp crack broke her thoughts, and she looked up to see Curtis stamping on a spear. He picked up the sections and then turned and asked for the strap to her shotgun. She handed it to him and watched as he started cutting it up. He'd divided it into several lengths when she heard bells jangling on the steps behind her and Jester brushed past and dropped their kit bag onto the floor.

She went back to staring at the corpses that were lying just yards away. Weaver had made the "guard animals" sound like a couple of fierce dogs, but what they'd just faced had been on another level altogether.

Eventually her curiosity became overwhelming, and when Curtis looked up she asked him what he thought the creatures were.

"Well," he replied, turning to study the bodies. "I think they're a kind of lycanthrope. Or perhaps caninethrope would be more accurate. They were normal animals once, probably huskies. They've mutated."

"But what had happened to them?" she asked quietly. "They were so tough. They healed so quickly."

"My guess is that there were infected by a kind of virus. Their cellular regeneration had been accelerated but it wasn't sustainable. They wouldn't have lived much longer than a couple of weeks." He tightened the last piece of nylon. "That's all we need to know for now. I think we've learned that we have to stay sharp and keep moving."

"Sure." Jester was studying the young black kid with both curiosity and admiration. "So what's next?"

"Next?" Curtis struck a match and lit the torches. "Another room of sick creatures—just as Weaver said."

His companion's eyes narrowed. "What, and you *know* this?"

"Yes," Curtis replied. "I've seen them. They're in a room near where you were attacked."

Jester looked at her with wide eyes. He obviously wanted her to join him in ridiculing their teammate's confident prediction, but she kept her face blank.

"Okay then," he eventually said with a shrug. "Let's go introduce ourselves."

A single thought nagged her as she followed the two men down the hallway. Weaver had mentioned something casually that now seemed pretty important. He'd warned them in the truck that there was something after the animals, something that sounded even more dangerous. If that was true then they needed to take things really slowly and do as much as they could to find out what they were dealing with.

When her teammates stopped in front of a large steel door she moved up quickly to join them. "Listen, wait a minute, perhaps we should think about doing this in stages." She took a deep breath and glanced back down the corridor. "I mean, that was tougher than we thought. How about we just try to get a look at what's in here and then go back up and report it to Weaver?"

Curtis nodded slowly. "I can see why you'd want to do that, Jodie, but I think it's a really bad idea. If we turn around then there's a risk we're going to become the hunted and not the hunters."

Jester nodded. "Yeah, I have to agree. That's a Special Forces strategy. Keep 'em on the back foot by attacking."

"Okay." She looked down and let out a sigh. "So how about we take some time to plan what we're going to do?"

"Yeah, sure." Curtis looked at the holdall that his teammate was carrying. "First we should have a good look at our gear. I think we're going to find things in there that will help."

"In the bag?" Jester swung the pack the floor. "I already had a peek. It's just ammo and flashlights and all that."

Curtis took it and after rooting around for a while produced a fat steel tube with a trigger at one end. He pulled a face, then passed it up to her and she examined it. It was bulky and heavy and the label on the handle announced that it contained two steel nets that could be fired at a range of thirty yards. Weaver had mentioned providing some kind of weapon to capture the creatures but there was no way she was going to try to catch something with that.

She handed it back with a shake of her head and Curtis gave her a knowing look.

"Yeah. A bit unwieldy isn't it? Don't worry. If we find the arthropod I'll pin it with a spear." He dropped the weapon into the bag and dug deeper into the contents. "That wasn't what I was trying to find though. Maddie said something about using the clips with the gray tape in the first rooms and I thought we should have a look at those." He lifted out a magazine with a metallic strip on it and passed it up to Jester. "Tell me what's unusual about those."

His teammate pressed out the top round and held it up. "Ah, right. Kinda shiny ain't they? I get it. These were for those furry fellas back there."

"Yeah," Curtis replied. "They're silver."

"What!" She turned to Curtis, open-mouthed. "So why didn't they tell us?"

"I don't know," he replied, shaking his head. "It seems they had a problem with all this. Especially Weaver. I don't think he really believed what it said in that archive he manages. They did all the preparation then got too embarrassed to tell us about it."

She found herself staring at the bag while Jester quizzed Curtis on the effectiveness of silver bullets. Was it really possible that the young academic had known those animals would be so dangerous and not told them? Maybe not. So far nobody had ever survived to get any information out. He had definitely mentioned that the next stage was going to be even tougher though, and she was finding her teammate's casual approach to the situation increasingly frustrating.

"Guys," she said, interrupting them at the first opportunity. "All interesting stuff, but perhaps we should focus on getting ourselves ready."

"Yes." Curtis nodded and pointed at the door. "And that's the other thing Weaver was trying to tell us. He skipped over it but there was something about the way he was talking that made it stick in my mind. I remember the language he used. *Upir,* he said, and that's a fairly dramatic concept. The word's changed and we don't say that anymore … now we call them vampires."

Jester's eyes widened. "Really?" He dabbed his thumb on his incisors. "You mean … all dentally enthusiastic, white faces, dark cloaks and all that?"

His teammate shrugged and glanced at the door. "I guess we'll find out."

"Sounds scary," Jester continued. "Maybe they'll do a lot of math and counting and shit …"

"You know"—Curtis squeezed his eyes closed and smiled—"More and more I'm getting why you're immune to the hypnosis." He delved back into the holdall. "Anyhow, if they've got the name crawlers then I'm guessing they'll be able to stick to walls, maybe even the ceiling. If they *are* some kind of bloodsucker they'll go for the throat and try to inject a virus." He turned to her and held her gaze. "Don't let them. If they do, I can't help you. Nothing can."

The warning sent chills into her bones. So far nothing had seemed to faze their young companion but at that moment his eyes were full of genuine concern.

She was just trying to imagine a creature that could be tougher or more horrific than the things they'd just killed when he pulled out a section of carbon-fiber and held it up to the light. The graphite weave shone like fish scales as he twisted the upper half until it locked at right angles.

"Crossbows," he announced. "My guess is that we need to get wood into their hearts to kill these things." When he'd passed the weapon to Jester, he delved back into the bag. "Yep"—he pulled out a couple of short arrows and weighed them in his hands—"and ash bolts too."

Jester nodded. "Okay then, dancing boy," he said cheerfully. "If there's a bunch of vampires in there, I think we're gonna need a plan."

She listened carefully to the briefing, amazed that their polite young companion not only knew where the fierce-sounding creatures were but that he had ideas about how to tackle them.

The place was like a butcher's freezer. As soon as the door opened she was hit by a wall of icy meat-scented air and her stomach lurched. They shouldn't be there. The foul stench and horrible stillness were meant to be left alone. This was a mortuary and it was hidden from the world for a reason.

Jester brushed past her and moved into the gloom. With the lengths of burning spear in one hand and his rifle swinging in the other, he strolled into the blackness, and she watched with her heartbeat pumping loud in her ears.

At first, the flickering torchlight revealed just his outstretched arm and the sharp profile of his face, but as he moved deeper she caught glimpses of steel-framed chairs and got the impression that he was moving through a large canteen.

Quicker than she would've liked, Curtis slipped into the room and vanished into the inky darkness to her left.

It was her turn. With a crossbow in each hand, she slid around the doorframe and slipped down the brickwork. Placing the second bow by her foot, she pressed her weapon to her cheek and looked up.

Jester stopped and threw the torches deeper into the room. They bounced off a table then skidded onto the floor, and he sent a spray of rounds after them.

His role was to act as a distraction and a decoy and he played it with conviction. After releasing another torrent of bullets, he started to sing loudly and tunelessly. "Flew in from Miami beach BOAC. Didn't get to blah, blah, blah ..." He belted out a few more lines of the song and then stopped abruptly and tucked his rifle under the crook of his arm. Pulling out his cigarettes, he lit a couple and blew smoke high into the air. "... you don't know how blah, blah you are, boy. I'm back in the USSR."

He was taking a second long drag when something moved on the ceiling above him. A smooth, mottled dome appeared in the light of the flames and then vanished. The shape appeared again and she was able to make out a couple of pointed ears and a wrinkled neck.

Adrenaline tingled through her feet and fingers. It was a head hanging upside down. The head of a crawler.

As she moved her sights to the top of the creature's spine, her whole body tightened and started to tingle. What would happen when she fired? Were there others that would come straight for her? Curtis's words echoed in her mind: *If they bite you, I can't help you. Nothing can.* Her shoulders locked and a strange paralysis slowed her thoughts. Some inner survival mechanism was telling her to stay perfectly still and never move again.

She sat frozen with fear and watched the hanging creature start to grow. A moment later, two claw-like hands emerged and reached down toward Jester. She stared motionless as the long talons extended toward her companion, and then a voice spoke in her head and she heard herself giving shooting lessons: *relax, stay fluid, follow the target.* The air that had been trapped deep in her lungs came out in a long slow breath. *You've won medals for archery. You can do this.*

As its torso stretched into view, she measured the proportions of the skull and neck and moved her aim to where its heart should be. Then, with her jaw clenched tight and an angry tension buzzing in her head, she pulled the trigger.

The arrow sank into the creature's back and it fell, skidding off her teammate's shoulder with a piercing shriek and crashing onto the floor. He spun and started to spray rounds into its head. The crawler shuddered downward with each impact until its skull was tight against the ground. "Here …" Jester pressed the tip of his barrel closer. "Have some more, you fucker." He started firing again and had emptied a whole clip into his attacker when a second wiry creature dropped out of the darkness onto his back.

Oh crap, there's more of them in here. Jodie lunged for the second crossbow and snapped it to her cheek. Her teammate was spinning left and right with a shriveled snake-eyed man climbing up his vest. She pushed herself to her feet but had only moved a couple of steps when the crawler started to lower its mouth toward his neck. Jester jabbed his rifle behind him and jerked from side to side but couldn't shake it off.

She swung her weapon in time with the violent twisting and turning, and then heard Curtis's voice ring out from behind her.

"Shoot!"

"Hold still!" she shouted.

Jester froze and the creature lunged at his neck.

She pulled the trigger; the bolt buried deep under its shoulder blade and it let out a nerve-jangling screech.

She dropped the bow, and before it hit the ground her revolvers were in her hands and she was blasting bullets into the creature's rib cage. It fell and she followed it to the floor, firing into its chest until both guns clicked empty.

Its yellow reptile eyes dimmed, then its arms and legs shriveled toward its chest and it lay still like a dead insect.

She stepped back and looked at her companion. He was opening his mouth to say something when his eyes lifted over her shoulder and he nodded.

"Another one," he observed casually.

She spun and saw a third crawler standing with its arms outstretched. Her fingers snapped both triggers but the guns clicked empty.

"Down!" Jester shouted.

She threw herself past her teammate and landed on the floor with a jolt of pain. A short burst of rounds was followed by the sound of an automatic clicking empty. Then she heard Jester again, his voice soft and thoughtful.

"Okay. Try this."

There was a room-shaking boom and a thump of hot air slammed her flatter onto the floor. A force like a wrestler's thumbs pressed into her ears and her vision darkened to nothing.

Prickles of heat on the back of her hands woke her. She got her eyes open and blinked away the seesawing floor until the ground fixed into position. Jester was lying unconscious a few yards away. His mouth was open and pieces of burning chair were lying across his thighs. She was trying to make out how badly injured he was when a crawler appeared in her peripheral vision. It was the one he'd just hit with a grenade, but somehow it wasn't dead. Starched-white bones were showing through the punctures in its upper arms but it still seemed strong and able to move.

She watched the creature walk forward with its fangs bared and tried to shout. Her voice was just a croak. Even worse, something was edging toward his feet. A second crawler with an arrow lodged in its shoulder was down on all fours creeping up his legs toward his chest.

"Jester!" She tried to push herself up but there was no strength in her arms. The explosion was still ringing in her head and her body refused to obey. *Shit. Those fuckers are going to rip him to bits.*

There was a scream and a pair of black baseball boots stepped into view.

Forcing up her head, she saw Curtis ramming a spear through the nearest crawler. A strong thrust sent it staggering against a table where it fell sideways with its mouth gaping.

The second attacker twitched and launched itself into the air. Curtis melted sideways and spun. Steel flashed and the creature's head flew off into darkness.

A wave of relief moved through her. The young black kid had done it. He'd finished them all off.

Dropping her cheek onto her hand, she allowed her eyes to close. There was a fire burning in her skull and she needed a few seconds to clear it.

Gentle hands cradled her head and she opened her eyes to find Curtis examining her with concern. She allowed him to help her into a sitting position and then sat getting her bearings.

The room was lighter, the men had rested the torches on the tables and she could see that they were in some kind of dining area. It had obviously once been a clean and orderly place to rest and eat, but now it looked like a bomb site. The rear wall was blackened and cracked by the grenade, and there were bullet cases and spurts of dark blood along the central aisle.

Curtis pulled her to her feet and guided her into a chair. She was bruised and her ears were buzzing, but her body seemed to be okay.

Jester was standing gazing at her from the other side of a cluster of chairs. One side of his hat and suit was covered in a layer of white dust and his face was powdered with dirt and streaked clean with rivulets of sweat.

She blinked at him for a while, trying to force her body to relax while she told herself again and again that she was okay.

When her head had cleared and her hands had stopped trembling, she pushed a handful of bullets out of her belt and started to reload her revolvers. As she worked, she tuned into her companion's conversation and was amazed to discover that they were discussing the impact of Jester's grenade with the casual air of a couple of pals reviewing a fishing trip. Where had they found these guys? Their bravery was astounding. None of what was going on seemed to faze them or even slow them down.

When she glanced up, Jester was smiling at her. "You did well, Jodie," he told her. "Good crossbow work, then you emptied your revolvers at a range of about ten inches."

"Yeah well," she replied. "Those things were terrifying. I freaked."

"That's okay," he said, nodding appreciatively. "You can freak around me any day."

"So, we did it," she said, trying to sound upbeat and positive. "We've done two lots now."

She'd made the comment with the hope that her comrades might suggest returning to the surface, but Curtis's response demonstrated his intentions very clearly. After scanning the corpses and the fragments of smoldering furniture, he agreed that they were doing okay and then set to sharpening his spear. His understatement was as bizarre as their surroundings and she could tell from his tone that he had no intention of quitting and going back up top. Her teammates were determined to carry on and she was going to have to stay with them and finish the job.

"These markings here on the neck—this pair of wings." Jester had strolled over to one of the dead crawlers and was standing scratching his chin. "It's a Spetznaz emblem. At least it was"—He glanced at Curtis—"till you sliced it in half."

"What's *Spetznaz*?" she asked.

"Russian special forces," he told her. "Good guys. Tough as hell."

Curtis moved to Jester's side and followed his gaze. "You're sure that was a normal human tattoo?" he asked.

"Yep." Jester nodded and flicked ash onto the neck stump. "I think these poor bastards got sent in and ended up getting an unexpected makeover. If they're what Joolsey meant by the 'crawlers,' then most of what he said is turning out to be true." He straightened his back and stood surveying the circular steel door at the end of the room. "Which means that's where the crab thing is."

She still had one last chance to slow things down, and with her heart in her mouth she asked quietly how they were going to know if she was protected from the hypnosis.

Curtis reassured her that he had done everything he could to shield her, then Jester sauntered over and flopped a hand on her shoulder.

"I'll keep an eye on ya, Jodie," he said cheerily. "Any signs of going under and I'll pull you right out of there."

She nodded and thanked them. It would have to do. Both men had given her their word. They were a team and she was going to have to learn to trust them.

When she looked back up, Jester was standing staring at the entrance to the next room and she knew what he was thinking. It was time to get in there and find the arthropod, and to do that they needed another plan.

Chapter 33

Cryboy

He couldn't talk to Weaver. He couldn't talk to anyone. There was no signal on any of his devices and this left him with nothing to do. They were standing in the most boring corridor in the world and his companions weren't being very interesting.

Soon after the others had gone down, Maddie had pulled the staircase door open and had been staring into the darkness ever since. It didn't look like she was ever going to do anything else and it was making things pretty dull.

Helga at least was active. The big Russian lady was slowly patrolling the hallway and the way she was systematically checking the corners gave the impression she knew what she was doing.

He could hear water gurgling in the pipes and sometimes there was a faint whistle of wind from the door they'd left open, but that was it. Dull, dull, dull.

The total tedium had gone on for ages, and then the sound of three battles had reached them, ending with what had almost certainly been a small explosion. Worst-case, they'd triggered a mine or an IED.

Best case, it was a grenade. If the psycho was using those then they'd hit a serious level of resistance, perhaps the mutant animals. Maybe they were fighting their way out. Maybe the girl had got hypnotized and walked away from them again. That would be a shame.

If he'd thought of it sooner he could have slapped some nanospies on them. With some booster relays he might have been able to see what was going on. God, that would have been so cool—his own real-time war game. Instead, he was left with nothing to do. No signal, no machine, and no decent tools.

He could have used the load shifter as a weapon. He'd requested a model with an oxyacetylene torch and a nail gun in addition to its impressive forklift. In simulations on a gaming platform he'd been able to hold back a mob of half-deads from more than a mile away. It had been fun and he would certainly have impressed the others with the way he could maneuver such a bulky machine. But it was stuck outside and now he was powerless.

And not just him. As a support team they were ridiculously short of guns, and it was their organizer who was the main problem. Maddie was not exactly the experienced sniper that the simulations had specified. That role had never been filled. Instead, Sophos and Glover had insisted on putting in their own person. Their organizer could theoretically shoot but she had no experience and was really only there to keep things on track and to make sure that billionaires could get their own progress reports if Weaver proved unreliable.

Normally the level of firepower wouldn't have been such a concern, but with the machine stuck outside, the building's outline had changed. He'd left it running as cold as he could, but the heat signature would still show up if the storm died down for more than a couple of seconds. Any time now the Russians were going to get curious and come investigating, send a drone at the very least. That meant that they were probably running out of time. And what was Maddie doing about it? Nothing. She was standing gazing down the stairs. She hadn't even come to ask him what to do.

Chapter 34

Jodie

The big slab of metal swung open and a high-pitched tone scythed through her brain like a cheese wire. It was the same thought-numbing frequency that had cut into her in the West Wing bunker, and it sent a spasm of raw panic through her chest. She scanned her body for signs of change but she seemed fine. The sound was inside her, but instead of pushing everything else out, she seemed to be able to function alongside it.

Curtis must have sensed the vibrations too because he glanced across and asked if she was okay. She nodded then slotted a burning arrow into the crossbow. It was good to be using fire. The heat and colors were strangely reassuring and the movement of the flames reminded her that she was conscious and alive.

Her partner tossed in his torch and then stepped through the doorframe with his spear at his shoulder.

She took a couple of steps into the room after him. Her breath clouded and the stench of rotting fish and stale urine invaded her nose.

He glanced back over his shoulder. "Noise and distraction, remember."

She swept for a target, and then sent the bolt into the paneling on the back wall where it lodged with a spray of sparks. With adrenaline pumping through her veins, she pulled her eyes away and started scanning around her.

The place was obviously designed for monitoring communications. The main feature was a circle of screens hanging above a mound of processors. Rings of leather chairs faced the displays and the scattering of pads, micros and water bottles reminded her of the Situation Room in the White House. There was a sense of a meeting coming to a sudden end that gave the room a sinister museum-like atmosphere.

Curtis went to stand behind one of the chairs and projected another command back to her. "More noise."

She lowered her crossbow onto the carpet and drew her revolvers. A couple of shots into a bench on the back wall broke the stifling silence and left her ears ringing. *There you go. Waste of ammo if you ask me.*

There was a crack behind her and she forced herself not to turn and look. It would be Jester slipping in behind them and they had to try not to give him away.

Curtis took a slow sideways step and she saw his eyes probing the shadows under the chairs and benches. His head stopped and he thrust his hand back.

She froze and watched his spear lower to the bump in the center of the room. For a long time he didn't move. Her heart rate slowed and she began to notice more of the details around her. Orange flames were flickering along the far wall and the smell of burning plastic was slowly starting to overwhelm the fish market stench.

Seconds became minutes. The stillness pushed in from all sides and the tendons in her calves started to twitch and throb. She wanted him to do something, or turn and talk to her, but he stayed motionless with his spear held in the air.

It got more and more difficult to stay still. A tremor ran up her spine and she started to worry that she was going to cough or sneeze. She had just started to inch up a hand to rub the end of her nose when the floor exploded.

Shit! She leaped backward as a tube of bone burst out of the mound and landed on multiple limbs. The thing flipped upward and charged. Long limbs flailed at her teammate's neck but missed as its body jerked to a standstill.

Curtis's spear was through the creature's shoulder and coming out of its back.

Its arms battered the wooden shaft, then it turned and she caught a flash of an eyeless face and fanged mouth. Her stomach lurched and a sound like the screech of bats screamed in her ears. *That's it. That's the cause of all this.*

She stood, strangely dizzy and tired, and watched the scene play out in front of her. It was amazing how tightly locked Curtis's arms and legs were. She found herself mesmerized by the way his whole being was focused on gripping and pushing. *He's all on his own. I should try to help him somehow*. She started to sway. *Not just yet though. I'll wait till the noise stops.*

The creature made a sudden forward thrust and pushed itself down the spear.

Curtis grunted in response, the veins on his hands and neck bulging as he tried to lever his attacker onto the ground.

But it was no use. She watched from a strange distance as his strength drained, knowing that in just a few seconds the thing would rip him apart. And where was Jester? They were only meant to be the sideshow. She let her hands swing uselessly at her side. He'd run out on them. He was probably back at the surface having a smoke. The thought sent an echo of emptiness through her stomach. *He's left me, just like daddy did.*

She started to cry, her ragged sobs spilling hot tears down her cheeks. When Curtis was dead, the creature would turn on her. Well, let it be. She was going to get the end she deserved. She should've done what Mom wanted. Should've stayed near home and married early.

Her revolvers slipped off her fingers and she stood rocking on her heels. Filling her blurry vision there was only Curtis, a spear and the creature, now just a single thrashing entity. Her nose was running and she let the mucus flow into her mouth. *That thing's so strong it'll soon be my turn. Good. Let's end this. Let's silence the scream in my head.*

It started to snow and she blinked. Small white flakes were falling from the overhead ducts and floating in the air behind their attacker. A dark hole widened in one of the ceiling panels and a tile came loose and glided to the floor. Bells jangled, a cone of cloth appeared and her heart leaped. The stock of a rifle then a familiar face lowered into view. Jester began to swing his gun in both hands, his eyes sparkling, a lunatic grin on his mouth.

"Knock, knock!" he shouted, directing the butt of his weapon onto the back of the creature's head.

The screeching stopped and it slipped forward on the spear shaft.

Jester answered himself in a fake scary voice. "Who's there?" He struck it again. "Jester." Splinters of plastic spun into the air. "Jester who?" His rifle hit again. "Jest a bang on the head!"

The oversized skull flopped and the shape began to crumple. Curtis dropped the spear and the animal slid down it and settled on the ground: skewered, silent and still.

They'd done it. She stood with her arms at her side and repeated the phrase to herself again and again. While she was struggling to get their situation to sink in Jester dropped to the floor and stood leaning on his rifle like a walking stick. She met his eyes and he flashed her a grin then started to survey the room.

Curtis moved to the nearest chair and leaned on its back. After a while the smile slowly slid from Jester's mouth and he started to scratch his chin.

"What's the matter?" he asked. "I knocked out the right thing didn't I?"

"Yes." She stepped toward him. "Thanks." *Yes, you have, you big crazy hero.* "Well done." She kissed his cheek and felt his hand tentatively pat the small of her back.

After dabbing her eyes and sucking in several deep breaths, she lowered her gaze to the creature and asked Curtis if he was certain it was unconscious.

"Yeah." He lifted his head and fixed her with tired eyes. "It's definitely out."

"And it's not dead?" she checked.

"No. We'd know about it if it was dead."

"Man!" Jester's eyebrows shot into arches. "It's certainly *quieter* in here! That thing was wailing like a banshee. Well, I'm assuming it was that thing." He gave her a mischievous leer. "For a while I thought you two might have been … you know … at it. I was trying to decide which one of you was doing the screaming."

Curtis snorted and shook his head while his teammate snapped a flame to his Marlboros and started to stare curiously at the crumpled body.

"So"—he blew out a jet of smoke and then glanced up at each of them—"shall we take a look at it?"

Curtis nodded, took a torch from one of the benches and went and crouched by the skewered creature.

With her arms and legs tingling with adrenaline, she followed. It seemed like they were finally going to get a proper look at the source of all the problems and she was desperate to see what it was.

The large mouth was a pit of blackness surrounded by plates of ancient bone. Long rattlesnake fangs curved out of the top jaw and in each corner a pair of pincers wiggled among a sprouting of wiry brown hairs.

She quickly shuffled backward. "Look at its mouth," she hissed. "It's moving."

"Don't worry," Curtis replied. "That's just a reflex action." He moved the torch closer and she was able to see that the large bulbous skull was covered in a honeycomb mesh that flickered yellow in the light of the flames. He studied it for a few moments and then traced his fingertips over the lines of interwoven shell. "Looks a bit like a compound eye. Like a fly's."

Bells jangled behind them and Jester's voice boomed out. "Well fuck me with an RPG! Never seen anything like that before. Well"—a cloud of smoke billowed past them—"maybe my first wife without her make-up."

Ignoring his teammate, Curtis spread his thumb and forefinger between the incisors then lifted his hand to the bridge of his nose. He observed in a soft voice that the spacing was the same width as human eyes, then sat back on his haunches and put his fist to his chin.

While he was lost in thought, Jodie's gaze settled on the serrated pincer that lay on the floor near her foot. Fused onto the top of the appendage were the unmistakable clean white bones of a human forearm and hand. A pulse of disgust swelled in her stomach and she turned back and tapped Curtis on the shoulder.

He swung around and started to study the strange limb, slipping his fingers between the sections to test the strength of the bonding. "That's an interesting thing to do, isn't it?" he commented. "It's glued human bones onto its arms."

"So?" she asked.

"I think it's a primitive effort to look like its prey."

"Its prey?"

"Yes," he said, flashing his eyes. "Us."

While they knelt in silence, she considered what it was like to finally study the strange creature. When it was moving and making its terrible noises it was horrific and unworldly, but examining it close up somehow reduced it to just a set of parts. Some were insect-like and some resembled sections of crab shell, and it left her feeling as if she was studying some kind of bizarre biology experiment. She was trying to come to terms with its overall strangeness when Jester cocked his head and asked what it was.

"No idea," Curtis said, shaking his head. "But it is an animal. A natural creature."

"Pretty unusual though," Jester commented. "Never seen one in a petting zoo."

"But what are they?" she asked. "And how do they do the hypnosis?"

"Well. The whistling noise is part of it," Curtis told her. "But there's more than that." His hand moved over its chest. "There are waves and vibrations coming out of them that you can't hear. As for what they are … Look at it. It's *that*."

She glanced back at the stinking creature and narrowed her eyes. "So they're just some rare species that was frozen and got free? There's no big political plan to why they're in here?"

He shook his head. "No. I don't think so. I think Weaver and the AIs were right. They're smart, but not any more so than a chimp or a whale. They seem to be able to inject a virus that mutates people and animals … but there's not much more to them than that. You heard the thing screaming. It's an animal. It can't talk or plan or strategize. Everything is does is out of instinct."

The thought was both reassuring and vaguely disappointing. She was beginning to resent the fact that they'd risked so much just to capture some kind of large insect, when she reminded herself of the chaos that the things had caused in the outside world and the half-dead guards they'd left shambling around the White House.

Jester blew a plume of smoke down at the faceplate. "That's a hell of a cool animal …" he said. "But we are on a mission, yeah? We should be getting out of here ASAP."

"Yes, you're right." Curtis stood and looked at his companion. "Can you cut out some of this carpet and get it wrapped up?" He turned and peered at the mound behind him. "I want to see what's under this black stuff."

She followed his gaze to the lumps of dark netting in the center of the room, and the skin down her back tightened and prickled. His cool, calm exploration was beginning to irritate her. All she really wanted was to get up and out into the fresh air.

He made a single long slice in the black mesh and she found herself staring at a cluster of smooth curves glistening in the torchlight. Eggs. Of course. That was why they were there. Dealing with the half-deads and the mutants had made her forget that the focus of the mission was to stop these things breeding.

She caught sight of a female face and her heart jumped. Just a few feet away there was a girl lying with her eyes closed. Her head was lolling on twisted blue-veined arms and she looked painfully thin and gaunt. And there were more of them. Next to the body Jodie could see the lower part of someone's back, the ridged line of their vertebrae clear under pale tight skin.

She peered deeper into the shadows between the shells and discovered that there were bodies twisted everywhere; pale emaciated humans laid out like packing around Easter chocolate.

Curtis pressed his fingertips to the neck of the nearest girl and Jodie held her breath. She wanted more than anything for them to be alive.

His eyes were closed for several long seconds before he pulled back his hand and told her that they were in some sort of deep sleep.

A ball of tension loosened in her chest. "So why are they here?"

"I think they're food," he replied. "For when the young hatch."

"You mean the babies would eat them?"

"Something like that."

"So can we help them?"

"Yes. We destroy the eggs. Then make sure the Russians send in a medical team." He picked up his spear. "You might not want to see this." He pressed the tip of the weapon against the nearest egg then glanced back over his shoulder. "How about helping Jester out for a bit? We've got to wrap that thing up and drag it till we get radio signal."

As she walked away there was a sharp crack and a sickening squelch that made her squeeze her eyes closed. *Good call. Didn't want to see that. Right now I only want to see the sun, some blue sky and the ocean.*

Chapter 35

Helga

The carrying wasn't as bad as she thought. For some reason Helga had imagined she'd have to take the heavy box all the way down into the bunker, but Jester and the team had already pulled the unconscious animal a long way up the steps when they first called in. Before that it had been one long agony of inaction. The big empty base was eerily quiet and for a long time they heard nothing at all. Then the sounds.

Dull distant pops that they knew were gunfire. Her legs had twitched and her pacing had got even more frantic. She'd known her teammates were in a battle and she'd wanted so much to go and help them. But she couldn't. She had to wait so that's what she did. Maddie had waited with her, flicking worried looks and whispering reassuring comments while the computer geek tapped at the reader on his forearm. The sound of three battles reached them, and then … even worse … silence. It seemed to go on forever. Minutes dragged by and then there was a crackle. Just a few moments of hiss. The static was followed by Jester's voice, a few words that they couldn't decipher, but calm, spoken not shouted.

She got the call down and went on her own. Maddie was a bundle of nerves. It was not meant to work that way. No one who was resistant to the hypnosis was supposed to go near the creature, but they had no other choice so they kept the channel open and made sure that Curtis and Jester stood waiting to knock the thing out should it show any sign of life.

It was darker and colder on the lower levels and it smelled bad. She had to go through a big empty room and down through a trapdoor. They were waiting for her at the bottom of a spiral staircase, dirty and dusty but uninjured. The place smelled of smoke and burnt plastic and just visible behind them there were animal corpses sprawled out in pools of blood. And there'd been even worse things. She listened while she hauled the heavy roll of carpet up the steps. Jester took the other end but she kept the bulk of the weight and staggered up backward. Her legs and back were screaming in pain, but she finally got warm, actually sweating by the time they got to ground level.

Maddie had retreated to the entrance corridor and triggered the beacon. She and Cryboy were huddled in the distance in their snow suits. They wouldn't come near them until the thing was in the box, and that made sense. The machine was waiting by the door. The hatch was open and it was easy to slide the animal inside and lock it shut. She never got to see the creature. It was long and heavy and that was all she knew.

They talked about it in the copter. Jodie was distressed, confused and unhappy. The Ferguson kid was silent and dreamy again and Jester seemed delighted, full of the glory and strangeness of it all.

The military took it and buried it in an old drilling shaft: several tons of concrete and the inevitable plug of ice. Somehow they knew not to celebrate too much. McDermott was cautious and restrained the whole time. He stopped them from giving him any details and quickly changed the subject. In a slow steady charming way he asked if they would consider flying to another site. It was hot there and they would be well looked after. The thing was, he explained politely, there might just be another job for them.

Chapter 36

Weaver

They were safe. They were all uninjured and they'd captured the creature. Weaver punched the air, almost letting out some kind of yell but then restraining himself. Instead, he turned the potential sound into a long exhalation then unclenched his fist and reached out for his water. So they'd done it. That was amazing.

He took another few long deep breaths and realized that the emotion from the news was still building. Euphoria and relief were making him giddy. He had to blink away tears that had risen from nowhere in order to watch the colors on his screen change one by one. Everywhere he looked, amber was turning to a pale green and he couldn't help feeling that the AIs were congratulating themselves. They seemed pleased with their decisions, as if a sense of smugness was rising off the circuit boards. They were now quietly confident that the Ferguson kid could protect himself and someone else. They were calmly assured that the wild predictions in the scrolls did indeed have a foundation in truth. There were mutant animals, and the arthropods did seem capable of turning healthy humans into either half-deads or some kind of vicious guard.

After taking a sip, he lowered the cup and let his gaze drift across the room and out through the slats of the blind. *So what had it been like down there?* He'd spent many years smirking at the superstitious nonsense that had been collected by one of his predecessor's PhD students and now it turned out that it all had a foundation of truth. All those crazy-sounding hybrids really existed and he had no idea what they looked like.

While he stared at patches of bright sky on the skyline, his fingernails started to scrape at the stubble on his chin. It would've been nice to have got some photos but one of the parameters of the missions was that they left no trail or evidence. Already there were reports coming in of attempts to hack their operational plans, and that meant that someone somewhere was getting curious about what they were doing.

A second monitor sprang to life in front of him. He started to read the stream of data that was pouring down the screen in Cryboy's super-fast shorthand, then closed his eyes and blew out a long breath.

Eggs. Shit. So that was true too. That means we really are in a hurry. The implications for Washington were serious. If there were a whole load of smaller ones to catch then the robots really were going to struggle.

Some of the details weren't great. It sounded like they'd nearly frozen because the power was off. Had the planning team known that? They can't have. If it had been inputted then the software would have allowed for it.

The load shifter specs had got messed up somewhere too. He'd take the blame for that. He was supposed to double-check things with the military. The situation was tough though. It was complicated and constantly changing and there were bound to be a few mistakes.

He typed the word "Requests?" and watched it blink on the display. A cascade of pre-prepared responses started to file down the screen. He reached out and made sure that the list was being relayed to the logistics teams and then started to read. They wanted smaller load shifters and a maneuverable military-spec machine to help them fight. Of course they did. Well, everybody was working on that. Trying to get a new type of UGV built from scratch or even getting bomb disposal machines modified was a tall order in just a few weeks.

What else? They wanted flamethrowers, more ammo and more flashlights. Easy. Fine.

A third screen lit up. That was interesting. Why was Maddie sending a report on her private channel? When the three words had sunk in, he fell back in his chair with his hand on his brow. *Oh shit. Major problem. That's worse than the eggs.* He dropped his forehead onto the tabletop. *So Jodie's quit. Bugger. The software says we can't do it without her.*

He spun his chair and sat with his head in his hands. The elation had gone and there seemed to be more problems than solutions again. He'd intended to talk to them, but he needed to get his head straight first. He'd send messages congratulating them and that would have to do. Face to face he'd look tired and weak and they'd ask him a ton of questions. He was ultimately responsible for leaving them out in the cold, and he'd not warned them clearly enough about the crawlers. Plus they were traveling and the signal would be awful. They'd either be in a storm or on a military base covered in scramblers. It was best left at a local level. McDermott could try to charm Jodie into hanging around. He could tell them about the creature leaving Nerchinsk and making it to Mongolia too. He could send them off to the Aras River.

Chapter 37

Trip

Curtis knows he is being watched. Ella has seen him slip down the eastern path and followed him to the boundary huts where she is studying his departure with a curious mixture of emotions. Concern, anger and envy are all etched on her brow and sit deep in her dark eyes.

After a brief nod of farewell he pulls his gaze away, turns and breaks into a jog, his bare feet padding softly on the leaf bed as he leaves his family behind.

They are in the cool shade of a towering mahogany when the healer touches his shoulder and points at a thin brown vine curling around the base of the trunk. Having bent to scoop up a handful of soil, he points to the nearby trees and the position of the hidden sun, all the time checking that he is being understood, that the boy is noting what's being said.

They collect several lengths of the creeper and a large handful of leaves from a nearby bush then press on. Just as the grip of the day's heat is loosening they reach a spit of land where a thin stream forks. Here they make the most basic of camps: a fire, a bent sapling shelter and a latrine.

The healer crouches next to the small blaze, feeding it with twigs while eyeing him intently. He explains, using a simple child's version of his language, that the sacred drink he is brewing is a *seer's* drink. It will help him to *see*. Then he adds with a toothless grin that once they've finished their journey Curtis will not be the person he is now. He pulls a leering face and Curtis feels an adrenaline flash of panic. *I shouldn't have come. Mom and Dad said no. I should've listened.*

He drains the bitter soup then sits in silence trying to swallow away the taste of bark and soil while watching a wreathe of smoke rise from the hissing fire. *This is a long time just to sit and wait,* he thinks, but has hardly finished forming the idea when his mind lifts slowly from his skull and peels open like an over-ripe banana.

He finds himself gazing up into the raven heavens with an unyielding smile lifting his lips. As he watches, the stars begin to misbehave. The tiny perforations of light start to grow, looming in front of his eyes like oncoming headlights until suddenly they're gone, ripped back across the cosmos on taught elastic.

He blinks and his smile deepens. Around him the pressing jungle becomes louder and more crowded. A crawling hive of life emerges from the treetops and expands toward his face. Birds, bats and insects dart and swirl around the canopy like excited electrons, dancing faster and faster until their crazed frenetic movement forces his head down and his eyes closed.

He can't stay long in the darkness behind his eyelids. Where there should be emptiness and peace there is now a throbbing riot. With his temples held gingerly between his fingers, he opens his eyes and focuses on the ground. He watches a double line of ants patrol and explore the underside of a branch and then he suddenly perceives the entire organism stretching in scent-marked lines to the nest under a nearby trunk. He becomes one of many, simultaneously a fraction and the whole, and follows his counterparts into the rich dark soil. Marching into the tunnels of his home, he is engulfed in the taste of plant life returning to the earth. Then everything moves and his perceptions start to fade.

A lurching jolt and he is sniffing at the bases of nearby trees. An explosion of scents and meanings fill his nostrils, and his movements become light and lithe. He is jaguar. He stalks his textured hunting ground in effortless overlapping steps until his feline senses fade and a distant body calls him.

Human again, and echoing inside a clumsy frame, he crawls to the latrine where diarrhea bursts out of him and he vomits up the soup, retching until acid eats at his tongue. When empty, he makes his way slowly back through the damp leaves and takes his place by the fire.

As he sits and contemplates the flames, his material shell slowly dissolves and he becomes transparent and gossamer-light. Around him the monkeys start to yelp and chatter, their sound penetrating the bones in his skull. Soon the wind picks up and sets him stiff and straight. Suspended flat above the ground, the wet air blows through him, opening his body into a woven mold of holes that gradually melts to vapor.

He's at the head of the valley, part of a forming cloud that circles the mist-capped mesa. He hangs for a moment and then descends the steep escarpments in an exhilarating swoop. Rushing through the stubble of trees, he charges into the thickening jungle where he weaves through innumerable trunks and branches; now, the life-breath itself, he penetrates everything.

Something switches. He spins through a rib-walled tunnel and emerges high in the night sky. As he floats above the forest, a flicker of colored shapes presses into his mind. He sees two twisting pillars rising next to a plume of smoke. The patterns have a familiar texture, and they pulse, rising and falling with the life beat of an old man and a boy. *It's me and the healer,* he thinks. *I can see our auras.*

He tumbles away, but as he's tossed around the sky his senses swell and all the life signatures of the jungle emerge.

The energy from the vast web of trees rises as a net of green cables. The monkeys send columns of cloudy gray light pulsing into the air then thousands of black and silver bubbles shimmer in and out of focus. *Those are the insects: the ants and beetles and spiders.* He flushes with elation. *I can see. I can see life.*

Looking up into the looping rollercoaster darkness that used to be the night sky, he discovers that the jungle's life-colors are the floor of another world. He swerves around rising shapes of energy and then stops. *What's that?*

Far away in the forest his body jerks and the hairs ripple along his neck and arms. There is a giant human towering in his vision. Curtis chokes and his breathing stops. The figure turns toward him, lifts a stone hammer and begins to laugh. As his strength and power ripple across time in suffocating waves, Curtis flinches and shrinks. *Who was that?* Fear, elation and nausea explode inside him and he gasps for breath.

He is slammed back into his own skull, peering at the outside world through blurry wet eyes. The heatless infant light of dawn is pushing through the eastern tree line and there's a vine leaf stuck to his knee. He looks down and studies it. The vascular structure zooms large and becomes the valley he's sitting in, the river and its many radial tributaries an exact copy of the tubes ridging the back of the foliage.

His view shifts to a range of gorges cutting their passage across the land. The seasons spin by and he sees the waterways swell and drain with the passing rains. The pattern of streams merges into the veins and arteries in his arms. He watches and listens to the pumping of his own blood, feeling it lurch then pause, lurch then pause around his limbs. In time the rhythm of his pulse fades and the surface of his arm solidifies under his fingertips. Now he understands.

When he looks up, he sees the healer squatting in front of the fire with a bundle of sticks in his hand. They smile at each other and start to chuckle. They laugh until his stomach hurts and he is gasping for air.

They return to the village at dusk and he is given a medicine man's rattle and privileges. He is a seer. He has become part of the everything and the everything has started to consume him.

The Aras River Base

Chapter 38

Jodie

She was tired and achy when she stepped out of the plane into the bright midday sun. Her body still seemed to hold the sensation of movement, and the constant humming of the engines echoed in her ears as she stood blinking and yawning with the others at the top of the steps.

McDermott had been very convincing. He'd told her that the Aras River base would be a nice place to relax. He'd told her she deserved a break and they'd be well looked after, and most importantly he'd told her that it would be hot.

His prediction turned out to be true. The air was wonderfully warm and while she stood gazing across the lush landscape she felt her breathing deepen and her muscles relax. She was just wondering what was going to happen next when Maddie spotted a vehicle approaching out of the heat haze and led them down onto the tarmac. The big limo stopped a few feet away and a tall athletically built man in a dark suit stepped out. As he shaded his eyes and looked at them Jodie found herself suddenly re-energized.

"Oh, it's Chris!" she said to no one in particular. "He was the guy who delivered my invitation."

"Yeah," Maddie nodded. "He came ahead to set things up." After raising her hand in greeting, their organizer shaded her eyes and looked back at her. "So," she said casually. "You coming with us? We don't actually go to the base straight away. We've got a floor at a local hotel."

Jodie squinted into the mid-distance while she considered the offer. She'd already chosen to fly with the team when she could have waited in Alaska for her own flight, and once again she had the choice of starting the return journey on her own or getting sucked along with the group.

"You might as well," Maddie said, stepping close to her. "You could get a proper rest and something clean to wear. We've made certain that there are clothes in your sizes."

Jodie nodded slowly. A shower and a big clean bed would be absolutely blissful.

She chose to ride in the front with Chris on the suspicion that he would be easier to get information out of than Maddie, and it turned out she was right. The handsome driver was much more than a well-dressed chauffeur and was actually responsible for setting up all the equipment and logistics at each of their sites. He seemed to know as much as anyone about what was going on, and in just a ten minute journey she found out a great deal.

It seemed they were in an enclave of land that bordered both banks of a river between Turkey and Armenia. The site was used by the US military to run operations in Asia and the Middle East, but officially didn't exist. They were going to be given rooms in a secure hotel, and it was from here that they were expected to carry out another mission in Mongolia. She asked him if there were going to be a whole load more jobs that were being kept secret, but he shook his head. It seemed there was something genuinely strange and unexpected about this one because the video footage only showed three creatures and yet they were certain there was something inside an old temple in northern Mongolia.

He also knew that she'd quit, but he didn't judge her or try to convince her to change her mind. When they'd parked in front of a very modest ten-story building she found herself asking him what she should do. He smiled and told her to have a good rest and then spend some time in the sun. He had no other agenda and seemed to be a sensible voice in the midst of chaos.

Six hours later she was standing under a gently flapping awning scanning the hotel's roof terrace. While she squinted into the bright sun her senses started to tune in to her surroundings. A background murmur of traffic reached her from far below and the heady fragrance of lavender and wisteria hung in the hot air.

Her gaze passed over the pool and several rows of sun loungers and then settled on a lone figure sitting at the glass barrier on the roof's edge. Pulling her robe tight, she pushed her fingers through her freshly washed hair and set off toward him.

Curtis greeted her without taking his eyes from the view. "Hi Jodie," he said softly.

"Oh," she stopped and rested her hands on her hips. "You knew it was me!"

He turned and with a shy smile told her that very few people walked or smelled like she did. She nodded and let her gaze wander across the woodland and the scattering of small houses that faded into a distant heat haze, torn between using the time to talk to him alone or to enjoy the refreshment that the water would bring.

"I was going to go for a swim," she said eventually.

"Okay," he replied. "Nice idea."

She started to walk to the nearest lounger and then paused and glanced back. "Do you want to come in?"

"Sure."

She was sitting on the edge when she heard the metallic jangle of a belt buckle and started to turn her head. The realization that he was taking his pants off stopped her and she lowered her gaze to her legs.

"What's the temperature like?" he asked from close behind her.

She waggled her toes and then looked over her shoulder to see him standing in a pair of plain black boxers. He was incredibly slim, zero body fat with muscles and tendons running through him like wires. "Fine. Fresh," she told him.

"Good. I hate it when they overheat it."

Three fast footfalls on the tiles and he entered the water without a splash and curved himself upward. When his head broke the surface she took her weight on her arms and started to lower herself in. *Now girl, swim natural but keep the damn water out of your hair. If you don't it'll frizz into tumbleweed.*

"So"—he stood next to her in the shallow end with his arms spread along the edge and examined her face—"how are you feeling? Did you get a good sleep?"

"Yeah, couple of hours." She watched the sunlight dancing on the water and then teased a wedge of wet fringe out of her eyes. "I'm tired though. My body clock's messed up."

"And are you going back? Are you going to ask them to take you home?"

Boy he gets straight to it. Yes I am. Done my bit. No way am I going down to face any more of those things. She nodded slowly and he lifted his chin, his eyes burning into the side of her face.

"You're going because you're afraid?" he asked. "Scared?"

She let out a quiet hiss of air. *Right. So finally we get to talk about how insane this is.* "Man! Course I'm scared!" she told him. "We could've got ripped to bits a hundred times back there. Weaver didn't warn us about the wolves and the crawlers. And that's just the start of it. There were a whole load of eggs about to hatch and nobody's told me how just the three of us are supposed to deal with a bunch of those things."

"Yeah," he said quietly. "I understand."

Her jaw clenched. He understood? For Christ's sake! One slip and they would all get ripped to bits.

She lowered herself in the water, trying not to get too frustrated with his cool calm questioning technique. It was important to remember that he'd saved her life at least a couple of times and that being laid-back was his style; it was just how he was. What she needed to do was go with the flow and try and find out more about what was going on inside his head. "So do you think we can do it?" she asked. "Even if the eggs have hatched?"

"Yeah." He tipped his head, his brilliant white teeth glistening as he flashed her a smile. "I think with you we can."

She turned away and squeezed her eyes closed. *Oh great. Pressure. Pressure from him.* She pushed away from the edge and broke into a gentle breast stroke. *Thanks for that. Not what I needed at all.*

She studied him as he got out, admiring the thick triceps that popped out of his upper arms as they took his weight and then watching his underwear cling to his buttocks as he moved to his lounger and dabbed his face. The whole time she wondered what it was that she found so fascinating about him. He was too skinny, way too young and much too poor, but there was definitely something.

She continued to consider the matter as she swam toward the pool's ladder. Was it the way he moved? His strength? His courage? That was it. It was his bravery. He had shown no fear. There had never been any doubt or shame or anger. Even after everything had fucked up in Washington, he had stayed cool, calm and collected.

"So you had an unusual childhood yeah?" After a brief moment of eye contact she leaned forward on her sunbed and started to poke a finger between her toes. "Lots of moving around?"

"Yeah, Mom and Dad are both anthropologists," he told her. "I traveled all the time. South America, Asia, Africa. Anywhere there are still traditional tribes."

"So what about your education?" she asked. "Your schooling?"

"I was supposed to do private study or go to one of the international centers, but I never went. There was too much going on! Men taking their boys out hunting, learning to use weapons. There was always something seriously cool to do. I got really into the witch doctors and they let me take part in the ceremonies. That was wild! To be accepted you have to do the initiations with them."

"Your mom *let you*?" she exclaimed. "She let you do all that when you were just a kid? I mean … it's serious stuff, yeah?" She touched her thumb to her collarbone. "Like the native Americans ripping their chests? Why would she allow you to do that?"

"Well"—he shrugged—"she did."

"And you did more than one?" she asked. "You moved around and did a whole load of them?"

"Yep. I must've done about eight or nine in total."

"So are you eight or nine times a man?" The comment was a lot flirtier than she'd meant and her cheeks flushed hot.

He shook his head without looking up. "I don't think it works like that. What you learn is humility."

He hadn't picked up on the innuendo at all, and she didn't know if she was relieved or disappointed. "You learned plenty of other things too, yeah? Handling a spear and a knife … and the magic stuff …" *Will he talk about this? Can he explain it?* "That thing was screwing with my brain but I didn't go under … neither did you. And you knew where to find the animals. How many there were."

"Yes," he confirmed. "I knew all that and I was able to protect you." He turned and met her gaze, his eyes holding hers with an intensity that quickly made her look away. "And I could protect you again."

She stared at her feet while the words sank in. *Boy, another loaded comment. Seems he likes hitting me with these guilt trips.*

They sat for a while in contemplative silence, then there was a chime from the other side of the roof and they looked up to see Helga step out of the elevator and give them a small wave of greeting.

Jodie ran her eyes up and down her outfit as she approached. Her large friend had clearly made a real effort, choosing a dress with a feminine floral design and matching it with expensive-looking leather sandals that brought an elegance to the ensemble without adding to her already significant height.

When she reached their loungers, the Russian lady rested her hands on her hips and looked down at them with a shy half-smile. Jodie complimented her on her dress and she seemed pleased, looking down and swiveling her toes while she talked about the great range of clothing and accessories that was always waiting for them at each location.

Although it was a valid observation, Jodie herself was not entirely comfortable with the huge selection of garments that were always lining the drawers and closets of their accommodation. It certainly confirmed that Weaver and his team were generous with their cash, but it also suggested that to get exactly the correct sizes and even the right brand of toiletries somebody had hacked their shopping records. It was very clear who that person would have been, and the thought of Cryboy pouring over a list of everything she'd bought in the last few years was extremely creepy.

They quickly moved on to more serious topics and had started to discuss how they were feeling about taking on another mission when a second chime and the sound of clinking ice reached them from the elevator. Jester came sauntering over with a pitcher of blue liquid hanging in one hand and a couple of cigarettes in the other. She realized that he'd probably raided the minibar in his room and then wandered through the hotel smoking and slopping drink onto the carpet. It seemed he never missed an opportunity to break the rules or rub people up the wrong way, and she smiled inwardly when she visualized the situation. He was a very big man in a heavily bloodstained costume and she suspected that nobody had challenged him.

When he reached them, he flashed his eyes in greeting and then turned to look at her big Russian friend. "Hi Helga," he said, running her up and down with his eyes. "You're looking pretty hot. I'm liking the dress." He palmed his Marlboros into his mouth and lifted the jug. "I knocked up a splash of pick-me-up. Anybody want some?"

Curtis swung his legs off his lounger. "Not me, thanks. I'd like to take in a little more of the scenery." He dipped his forehead at the far rails and then looked at Helga. "Would you like to come look at the view with me?" Jodie noticed a blush rise in the other woman's cheeks as she nodded and murmured her agreement.

When her two companions had gone, Jodie sat up and pushed her hair up at the back of her neck. Her eyes settled on the jug of liquid sloshing by Jester's side and she gave him a blatantly manipulative smile. "Now, do you reckon you could be a true gent and go and get me a glass of decent white wine?" she asked. "Something crisp and really, really cold."

He bowed his head and, using a rather posh-sounding British accent, told her that it would be his absolute pleasure.

She watched him stroll to the bar in a slow rolling gait and pulled her fingers slowly through her damp hair. He was another one that she hadn't quite made up her mind about. One of the strangest men she had ever met: angry, sad and funny at the same time.

The late afternoon sun sparkled in her wine as she raised her glass and thanked him.

He acknowledged her with wide sincere eyes and then gave a short bow which he finished by knocking an entire cup of liquor down his throat. After settling the empty beaker on the floor, he lit a couple of cigarettes and asked her if she was heading home.

She nodded and looked out across the horizon. W*hat does that make me? Smart or chicken?* Before she knew it, she had caught his eye and was blurting out a question. "Do you think I'm a quitter?"

He lifted his chin then slowly shook his head. "No I don't. I think you're one of the toughest goddamn fighters I've ever worked with. You've done a job. You want out. Fair play to you. Just make sure you get paid a good whack."

"I feel bad about going," she confessed.

"Don't. You've done your bit."

"But what will you do … if I go?"

"Well"—he grinned and then shrugged—"Maybe just the two of us can do it." His eyes drifted across the roof. "Or maybe dancing boy there can protect someone else."

"Do you think he can?" she asked.

"Yep. I reckon that's why he's getting to know Madame there."

She looked over to where Curtis was standing at the rail, deep in conversation with Helga. As she watched, the young black kid reached out and touched her gently on the shoulder, and Jodie felt a cold spike twist in her chest. What was he asking her? He was so perceptive. He'd got so quickly to where her pain and doubt were and she was sure he was doing the same thing again.

After a few moments she forced herself to pull her eyes away and continue the conversation. "So you're not worried that the eggs might have hatched?" she asked. "I mean, you're not in a hurry to get in there?"

"I'm in no rush." Jester shook his head. "These guys have got to organize things. We're getting new weapons and they've got a whole load of political shit to sort out with the Mongolians. I managed to drill Maddie for some information and it turns out they're actually paying to get us in to try to catch that thing."

She sat nodding while he took a hard suck on his cigarettes. *Oh well. None of my business, I guess. I should be getting out of here.* Her gaze drifted back to Curtis and Helga and she took a sip of wine. *Or maybe I should go along and stay up top.*

She lowered her glass and made her voice sound as casual and friendly as she could. "So, back there in Chicago, you live on your own? No girlfriends or family or anything?"

He shook his head.

"And you don't get lonely?"

His face went stony and he shrugged. "I choose to be alone. When I was young I spent a lot of time in barrack blocks, sometimes thirty, forty guys to a room. Then I ended up in a rehab hospital. That's pretty intense. They put you in this clean white place and fill it with people on fire. People screaming blood. You know what I mean? I made some friends but it doesn't mean I want to live with them."

"But wasn't there some good stuff?" she asked. "I always thought vets got looked after."

A light sprang up in his eyes. "There was drama class. We set up our own theater and the plays were cool. Shakespeare is hot shit, man! I don't know why the high-school kids don't get it. There's always someone going nuts and yelling their guts out. Boy, did we love that."

She nodded slowly and looked down at her glass. He might be angry and strange but if he trusted you this man gave you everything. He wasn't afraid either; there was no fear in him at all. His lack of apprehension made her think that maybe she was overreacting about the missions. Perhaps he wasn't scared because they weren't as dangerous as they felt.

She drained her wine and was tucking the glass under her lounger when a second thought occurred to her: or maybe it was because he was a nutcase.

They were lying enjoying the warmth of the sun when he stood and started to saunter toward the elevators. Curious to find out why he was suddenly so focused and full of purpose, she shouted after him and asked him where he was going.

"Find Maddie," he replied.

"She usually finds us," she commented.

"I know, but *I* want *her*. I want her to call Joolsey." His head lowered and he gave her a pointed look. "I can keep him on the line for you too."

She cocked her head, suddenly intrigued. "Why?"

"Well …" He came back, crouched and gripped the frame of her lounger. "Last mission a success. Capability proven. Our skills irreplaceable. Now's a good time to negotiate our cash."

"I reckon you've got some sharp business sense there," she told him. "I didn't think that would be your thing,"

"Oh, I spent plenty of time getting screwed by *the man*," he replied. "I know *plenty* of tricks." He stood and walked into the elevator, then turned and held her gaze. As the doors started to close, he folded his hand into the shape of a pistol and aimed two fingers at her. "Dodge the bullets or carry the gun?" he said, arching his eyebrows. "The choice is yours."

Chapter 39

Helga

Helga watched the curving width of river roll away into the distance and felt some of her optimism drain. Somehow she knew that their luck was going to run out. They'd had a tough time down in the bunker on Kotelny and it was just a matter of time before somebody got seriously hurt, or worse.

Curtis had spent the last half an hour trying to read her and it had been an interesting experience. He'd asked all about her childhood and about losing people and this probably helped him do his magic. So now he knew about the side effects of the Smetna Program. He knew it had left her barren, and she knew what it was like to have those big deep eyes fixed onto you, to look inside you.

Movement caught her eye and she turned to see Jodie walking across the terrace toward them. The sight of the poor young thing filled Helga with two simultaneous emotions. Pity that the girl had had to learn so much about violence so quickly, and relief that while she was around there was less chance that she herself would have to go down into the bunker.

When the pretty American reached them, Helga found she had to ask her why she hadn't been taken home yet.

"Well, I haven't really asked," Jodie told her with a shrug. "I was thinking I might come along but just stay up top."

Helga nodded slowly. *No don't. We'll figure things out without you. You should never have been involved in all this.*

Jodie was obviously keen to talk about something else because she quickly turned to Curtis and asked him if they'd been talking about the crab creature.

"Yeah," he told her. "Helga didn't see it. She's curious."

Curious! I wanted to rip open that carpet and get a look at that thing. Too late now. We've buried it. No analysis or anything, it's gone. And what about the weight of it? How can shell and bones have all that mass?

She noticed Jodie earnestly studying her face.

"I tell you, Helga," she said. "Everything about it was freaky. They're terrifying. They mess with your head. And that's not the half of it. The wolves and the crawlers we told you about? They're fast and fierce and they can regenerate."

She nodded. *I know you told us that, but is it true? Did they really heal in front of your eyes or did you panic and miss? Did all your shooting expertise fail you and you're explaining it away with these stories?*

"Aren't you guys freaked?" Jodie pushed her hair behind her ear. "I mean, everything that Weaver said is real. The crab things really do have a hypnotic effect. The dogs are like werewolves, the crawlers like vampires. All that crazy stuff he was talking about in New York is true."

Curtis nodded. "I know. I was doubtful too. When we got here I asked to look at the archives. I've been reading through the scrolls he told us about."

"What do they say?"

"A lot. The main problem is that there's a lot to wade through and it's all in scraps. It starts with ancient Norse stuff and then there's Sanskrit and Aramaic from around the time of Christ. There's a ton of stuff from medieval Europe—"

"Okay, Okay," Jodie said quickly. "But what is there that we need to know?"

"Well." Curtis nodded patiently. "Weaver gave a pretty good overview. He told us the important stuff. What amazed me was the consistency. The stories all mention the half-deads, some type of strong wolf and the crawlers."

Jodie rubbed the back of her head and looked out across the river. "But why've we never heard any of this before?"

He started to nod. "Cause we're not supposed to. Once the creatures have been buried, the only risk is from curious people digging them up. It has to be done secretly. No records except for a special group. There's accounts of these captures from the time of Christ and the most recent from Europe in the middle of the fourteenth century. There was a massive outbreak of half-deads, people collapsing with hemorrhaged eyes, but they cleaned it up and blamed it on some sick rats."

"Right. But did it say anything about the young?" she asked. "The babies? If we could kill them then maybe this thing wouldn't be such a problem."

The young black man gazed into the middle distance. "Yeah, that was what I was looking for."

"So?"

"Well, as Weaver said, there's nothing about the eggs ever hatching. Seems it's never happened."

A couple of bleeps came from Jodie's arm and Helga looked down to see the younger lady squint at her chip reader.

"I thought I'd switched this off," she commented, staring at the display. "Override?" she tapped the screen and Maddie's voice filled the air.

"Jodie? Sorry to cut in, but it's urgent," their organizer said.

The two American ladies had a short conversation and Maddie informed her of a dramatic development. It seemed that the timetable had been updated. The Mongolians were willing to give them a shot at capturing the creature and wanted them to start straight away. Their car was already waiting to take them to the airfield.

Helga looked at each of her companions and tried to read their reactions. The Curtis boy was as calm and inscrutable as ever but the girl looked distinctly uncomfortable. That wasn't really a surprise. The poor young thing was meant to be going home, and now it looked like she was getting sucked in again.

Chapter 40

Cryboy

She still clicks through all the logons. I showed her the shortcuts so why doesn't she use them? She's supposed to be systems literate.

Cryboy's hands tightened into sweaty fists as he pushed himself to the edge of his seat and watched Maddie link to the limo's comms system and open the connection to the New York office. *Why am I the only skilled person in this team? These guys are so dumb and sloppy.*

There was a pop from the speakers, a flicker of colored light and then Weaver's head appeared.

"Hi guys," he said cheerfully. "You getting a clean signal?"

"Yep," Maddie replied. "We hear you, Julian."

"Good. Well, thanks for getting together so quick. Sorry you couldn't have a bit more of a rest but there's been a breakthrough with the Mongolians. Firstly the good news though. Let me congratulate you again on the Kotelny job. You were all fantastic and I can't thank you enough. Also let me tell you that we took your requests for new gear very seriously. You're not going to be short of firepower this time, I can assure you."

Cryboy stroked his fingers down the controllers on his wrist. *Yes. Now they can see my expertise. My weapons skills.*

Weaver lifted his head. "The other bit of good news is that the mechanized operations at Fort Wainwright and the White House are about to start. By the time you've finished this job they should be complete and the whole situation resolved."

While they sat absorbing the news, Cryboy studied Jodie's face for signs of a reaction. *She was going to quit. Why's she still here? Why did she even get into the car?* He pressed his fingernails into his palms then sprung his hands open. *She's emotional. I mustn't expect her actions to follow a logical pattern. Her thinking's governed by the moon. Gravity pulls blood out of her and different hormones affect her moods. She's a variable.* He started to gently rock backward and forward in his seat. *Unpredictable but mission critical. How did we let that happen?*

Weaver's voice filled the cabin again. "Jodie, hi. It's good to have you on board. I need to let you know that although we'd like you to stay, we have been considering possible replacements … that is … you're under no obligation."

Cryboy gripped the seat and watched her nod. *That was slick. He wants her to stay but doesn't want to use coercion. It's unethical. Maybe he should force her though. We need her tonight. The chances with her are thirty to forty percent. Without, it's all under ten.*

Jodie leaned forward. "Just going back to the firepower though, Dr. Weaver. Yes that'll help with the wolves and the crawlers, but the real problem's the crab things. What are we supposed to do if the eggs have hatched? I mean, if there are young and they attack us. Can we shoot them?"

"Right, yeah." Weaver pursed his lips. "That's a critical question and obviously something we've been discussing here. We think there *are* risks in killing the young so we'd like you to catch them alive too."

Jodie scowled. "Even if there's ten of them?"

"Yes, I'm afraid so …"

Cryboy watched the young academic take a deep breath and start to stroke his chin. *Now's the time to state the hypothesis. We've got even more evidence: the fangs, the bodies with the eggs, the weight of the creatures. It all adds up.*

"Here's the issue," Weaver said, leaning forward. "We mentioned that the creatures contain part of a human that mustn't get out. As you saw in Russia there were bodies with the eggs—alive, but in some kind of coma. We think they were there to provide food for the young."

"Yeah, so they eat people." Jodie dropped her hands onto the table. "In my book that's even more reason to kill them."

"Yes. But it's not just that they eat people but that they suck out part of their life force, their consciousness …" Weaver grimaced. "What some might call … their souls."

"Souls? That's what they eat? That's what's in them?"

"Well, we don't always work with that name here, but, if there is some kind of energy force inside a human, we think they can extract it."

Curtis turned to Jodie with raised eyebrows. "And we can't let the souls get out because then they would possess the nearest living thing."

"And you believe this?" Jodie asked, her voice straining. "After seeing one up close?"

Curtis gave a single short nod. "Yes."

"And the scrolls say this too? That's why you looked them up?"

"Yes. When you read the historical accounts, all the pieces start to fit. There were four of these things. A few thousand years ago, one of them was killed. There were possessions and hauntings all over the world from then on. Every society has pretty much the same idea of being invaded by an evil spirit. It seems to explain where it comes from." He paused and rubbed the side of his neck. "My guess is that they're basically a parasite. They've evolved to extract blood and a type of life force from us but there's no reason to think they're actually evil or even self-conscious. They're just behaving like any sort of leech: They burrow in and suck out as much food as they can."

Jester blew out a jet of air. "Boy. That's a hell of a theory," he said, grinning. "So they're not giant crabs. They're giant fleas!"

Jodie turned to him with a scowl. "I'm glad you find this so funny. Personally I don't like the idea of having my soul sucked out or the fact that we … that you … won't be able to kill the young."

Weaver glanced down at something and then looked back into the camera. "I hate to do this to you guys but I'm afraid we've kinda run out of time. My tracker says you're approaching the airfield and the scramblers there will cut us off. Before that happens, I really want to say good luck with this one."

There was a chorus of half-hearted "thank yous," and then, just as Jodie lifted her chin to ask another question, the speakers emitted a pop of static and the young academic's head vanished into thin air.

Cryboy listened to his teammates groan and mumble a few complaints. It seemed that they'd realized that Weaver's timing was not entirely accidental. He made sure that when he spoke to them he could cover the basics but never let them drill him in too much detail. That was because a lot of the possible scenarios were extremely unpleasant and the young academic liked to focus on the positive.

He felt his hands tighten on the controllers strapped to his forearm. *He's right to be elusive. Even three of them firing steel nets isn't going to be enough. The platforms can do it though. I can operate them remotely. It needs her though: She's got the speed and the accuracy. Her and me working together. A team. A couple.*

Chapter 41

Jodie

It shouldn't have been but it was pleasant. Jodie found herself enjoying the late evening walk much more than she'd expected, and as they wove their way up the side of the remote valley, she found herself increasingly appreciative of her surroundings. The air carried the scent of exotic spices and there was a gurgle of distant water that was strangely relaxing.

Their entrance had been slick and uneventful. A short flight had ended at a commercial airport where a trio of trucks had been waiting. Once on board, a line of army jeeps had escorted them up into the mountains where they'd passed groups of bored-looking soldiers sitting on top of tanks and troop carriers. Finally, after passing through a couple of checkpoints, they'd been left alone in a parking area overlooking a lush green hillside.

Everything they needed was packed ready for them inside their vehicles. She knew from her short conversation with Chris that the necessary weaponry and equipment had been gathered from all over the world in less than twelve hours, and this was incredibly impressive. But then if Weaver and his team did one thing really well it was logistics. She'd been reflecting on this ever since the meeting in New York, and it made perfect sense. Political influence was the foundation of their day-to-day business. Buying equipment and moving it around the globe was what they did for a living. Even getting access to the sites didn't seem to be much of a challenge, but she had to remind herself that their expertise seemed to run out where it really mattered. In the cold and dark of the basements their knowledge and power thinned dramatically. Even though they were clearly getting distant and secretive help from the military, the approach to the combat side of the missions seemed a bit vague and optimistic. When it came to having the right information and the right gear, it always felt like they were playing catch-up.

Weaver had listened to their demands though and they now had considerably more weaponry. He'd given them robots. Cryboy was controlling them from pads on his forearm and the three pyramid-shaped combat units were at the front scanning for threats while a bunch of load shifters rolled noisily on caterpillar tracks behind them.

They'd also been given an impressive-looking flamethrower that promised to both give light and the power to incinerate.

But she tried to ignore all this. Catching the sunset as part of a heavily armored team was bound to feel good. She had to remind herself about the bunkers. Reliving the horror of the savage animal attacks would make sure she didn't fool herself into going down there again. She'd come to help out up top. It was a compromise, but she'd still get a significant payment and wouldn't feel like she was abandoning her teammates.

They climbed a gradually narrowing walkway that curved around the foot of a large stone wall and ended on a broad terrace with spectacular views of the sweeping grass plains far below. Set in the middle of a scattering of trees, there was big pond, and Curtis went straight to it and stood gazing across the water. Jodie was curious to see what had attracted his interest but there didn't seem to be anything unusual. Bulrushes stood thick and proud around its edges and darkening clouds sat sharp in the mirrored surface, but it otherwise seemed nondescript and ordinary.

Maddie lead them around the top of the pool and pointed to an archway cut into the fortifications. Cryboy sent the three UGVs ahead through an open gate and they followed.

They passed through the short tunnel and were climbing a paved ramp when the roof of a giant pagoda appeared on the skyline. Each step revealed more rows of cascading brown tiles and then the full height of the wooden pavilion came into view and she stopped dead in her tracks. The building stood alone in the middle of a huge courtyard and was far bigger and much more splendid than she'd expected.

"Quite a place," Jester commented, stepping up to join her.

"Yes it is," she replied. "It's beautiful."

"Right." His voice was hard and businesslike. "And now you've seen it you've got a good memory to take home, yeah?" He tipped his head at the gun platforms rolling across the enclosure. "You've been replaced, see, my love. Those things are worth a hundred of you. Fielded and armor plated, they spit out a thousand rounds a minute. So you can go back to the truck. I'll tell the others—say goodbye for you."

Shit. Doubt and disappointment sank through her like heavy stones. He'd said all those nice things back at the hotel. "I could still be useful, no?" she asked.

"You are useful," he told her. "You're more than useful. But you could be useful on a plane, useful in the hotel, useful back home."

She couldn't think of anything to say, and it wasn't until he was several yards away that the words came to her. "Didn't know you cared," she shouted after him, not bothering to keep the sarcasm from her voice.

"No." He stopped and stood scratching the back of his neck. "Neither did I."

Passing through the pagoda's carved doors took her into a massive wooden hall lit by the searchlight beams from their robots. The first thing she saw was the throne, a huge monument to authority that sat on a high dais in the middle of the room and effortlessly commanded the space around it. Every inch glinted with intricate decoration, and she had to force herself to pull her eyes away from the carvings of intertwined dragons to scan the rest of the big dusty space.

Helga was a few yards away, peering into the shadows with her rifle braced, and the others were standing at the top of a staircase by the far wall. Maddie was pressed close to Cryboy and the two of them were staring at the controllers on his arm.

They'd obviously sent a gun platform to check for threats below and it was a comforting thought. The miniguns the machines carried finally gave them the firepower they needed to make the missions easier, and that had to be a good thing.

She set off toward them. Jester had made her feel that she wasn't needed, but if that meant she could stay at the back while the machines did all the fighting, then that was fine by her.

The stairs took her down to a copy of the first floor except for one crucial difference. The second throne was painted entirely in black and was oriented in the opposite direction. This one was facing a pair of ornate tapestries that had been hung to form a screen in front of a set of stone steps.

She stepped over to peer between the curtains and felt the skin around her spine tighten. The creatures were definitely down there. There was a distant tension in the air that set her nerves on edge.

Curtis walked up to the big chair and started studying it. After squinting at the intricate engravings, he closed his eyes and held his hand close to the wooden panels as if warming his palms. After about thirty seconds he stepped back and tentatively knocked his spear on the floor. "There's another way down under the throne," he said softly.

"You sure?" Maddie asked, looking up from her reader.

He pressed the base of the platform but nothing happened. Frowning, he shifted his balance and pushed sideways. A crack appeared along a dragon's tail and the panel slid open to reveal a set of wooden steps curving down into darkness.

"You've found another way down?" Jester asked. "Nice work." He turned to Maddie. "You want to send a robot with us don't you?"

"Yes. Dr. Weaver and the analysts—"

"Yeah yeah, I can guess all that." He held up his hand and squinted at the embroidered rugs. "Proposal for ya. How about the machine goes in the front door …" He turned to the gap in the side of the throne. "And we sneak down the back?"

It sounded like a good idea and Jodie studied Maddie's face to see if she'd agree.

Their organizer's eyes glazed—there were a few moments of silence—and then she turned back to Jester and nodded.

"Good," he continued, casually popping his lips. "So the only thing now is to figure out who's coming down with us."

Jodie's stomach lurched and she looked down at the floor. *Shit. Decision time.* She avoided saying anything for as long as she could, but when she eventually glanced up, she found Maddie staring at her.

"You're still the first choice, Jodie," the other lady said softly.

"It would be good if it was you," Curtis added.

She allowed her vision to glaze. Would it be easier if it was her? Was that what he'd been saying in the pool?

When she refocused, they'd all turned away. Maddie was looking intently at the gun platform on the far side of the room and Jester was sucking gently on his cigarettes with his eyes fixed on the big throne.

Jodie looked at the gaping black space between the tapestries and her hands tightened around her twelve-gauge. What would happen if she didn't go? Curtis hadn't been able to protect her the first time. It had taken two tries. That meant that there was a real risk that Helga would get hypnotized. If she did, then the guys would have to wrestle with her, and if those three fought then somebody would get killed and that would be one sick ending to the whole thing.

As she breathed out a long sigh, she became increasingly aware of the passing of time and of the others' careful efforts not to appear to be waiting for her. *This is fucked up. They won't ask and they won't force me. But who are they trying to kid? We all know it has to be me. Even I know that deep down. That's why I never went home.*

With a sudden sense of resolve, she reached down and cupped the handle of a revolver. It was time to step up again, time to show the world what she was made of. "Yeah," she said, trying to nod casually. "I'll come."

Chapter 42

Slipstream

The roots of the Lifetree were gnarled and twisted. Each sharp turn set him spinning faster and faster until he tumbled into the void and found himself floating in silent weightlessness. As he hovered in the dark, he watched the tunnel mouth and waited for the slow-churning vortex to solidify and show him a route. Eventually it did: the helix of blended light sharpening into a wall of rock perforated with beams of polished wood.

He drifted into the material and started to stretch upward, passing through a series of hollow chambers until he found himself floating inside a rectangular hall surrounded by familiar life forces. He immediately sought out the young woman, bouncing off the hard surfaces until her rotating ovals of orange and yellow came into view, and then cocooning her in protective layers until she became slippery, just a wrinkle in a pulsing skin of energy.

He let go and started to sink, dropping past the carved forms of animals to emerge in a cavern where near-lifeless creatures were surveying a dark pool. He was there for just an instant before everything shifted and he found himself entombed in polished marble with his male companion. They were islands in a lagoon of thick blood, their light fading as one of them slipped toward death.

Another lurch and he was deeper still in the earth's bedrock. Here an unbalanced life-form was thrashing and writhing uncomfortably. While he watched, the patterns of a scream rippled through the energy field and a male and female human died—infected, tortured and in pain. The shock of the deaths exploded around him and set him drifting again. With the anguished cries still ringing in his head, he rose and floated back through the hard-packed strata. Here he was pulled to a single point where time and space overlapped and then released into his mind with a snap like a bubble popping.

Chapter 43

Jodie

For the first time, Jodie watched their companion's meditation with real interest. He'd protected her in Kotelny and had somehow been able to see in advance where the creatures were. This meant that he really was able to do something when he was in a trance, and she was becoming more and more curious to find out what it was. Unfortunately he wasn't at all communicative about his powers, and watching him sit with his eyes closed gave nothing away.

Her gaze had left him and had started to drift around the throne room when a sudden movement caught her attention. She saw him shudder sharply and then sit with his eyelids twitching. A moment later a second set of trembles rose through his body, his eyes shot open and he blinked at her.

"You okay?" she asked.

He rose slowly to his feet and nodded. "You're protected."

"Good. Thanks. You sure you're alright?"

He picked up his spears without looking at her and then walked to the base of the throne and flashed his eyes at his waiting companion. "We should get going."

Jester nodded and pointed the barrel of the flamethrower down the steps. His cigarette filters flew out of his mouth in a gob of spit and he glanced back at her. "Well, Jodie," he said with a grin. "Can I take you in the back passage?"

After a few minutes of careful descent the wooden staircase opened out to a sloping stone floor. Jester cracked a light stick and the faint glow revealed the outline of an arch-roofed walkway that stretched into total blackness in front of them.

She glanced over her shoulder. Curtis's silhouette was a dark outline in the corridor behind her, the whites of his eyes just visible as he cracked a thin smile. She returned his greeting, not sure if he could see her, and then turned and quickened her pace.

The gradient started to bottom out and the floor became uneven. She steadied herself against the wall and peered down and saw that a ridge of disks had risen in the middle of the corridor. She was trying to work out what they might be when Jester came to an abrupt halt. Her heart jumped, and with blood pumping loud in her ears she watched him squint into the gloom and then lower himself into a squat. He cracked another light stick and tossed it into the void, where it skidded along something metallic and disappeared with a faint plop.

She heard a few distant splashes before a damp breeze brushed her cheeks and carried a meaty slaughterhouse smell into the back of her throat. Her instincts told her that they were about to encounter something bad, but she couldn't be certain. The only thing she was sure of was that here was a big space in front of them and something out there smelled disgusting.

Curtis moved up and stood behind her and together they stared into the inky blackness.

That's humming. No. Gone. Back again. A single note was droning in the distance. The sound gradually became a buzz and then a rectangle emerged in the dark velvet in front of them. A faint pearly glow seeped down inside the shape and a series of horizontal lines emerged. The slats became shelves, the buzzing became a whirring motor and the scene clicked into place. It was the main staircase and the noise was Cryboy's robot coming down the steps.

The light continued to grow, sending a milky iridescence down the stairwell that revealed a massive tiled chamber that curved into a large dome somewhere above their heads.

The sound of the machine got louder and her eyes were drawn to the highest, brightest part of the opening where a set of triangular wheels had appeared and was lowering itself toward the top step.

She cracked a thin smile, the tentative exploratory motion reminded her of an old man feeling his way in the dark, and she found some humor in the difficulties that the stairs were presenting to such an advanced piece of military hardware.

The robot itself appeared and the process was repeated until the pyramid of fielded metal reached the floor. Searchlights sprang out left and right, each illuminating passageways leading off the central chamber.

She shuffled forward and peered down. The golden walkway curved like the prow of a ship over a basin of dark liquid. The edges were lined with spindly railings that ran up the walls and faded into shadows, but they were only an inch or so wide and there didn't seem to be a way to get to the other side.

"No way around," Jester confirmed, turning back and grimacing. "We've got to go through."

She was about to pass on the message to Curtis when he appeared at her side.

"I know," he said, nodding. "It's a baptism pool." He tapped the walkway with the shaft of his spear. "The dragon's water gives long life and wisdom."

Jester peered between his feet. "Oh yeah. So you think it'll work for us?"

"No," Curtis answered. "This place is corrupted now. Contaminated."

"Right, well …" Her big teammate looked back at the pond and then announced that he was going to find out how deep it was. He dropped a light stick and they watched it slowly fade to nothingness. "Too dirty to tell," he commented. "I'll give it a try."

Lowering his legs into the thick water, he slid down the edge of the bowl.

"Waist height and gloopy," he whispered. "Kinda tight against my thighs. It's actually very nice …" He looked back with the expression of a gourmet analyzing a sip of wine. "In fact, I think I'm getting an erection."

She snorted and he started to cross the pool, moving slowly with his rifle on his back and his flamethrower held across his chest. Her head filled with images from history documentaries. She saw visions of troops wading through waves with their weapons above their heads, and the pictures disturbed her. The young men smiling into the cameras never lasted long. That was when the machine guns and the bombing started.

Jester reached the far side, hauled himself out and stood scanning the room with dark liquid dripping from him. His eyes swiveled back and he looked at her expectantly.

She sat and shuffled to the edge. *My turn now.* She took a deep breath and swung out her legs. The fluid pressed tight against her boots and ran over the tops, sending chilling wet fingers creeping down her calves. With a sudden intake of breath, she slid down the side of the bowl and pushed away from the rim.

After just a couple of short steps she became overwhelmed with the sense that something significant was happening behind her and stopped to look over her shoulder. Curtis was crouching on the jetty with his eyes flicking from the walls to the domed ceiling. Her stomach tightened and she followed his gaze up into the shadows. She could see nothing but blackness, and when her neck started aching she reluctantly turned and pressed forward.

The vision of Curtis's face lingered in her mind, and a few moments later she found herself looking back again.

He had lifted his spear and was pointing the tip into the dome. "Keep moving, Jodie," he told her. "Fast as you can."

She turned and started again, placing her boots carefully on the slick metal and pressing her legs forward as quickly as she could. After just a few steps her neck started to tingle and she stopped. Peering up into the darkness, she was just beginning to make out some faint shapes when Curtis's voice cut the air.

"Down, Jodie! Low as you can. Fast!"

The urgency in his voice set her moving. She squatted and started to turn toward Jester. There was a ripple of movement and the railings started rising up and buffeting her with cold air.

His voice rang out again. "Jester, the walls. Torch the walls!"

Her companion lifted his weapons. She turned and saw flashes of sickly pink and then a giant bird with a scarlet beak and massive bulbous eyes plummeted toward her. She let out a sound—half-scream, half-yelp—and threw herself forward. Curtis's spear whistled through the air and skewered it. The body hit her shoulder and splashed flapping into the pool. Searing flames roared over her head and the rim of the basin came alive with yellow flickers.

She squatted lower. Squawking and screeching filled her ears and the dark liquid splashed her cheeks. Another jet from Jester's flamethrower swept above her and burning air filled her nose.

Bullets zipped around her and a white beam cut across the basin. Her feet were struggling to find grip when the room exploded with a brutal hammering. Streams of heavy-caliber rounds whistled past her ears and then the surface of the pool exploded with crashing birds and fragments of burning flesh. Her hat shuddered as something scythed through her hair and she heard Jester's voice.

"Cryboy, too close," he shouted. "Too close! Switch it off."

The staccato thumping stopped and she reached the side to find her big companion tracking both weapons above her head. She pulled herself out, dropping wet onto the floor among the charred bird corpses, her lungs raw with smoke and fumes.

"Sorry, Jodie." Jester said, flicking her a split second glance. "You took too long. I lost my hard on."

She saw Curtis set off across the basin then lifted her hands and studied them before peering at the liquid dripping off her vest. Her stomach gave a sickening lurch and she swiveled her gaze into the dome above the pool.

There were mutilated faces looking down at her. Iron chains layered with hooks were dangling from the ceiling and hanging from the spikes was a hideous pendant of human limbs and heads. The features were twisted and disfigured. Eye sockets gaped empty and cheekbones were glistening through flaps of torn skin. As she stared, there was a flash of movement and one of the severed arteries disgorged a droplet from its glistening tip.

Oh sweet Jesus. She patted her vest. *Blood. That was blood I just waded through.*

Jester stepped close and rested a hand on her shoulder, his eyes and both his weapons still tracking between the dome and the room's exits.

"Those are bodies up there," she said in a soft voice. "People ripped up."

He nodded without lowering his gaze.

"That was blood we came through," she continued.

He nodded again but stayed mute, his eyes still scanning for threats.

They were standing in silence, her head throbbing with the memory of everything that had just happened, when a sharp pop broke the air and Maddie's voice filled the chamber.

"You guys okay?" she asked.

Jester glanced over at the metal pyramid and slowly lowered his weapons. "Yeah we're okay." He took a couple of squelching steps toward the machine. "Did you see that?"

"No not really," their organizer replied. "Bits over Cryboy's shoulder."

The big man nodded and pressed a packet of Marlboro to his mouth. "Giant fuck-off mutant birds," he said in a mumble. "Cranes I think. Came at us from the ceiling."

"Yes. Cryboy took out some of those from here."

"Yeah …" He flicked open his lighter and looked down at the remote-controlled weapon. "And some of those rounds were pretty close to my lady friend here."

There was no reply. After a few seconds, Jester started to walk toward the robot and gestured for Curtis to follow. "You know, I reckon we stand a better chance against mutant animals than a bunch of overexcited miniguns." When he reached the rear of the platform he bent and examined the cable that ran up the steps. "You hear that, Cryboy? Deal was that the machine always fired away from us."

"Well, that wasn't the machine actually, that was me. I was operating manually." It was the IT specialist's voice, distant and slightly muffled.

"Right." Jester pulled a face and started to shake his head. "I don't really think you're getting my point." He beckoned Curtis to him and turned to the robot. "What you looking at now? What's on the screen?"

Cryboy cleared his throat with a short cough. "I'm covering the ceiling and the two exits."

Jester nodded and jerked his finger at his comrade's machete. Curtis pulled out the long blade and frowned. Jester pointed at the wire snaking up the staircase and she heard him whisper something about the power supply being inside the unit.

His companion looked at him blankly.

The big man raised his arm and then dropped it in a chopping motion. Curtis gave a slow nod and stepped forward. With a single swipe he sheared the cable and Jodie felt something twist inside her. There was something good and bad about what had just happened, and while she was staring at the disabled machine Jester strode to the front and stuck his face close to the camera.

"You hear us now?" he asked, blowing a cloud of smoke into the silver-white fielding. She waited to hear the crackle of the radio channel but the machine was silent.

She stood in cold wet boots and a clinging bodysuit and started to feel along the crown of her hat. Her trembling fingers poked through a pair of bullet holes and a flash of anger rose through her. Yes, they'd just been attacked by some horrific things, but Cryboy's shooting had definitely put her in danger. That was why Jester had cut it off. It made sense, but at the same time losing all that firepower made her feel strangely small and vulnerable.

There was a click and a rattle and she turned to see the men rummaging through a drawer in the base of the gun platform. She lifted her chin and, making her voice as strong and clear as she could, asked if there was any water.

Curtis grabbed a bottle and walked over to her, his pants clinging to his legs and blood dripping from him with each step. "You okay?" he asked.

She took the drink and deliberated on the question while she unscrewed the cap. What could she say? She was very un-okay. They'd just been attacked by giant birds. She was cold and shaky and terrified about what they were going to meet next. They'd planned the mission around a powerful robot gun but it had been operated by an asshole so they'd been forced to disable it. Her face and clothes were covered in other people's blood and there were ripped up bits of bodies hanging above her head. She'd definitely been better.

When she'd taken a gulp she gave him a nod. "Yeah, I'm fine," she said casually.

She was tipping her head back for a second swig when she noticed a swirling red shape with a feathered tail and a beak carved above the entrance to the hallway behind him. Glancing back at the opposite arch, she saw that it was decorated with a turtle made of black gems.

The dragon over the basin and the animal imagery on the tiles suggested that each area of the temple had a specific meaning and she was keen to know where they were heading. "So where next?" she asked. "Red bird or black turtle?"

Curtis studied the design on the far arch. "It's a phoenix …" he said, turning to look over her head, "… and that's a tortoise." Blood dripped from his sleeve as he lifted his arm and pointed. "We go down there. There's a big room with a statue in it. That's where the crawlers are."

"Ah, right. So you've *seen* this again have you?" Jester asked, moving up to join them and eyeing the young black kid with a strange mixture of suspicion and admiration. "In that case, maybe you know how many there might be?"

"Not sure exactly," Curtis replied. "But more than before."

She let out a long breath and felt her last reserves of hope drain away. The last time they'd just scraped it. Even with the flamethrower she couldn't see how they could deal with any more of the creatures.

The next thing she knew, Jester had spat out his cigarette ends and was fixing her with his watery blue eyes.

"I think we need you on crossbow duty again, Jodie," he said calmly.

She glanced back and gave a single nod. The situation was really dumb. They should've kept the robot. A thousand rounds a minute would have pulped the crawlers and now they wanted her to go in armed with pieces of wood and string.

They needed to get weapons and ammo from the base of the robot and this gave her a little time to think about improving their tactics. Both men were insanely brave but she was sure this would eventually be their downfall, and while Curtis crouched and rummaged in the big drawer, she tried to think of how they could slow things down or tackle the crawlers from a safer distance.

After inspecting each of the items, the young shaman pulled out a wooden stake, settled it in the palm of his hand and started to reshape it with his machete. As he took short controlled blows he gave her a lecture on the design of hand weapons. He explained that if knives and spears were perfectly balanced they could be wielded easily and almost at the speed of thought.

She studied him as he spoke, interested in his new teacher-like persona and curious as to why some of the words and phrases he used didn't always sound quite his own. She realized that he was passing on what he had learned as a boy. He had spent his childhood being taught by the elders of many different tribes and what she was hearing was a kind of echo. He wasn't the junior anymore. He was the only one with the skills and knowledge to deal with their attackers, and without realizing it he'd become their mentor.

A mixture of pride and excitement rose into her chest. Christ, they'd been smart to find him. There couldn't be anyone else on the whole planet who had learned the customs of so many different tribes. He had the skills and speed to deal with the mutants *and* he knew all the magic stuff. He was their secret weapon.

When he'd finished making a couple of short stabbing spears, he laid them by his feet and pulled out a rifle clip. "Ammo?" he asked, glancing up.

She nodded and reached into the drawer. As she was picking out a selection of bullets she caught sight of a coil of rope and held it up. "Let's bring this too. We could use it."

"Go on."

"We could tie it to the crossbow bolts and make a sort of harpoon." She used a tugging motion to demonstrate her idea. "We might be able to control them a little more easily."

"Yeah? Interesting." A light sprang up in his eyes. "Yes! They regenerate. If we get an arrow deep into a limb it could seal the rope inside. You know, you might just be on to something there."

She nodded. It was the best she could think of but, as they turned and made their way toward the room where the crawlers were waiting, she had a sinking feeling that it wasn't going to be enough.

Jester went in first and casually hosed the darkness with a sweep of flame. A couple of long strides took her to a position behind him where she stopped and scanned the planes of white marble that formed the large rectangular space around them. Hot sooty air billowed back in her face but it seemed empty. The alabaster surfaces ran clean for about forty yards in every direction and there were no features or furnishings except for a large hulking presence squatting in the center. A second blast of fire revealed that it was the statue of large tortoise facing the opposite direction. She ignored it and set her mind to searching for possible cavities and bolt-holes. The glow from the burning napalm spread a soft light all the way to the far walls but her probing eyes failed to find any possible hiding places. Even after leaning and bending to peer into every dark corner, the room seemed strangely bare.

They started to move forward. Without communicating any kind of strategy, they naturally divided the room in half. Jester continued toward the left of the statue and she stayed on the right nearer the door. The taste of burnt gasoline flooded her mouth and with each step her throat tightened and dried.

She drew level with the turtle's feet and saw that the smooth line of shadow that ran under the far wall was in fact a series of holes. Just as it occurred to her that these were the obvious places to hide, Jester dropped to one knee and looked back over his shoulder. He had a grenade in his hand and was jabbing his finger at the pits. She nodded, and he pulled the pin and set the small bomb rolling toward the back of the room. When she met his gaze again, he flashed her a dumb grin and passed back the steel ring.

"Nice," she mouthed, cracking a fake smile. "Thanks." The dry humor of the situation made her shake her head. She had to survive all this just to be able to tell Hannah. A guy finally got down on one knee and gave her a ring. The problem was, one: They were in an underground room hunting some kind of horrible mutant, two: He had just thrown a live grenade, and three: He was totally covered in blood and quite possibly insane. That was so not how she'd imagined it.

The explosive passed the statue and then curved away to the right and dropped into the furthest hole.

"Yep," he said, giving her a confident nod. "If they're in there, then someone's going to get a real headache."

They turned and covered their heads. A loud crack shook the floor and a shock wave of hot fumes pushed past them. When she turned, Jester was back level with the statue swinging his weapons in each arm.

"Knock, knock!" he shouted, spraying a torrent of bullets and flame into the pits at the back of the room. "Wake up you cuntbags!"

She moved up to join him and a few yards from the nearest pit he stopped and lowered the tips of his weapons. A series of tiny creeping movements caught her eye and set the skin along her spine tingling. Bony claws tightened on the edges of the pits and then a trio of crawlers vaulted up and landed in squat shapes of tensed muscle.

Fuck! She jolted and was trying to juggle her crossbow back under her control when the nearest came flying straight at her.

Wiry arms stretched toward her throat but never reached her. A torrent of fire and bullets knocked it onto the floor where it rolled onto its back with holes exploding across its chest and stomach. Jester moved closer, keeping both weapons trained on it until his rifle clicked empty. As he ripped out the magazine, the creature pushed itself onto its feet and started to wade toward her.

She fumbled with her weapon as it approached. *Oh Christ. Somebody please stop this.* It was just a few feet away when a streak cut across the room and a bolt sunk into its shoulder. Its head flung back, a shrill scream cut the air then the rope snapped taught and it was yanked toward the door. *Good.* Exhilaration swelled in her chest. *Curtis's pinned one. The next fucker's mine.*

There were two more behind the leader. She was squeezing the trigger when their heads went down and they came tumbling forward in tight-clenched balls—one wheeling at her and the other at Jester. The chamber burst to life with the heat and noise of her partner's weapons and she aimed and fired. The bolt sank deep into her attacker's spine then snapped as it continued its roll. When its back appeared again the rope had wound into a loop. She turned and started to sprint toward the door. After a few strides the line snapped taut and the bow twisted in her hands. She rammed it under her arm and spun. The creature was just a few yards away, hunched and snarling, its clawed hands snatching at the cords around its legs and back. She yanked it onto its side and stamped the bindings onto the floor. Its reptile eyes fixed hers with a cold menace and it let out a hiss. She let the crossbow fall and snatched out her revolvers. "Now that's no way to address a lady, is it?"

She fired both guns at the same time, one into its forehead and the other into its heart, only stopping when the cylinders were empty and the vampire lay gnarled and still underneath her.

As she stood over the tight-curled skeleton a thin membrane started to grow over the entry wounds and its yellow eyes flicked open. She holstered her pistols and swung up her shotgun just as its arms braced on the floor and its wiry muscles flexed to push itself up. "No you don't," she said, shaking her head. "No you fucking don't." She blasted two loads of shot into its forehead and Curtis skidded to a halt at her side.

"Stand back," he said, and separated skull from neck with his machete.

She gave a nod of thanks then looked past him and her heart sank. On the other side of the room Jester was staggering backward with a crawler high on his chest. He was holding the creature's ears in a vice-like grip but she could see from the strain on his face that he was only just managing to keep its mouth from his neck.

Curtis followed her line of sight and then left her side, lifting his big knife as he bound away.

She stood transfixed and watched the creature make a lunge at Jester's jugular, its fangs almost reaching his skin before being hauled back. The two combatants seemed held in perfect balance then the vampire let go of a vest strap and lifted an arm high in the air. The sinewy limb came down in a blur and hacked at Jester's collarbone. There was metallic rip, like a knife slashing foil, and his suit fell open at the shoulder. The crawler struck again. Its black talons sliced a long deep gash under her teammate's jaw, a pulse of blood spurted across the floor and he slumped onto his knees with a soft moan.

Oh shit. A rush of dizziness left her swaying on her heels, weak and clammy cold. *We've lost Jester.*

Chapter 44

Cryboy

He was impotent. Cryboy tried to refresh the feed from his lead robot but the screen stayed blank. He'd lost signal when they were talking to the others and it hadn't come back. Although part of his mind knew that checking again and again wasn't going to change things, he couldn't help himself.

Eventually he shifted his finger a little lower and started moving through the other views. The second camera showed the staircase to the upper floor, the third the double doors in front of the throne and the first … nothing. He kept hitting the smooth plastic. No signal. Staircase. Double doors. No signal. Staircase. Double doors.

After a couple more cycles he sucked in a long breath and squeezed his eyes closed. He had to stop hoping the machine would come back online. Obsessive behavior was unproductive. He had to do something else.

When his lungs felt unbearably swollen and fizzy, he exhaled and started to walk along the side of the dais. At the front of the throne he turned and retraced the seven short steps, his finger dabbing through the same points on his controller. *Blank. Staircase. Double doors.*

At the end of his route he stopped and forced his legs to stay still. *Seventy circuits. Nine hundred and eighty steps. That's* ... His head gave a sudden violent shake. *Mustn't do any more math. Must stop the math.* Although he tried to stand still and concentrate on relaxing the twitching muscles in his legs, he soon found his mind racing again. *He cut off the biggest machine. My weapon got too close to his girl so he threatened me with castration. That's territorial behavior. Like an ape or a big cat. Cut off my tool. Dumb testosterone shit. Might just get him killed. Might just serve him right.*

He flicked his eyes between his remaining gun platforms and started an assessment of their firepower. *I've still got two. I can still show her how good I am. They might come up and ask for them. Got to be quick though. The eggs are hatching now, we know that. Then the creatures disperse. Dispersal's an end-gamer. Exponential breeding. Way beyond our resources. Beyond anyone's.*

There was a faint scratching sound from behind him and he lifted his gaze to see that Maddie had pushed herself off the wall and was standing next to the robot at the top of the steps. He watched her peer along the spotlight beam into the darkness below and felt his eye muscles twitch. *She should let me send another one down. Should be keeping the hired guns under control. UGVs are part of the plan now. She's letting that dumb sack of muscle run the show. No leadership. Four, five, six.* His feet had started moving again. *Seven.* He turned. The controller on his forearm was back up in front of his eyes, the three camera feeds rotating at his touch. *No signal, staircase, double doors.*

He sensed Maddie turn and look at him but kept his eyes on his wrist pad. *Nine twenty-three local. Four minutes since the last gunfire. All quiet now. Impossible to analyze a single data event. Anything could be happening down there. She could be dead.* His buttocks tightened and he felt his tongue push against his teeth. *Hope not. Maybe lizard brain got taken down. Be good to see her and the black kid come out. He's okay. Respectful. Been negotiating with Weaver for cash though and that's strange. Supposed to be a shaman. One thing the databases all agree on is that witch doctors can't take payment. It weakens them. So if he's really got any powers they're going to run out. Potential disaster. But does he know that?*

Chapter 45

Jodie

Jodie looked on with a sense of total emptiness as her companion rocked backward and forward with a stunned expression on his face. The crawler yanked its head from his grip and started to move its jaws toward the pulsing wound. Blood splattered across its cheek and was just about to spray into its gaping mouth when Curtis reached them and his foot connected with its skull. It flew backward onto the floor, immediately jerking itself into a sitting position and meeting its attacker's eyes with a hiss. An instant later its head was spinning away into the shadows in a flash of metal and a spray of inky droplets.

Curtis sank to his knees at Jester's side, clamped his hand against the deep gash and started to ease him backward. When he'd laid him flat on the ground, he looked up at her and jerked his head toward the back of the room. "Over there," he said, flashing his eyes at the pits. "There's one left."

She followed his gaze and saw a hunched figure near the head of the statue. Her shotgun went to her shoulder and her feet started to move. *This one's all mine. If Curtis has to help me, Jester bleeds to death. Simple as that.*

She saw glistening pink strips on the crawler's skin and realized that it was the grenade victim. It had obviously been badly injured and only just managed to get out of its hole. *Well* ... She emptied both barrels into its skull, watching with satisfaction as it shuddered and staggered backward ... *It can damn well go down again.*

The mechanism gave an empty click but she kept on anyway, swiveling the hot barrel in both hands and lifting the gun above her shoulder. The vampire was raising a skinny blistered arm when she reached it and smashed at its skull. It fell backward and then stood swaying with its head lolling at a hideous angle. Her second blow took it down, and then she was standing over it ramming the stock of her weapon hard onto its forehead. She heard metal scrape against stone and Curtis's machete slid up against her boot. She dropped her twelve-gauge and snatched it up. *How difficult can this be?*

The big knife came down again and again, sparks flying as the metal tip glanced off the marble floor. Sinew, muscle and serrated bone all fell away under her blows then the grimacing skull rolled away.

She straightened her back and stood panting, her hands raw and throbbing. *This is all wrong. No one should ever have to do this. That was once a normal man and I just hacked his head off.*

When she turned, Curtis was on his knees with his hands pressed against Jester's neck. Blood was seeping between his fingers and running in thick trickles into a pool on the floor. He looked up at her with blazing eyes as she approached.

"Could still be more," he said curtly. "Check the pits. Check for more pits."

She turned and moved away in a daze. *Bastard. I take one out on my own and now he's shouting at me.*

Her shaking hands groped for the flashlight on her vest as she walked to the first of the holes. Clicking it on, she leaned forward and directed the beam into the rough-hewn hollow. At the bottom there was a pile of rifles and what looked like human bones, but no crawlers.

After quickly checking the others, her eyes were pulled back to her comrades on the other side of the room and she strode back to them and dropped to her knees. As she watched, Curtis tentatively released the pressure on the wound and reached inside his jacket. Jester's mouth moved, and when she shuffled forward he met her gaze with a grin and a roll of his eyes.

"You look all flushed, Jodie," he said softly. His eyelids closed and she reached out and rested her hand on his shoulder.

"Are you okay? You …" she searched for words. "Hold on there, pal. Stay with us. We need you." A freezing cold expanded from deep in her stomach. *Dumb bitch. What a pathetic thing to say. You're useless here. No medical training. Too weak to drag him out. Too slow killing the crawlers.*

As she stared at his tight pained face, his eyes flashed open again.

"I was sensing a lot of hostility in here just then …" he said quietly. "Were you guys picking that up at all?"

She reached down to hold his wrist. His skin was cold and the light in the center of his pupils had started to dim.

"Oh guys!" he said, his words hanging above his mouth like a tracing in the air. "Quit fussing, yeah? It's a scratch. Just a scratch." His eyelids fluttered closed and his back and shoulders flattened against the floor.

She called his name and squeezed and yanked at his arm. When he gave no response she turned to Curtis. "Do something!" she shouted. "Save him!" Her voice choked hoarse. "Save him."

"Yes, Jodie." Curtis caught her eye and gave a curt nod. "What the fuck do you think I'm trying to do?"

With Jester's cold hand in hers, she sat on her haunches and watched her young companion produce sticks and leaves from a small pouch. As he busied himself stripping and crushing the roots, her eyes slowly glazed and she allowed her shock and emptiness to overwhelm her.

For a while there was nothing but a kind of roaring noise in her head, and then a small flame sprang to life in her peripheral vision and reminded her where she was. A sweet smoke reached her, and as she inhaled it she became conscious of the cold limb that she held across her lap and started to wonder what Jester's loss would mean to others. Her mind tried to produce images of his friends and family, but failed. She had no concept of what they might look like and in their place there appeared a swirling procession of all the people who meant the most to her. She saw the warmth in her mom's eyes as she greeted her through the screen door. An image of Hank smiling quickly morphed into a blur of memories of her father, then she had visions of Hannah and her brothers running around in the yard.

She felt somehow that she'd let them down. She now knew for certain that she'd put herself into terrible danger, and the thought that she might become separated from them or that her death would cause any hurt and distress brought icy crushing pains to her chest. A flicker of awareness gave her the bitter realization that she had been thinking about herself when she should have been thinking about Jester. It was a betrayal that only added to her wretchedness, and when she felt hot tears flowing freely down her cheeks, she welcomed them as a release.

Through the gentle breaths of her weeping she became slowly aware of a soft low humming. The sound wove into a looping melody then got louder and became a chant: a cycle of notes that snaked around her while she sank deeper and deeper into her thoughts. She wanted to go back and change things. She wanted the power to make a small adjustment to the past that would prevent Jester from getting taken down, but wherever she looked there was no answer. The universe told her the truth. Reality was as brutal and unyielding as the stone around her. Time could not be changed and the dumb pretense that they were succeeding was over. A life was ending and they were all to blame.

A movement caught her eye and she became aware that the boy had lifted his palm to his mouth and there was a dark pool growing in it. His hand moved to their teammate's neck and stayed there. There was a period of stillness and then she saw that her companion was gently rocking and the dark pool under the sick man's head and chest was creeping down the side of his legs.

She started to move. Her arms hugged her knees and her hands started to squeeze some warmth into her shoulders. A sudden violent bout of shivering shook her body and then made her blink. She became aware of some certainties. She knew that she was cold and she was sitting on hard marble looking at a young black man whose eyes were closed.

Curtis's eyes flicked open and the movement and sudden attention of another human being pulled her into focus. "So? How is he?" she asked. "What have you done?"

"Lots of things. On many levels." His eyes rested on Jester's chest and he shook his head, a faint smile of puzzled admiration on his lips. "That man's immune system is like nothing else, I can tell you that."

"Yeah but how is he?"

He shook his head. "Don't know."

"Is he dying?"

"He's in a kind of coma."

She jerked her chin toward the door. "We could drag him back to the steps. The guys could get him to a hospital."

"Wouldn't make much difference."

"But we could get him to an ICU."

"Only thing they could do is give him some blood." He looked at his hands and started to wipe them on the pants of his suit. "It looks worse than it is. He's only lost about a quart. Not an issue for a man as strong as him."

"So you're going to just leave him there?" she asked.

"Listen." He started to drop the roots and twigs back into his bag. "I'm a healer. It's what I do. It's what I am. The crawler's nails were infected. That's all that's threatening him now. There's some kind of virus in his bloodstream, but it's not something that will be known to regular science. I've purified the wound and stimulated his own defenses in every way I know. Now we wait. The two forces fight it out. One will win."

"And they can't do more than that in a hospital?"

"With what? Electric lights and white coats?"

She nodded doubtfully then rested her hand on Jester's forehead and closed her eyes. Forcing her mind to consider as many options as possible, she tried to think of a better alternative. She realized that dragging him out of the temple would take a huge amount of time and effort and she wasn't at all sure what medical support there was nearby. A voice in her head reminded her that Curtis had been right about every prediction he'd made so far, and in the end she gave in to it. Maybe she needed to trust him again. Maybe there really was nothing else they could do.

She pushed herself to her feet and started loading a revolver. *So this is it. Just the two of us now.* The brutal reality of the thought sank in, and while her fingers fumbled with cold metal, her vision went blurry and she felt water dripping onto her hands. "Damn it!" she said angrily.

He was suddenly at her side, his arm pressed across her back, a hand gently patting her shoulder. Tears swelled again. "I'm okay. I'm okay," she told him, shaking her head. "Just getting used to all this."

He squeezed her arm then stood studying her. "That's fine but we need to keep moving. I'm going to make some more torches and I need you look for an exit."

She started to scan the room, realizing for the first time that it seemed to be a dead end. She asked where the entrance to the nest was and he glanced around the chamber.

"Exactly. It's got to be in here somewhere," he told her. "And it goes down. The creature is deeper still."

They had extra light sticks in their vests and she cracked a handful and threw them into the corners. The rising glow illuminated more detail in their surroundings and a set of shapes emerged high on the walls on either side of her. There was a white tiger on her left, and when she turned to her right she found a blue dragon looking down with a cold impassive gaze. They had to have some kind of meaning but she had no idea what. Curtis would know but he'd gone back to examining Jester and there was no way she wanted to disturb him. This was something she'd solve on her own. Drawing a revolver, she moved to the wall and started tapping the stonework.

She found nothing of interest, and after a while her attention was drawn back to the statue of the turtle. It seemed as if it had some kind of special significance in the room, and there had to be some reason why it was standing staring at a picture of itself. She followed its gaze to the stonework in front of it and then went and knocked the butt of a pistol gently against the marble. The sensation of solid stone reverberated up her arm. Stepping back, she noticed a series of smudges on the floor and hunkered down to examine them. They were footprints that vanished into the polished surface.

Curiosity led her to the front of the animal where she rested her hand on the back of its neck and looked closely into a single wise eye. Without any specific intention or forethought she pressed down hard and the head moved smoothly under her touch. There was a dull echoing clunk and the section of floor in front of the statue lowered and revealed a ramp descending into darkness.

"Well done," Curtis shouted. "I think you've found the nest."

Chapter 46

Weaver

He couldn't taste any stone or fruit. They'd described his bottle of Pinot Gris as flinty and citrusy but Weaver suspected that coffee, adrenaline and sleeping pills had numbed his taste buds. He put down his glass, dabbed at his mouth and then found himself using the expensive square of linen to wipe the smudges off the rim. Even in one of the swankiest restaurants in town he found he was unable to stop himself compulsively cleaning and tidying. It was a new habit. Some deep-routed desire to feel he had some control over his environment when in fact he had none. He'd come to relax, but not even the eye-wateringly expensive wine was making any difference. The midweek crowd squeezed around him was making an unimaginable amount of noise, and with each squeal and peel of laughter he was becoming more stressed, more angry and more isolated from his fellow New Yorkers.

Two critical missions were being carried out at the same time and this was a new high in tension. The army had sent the robots into the West Wing and his own guys were creeping around some remote Mongolian temple. There was nothing he could do to affect either outcome. He just had to sit and wait. It was as simple as that.

A chorus of shrieks came from one of the biggest tables and he allowed his eyes to drift over and examine the occupants. He hadn't mixed with the ultra-wealthy very much before and they weren't hugely likable. A handful of them were wearing immersive glasses, and judging by the smutty comments and giggles they were playing online sex games while they ate. *Seduction Three* was in its final stages and there were already a wealth of incredibly popular spin-off shows and video simulations.

He pulled his gaze away and jabbed his fork at his appetizer. Had the population always been this stupid? His colleagues had long moaned and joked about the ridiculously poor quality of undergraduates they received but somehow this seemed worse. On the surface it looked like the Interim Authorities were keeping everything running as normal so people seemed to have forgotten about the missing administration and were just getting on with their pampered, blinkered lives. The immigration flood and the chipping and gating of citizens had probably only worsened things. The city dwellers were now safe from any sort of obvious crime and this was making them complacent. With the remaining population desperate to get gated, and a mass of starving immigrants on their doorstep, they had an endless source of cheap or virtually free labor, and this meant that comfortable wealth was taken for granted. Perhaps his more left-leaning colleagues were right. It was a return to serfdom. Hunger slavery.

In a deliberate attempt to close his mind from what was going on around him, he looked down at his reader and stared hard at the screen. A single tap refreshed the comms and data, and the operational status reassembled in front of his eyes. The top risk remained the hatching of the eggs, but this was pretty much academic. The emergence of the young arthropods was now beyond anybody's control. They'd started too late and that was his fault. He'd been too slow in finding the Ferguson kid. He had to live with that.

Moving down the list, he came to the possibility of the robots failing and this was a different matter. Cryboy had sourced and refitted a specialist Sentinel for the team but it was clear that the military were struggling. They were massively tied in to Brutetek and the hardware firm could name their price for the modification and didn't seem to be in any hurry to get things right. Hernandez and O'Keefe made plenty of unsubtle references to the fact that Canmore's company was being passively uncooperative, and why not? They could make money on the new UGVs and even more if they weren't quite up to the job. Canmore was making much more cash while he manipulated the Interim Authorities than he ever could under the elected government, so maybe the new droids wouldn't be quite up to spec and the situation would drag on.

Weaver sighed and took another huge mouthful of wine. It seemed that the business-minded senator didn't know about the eggs and the possibility of the young escaping quarantine and spreading. That would be more than convenient political stagnation; that would be a national disaster.

He shook his head. It was no good letting himself get worked up about these things. He had to focus his mind on what he *could* change and keep from pointless fretting. His guiding AI still put forward anomalies and puzzles for him, and he was meant to use his human intuition to reframe the problem. Again and again it had asked him to investigate a broken air defense platform on the roof of the West Wing, and once more he found himself reading through the details. A missile system had been delivered to the White House and never worked. The motors and ammunition loader had all failed and it had been sent for repair. Yes, this was unusual, but it didn't seem to have any other relevance. It had happened well before the outbreak there and most of the big defense systems were switched off now anyway. But the AIs were picking at it like a scab. They couldn't fit it into a simulation but they wouldn't leave it alone.

He decided to send it to Cryboy. The kid couldn't stop analyzing stuff so he might as well use him. He hacked from the truck and actually worked on things while he was waiting down near the bunkers. He had Asperger's at the very least. He could somehow concentrate with a firefight going on below him, so maybe he could find out a little bit more about this broken machine and then delete it from the system.

Another burst of laughter and dumb shouting set Weaver's teeth on edge. Most of his fellow citizens were wandering through life with their brains totally unused. They learned little and noticed less. But he wasn't doing it just for them. Most of the simulations showed what would happen if the young hatched at any of the locations. They were likely to disperse and they'd soon be out of gate wandering the countryside. Out there it wouldn't be possible to contain them. Out there they'd feast on the immigrant families and the decent hardworking people who couldn't afford to go gated. People like Jodie.

Chapter 47

Jodie

On their right was a stone block wall, but on their left nothing. The white marble fell away to an ocean of darkness, and with each cautious step she got an increasing sense of scale, as if she'd been swimming near a beach then drifted out above a chasm in the seabed.

After a few yards, a thin whistling sound clarified in her head, like a thin wire had tightened between her ears. She glanced at Curtis but he was stalking downward undisturbed. The shrill tone quickly thickened into a buzzing that set her teeth on edge and triggered an echo of fear deep inside her. She knew it was in there. They were approaching one of the creatures again and there weren't enough of them. They were just a couple of kids messing with something they shouldn't.

About thirty yards down, Curtis stopped and stood squinting out into the shadows. "This place is big …" he said softly, "… really big." He hurled his torch out into the void where it hung in the air above a grid of curved shapes before landing at the foot of a row of grim-faced soldiers. She jerked and started to squeeze the trigger on the flamethrower, and then realized that the men were all identical: each expression fixed. *Statues.* She eased off the tension in her hand. *Lots and lots of them.*

They stood surveying the strange scene for a moment then he moved to her side and gently steered her weapon down the slope. "How about some light down there?" he asked. "A blast on the edge of the ramp?"

She complied, laying down a strip of burning napalm that illuminated even deeper ranks of clay soldiers. "Hell of a lot of statues," she whispered.

"Yeah," he confirmed softly. "An army for the afterlife."

"And what about the target?" she asked. "Do you know where it is?"

"No." He pulled his spear closer and rested his chin on his fist. "But it's in here somewhere. Can you hear it?"

She told him that she had the buzzing in her head, and he nodded while staring out across the vast hall.

"So if you were it, where would *you* hide?"

She gazed down the lines of terracotta figures and felt an ache of anxiety grow in the pit of her stomach. "Somewhere right in the middle."

"Yeah. Me too."

"So how are we going to catch it?" she asked.

He stood and gazed thoughtfully into the mid-distance then shook his head and set off down the ramp. She followed slowly; icy doubt sinking deeper into her bones with each step. *Now he's Mr. Silent again. There's just two of us down here and he wants to make it up as we go along.*

As they approached the bottom he slowed and lifted his spear. She saw him study the patch of dusty ground that ran between the ramp and the first statues, and then he asked her to put down another line of fire. The crescent of flame revealed a mass of footprints and dark streaks and her heart sank. There'd been a lot of people down there, and most of them had left bloodstains.

Her partner seemed unconcerned and led her off the marble ramp onto the sandy floor, where he stood peering into the lines of soldiers. Flames were jumping and flittering around their legs, and whenever she turned or looked away, the line seemed to loom forward, a faint menace oozing from the blank eyes and the dark spaces between the rows.

A single relentless thought grew in her mind while she waited. *I do not want to go in there. We cannot go creeping into the middle of those things.*

Eventually, she shot him a sideways glance and shared her fears. "We can't go in there," she hissed quietly.

"I know," he replied. "But there's something else we can try." He walked to the nearest soldier and gave it a gentle push. After watching it rock on its booted feet, he turned back to her. "I really hate to say this, because these statues are all priceless relics …"

"But?"

"But …" His eyes widened dramatically. "Have you ever heard of the domino effect?"

With a handkerchief tied across his mouth, he moved to the leading soldier and looked straight into its colorless eyes. "Excuse me sir," he said, bracing his legs and pressing its shoulders. "Forgive me, but this is for the greater good." He pushed hard, like a playground bully starting a fight, and the clay man started to rock. A second shove sent it crashing into the soldier behind, which toppled backward and set the line falling.

He came striding back to her, head after head dropping out of sight behind him with each step. The thuds became a long, low rumble, and then he was at her side guiding her up the ramp.

Jets of powdered clay rose into the torchlight as they climbed. The noise was soon a rising roar, and when she looked out again, the dust had become a cloud billowing toward them like the sails of a giant ship. *Oh shit.* Panic flushed through her as the thick fog enveloped her head. *We've given it perfect cover to attack, and that was definitely not part of the plan.*

Everything blurred. Curtis's face loomed close, and he shouted something and pointed along the front of the ramp. She nodded and lowered the flamethrower, keeping her finger tight on the trigger as the heavy air swam around her.

It was a false alarm. None of the swirling demon shapes solidified and she was squinting into the darkness when the rumbling suddenly stopped. The flicker of flames grew sharper, and then the remaining statues emerged out of the gloom.

He swept his arm across the columns. "I thought the one line would knock over the others but we're going to have to do it again."

"Do you think it'll definitely come out?" she asked.

"Yeah," he replied. "It has to eventually." He glanced back as he moved down the ramp. "Stay here. When I've pushed it over I'll come and stand behind you. I'll skewer it. Then you need to get around the back and knock it out."

"Yeah. Easy." She cracked a thin smile. "And if there's a load of them?"

He shrugged. "We improvise."

"Right." The flamethrower swung onto its strap as she dropped her arms. "Sure."

He turned and walked back to her. "Listen." She felt a hand on her shoulder. "We've got everything we need." His gaze intensified, his deep, dark eyes sucking her somewhere deep inside him. "*You've* got everything you need. Remember that."

Moments later, the great hall was shaking with the sound of falling statues. Crashes and rumbles filled her ears, then a wall of gray particles rolled over them and she was blinded.

With her finger tight on the flamethrower's trigger, she swung the barrel and stared into the haze. Her blinking eyes found no movement. Nothing appeared out of the gloom, and when the gritty particles started to thin, she felt herself breathing again.

She was turning to Curtis when a dark shape zoomed at them. A taloned arm smashed at her gun and then swung at her throat. She got a fleeting glimpse of an eyeless face and threw herself backward. Her teammate was braced solid behind her. The spear shaft shot over her shoulder with a crunch and a piercing wail. Something whipped into her stomach and knocked the breath out of her, and then a shove sent her staggering sideways. She opened her eyes and saw Curtis throwing himself off the ramp toward the skewered creature.

"Move!" he shouted.

She tottered for a moment, and then she found her balance and sprinted down the ramp to join him.

When she got to the bottom, he was standing braced with his back to her. She caught glimpses of the animal behind him; at first just flashes of thrashing limbs and then a stomach-churning vision of a large eyeless head.

Her hands dropped and she became aware of the unusual beauty of the scene. She noticed, as if for the first time, the rippling flames giving an orange warmth to the legs of the statues. She admired the way Curtis's jacket swung open when he pushed forward and the deft movement of his baseball boots as he fought for ground. She studied the sharp proud veins on his neck and the back of his hands and deduced, in a slow and distant way, that his body was straining at full exertion to hold his attacker at bay.

But it was winning. In push after push, Curtis's feet were skidding closer toward her. His arms and legs seemed to be shortening and his movements getting tighter. As she listened to the clattering of the insect's arms on the spear and the squeak of rubber soles on the stone floor, a few lazy thoughts started to form somewhere high in her head. *I wonder how long he can keep fighting it like that. It's so strong. So relentless.*

Her hands had settled comfortably on her flamethrower and her eyes were beginning to glaze when he flicked back his head.

"Need help," he hissed. "Soon."

Shit. She found herself moving, a sudden snap of adrenaline pushing blood into her arms and legs. The thing had been messing with her head. She had to get behind it and knock it out.

She started to push her way between the soldiers but was only halfway around when a crack and a short cry stopped her dead in her tracks. Framed between two statues at the end of the column, she saw

Curtis lying on his back with a length of broken wood in his hand. When she saw the grimace of despair on his face, the scale of their mistake became clear. They'd left all the doors open. His spear had broken and now the creature could get to the others and out into the countryside.

Curtis was already on his feet, moving after it. She caught glimpses of him sprinting along the front row and then he stopped. His keen eyes found her in the shadows and his arm shot out behind him.

"The weight," he shouted, jabbing a finger at the far wall. "Shoot it off."

She followed his arm to a giant section of tree trunk hanging under the top of the slope and his idea became clear. The wood was a counterbalance. If she could cut the rope, then the ramp would rise and the creature would be trapped.

She drew a pistol and rested it on her forearm. The cord was a faint sliver of gray against the darkness. *Can't get it with this. Nobody could. This is a rifle job.* She braced and fired. The crack rang loud in her ears and the bullet disappeared. *Damn it*. She caught a glimpse of the creature approaching the foot of the incline, sighted again and squeezed the trigger. The shot went somewhere to the right. *Crap! Can't do it. That thing's going to get out.*

As she stood squinting down the short barrel, she felt time slow and became acutely aware of the tiny flickers of movement in the room: the dance of the flames on the napalm along the front row, the snowstorm of dust floating in front of her eyes and, away on her left, the two dark shapes hurtling toward the foot of the slope. She sucked in a deep breath and heard Curtis's words playing in her head. *You've got everything you need.* Her world steadied and solidified. *He's right. I'm the one. This is mine.*

She fired. The rope shuddered and started to twist and she flicked her eyes sideways. The creature was just a few feet from the ramp. She fired again. The last strands of rope burst and the log hit the floor with a deep thud. The ramp jerked up into the air and the creature's bony claws started to pull at the edge. She turned to watch Curtis sprinting fast down the front of the room and then noticed the short stump in his hand. The brief swell of elation drained straight out of her. What was he going to do when he got to it? He couldn't fight it bare-handed, and his other spear was on the ramp.

He started to curve away, picking his way over the broken statues until he was running straight at its rear. When he was a few yards away, he launched himself into the air and bounced off the stub jutting from its back. His second step took him onto its head and then he was on the ramp and sprinting up toward his spear. There was a creak and a rattle of chains and the long marble slab started to lower. An instant later he'd snatched up his weapon, spun, and was charging back down the slope. The creature reared up and was flailing its boney limbs when he steered the wooden point into its chest and the two of them slipped backward onto the ground in a cloud of pink dust.

She heard grunts of exertion and the whiplash crack of bone on wood and started to walk toward them, her feet gaining pace with each step. *My turn. Got to be quick this time.*

At the edge of the clearing she hesitated. Curtis had shoved the thrashing animal toward her and now it was only a few feet away. She became aware of her arms swinging loosely at her sides and doubt flooded her mind again. She didn't want to go out there. Now was the time to take her chance and go and find somewhere to hide.

The indecision left her frozen until a voice in her head gave her new courage. *The hypnotism is slowing me, but I can resist it. I'm here for a reason. I'm the one who can do this.*

With the warm barrel of the flamethrower tight in both hands, she slipped out of the line and focused on the back of the creature's head. *Don't hit it. Hit through it.* She lifted the weapon and swung it with all her might. A sharp crack cut the air. The impact shuddered down her arms and a splinter of casing flew into the darkness. For a horrible moment nothing happened, and then the giant insect crumpled to the floor and she was left standing face to face with Curtis.

He congratulated her, but his words were just a whisper, and before she could do anything he slumped slowly to his knees. Too stunned to move, she watched him sway for a few moments and then his eyes closed and he flopped sideways, his head dropping against the dusty ground with a soft thud and a puff of red powder. *Oh shit. Not him. Not now.* She dropped and checked his vital signs and then tried to revive him. She hit his face until her palm left a mark, then shouted and swore but nothing would wake him. He was out cold.

Pushing herself to her feet, she stood and squeezed her hands into fists. Her eyes flicked desperately around the big dark hall, but it didn't matter where she looked, the horrible truth was that she was on her own.

Chapter 48

Helga

The smell arrived before the smoke. The pungent aroma of burning gasoline coated Helga's nose and throat and loosened chunks of raw emotion from deep in her memory. She didn't want to deal with the feelings so she nudged them away, choosing instead to push herself to her feet and refocus her mind on the deadly battle that was going on in the depths of the temple beneath them. It had been ten minutes since the last faint pop of gunfire and the tension was slowly tightening knots in her stomach.

They should let us go down and help. It's always worse to hear a firefight than be in one. Once they start, time changes. Everything is slow. You have total focus then it's over. You survive, you're screaming for morphine or your light goes out. Not much in between.

Another strong waft of the petroleum scent came to her and this time the memories were irrepressible.

She was at the refinery on the Black Sea and the stink of smoldering oil was mixing with the salt spray blowing from the beach. It was dark and there were fumes curling around their heads but she wasn't alone. Vasily, Sergei and Klara were with her. They were four when they should've been eight. A Jeep had broken an axle and they hadn't had time to wait.

They had five minutes to clear a digger from the gate and secure the driveway for the regulars. Three of them had to take the perimeters and that left Vasily on his own, but that was okay. Nobody was strong like her Vasily. She couldn't watch because she had sixty degrees to cover, but she could listen. His grunts were loud and guttural and then there was a sudden creak of metal and something more like a scream. They'd known he'd done it then: pushed a four-ton barricade clean across the road.

When the uniforms had taken over, he'd been standing gripping the fence. At first they'd thought he'd been shot, but there were no holes, no blood. He'd looked at her with pride, moving close as if to kiss but with his smile turning to a grimace. His fingers had slipped from the mesh and he'd fallen and died at her feet.

They'd taken him back themselves and she'd sat in the morgue till dawn. Light had come from his face all that night, his features so clear and peaceful. She loved him more then. More in those five hours alone than any before. More than she'd thought possible. And all the time the burning gasoline smell had clung to their skin, hugging them like a shroud. It had taken days to scrub it off and maybe she hadn't wanted to. Maybe the kerosene aroma was a parting gift. Carbon rising to the sky while he went to the ground.

A shiver shot up her spine and she shook her head to snap the memory clear. *Coronary rush, they called it. They'd made us too strong. We had too much power. Too much pressure on the valves. Vasily was the first, but we've all got it. It was more than his heart could take.* She snorted away her welling tears and forced her fingers to run their habitual checks around her rifle. *More than mine could too.*

Chapter 49

Jodie

There was only darkness and uncertainty ahead of Jodie. Silent soldiers pressed close, and she kept the spear ready in one hand and the flamethrower swinging a protective arc in the other. With each step she got further from the flames at the front of the hall and her nervous glances revealed less and less of what surrounded her. The faces and woven tunics dimmed to a blur, and then the silhouettes slowly softened and she found herself creeping between lines of vague dark shapes.

Eventually she stopped, choked to a standstill by her fear of what might be waiting ahead. She chose a point in the mid-distance to lay down a blast of fire and was just tightening her finger when she noticed a faint iridescence and paused. About ten yards away the rows thinned and there was something white spread across the floor. She edged forward until the scene sharpened in front of her.

Just ahead, the statues had been pushed back to form a clearing, and in the middle of the space there was a circle of smooth white shells. It was the nest.

A flicker of movement made her jump. A low shadow had moved from left to right at the back of the site and then vanished. She heard a series of soft taps and her body jerked into action. The flamethrower was suddenly moving in her hand, hosing the perimeter with jets of orange flame.

When she released the trigger, thick smoke was stinging her eyes and the site was ringed with fire. She scanned for threats and noticed that just a few feet away there was a human arm bent awkwardly. She stepped closer and the mesh around the base of the eggs sharpened into a mass of twisted bodies. Faces emerged: sallow-cheeked Mongolians with their mouths open and their T-shirts thick with pink dust. She surveyed them with a mixture of pity and disgust. *Food. Food for the young.*

She was about to examine the bodies when one of the shells shivered and gave off a faint creak. She whipped her weapon around. *Oh shit. Those things are just about to hatch.*

Dropping the flamethrower onto its strap, she gripped the spear tight in both hands and stepped up to the nearest egg. With the point pressed hard against the middle, she lunged forward with her full strength. The casing gave way, the wooden shaft sank inside and then something moved. She leaped backward. The memory of the squirming sensation quivered up her arms, but something hardened inside her. As she watched the spear bouncing in the air in front of her, she replayed Curtis's words in her head. She had everything she needed. This was a job that just had to be done. No time for squeamishness.

She rammed the weapon deeper. A foul-smelling fluid slopped over her boots, but she kept on, driving the point toward the ground until the solid form inside was still.

Her fear kept her working. She moved around the big circle methodically destroying the eggs and the things inside them until she reached the final shell and found it broken and empty. Studying the ground in front of her she discovered a shiny trail leading out of the back of the clearing. *Oh crap.* She swung the weapon across the first row of soldiers. *One of those things is out there somewhere.*

There were long shapes stretched out on the ground where the wet dust vanished into the statues. When she got closer she discovered a young man and woman lying open-mouthed. Their cheeks and temples were striped with what she thought was tribal war paint but soon realized were streams of blood.

She flicked up her head and scanned the darkness. It was no use going hunting for it, the remaining lines of statues still left thousands of places to hide. She'd have to do what Curtis did; start knocking things over and hope that it came running out.

She stepped up to the nearest terracotta figure and prodded it. A firm shove started it rocking and she was about to push it over when something scuttled between the rows. *Fuck!* She threw herself backward. The creature burst out of the line and reared up. She pulled the trigger and her attacker was engulfed in a billowing mushroom of fire. Limbs flailed in the flames then its jaws stretched open and a mind-numbing screech cut the hot air.

She turned and ran.

The spear caught and was wrenched from her hands. The flamethrower snagged but she slipped it from her shoulder and kept moving, her shaking legs taking her fast down the column toward the front of the hall. She ignored the bumps and nudges and was soon bursting out of the line and running full pelt toward Curtis's body.

She dropped at his side and spun. Her pursuer was close behind, scuttling fast toward her like a scorpion. It was smaller than the adult but fast and fierce with sharp-looking fangs.

Her hands found her revolvers and she let loose a hail of bullets. It stopped, quivering and screaming until she'd emptied both guns. She grabbed Curtis's machete, and when she looked back it was rearing up a few feet away, its honeycomb faceplate blackened and sooty. She stepped forward to meet it.

Her first swipe knocked away a flailing arm and sent chips of bone into the air. She kept rhythm and swung back with full force. The blade sank into something soft, and stuck. A pair of spindly arms whipped across her shoulder. She yanked the knife free and swung again. It hacked through to thin air and the creature's head bounced off. The body swayed then fell and landed with tight-curled legs.

Holy fuck. I've killed it. Her hand found the ramp and she fell back. For a few moments there was a blissful silence, and then a rising haze blurred her vision and her world turned inside out.

Something fizzy buried into her belly and pushed a wave of nausea into her throat. Acid flooded her mouth and she buckled onto her knees and vomited. Her head spun and a babble of foreign voices chattered somewhere behind her eyes.

A second wave rose through her and she retched again. Hot stinging sweat broke out all over her body and she fell onto her side with a groan. The strange words boomed louder, like hundreds of transistor radios scanning through her brain. She spat out a mouthful of bile and then, as suddenly as it had begun, the pain vanished and there was calm.

She lay panting while the salty droplets cooled on her clammy skin. With each lengthening breath, a feeling of restfulness and well-being spread through her trembling muscles. *Jeez. What the hell was that? Thought I was going to die there.* Out of the corner of her eye she saw a cloudy haze float away from her and vanish between the rows of silent soldiers.

After propping herself up on her elbows, she lay staring at the point where the mist had vanished through the rows of statues. Tension began to creep back into her body and a sense of malice seemed to grow in the shadows that surrounded her. She pushed herself up into a sitting position and wiped her mouth. There was a steady crunching sound coming from deep in the hall that set her heart pumping loud in her ears again.

She snatched up the machete, rose shakily to her feet and hurried toward the foot of the ramp. At the base of the slope she paused and heard the unmistakable rhythm of footsteps. Her eyes darted across the rows of clay soldiers and caught a glimpse of movement. A young man and woman were marching slowly and mechanically down the central column.

She ran up the incline then stopped again. They had reached the front and were emerging from between the statues. The faint green and orange stripes on the girl's T-shirt triggered an image in Jodie's mind. It was the couple who had been lying by the empty egg. She'd been certain that they were dead but here they were coming toward her.

As she watched, their heads swiveled upward and their punctured black eyes locked hers. Their pace quickened and their lips peeled back. With their wet white teeth shining in the firelight, they moved straight past Curtis's body and broke into a run.

Fizzing with a massive pulse of adrenaline, Jodie turned and sprinted up the ramp.

She glanced at Jester as she ran into the statue chamber. *Oh, please be awake.*

He was lying exactly as they'd left him: flat and motionless with an ashen face.

The patter of fast footfalls was loud outside when she reached the weapons. She grabbed her shotgun and turned. The girl was close, her face twisted into a sickly grin. Jodie took aim and squeezed the trigger. *They're not people anymore. They're already dead.* When she'd fired both barrels, she reloaded and emptied the gun into the boy.

Her attackers slumped sideways and hit the floor with a thud. Without a second's hesitation she strode up to the corpses and lowered the weapon to their foreheads. *Quick and without doubt. Just like Curtis.* She put two loads into their brains and then walked slowly to the wall and leaned against it. With her gaze held on the limp bodies, she slid slowly to the ground. When she was certain that she was safe, she closed her eyes and let hot tears cleanse her cheeks.

Exhaustion dragged her into a kind of half-sleep and her dazed mind replayed the horrors of the last few hours, putting order to the scenes of violence and carnage, trying to reassure her that everything was going to be okay. Some survival processes deep in her brain kept her ears monitoring for sounds, and while she was putting together a plan of what to do next, a rustle from a few feet away jerked her into action. She pinged her eyes open and saw Jester sitting up, tapping the wound on his neck with his fingertips.

"Sorry Jodie," he said, taking time to coolly examine the ramp and the bodies before turning back to her. "Must've drifted off for a bit there. You were saying something about how much you needed me?"

Chapter 50

Cryboy

They left it at the bottom of the steps. Just sitting there. Useless. A total waste. A winch engine buzzed and Cryboy twitched up his head and watched the crane swing the metal lozenge out over the shaft. *Sliced straight through. Clean cut. Looked like machete work, so maybe Curtis did it. I thought he was on my side.*

Sudden movements and a squelch drew his eyes to where Jodie was hugging herself and treading her feet in the thick mud. He examined the inkblot patterns that were forming on the calves of her boots and felt his hands tighten to fists. *They needed those guns. She had to finish it on her own. Close call by the look of it. Nutjob got taken down. The kid collapsed. Whole thing nearly failed. I should have been with her. My weapons would have made the difference.*

The shadows from the floodlights started twisting on the damp ground and he looked out to see the coffin spinning above the center of the borehole. As he watched, a guy rope pulled it steady and an analysis of the forces that were playing on the suspended load started to run in his mind then got snapped clear by his frustration. *I get called in when the action's over. Then they want the UGVs. I move the box. Cover the withdrawal. Dumb outsourcing shit. Clean-up work. Weaver should know better. He knows how good I am with the robots. He should be telling Maddie to use me more. As soon as they realize that the eggs in Washington have hatched they're going to come begging for help.*

A steady clunking sound cut the air as the chain started to lower link by link. He glanced at the reader on his forearm and checked that his inbox was still empty. *I wonder what he made of my report. The evidence was all there to see. The young were hatching. Two of the victims were sucked dry then got reanimated and walked up the ramp. Her story rings true. No reason to lie.*

He started to rock backward and forward, his arms straight at his side, his hands opening and closing into fists. *This stuff is changing all the rules. We should be taking it more seriously and trying to learn from these things; scanners and analysis gear in the coffins at the very least. At the start it made sense to keep it secret, but maybe it's too late for that. These hacking attempts Weaver's fussing over. They're routed through an offshore platform, but it's got to be Canmore. He's got good reason to keep his eyes on Sophos and must have got a leak about the missions. He's got no detail though. No way his guys will crack my core firewalls, and that leaves him guessing. He either wants to stop us or get his hands on these things himself, and who can blame him? They'd make a hell of a bio weapon.*

The steel links loosened and started to rise. There was a series of insistent beeps then a dump truck backed to the edge of the shaft and started to dump a slurry of concrete into the darkness.

When the first load had been emptied, Maddie turned and flashed them a pointed look. "Okay," she said loudly. "Let's get going guys. The Mongolians don't want us hanging around."

He moved past his teammates toward the nearest of their three waiting vehicles, eager for the warmth and seclusion of its powerful comms booth.

There was a distinctive call tone from Maddie's communicator and he stopped. Three fast triple chimes was Weaver's direct line and it meant something important. He turned and saw their organizer lower her chin and study the controls on her collar.

"Hi, Julian. You got my message?"

"Yes …" Weaver's voice boomed out of the radio. "Literally about three minutes ago. The truck diverted to your personal."

"Good …" She turned to look at the group. "You're on speaker now. We're all here."

"Ah. Right. Brilliant! I have to say, well done guys. I'm absolutely over the moon. You all okay? Has the box been buried?"

"Yep," Maddie glanced over her shoulder. "Concrete's going in now."

"Good. And what about the injuries?"

Cryboy shuffled a little closer. It would be interesting to see how she replied to that. The truth was they'd all been knocked out or injured in some way and Weaver knew it because he himself had filed his own report. Most curious of all was Jodie's account of voices in her head. The timing was too close to be coincidence. It had to be a sort of possession, and that meant that even some of the wildest theories in the scrolls might be true.

He noticed that Maddie examined each of the strike force carefully, waiting until they met her eyes and gave her a nod of affirmation before she replied.

"Not so bad. A few cuts and bruises but we're all okay."

"Great," Weaver replied. "That's good to hear. I'm afraid I've got some mixed news for you though. The best part is that the UGV mission at Fort Wainwright is one hundred percent complete and they found nothing at all. There were some bodies, some half-dead guards, but absolutely no sign of any creatures. The bad news is that in Washington the robots failed and that means we'd like you to go back and try again."

Cryboy scanned his teammate's faces looking for clues but saw nothing that was obviously decipherable.

"So does that sound okay?" Weaver asked. There was a pause and then a short muffled cough. "I mean … are all of you up for that?"

Jodie started nodding and the others turned to look at her. Her face was more serious than usual, somehow stiff and fixed. "Yes. We can do it," she said loudly. "We're the only ones who know how."

"What about equipment and supplies?" Weaver asked. "Anything we can get for you?"

Curtis lifted his head. "Yes. I've got some plans I'm going to talk over with Cryboy. We'll need some gear ready for when we land."

That sounded intriguing. What kind of plan would the young shaman need him for? It would be good to see how they could work together. He did actually seem able to do some cool stuff and they'd definitely make a good team.

"Fine. No problem," Weaver replied. "That's what we're here for. We hope to get you into the White House in about six hours from now. Anything that's humanly possible in that time will be done."

"Good. Thanks." Curtis took a step forward and put his hand to his chin. "And another thing …"

"Yes."

"I need to ask you about the history of all this."

"The history?" There was a note of surprise in Weaver's voice. "Sure."

Curtis leaned forward and his face took on a new intensity. "We need to be invested now."

"Sorry?" Weaver's voice was strained. "I'm not with you."

"The history of this. The manuscripts you've got. The different sources. They all talk about what to do when this happens."

"Well, yes … there's some variation but—"

Curtis took a short step closer to the microphone, his voice suddenly louder and clearer. "They suggest forming a group of warriors to tackle the infestation."

"Uh … yes," Weaver confirmed.

"Well, we've become that group. The person who brought us together needs to name us. There's power in the naming."

Power in the naming? Cryboy could see that the other team members were just as confused as him. Jester was pulling a face and the girl was frowning with her head on one side. She looked good like that; her hair was blowing in the breeze and he wanted to go over and touch it.

Weaver cleared his throat. "Right. I think I'm kind of following you … Did you say 'There's a power in the naming'?"

"Yes." Curtis continued to nod. "Yes I did. There's a name for this force, this group of warriors, isn't there?"

"Yeah. Well lots. Each account …"

"Roughly the same name in all the different languages?"

"I suppose so. Yes."

"We need the name. Tell us what it is."

"Well … right, I see what you mean. *Hammer against our enemy* is the common translation. *Foehammer* in the ancient Norse."

"Yeah." Curtis cast his eyes slowly around the group. "That's it. Now you need to name us, Dr. Weaver."

"Name you?"

"Say it. Say who we are."

"Well." The line fell silent. "Okay. I see what you mean. For these jobs … yes, I see your point. I suppose you are."

Curtis studied each of the group in turn, and then Weaver's voice cut loud and clear through the night air.

"Everyone. Everybody who is working together to do this. Firstly, I thank you, and secondly I name you. I name you *Foehammer*. You are *Foehammer*."

Curtis gave each of them a pointed look then turned and started to walk to the truck.

Cryboy stood transfixed while he allowed the conversation to sink in. In a way it made sense. The scrolls did all talk about a team called Foehammer. Maybe the Ferguson kid was right. Maybe they needed to take the role more seriously. It certainly sounded cool. The secrecy requirements were a total bummer though. He'd have *loved* to have got online and told the hacking community that he was part of an ancient warrior cult. The problem was, nobody could ever know.

Chapter 51

Helga

The whole experience had been strangely frustrating. She'd had nothing to do in the temple, and even when they'd heard that the creatures needed boxing and moving out, her strength hadn't been required. Cryboy had wheeled in big load shifters and the job had been completed deep in the bowels of the building. It was how it was supposed to be. They were just backup and if things went according to plan they weren't meant to be needed. This was important. What had happened down there sounded pretty shocking and they now knew for certain that all the terrible things that Weaver had warned them about were true. That meant that she had to stay well away from the arthropods or risk hypnosis and a horrible death.

It helped to remind herself what she *had* done. According to news reports and messages from her friends, their secret mission on Kotelny had already changed things in Russia. The conspiracy theories had faded away and faith in the democratically elected government had been restored. There was peace on the streets and growing confidence in the economy.

She'd been part of that. Just a handful of them had changed the fate of her country, and the feeling of satisfaction kept growing with each passing moment. But it was keeping her awake. Maybe not just the good stuff. It was probably the strange combination of exhilaration and frustration that meant she couldn't relax, and this left her almost on her own. Her companions had all fallen asleep in their seats and only Cryboy was making any noise, tapping at his micro while their vehicle crept through the darkened Mongolian countryside toward the airport.

When they finally reached the plane, their organizer stood in the aisle of the truck and addressed her with her hands on her hips.

"Helga, honey …" she said, sweeping her eyes across the sleeping forms of her comrades. "I know you must be just as tired as these guys, but do you think you could carry them onto the jet?"

"Carry them?" Helga smiled at the American lady. She obviously didn't know her yet if she thought that she was tired or would struggle to lift a human body. "Even strong Curtis and the big heavy Mr. Jester here? Yes, Maddie, I can."

She dropped into a squat in front of Jodie and slipped her arms under her back and knees. The girl hardly weighed anything and she quickly pushed herself upright and moved carefully down the aisle to the rear door.

When she got back, both the men were still asleep. She slid along the seat toward Curtis and reached for his arm. As she gripped his wrist his eyes flicked open and he met her gaze with a tired smile.

"Hi Helga," he said sleepily.

She wasn't surprised that he knew what was going on around him. Even when he was asleep he was aware of what was happening. She slid off the seat and let him move past her. He stood for a moment gazing at the rear door and then patted her gently on the arm before setting off down the central aisle. Her eyes followed him sympathetically. He'd been working hard. It wasn't just the fighting, it was the shaman stuff too. The whole time they were down there he had to protect the girl and that meant part of his mind working on another plane.

She moved to the other side of the table and surveyed Jester's sprawling body with a faint smile. He could be angry and nasty to some people but he'd always been polite to her. She knew why. It was because she'd served and she somehow knew that he divided the world into those who had and those who hadn't.

She had tucked herself under his shoulder and was just starting to pull him along the seat when he groaned and his eyelids flickered. A moment later, he lifted his head and opened his eyes.

"Hi, Mom," he said, looking around the cabin and fighting back a yawn. "We at the plane?"

She nodded and then felt a firm pressure on her shoulder as he started to nudge her off the bench. "Come on then. We can't keep the others waiting just 'cause you wanted a secret snuggle."

"No!" she said quickly. "I going to carry—" She saw the twinkle in his eye and checked herself, moving out of the way to let him slide off.

He stretched and dabbed at the gash on his neck before looking back at her. "Totally understandable. There's not a woman on the planet doesn't give it a try if she's left alone with me."

He stuffed a couple of cigarettes into his mouth and started for the door. A few steps later she came close to bumping into him when he stopped suddenly and sparked up his lighter.

"It's not that you're not an attractive lady, you understand. Just that you're going to need all your energy for this next mission."

"Thank you," she replied, smiling to herself as she followed him out into the cool night air. "But somehow I manage to control myself."

The jet had leveled out and they were being propelled through the sky at some insane speed when Maddie sighed and rested her hand on her leg.

"Thanks Helga," she said kindly. "And well done. We did good tonight."

"Yes we did," she replied. "That poor girl had a bad time down there, but she did it. She's tough. Strong inside."

"Yes she is." Maddie confirmed. "We all did okay. We're a team now. We all do our bit."

On hearing the last few words, Helga felt a tightness in her chest and found herself struggling to contain an ocean of feelings she couldn't quite define. Without planning what she was going to say, she found herself trying to describe her emotions to the American.

"You know, it is good to be working with these people," she said slowly. "I am glad to be part of this team." She tapped Maddie's thigh. "Let me tell you something. When I was child, both my parents died. I went to a special school. A good place, but for children who are alone. They were hard and strict but we were safe." She took a long breath, still unaware of the exact sentiments she was trying to express but compelled to keep talking. "There was a man, Mr. Sidorov, who taught us sports. He was old but very strong. I liked him. If we went out from school on buses, I would fall asleep. When we came back I would keep my eyes closed and pretend to still be sleeping. Mr. Sidorov would walk down the bus and I would be very happy to feel his weight on the floor. I would try not to show smile on my face. He would lift me. So strong but gentle, I would smell him, his shirt, the smell from his body, you know? He would hold me and carry me to my bed. And I would like to pretend. I would imagine …"

She found herself needing to clear her throat, and after several short coughs she continued. "I would imagine this man was my father. Hugging me, taking me to a bed in our own house."

Feeling briefly exposed, she turned and looked out of the small window at the blank, dark sky and wisps of passing cloud. Further out on the tip of the wing a single red light blinked on and off and the outline of her face was reflected back at her. She felt Maddie put her hand on her knee and give it a squeeze and reminded herself that it was okay to say these things; it took bravery to share your emotions with your teammates, and in the end it made everybody stronger.

When her breathing seemed easier again she looked over her shoulder at the figures in the seats behind her. "Tonight you know, when I was lifting them and they were sleeping, something similar happened, and I think that these people … were mine. My children … my babies.' She pressed the back of her hand to each of her cheeks, smudged away the moisture and turned to look at Maddie, who smiled and gave a couple of gentle nods.

She had nothing else to say, and as she sat reflecting on what she'd just confessed, she realized that she was exhausted, not physically but emotionally. They had underestimated the strain of waiting on the surface while three of the team went and did battle below. She would have preferred to have more to do but she knew the hypnosis was real and she knew that the Curtis boy was struggling even to protect himself and the girl. That left them with the nerve-straining job of just waiting and listening. It was tough, but she was going to have to get used to it.

After a long yawn she let her head fall back and started to drift into a doze. Maddie had also closed her eyes, and the rest of the team seemed to be asleep. She remembered that there was a mild sedative released by the plane's air-conditioning system and was glad of it.

After just a few minutes she found herself floating on the line between wakefulness and stupor and her mind filled with a series of images. She saw Maddie's face lit in the warm glow from the warning flash on the tip of the aircraft's wing, and then she had a vision of the small plane from the outside, whirls of vapor spinning off its stubby wings as it hurtled through the darkness toward the top of the world and the very edge of space. She found the idea strangely comforting and allowed herself to fall backward into the weightless embrace of sleep.

Chapter 52

Spiritwalker

As their vehicle bounces down the slope to the ancient flood plain, Curtis hears the shouts of youngsters he cannot see but presumes hidden in the grass. The children soon appear, running alongside the jeep pointing and laughing with a raw uncontrolled delight. The words and sounds are an echo to him. Faint but familiar impressions that rise from somewhere deep in his mind and wait to be given a meaning.

He ignores the kids, keeping his chin high and his eyes straight as they pull to a halt by the gate in the mud wall. He is tested and proven, a returning traveler with the double-swiped scar of the warrior clear and vivid on his brow.

The seer arrives in the village when the shadows are long and the women are slapping dough onto hot rocks. Standing hunched on the edge of the meeting circle, he carefully scans each new face but avoids looking anyone directly in the eye. When the food is ready, he takes a loaf and slips inside the darkness of the main hut. Curtis keeps his gaze on the low doorway while he stuffs strips of bread and bean paste into his mouth. He eats, he watches and he waits.

When every bowl has been scraped clean, the chief and the seer emerge from the dwelling and stand talking. The two men briefly squeeze each other's shoulders and then the chief walks into the firelight glow and takes the prime position in the circle. The seer doesn't join them. Curtis's eyes follow him as he slips into the shadows between the nearest huts and disappears.

After making a short speech of introduction, the chief asks Curtis to join him and they face each other in the center of the group. "You have grown tall ..." he says, "but fat." He pinches the tiny roll of spare skin around Curtis's stomach and there is a peel of laughter from the group.

Next there is a trial of strength. The chief offers his raised palm to push against and Curtis puts up enough resistance to earn respect and then allows himself to slip backward across the smooth baked ground.

The onlookers laugh and clap.

"A strong man!" the leader announces. "He will hunt with us. He is welcome."

"Leave the village now." The chief is whispering in his ear, his breath brushing his neck while an acid tang of sweat rises from his dusty skin. "Find the seer. He has gone north. You must follow him."

Curtis steps slowly backward out of the firelight and then turns and slips into the darkness between the huts. Dogs bark and jump at his heels, following him to the gap in the wall where they collapse onto their bellies and watch him walk out onto the dusty plain with lazy thoughtful eyes.

A short distance into the savanna a branch has been broken from a bwazi shrub and used to sweep the ground. Dropping to a crouch, he presses his fingertips against the earth and scans for markings. He nods and finds himself smiling. There is a drawing of a wolf scratched in the mud. His power animal. Nobody knows this. He has told no one.

He rises and peers across the plain. The night is clear and the African stars are glittering in the vast ebony dome above him. A few yards ahead he spots another patch of swept ground and treads forward to examine it.

It's another simple artwork: the outline of a toad. He knows instantly that this is the only clue he will be given. It's a test. There will be no tracks to follow. The message is clear: *Find me and you will be worthy.*

He sucks in a deep breath and feels the anticipation build inside him. This is the opportunity of a lifetime. The seer is one of the most powerful and respected in West Africa. Passing the test will bring new insights and powerful secrets. He is certain that no one so young has ever been offered this before.

He moves a little further into the bush and settles in a shallow bowl between the roots of a gnarled yohimbe tree. With his legs crossed and his eyes closed he begins to rock. A low murmur emerges in his throat and he shapes it into his chant. The noise is at first slow and quiet but as he sways it finds its own voice and rhythm, becoming so regular and so constant that it soon vanishes altogether. His body goes and only the faint sounds of the night insects remain. For a while they too fade to nothing then return, along with all the traces of life around him, deafeningly loud. He hears the tree's microscopic roots pushing into the soil deep below him and feels the moisture being dragged out of the ground. He focuses on these sensations until there is nothing else, and then he unbalances himself and prepares to embrace the abyss. He sways, almost weightless, on the brink of a high undefined darkness then the tunnel opens behind him and he falls back into it, tumbling and twisting through loops of spinning air until pressure slowly builds below him and he slows.

The next thing he knows he has settled upright and is floating toward a couple of smooth-worn footpaths on a landscape of baked earth. His descent takes him to the crossroads where the two tracks meet and places him in front of a hunched figure sitting on a tree stump.

The old man is wrapped in a simple blanket woven from undyed wool. His skin is deep mahogany and creased like shriveled leather. There are red markings on his brow and a walking stick propped between his withered legs.

Curtis waits until the dust settles then lands, kneels, and draws a toad quickly on the ground. When he looks up, the man is holding a thin slab of rock between both palms. He opens his hands and the stone splits. The inside is trickling with moisture. Two skin-smooth lids open on a pair of large domed eyes and a toad is visible nestled into the contours of the rock. The old man laughs and Curtis smiles and nods; he already *knew* this. This knowledge is part of an infinite recurring dream.

The elder and the pathways have gone. He opens his eyes and looks out across the dimly lit plain, gradually aware that he is a young man with aching legs and a stone sticking into his calf. After a few minutes, he stands, dusts himself down and sets out in a new direction, this time due east. In his mind he can see a low line of hills. Somewhere among the mounds there is a crack in the rock. At the bottom of the ravine there's a cave where moisture trickles down the cool stone walls. The seer will be waiting for him there.

In less than an hour's walk, a low ridge emerges on the horizon. He climbs the lower slopes in the milky starlight and allows himself to be drawn to a long seam of granite sticking up near the crest. He crouches and spots a fissure that broadens into a thin trench. He slips through and finds himself on a ledge at the top of a narrow ravine.

The seer is lying in a hammock when Curtis drops in front of him. The old man opens his eyes, fixes him with an infinite glassy stare and then starts to laugh.

The sliver of sky above them is brightening by the time they have finished drinking several cups of bush tea.

"You travel." The shaman has leaned forward and is addressing his words to the top of Curtis's chest. "Your father and mother take you to other tribes."

Curtis nods hesitantly, his brain slow to process the words then struggling to identify what is being phrased as a statement and what as a question.

"And not just here." The old man taps the ground with his stick. "Not just on this soil. You go to other lands." Here the seer drops in three words in English, pronouncing them carefully as if his mouth and tongue were actually summoning them into being. "Europe, Asia, America. In these places, you have learned with other seers."

Curtis nods and his companion stands and starts explaining how they will work together while pacing up and down the narrow gorge. The deal is going to be two-way. Curtis will learn but he will also share. There is a balance to this that he finds instantly acceptable.

After a handful of cold dry bread and many more cups of tea, the old man leans forward again. "So tell me of your dreams. You are visited. This I know. Tell me of those who come to you."

Curtis lowers his gaze to his feet. "There are people … on the other side … when they come they're very strong. Very big." He lifts his hands in front of his face, slopping hot tea onto his bare toes. "They fill the space. They are like us. They are like humans, only bigger and stronger."

The seer nods slowly and knowingly and then questions him. "How many? How many have you counted?"

"Twelve," he replies.

"And who came to you first?"

He describes the massive figure wielding the stone hammer, and the shaman bends forward until he is almost touching his knees. "And the others?" he asks. "Tell me of them."

Curtis recalls everything he can about the size and shape of the twelve entities, the colors that fill them and the sense of immense power that they pervade.

When he has finished, the older man leans back and nods. "What you have seen are called the mysteries," he says. "Have you heard that we can use their strength? Have you heard that these can become one with you?"

"Yes." Curtis tells him.

"And you would like to be able to use their power?"

"Yes."

"And me!" The seer slaps his palms on his thighs. "I will help you and you will help me. Together we will learn to break mountains!"

Back to Washington

Thursday, July 15

Chapter 53

Weaver

Dr. Julian Weaver stood at his office window staring down at the dots of people scurrying around on the streets below and scrunched the data printout tighter in his fist. The background level of frustration that he'd been living with for the previous few weeks was building into an urgent anger and he was unable to stop it. He'd been operating on his own for too long. He had assistants and co-workers but nobody who understood his position and nobody he could share his fears and doubts with. More than ever he felt alienated from the New Yorkers surrounding him, and he'd suddenly decided that it was their fault. After all, why weren't they doing anything? Why didn't they read what was on the opennet? He wanted them to protest or to demonstrate. He wanted them to do *something*. At least then he wouldn't feel so alone in his struggle. Instead, they seemed happier than ever to float around in a bubble of inane distractions. TV voting was at a record high. Sixty percent of the population were watching *Seduction* or one of its many spin-off shows. Virtual networking was up fifteen percent since the start of outbreak and it was driving him crazy. Did all those guys really still believe there was a virus? How could they be so brain dead?

"Wake up!" he shouted, flinging the ball of paper onto the carpet. "Do something! You haven't seen your president for seven weeks. Doesn't that bother you? Are reality shows enough? Is that all it takes to keep you quiet? Are you asleep out there?"

Turning from the glass, he paced backward and forward with his arms flapping at his side and then stopped and let his shoulders drop. He took a few deep breaths, and when his heart rate had slowed he slowly circled the room, switching off the monitors and AI suites that lined the walls before slumping into his chair.

For a while he sat staring at the dark pools widening on the surface of his coffee, then he rested his forehead on his knuckles and watched the vapor from his cup float up through the slabs of sunlight that penetrated the blind.

He hadn't done enough. He hadn't found that extra something that they were going to need that night, and the thought was eating him up. The eggs in the West Wing had hatched; he knew that, and he suspected that everybody else did too. The net guns in the robots probably weren't going to help much either. The target recognition systems were suspect and everybody except the salesmen doubted them.

All they really had was Curtis's plan and that didn't sound like much. The drills had a lot of reinforced concrete to get through and then what? He couldn't see how any of the cloudbuster stuff was going to work at all. No. He had to be honest. The situation was hopeless. And while he was sitting fretting about the team, where was his support? Sophos and Glover made the right noises when he gave his updates, but once they'd chucked more money at him all they did was retreat to the safety of their yachts and airships. Even worse, now they'd decided that the job was doable, they'd started pulling staff onto other projects. He only had seventy percent of the analysts he'd started with, and now that Cryboy was away they were missing a cyber-defense specialist. It shouldn't have mattered but the reports of hacking attempts were racking up, and as the whole mission was meant to be top-secret that was something of a concern.

He allowed his arms to slide until his forehead was pressing onto the tabletop. Fatigue was starting to overwhelm him and he found his mind flooding with the worries and fears that he normally managed to keep at bay. Worst of all was the idea that he might soon be sitting in the same spot reading the news that they were all dead. The thought was both devastatingly tragic and incredibly unfair. He'd done his best but he'd never been right for the job. They'd only picked him because he had a good knowledge of the scrolls, but in reality he probably hadn't taken any of the accounts seriously enough at the start. It wasn't all his fault, though. The billionaires had made all the early decisions and it was them who'd decided to get an academic to run a military operation. Now perhaps they were about to discover that throwing cash at a problem didn't always deliver the right results.

Chapter 54

Cryboy

He had so many camera feeds that he'd had to divide one of the spare screens into sixteenths just to fit all of them in. Some of them were perhaps not necessary, and some of them he was perhaps not meant to be viewing. The parking and security cameras on the other trucks had taken a little while to hack but they'd been so close and so tempting it had been impossible to resist.

When he had each image exactly the size he wanted it, he sat back on the comms booth's bench and gave himself some time to reflect on the big picture. He knew he could be too easily sucked in to the detail, but now more than ever it was important that he looked at the whole and not just the parts. First, he needed to be certain that he could deliver everything that Curtis needed. He wasn't exactly clear how the end stages of the plan were meant to work, but he was determined that his contributions would be a hundred percent precise.

His eyes settled on the central interface, and he checked the readings from his high altitude blimp. It was still tracking the progress of the lead truck with pinpoint accuracy. The silver iodide dispersal was running smoothly and he could already see hot wet air forming in convection currents above its envelope.

His middle machine was set to cracking a strange little puzzle that Weaver had sent him. The AIs were freaked by this broken missile platform on the roof of the West Wing, and they were right. There was something odd about it, and whenever his other simulators slowed down he would turn and give it some brain time.

Next to grab his attention were the UGVs in the trucks behind them. He was soon going to get the chance to operate all seven simultaneously. There weren't many who could handle that many, and he was fairly certain that this time she'd notice how easily he did it.

Just as he was starting to fantasize about her, a hand with slim fingers and painted nails gripped the curtain, the fabric was pulled back and Jodie looked in at him.

"Hi," she said casually. "Maddie says you can help me look things up."

He swallowed hard while he selected the best response. "Yeah, I can help," he told her. "Don't have long though." His eyes flicked to the navigation app in the corner of the display. "We'll be there in seven." He waited for a reply and then looked up and saw that she was squinting curiously at the cloud-seeding sequence running on the main monitor. He was trying to figure out how much of it she might be able to understand when she turned and widened her eyes expectantly.

"She says you can tell me anything I need to know."

The scrolling data streams in front of him drifted out of focus as he considered the comment. *Yes I know more than anyone else, but there are gaps. In complex systems it's not possible* ... He checked himself. *She doesn't literally mean anything. It's just an expression.*

A quick sideways glance revealed that she was still staring at him expectantly. When he met her gaze, she flashed her eyes at the bench and he flushed hot. *The seat. She wants to come and sit next to me.* For a while he stared at the array of keyboards and controllers in front of him and then he slid against the wall.

"Thanks." Before he knew it she was right next to him, the scent of warm sweat rising from her body. Her thigh touched his and electric tingles ran through his groin and stomach.

She directed a finger at the central screen. "Team choices. Personnel selection. That kind of stuff."

"Yes. It's all here," he told her. "All accessible. Transparent. Weaver wanted it like that."

She pushed up the curls at the back of her neck. "Yeah, So I heard."

For a while she sat rubbing her left ear, and then she spoke in a long-drawn-out voice, stretching her words lazily in a way that sounded startlingly similar to the actresses in the opennet videos. "Thing I want to know. Thing I want you to help me look up … is why me?"

"Why you?"

"Yeah." She flicked her head toward the lounge area. "Those guys are all unique. All experts. You too. But why me? I can shoot, but I had no combat experience." She lifted her hands off the desk, palms held upward. "I'm just a girl. They must have known it was going to be physical down there."

He let his fingers dance over the controllers. *Finally she's interested in selection. I can show her how thorough we were, the quality of the research and analysis.* "There you go," he said, nodding at the screen. "Decision synopsis. There were multiple analysts, mostly AI with some—"

"Yeah, yeah." She waved her hands and squinted at the screen. "Bonding and cohesive effect? Mediator, moderator, connector? Were you involved in this? Do you know what it means?"

He nodded. "Well, yeah. Curtis and Jester failed the team tests, see. Both mavericks … lone players."

"So?"

"So, you three needed to be a team. The third member had to be able to pull everyone together."

"But why not a guy?" she asked. "Someone strong and experienced?"

"No space for a man. Too many egos. Had to be a young female. Look … 'Fraternal and paternal bonding will aid cohesion and encourage supportive combat behaviors.'"

"Wait a sec. *Paternal*? Jester's got a daughter?"

"Yeah. I found her actually. She's in Seattle."

"And she's around my age? Jeez."

"Yeah. There's a detailed psych profile …"

Her fingers touched the back of his hand and he felt his buttocks tighten.

"It's okay, I get it. Same age as Curtis's sister and Jester's daughter … Wow." She pushed herself up on her arms and started to swivel off the bench. "Okay, thanks."

"Wait a sec." He showed her the link on the screen. "There was a second deciding factor."

"Yeah?"

"Yes. Latent potential."

"What's that?"

"That's kind of the energy that a system isn't using yet."

She snorted and pushed her way through the curtain. "Yeah, well … that's good. 'Cause I reckon we're about to need that one."

Chapter 55

Jodie

The first part was a blur. Jodie hovered near the rear door watching Cryboy guide a line of UGVs across the driveway and then she was out of the truck standing on the darkening tarmac scanning her surroundings.

The evening was warm. Spirals of leaves were blowing around her boots and the air felt tight and heavy. The floodlit facade of the West Wing was casting a ghoulish luminosity onto the lawn, and the overall effect only added to her sense of drifting into a recurring dream.

When the column of gun platforms and mobile drilling rigs was lined up along the side of the building, Maddie turned and gave her an expectant look. Their organizer didn't need to speak. They knew the plan and it was the same as usual. The three of them were to go ahead while the others waited as backup.

Creeping in behind one of the big battlefield robots would have been nice, but Jester still refused to work alongside them. There'd been plenty of heated debate over the previous few days and it seemed a compromise had eventually been reached. The slim cylindrical machine left at the back of the truck obviously met his stipulations, and when he'd given it a playful kick they followed it toward the covered walkway.

As they approached the service entrance, she looked down at the tower of armored metal and asked him why he'd agreed to use it.

"It's specially adapted for us," he told her. "Manual control only. Let me show you how it's set up."

She didn't particularly want to learn how to operate such a brutal piece of military hardware, but after he'd stressed very pointedly that she might need to use it on her own, she allowed him to guide her through the controls.

It had been specifically designed to fit through the squeeze space in the bunker and held custom-made ammunition such as steel nets that were meant to be able to capture the insect creatures. It was impressive and she couldn't help thinking that if they'd had two or three similar devices from the start they would have found life much easier. But then she remembered that initially nobody had really known what they were going to encounter. It seemed that the truth about combat operations was that you never knew exactly what you were going to need until after the event.

The entrance area was exactly as she remembered it. The trolley of stacked linen stood unchanged against the wall and her heels made the same sharp click on the tiled floor.

Jester stopped at the fire doors, and when she saw the warm yellow light through the porthole windows she flooded with vivid memories. She felt herself moving along the same space just a few days previously and an echo of trembling weakness returned to her legs and stomach.

Metal clinked behind her and she turned to see Curtis shifting a long canvas bag on his shoulder.

Why was he dragging something heavy around when he hated being weighed down? He'd remained typically tight-lipped about his special plan and she got no time to quiz him. Jester took his teammate's arrival as a cue to continue, and for the second time that week he pushed open the doors and led them inside.

Snapping her weapon left and right revealed nothing new; the terrible sewage smell had intensified and the scattering of shapes at the T-junction suggested that the half-deads they'd shot were still there, but there was no sign of danger.

The sense of unreal repetition intensified with each passing moment, and she had to force her eyes to move quickly, struggling to keep her movements alert and focused when part of her felt as if it was drifting through a dream. It was all the same but different. They'd followed a machine down there before and here they were again.

They caught sight of a pair of figures lying in a window bay and set off toward them. The stench thickened as they approached, and they were soon able to make out a couple of half-deads with their heads slumped and their arms hanging at their sides. There was something different about them, and when she saw the tight transparent skin on the men's cheeks and hands she became certain that they weren't a threat. They were dead. Properly dead.

Jester sent the robot to monitor the intersection and Curtis crouched and started to examine the corpses. After a brief inspection he announced that there were no bullet holes and that the guards had probably just wasted away.

Jester responded with a shrug and they turned and continued down the passageway.

The building stayed eerily quiet and they moved without incident around the sad sprawl of dead guards and were soon through the nanoscanner and into the Situation Room.

They followed the softly whirring machine down the side of the long meeting table and came to a halt at the entrance to the bunker. There was a UGV parked at the top of the steps that hadn't been there before, but otherwise the place seemed unchanged.

Curtis sat and began the ritual of putting himself into a trance and they found themselves waiting.

Jodie struggled to remember how many times they'd watched the young black kid slip away into the spirit world and found that her recollections of the previous few days were confused. They'd done too many things in too many places and she was glad that one way or another it was all coming to an end.

After a couple of minutes Jester caught her eye and asked her how she was. She pursed her lips and shook her head but he pressed the issue.

"What we are about to do," he insisted. "How do you feel about it?"

"Nothing," she replied with a shrug.

"Nothing!" he said dramatically. "Nothing will come of nothing. Speak again."

She took a while to gather her thoughts and then told him that she just wanted to get the job done. He started nodding and she added with an ironic smile that it would also be really nice to come out alive and unhurt. He seemed satisfied with her answer and grinned at her while he teased a couple of cigarettes out of their packet.

"So what about you?" she asked. "How has all this been for you?"

He stuck a flame to his Marlboros and sucked them to life. "This? This is good." He blew smoke at the ceiling. "I was bored. Now I'm not."

That was him. She was finally getting to know this sad angry man and that last comment was just him all over.

Chapter 56

Dry irritable skin

The roots of the Lifetree rolled Curtis backward into the void. When he'd spun for a time that couldn't be measured, he emerged at the intersection of a myriad tight capillaries and waited for them to solidify into tunnels.

The first channel showed him just energy, and he was quickly able to find the yellow glow of the female and cover her in protective layers. Next would be an exploration; he needed to push himself outwards and find new views and visions.

A pulse of suction took him onto the hot sand of an endless red desert. Around him, cactus and thistle were contracting their leaves in mourning to the departing sun. As he sat waiting, a double line of black ants started to cross his outstretched legs. He sensed birds, large raptors circling on high thermals above him and smaller insect-feeders hopping around his feet. The ground under him resonated with the scuttling of tiny paws as rodents sniffed and twitched their way from burrow to burrow. His body felt their passage, the tiny avalanches of silica rising through his buttocks and echoing faintly in his jaw bone.

Soon he was a leaf spinning and tumbling in the breeze to the nearest wall. Pressing himself against its skin, he gave his imprint in return for a sensation of what lay on the other side. There was a faint sign of a wolf creature, angry, hungry and burning in an unnatural heat, and then he was bounced away.

As a yellow-white butterfly, he rose and brushed against a second pulsing wall. The skin flashed him a mass of writhing snakes twisted with incurable hunger, then the sensation numbed.

Now a darting woodrat, he brushed the tips of his fur against another barrier. The contact was enough to open a yawning sense impression of a host of dry hungry insects. He felt a splinter of time flash into human panic then flattened himself to nothing.

The nectar taste of the pollen stayed with him. The gritty quartz patterns of the cooling sand remained pressed into his skin but he started to change. Having protected the female and learned what he needed to know, he was ready to leave. Now he needed to divide. As a knot of tumbling thorn bush, he would stay and seek his spirit guides. The human he would send back. He filled the boy with all the experiences required and then released him.

Curtis opened his eyes and studied the two nearby figures. As he began to match their energy patterns with names and memories, he became aware of something uncomfortable that had traveled with him. His experience of the nest of insect creatures had solidified into a web of tar-like essence that had lodged between his stomach and chest. It was dangerous to transport this thing between worlds and he immediately began to break it down. He had to dissolve every last taste of it before he was fully awake. For him, this sensation was something deeper and richer than language, but for them it had a name. They called it *fear*.

Chapter 57

Jodie

"You okay, dancing boy?" Jester asked, standing and grinding out his cigarettes with his foot.

She watched Curtis as he nodded, observing the hesitant movement of his head and the dullness of his eyes with concern. He looked wiped out. He seemed to be getting more tired all the time and that was a worry. One thing she was sure about was that they'd need him on this mission more than ever.

The young shaman pushed himself to his feet and slipped a hand inside his jacket pocket. When he'd teased out a length of gnarled root, he moved up and stood in front of her. "I'll just give you the third eye again, Jodie," he said softly, and she gave a nod of acknowledgment.

She listened to his strange hypnotic chant while he traced ellipses on her forehead and spent the time refocusing and remotivating herself, using the circular sensation on her skin to try to pull strength and energy from somewhere deep inside her. *We've nearly finished. This is the last time we have to do this. I've got to trust him and allow him to protect me. We're a team now. We're Foehammer.*

"Empty." They'd moved down two flights of stairs without incident and Jester was standing looking into the room where she'd been hypnotized. "Bit of a mess though," he continued with a grin. "Looks like a bomb's hit it."

She peered inside but it wasn't as she remembered it. She had an image in her head of a calm lounge space filled with sofas and a snack machine, but she was looking into a war zone. The doorframe was a twisted spiral of metal, the carpet was littered with shell cases and the furniture had been shredded into splinters. "Is this how we …?" she said slowly. "I mean … was this us?"

"'Fraid so," Jester said, nodding. "After you dozed off we had this crazy frat house party … seems nobody hung around to do any clearing up."

She ignored his joke and looked over at the big yellow blast door that the half-deads had come through. It was standing open and there was no sign of any bodies. The only indication that the guards had ever been there was a scattering of assault rifles along the wall.

They moved slowly toward it. The large steel slab had a length of armored cable snagged underneath it that she guessed was a remnant from the failed mechanized mission.

When they were just a couple of feet away, the spotlight from their robot swept across the casing of a machine trapped in the corridor beyond and her suspicions were confirmed.

They paused on the threshold and found themselves looking down a long walkway at another blast door, this one bright orange, in the far distance. About twenty yards away there was a water cooler and behind that an opening in the wall marked by a throw-image of the Stars and Stripes rippling in an imaginary wind.

Jester gave their gun platform a nudge and they moved through the huge metal portal into the long, seemingly empty, space.

It quickly got colder. The air was sharp and dirty-tasting, and as they crept slowly and deliberately toward the opening below the flag, goose bumps rose on her arms and legs.

They passed a couple of small sofas and a row of telephone booths and then the corridor opened into an alcove bathed in a faint scarlet glow. The far wall was lined with workstations, and floating in the center of the space was a large map of North America with the state of Alaska pulsing red.

They stopped to peer down the line of desks, and she became aware of a low rasping sound, like the buzz of a distant chainsaw, coming from the back wall. There was nothing on the floor or any of the chairs but the growling stayed constant: an angry bass rumble that occasionally broke into a series of muffled snarls.

The robot crawled forward a couple of feet then parked and primed its guns with a reassuring click.

Jester gave the command for secondary lights, and a further trio of blue-white beams sprang out. The swivel chairs sharpened to a mass of stainless steel, and bundles of cables appeared under the cubicles.

She swung her gun and searched for movement in the footwells. They seemed empty, and the longer she looked the more puzzled she became about where the noise was coming from. She shot a curious glance at Jester, who returned her look with a flick of his eyebrows and a shrug.

Curtis came to her side and stood peering into the corner. He focused his gaze on what looked like a scattering of small white rocks, and while her mind was struggling to place the objects, he leaned close to Jester and pointed at the robot. "Can you switch that off?" he asked in a whisper. "I want to go take a look."

Jester nodded, and as the young shaman moved up to the machine she felt her heart leap into her mouth. *Heh! Not so quick. Maybe it's really nice to have those big guns in front of us.*

The gun platform powered down and Curtis crept into the room then crouched and studied the floor. After about thirty seconds he placed his hands on the ground and peered under the corner workstation.

Long silent minutes dragged by before Jester hissed out a whisper. "So where are our furry friends?"

Curtis lifted a hand, his eyes still straining into the gloom. "They're dead."

"All of them?"

"There's one left."

"Okay. So what's with the teeth?"

Teeth! Of course. That's what they were.

"That's what's left of the others," Curtis said softly.

"Right. Cool. So where's Mr. Survivor then?" Jester asked.

"I'm looking at him." Curtis said, staying perfectly still.

They exchanged glances and then moved up with their weapons primed. Her eyes took a while to adjust but she was soon able to make out a dog-like animal curled up against the back wall. Its fiery red eyes had dimmed to a faint orange and the line of its jaw was obscured by some kind of hairy tube that curved from its haunches to its mouth.

As she watched, the creature tried to hook the thing deeper into its throat then let out a whine. With a sickening jolt she realized that the object in its teeth was its hind leg, and it was gnawing at its own flesh.

She turned and pushed herself to her feet. The hunger and pain in the sound was making her stomach heave. *Oh man, that's gross. I feel sorry for it now.*

She asked the men what they were going to do, and Curtis stood and moved to her side.

"We put it out of its misery," he told her, and Jester glanced at him knowingly and braced his flamethrower.

She started to turn but saw the jet of fire out of the corner of her eye. The roar of flames was followed by a yelp and a hideous crackling. A cushion of hot air hit the back of her neck and then the smell of burning fur and barbequed meat sent her rushing into the corridor where she stood coughing and fanning her face. Curtis joined her and then Jester came strolling toward them through the thinning smoke. He was nearing the door when a light flashed on the ceiling and he was caught in glistening sprays of water.

"Ah, yes …" he said, looking up with an expression of contentment. "My old friends, the sprinklers."

After wiping his eyes and shaking his head like a dog, Jester turned to her with a look of childish enthusiasm. "So. Interesting heh?" he commented. "A werewolf donut. Never seen one of those before."

"Yeah," she replied, fixing him with a disapproving stare. "Dream come true. Always wanted to see that."

He shrugged and pulled out his cigarettes.

While he smoked, she stood gazing down the corridor toward the big orange bomb door at the far end. It would be fantastic if all the creatures had died out or eaten each other, but she had a strong sense that things weren't going to be as simple as that. Although what had happened to the guards had made their progress easier, something about the changes they were finding was deeply unsettling.

Jester was grinding his stubs into the thick carpet when she caught Curtis's attention and asked him what he thought was happening.

"Good question," he said, rubbing his chin. "I think the half-deads just wasted away and the mutants … well, I think they've gone hypermetabolic."

Jester stuck himself between them. "Hyper what?"

"Hypermetabolic," Curtis continued. "Looks like in the final stage of the virus the body's systems go into overdrive. In the case of the dogs, they got so hungry they ate each other."

"Figures," Jester said, nodding. "But if that's right then I guess we have to consider *why now*."

"What do you mean?" she asked.

"The timing's significant. These things have a sophisticated protection system: the half-deads, the animals and then the crawlers. And right now they're all wasting away."

"So?" she asked.

"So when do you let your guards die out?" he asked pointedly.

The question swam around her mind, and when the answer came she said it out loud, a chill creeping into her bones as the full implication of the words sank in. "When you don't need them anymore," she said, and both men nodded.

Just twenty yards ahead of them there was a door standing ajar with a throw-image above it stating *Conference One* in bold lettering. She saw her companions eye the entrance and then exchange glances and move toward it. They passed a small seating area and then stopped and started to organize themselves. Curtis dumped his bag against the wall and stood gazing into the room while Jester pushed the UGV to the doorway and beckoned her over. Crouching at the drawer in the machine's base, he pulled out a rifle with a fat barrel and passed it to her.

She examined it and found six long chambers primed with wooden stakes. "Harpoon gun?" she asked.

"Yeah. I suggested them after Kotelny."

She spent a while lifting and aiming the new weapon and then swung her shotgun behind her and straightened her back. The men were standing watching her with calm, almost blank, expressions, and she let her gaze drift to the door and the darkness behind it. Tension crept into her muscles and her mouth dried. They all knew the crawlers were in there. The mood since they'd arrived at the White House had been casual and businesslike, and although she was still doing her best to project this image, the thought of facing the vampire creatures left her deeply unsettled. She tried to remind herself that the extra firepower from the robot would make it easier, but what she really hoped was that the hideous things had eaten each other.

Suddenly keen to get the ordeal over with, she lifted the new gun and gave an assertive nod to indicate that she was ready.

Jester maneuvered the UGV inside, and when she took up a position behind him, he leaned close.

"Robot's armed with wooden stakes," he whispered. "It's set to maximum target certainty, but make sure you're always standing behind it."

She nodded, the edge to his voice reminding her that he'd had friends killed by similar machines.

He barked out the command for searchlights and three new beams cut the gloom. The room sharpened into detail and they found themselves looking at a long table dotted with pads of paper and bottles of mineral water. The walls were hanging gardens of colored wires. Clearly once lined with monitors and screens, the hardware had been ripped out and a cascade of tangled cables hung from the recesses.

She moved the unfamiliar gun up and down and scanned the ceiling and floor but it appeared to be empty.

Long moments passed, and then from somewhere high above, the sound of distant drilling rose in pitch.

The long rifle started feeling heavy but she kept tracking while forcing herself to breathe deeply. *I know they're in here. Something about the smell and the tightness in the air.*

There was a rustle, and Jester started to reverse toward her. With their weapons still trained into the room, they stepped into the hallway and he flicked his eyes over his shoulder. "They're not coming out," he told their teammate.

"Yeah." Curtis's voice was close behind them. "It's a guard zone. You either need to walk further in there … or we need some kind of bait."

Jester nodded. "Yeah well, I guess that's my job."

She felt a flash of frustration. She didn't want to see those things jumping all over him. Not again. "Hang on guys …" she said suddenly. "Can't we send the robot in?"

"It's no use," Curtis replied. "They're not interested in it."

"But what about the scanners?" she asked. "Can't it find them and kill them?"

"Well …" Jester examined the UGV with his head cocked. "… It's got state-of-the-art heat, motion and sound sensors, but they're fuck all use if your targets are cold-blooded and staying perfectly still."

She let out a long breath, anger and irritation tightening her jaw. *Weaver knew all this. Everyone did. The whole world's out there laughing at us. We get the best technology money can buy, but it's useless, and in the end we're the suckers risking everything.*

Jester rooted in the pocket of his vest. "Just thinking …" He stepped back into the room and brandished a foil tube. "Maybe some smaller bait would do it." He clenched the beef jerky between his teeth and pulled it open. "I reckon I could just—"

The room exploded with movement. The underneath of the table fell away as a mass of crawlers dropped from their hiding place and snapped up their heads.

The meat was still falling from Jester's mouth when his rifle started barking. The crack of automatic fire hammered her ears as the shriveled bodies sprang onto the chairs and table. The leader leaped toward them but a hail of bullets knocked it into a backward somersault. It landed and knelt shuddering with holes exploding in its torso.

She aimed and put a spike deep in its chest. It fell sideways, mouth open but mute, its arms locked stiff.

The next group came as a wave, five skeletal figures scattering papers and bottles as they scrambled across the polished mahogany.

She swiveled to the nearest and pinned its arm to its stomach. With a screech it bounced off a seat back then lay writhing on the floor.

There were four left. As she snapped up her weapon, an arc of flame curved across the room and their attackers wavered, their skin blackening and sizzling. She picked a target and put a bolt into its left pectoral.

The others were almost on top of them but she only had time for one more shot. She was just about to fire when a faint beep was followed by a drum roll of bangs and her vision filled with a blizzard of projectiles. The crawlers flew upward with wooden shafts springing out of their torsos and were left nailed to the ceiling.

Well ... She let out her breath while an alarm sounded and jets of cold water splashed her hands … *looks like the robot's stake gun works.*

Chapter 58

Weaver

He was watching a kind of horror film. A strange thing to do, but he'd had no news from his guys and that had left a void to fill. For as long as he'd been able, he'd sat in the gloom with his super-intelligent machines switched off. For a while it had been calming, but then his imagination had started to kick in. The terrible things he was conjuring up in his mind had just got worse and worse until he'd decided that anything else would be preferable. That was why he'd rebooted the systems and diverted the latest data from the "soft probing" of Canmore's servers into the simulator. That was why he was using its animation mode to display the senator's intentions, and that was why he was watching the United States fall into tyranny.

The software didn't seem to think that Jester and the team would succeed and had quickly moved on a few days. It showed the arthropod breaking out of the West Wing at night and then explained that there were hints in Canmore's plans that the Brutetek platforms guarding the quarantine zone might "accidentally" open a hole in the fence. Once the thing was free, local citizens would be attacked and Brutetek robots would capture the creature and attempt to take it to one of their research centers. When it was outside the city the thing would be allowed to escape and the robots would consistently fail to recapture it. The arthropod would be left roaming the hinterlands and, to protect the terrified population, the gated perimeter would be strengthened and pushed back. Metropolitan areas would be divided into sectors and a fee charged for passing through the barriers. The senator's companies would provide the hardware and software for the transactions and make a few cents from each crossing. Across the country this would add up to hundreds of thousands of dollars a day.

But even this wasn't enough. The hacking software had found Canmore's plans to pass a law requiring everyone to take regular inoculations against the nonexistent virus. His life sciences business would sell placebo pills and injections that would be taken by millions every month and the profits would be astronomical.

Weaver sat back in his chair and stared in disbelief while the simulator showed him document scans that supported its hypothesis. A cartoon hand appeared and highlighted the title of a presentation and then zoomed to a few bullet points on a business plan. This was Canmore's Project Dublin. It was nothing at all to do with the Irish capital and just a play on words. Dublin was a pun on *doubling*. It seemed the senator wanted a twofold increase in the value of his biggest companies, and to achieve this all he needed to do was let the creature escape.

There was just one big remaining obstacle, and Weaver didn't need the simulator to tell him what it was. Canmore needed to win the vote later that morning and that depended on the presidential situation remaining unresolved. If Jester and the others failed then it was likely the Interim Authorities would become just "The Authorities." The White House would be abandoned and Canmore would effectively take control of the country. The republic would quietly become an empire.

It looked bad. It looked very bad, but, before Weaver had time to contemplate what he'd just been shown, a dialog box appeared and the software politely asked if it could incorporate its own data and insights into an updated simulation. He agreed and found himself watching something even more chilling.

Once again the AIs didn't think that the team would succeed, and they began by showing Canmore winning the vote and getting free rein to take over the operation in the West Wing. The Brutetek robots were reactivated and used to open a path for the arthropod to escape. This is when it changed. A red box flashed announcing "Unintended Outcomes" and a line of smaller creatures was shown crawling along the Washington streets.

Canmore didn't know about the eggs. He didn't know that he would be releasing as many as ten, and he didn't know that killing them was an extremely bad idea.

Weaver felt his stomach twist as the screen split and a variety of hideous scenarios played out in front of him. He saw the young scuttling across the city and making their way into the countryside. They produced more eggs and their growth became exponential. The problem spread rapidly from state to state and the greedy senator's plans were put into action without him having to suggest them. The urban areas were locked down and the rest of the country abandoned. In rural communities the immigrants and less wealthy US citizens were left to become victims of the infestation. They became food.

With his heart beating hard in his chest, Weaver scanned the attached notes. Did O'Keefe and the others know this?

It seemed they did. *This is why your guys are so important,* had been posted just twenty minutes previously. Plausible deniability meant there was no name with the comment, but it was certainly from one of his powerful backers. They knew, and although they would be trying to gather as much political support as they could, it was clear there was no plan B. His team were the only hope.

It was nearly two a.m. The vote was in seven hours, and in that time his guys had to finish the job and ensure that the investigators could get in and identify the president as either dead or alive. It should be possible, but he didn't feel at all confident. The only thing he was sure about was that they were all in way above their heads. Every day things had got more serious and more complicated, and now their options had run out.

He was going to sit and wait, but for the first time since the start of the missions he was glad of the two hundred miles between him and the rest of the team. He would keep faith and he would try to stay calm, even though part of him very much wanted to start browsing for tickets back to England.

Chapter 59

Jodie

Curtis had been gazing thoughtfully at the big orange blast door for some time. They were both standing watching him, and although she desperately wanted to get on with the job, she kept perfectly quiet. It was a sign of their respect that they now indulged his long moments of contemplation, and it wasn't until his posture changed and he took a couple of backward steps that Jester broke the silence and asked the young shaman what his intentions for the next stage were.

"Well, let's start by talking about you guys," he said, turning and rubbing his chin. "What would you do if I wasn't here?"

"Well," Jester shrugged. "I'm guessing there are juniors. I think we should get that out in the open. So I suggest we deal with them and then take on Mom together."

It didn't sound like much of a plan, and once again Jodie found herself asking if they could use their high-tech machine to take on the bulk of the fighting.

"Well, we can certainly give it a chance," Jester replied, studying the robot through narrowed eyes. "Weaver's had net guns put in, but they're pretty much untested. We'll just have to hope they turn out to be useful."

She knew that the ex-army man was deeply cynical about the effectiveness of the UGV and was relieved that he was at least prepared to give it a chance. Their mechanical assistant would help but Curtis was even more important. It was his lightning-fast contribution with spear and sword that had made the biggest difference to their battles, and although he'd cooked something up with Cryboy that involved a lot of drilling, she still didn't know what it was.

She caught his gaze and asked him what he was going to do but he remained vague and unforthcoming. He said that giving her any details wouldn't help and asked them just to get him inside and keep the creatures busy for a few minutes.

She was opening her mouth to question him further when he turned away from her and sat cross-legged on the floor. It was clear he was going to start one of his rituals, and she watched patiently while he made a small bonfire out of twigs and bits of paper and started staring into the flames.

Jester came and stood with her, and together they studied their companion's motionless form. Anxiety started to bubble away deep inside her but she forced herself to breathe slowly and ignore it. She didn't understand where the young shaman went or what he did there, but she knew for certain that he was their secret weapon and she was determined not to disturb him.

When the fire had burned down, Curtis lifted his head and started to work the cinders into a thin disk with the tip of his machete. "I'm going to invite someone to join me," he told them without looking up. "So if he appears, just try to stay out of his way."

"Someone to join you?" she asked, frowning.

"Yeah, well, *replace* me actually."

"And who is this person?"

"Well … To a lot of people his name's Shango."

"Right," she said hesitantly.

She looked back at Jester but he didn't meet her gaze, choosing instead to continue staring at his young teammate with soft thoughtful eyes. *I guess we just go along with this. It's his plan after all.* "Okay." Her voice sounded strange to her own ears, a confused old lady talking to a group of youngsters. "Well … good luck."

Curtis nodded and then struck his knife hard on the ground and dragged it across his wrist. At the end of the movement he gently laid the blade onto the ash and held his arm out. His blood was forming trickles on the steel when he spoke again. "I asked Weaver to make something up for you," he said. "It's in my bag. Long case about the size of a baseball bat." His eyes closed and a strain entered his voice. "I'll be gone for a while now, guys. Good luck and don't talk to Shango when he comes. Just get him in there."

Jester took a wooden box from the holdall and levered the lid off. When he saw what was inside he nodded with approval. "So, we finally get something to knock those things out with. Makes sense, we are *Foehammer,* after all." He passed over a long-handled hammer. "Here, get the feel of this and then I'll strap it on my back."

She sat swinging the long weapon from palm to palm while he lit a couple of cigarettes and blew smoke up at the ceiling.

"That was good work back there you know, Jodie." he commented. "Bulky new weapon and all three shots bang on. I can't help noticing that you're kinda good at this."

She thanked him, and then Curtis let out a short gurgling noise and they turned to see him jerking and making sounds as if he was about to vomit. They watched in silence until the fits faded away and then she changed the subject. "So what about the big plan?" she asked. "All this drilling stuff? Do you think it's going to work?"

"I don't know," Jester replied with a shrug. "I mean, what did he say? He's gone off to find his inner fruit and come back as a mango?"

"Shango," she corrected. "He said Shango."

"Yeah, whatever. Mango … Shango … can you do the fandango? It sounds pretty wacky even for him." He held up his hand. "No, I'm just messing with you. I don't know what he's trying to do, but I trust him. I mean he's really something else. Working with him …" He looked down and shook his head. "… Working with … working with both of you has been an honor."

"Heh!" she slapped his thigh. "It's not over yet. What about a bit of optimism here? We'll get this done and then you can take me samba dancing. Someplace here in Washington."

"Sure."

"And you've got to buy all the drinks and keep your hands off my ass."

"Well"—he cracked a sly smile—"I can promise to buy the drinks."

There was a rustle and they turned to see Curtis pushing himself to his feet. He bent slowly, picked up his canvas bag then hitched it onto his shoulder and turned to face the orange door.

They stood and she called his name but there was no response. Jester shook his head and told her to leave him be. A nudge from his foot set the robot moving toward the door and they followed.

The massive rectangle of steel came swinging toward them and a high whistle pierced her brain like a skewer. Jester stepped back, dropped his hand to his flamethrower and she was hit by a second assault: a slap of cold air filling her nostrils with the stomach-churning stench of ammonia.

"Great," her teammate said, staring into the gloom with the face of a man facing a laborious decorating job. "Here we go again. Cold and dark and stinking of piss." He let out a series of disapproving tuts. "It's like these things haven't even heard of scented candles."

They went further in; a single step taking her onto the metal threshold where she stood swinging her shotgun and squinting into the shadows.

The place was big. A long auditorium lit by faint blue radiance from a giant hologlobe that floated at chest height about thirty yards away.

Jester gave the machine a command, the headlights flicked on, and suddenly they were looking at a cavernous hall, part conference center, part hotel lobby. Lines of leather armchairs sat expectantly below the enormous un-spinning earth, and sofas ran the full length of the walls, each separated by a giant palm standing over a glass-topped coffee table. The left side was taken up by a low stage just a couple of feet high. A lectern stood in the middle with a bundle of cables hanging down the front. The space was eerily still and the air tight and expectant.

Jester glanced at the robot's info panel and she moved up behind him.

"What does it say?" she asked in a whisper.

"*Thermal*, nothing. *Movement*, nothing. *Sound* says the whole place is full of screaming banshees."

She raised her eyebrows. "Useful."

He started to take slow steady steps toward the seating under the globe and she followed with growing unease, the skin along her spine tightening with each passing second. *I know why he's looking there. The nest will be right in the middle. We know how they operate now.*

She was just a few yards from the nearest chair when she sensed movement and spun. Curtis was shuffling toward the front of the hall with his head bowed and his arms swinging at his sides. He made slow shambling progress to the stage and mounted the steps. His hand moved to the strap on his shoulder and in a series of jerky movements he untied the string and poured out the contents. There was a rattle and she caught glimpses of steel glistening in the robot's searchlight beam as a cascade of spears spilled out.

Weird, she thought as she pulled her gaze away. *I hope he does whatever he's going to do soon. We're gonna need his help.*

Jester had reached the first row of chairs and was training his weapons on the area under the holosphere. She caught a glimpse of glossy white domes then stepped up and saw that each of the shells was broken and empty. Something twisted deep in her stomach and her chest tightened. *Fuck it. They've all hatched. Worst-case scenario. The young are around here somewhere and there's a lot of them.*

They crept forward to investigate the dark tubes that were woven between the eggs and her worst fears were confirmed. The shapes on the floor were human corpses, their eyes bruised to purple jellies. There were rips in their clothing and what had at first appeared to be shadows materialized into bloodstains. With a sickening jolt, she saw exposed bone and realized that the bodies weren't intact; there were chunks of flesh missing from the chest and arms. She allowed the fact to sink in, surprised at how calm and accepting she felt. *Seems the young eat meat too. Fair enough. It's sustenance. They're animals.*

They studied the scene in grim silence for a few moments then went back to scanning the walls and corners for threats.

She was flicking her shotgun from one possible hiding place to another when the sound of drilling above their heads got louder. There was a noise behind her and she turned to see fist-sized chunks of concrete raining onto the floor and a long crack widening in the ceiling near the stage. *Great. There's a bunch of those things hiding somewhere, Curtis's a basket case and now Cryboy's bringing the roof down on us.*

It was clear that they needed some kind of plan, and when she'd completed another slow search, she started to move toward Jester. She was just a few steps away, her gaze still probing the shadows, when a series of thoughts started to slot into place in her mind. She realized that the divan bases around the room were all irregular. The dark squares that she'd assumed were footrests were in fact cushions lying haphazardly on top of each other. *If they've been pushed out then that makes space* ... "They're in the sofas," she said in a voice that was surprisingly soft and steady.

Jester was already squinting at the nearest line of seating, and when he heard her he nodded slowly.

Her mind flooded with thoughts. She considered the vulnerability of their position in the middle of room and started to wonder how they could tackle so many creatures at once. Her mouth slowly opened but her words remained jumbled and unvoiced. Before she could speak, Jester swung his flamethrower toward the nearest couch and tightened his finger on the trigger. *He's just going to start. Quick and aggressive. Okay then.* She pressed the butt of her shotgun against her shoulder and tracked with him. *Let's get this done.*

The jet was strangely beautiful; a mass of orange and yellow that reached out and caressed the divan with a lick of rolling fire that triggered a nerve-jangling screech. The upholstery bubbled and blackened and a bunch of spindly limbs and a dome of bone popped out of the smoldering frame. When the creature's gaping mouth appeared, she fired a shot into its body then scanned around her. Legs, heads and shiny carapaces were emerging from all of the sofas. Multiple jaws opened and a second shriek was followed by another and another until her mind was pulsing with a chorus of caustic screams.

Jester stepped forward, waving twin arcs of bullets and flame on the insects in front of him while he cursed under his breath.

She spun to cover the rest of the room and spotted the adult coming fast toward her. A double blast into its chest slowed it then she swept her shotgun through a half-circle and put a cartridge into her nearest attackers. They paused on impact, stopping and shivering before pressing forward again.

The next thing she knew, her gun was empty and she was surrounded. She let the weapon drop and snatched out her revolvers just as the adult reared up on two legs in front of her.

The robot burst into life. A whir of motors was followed by an explosive pop and a cigar-sized torpedo flew out trailing a steel mesh.

She felt a surge of hope. *Good, finally we're not alone in all this. Maybe the machine will wrap them up for us.*

The weights missed the arthropod's body but encircled two of its upper limbs and spun until the cord had tethered the appendages together. One of the young scuttled to its parent's side and the machine spat out a second net.

Jodie watched the package hit the creature and fall to the floor unopened and her optimism drained. *Oh crap. It's useless.*

Another cough sent a third projectile hurtling toward her teammate and she watched its progress in slow motion.

Jester ducked and snapped up his flamethrower, but the wires wrapped around the barrel and a weight hit him on the temple with a crack. A flicker of pain crossed his features and he threw himself sideways.

The machine fired again. The bundle smashed into his raised forearm and bobbed around his gun.

Fuck! She ran toward the machine. It fired again as she slid across the carpet on her knees. The buttons swam in front of her and then she saw the word *Disarm,* punched it and heard the motors wind down.

When she looked up, Jester was tugging himself free of the cables with blood running down his cheek. He got up onto his knees and started firing both weapons just as the creatures started moving again.

"Get to me," he shouted.

She sprang up and aimed her revolvers, putting shots into the young insects' chests as she threw herself toward him.

When she reached his side her guns were empty and the sprinklers were soaking them with water.

"Onto the stage," he said, glancing at the podium. "Stay behind me."

They turned and ran.

A creature moved into their path and reared up. Jester hit it with both weapons and flicked out a leg, knocking it backward with a kick boxer's strike. It turned and landed neatly on all its limbs but by then they had passed it and were at the foot of the steps.

She felt her teammate's arm around her waist and found herself locked to his hip and hauled onto the platform.

They made a stand on the stage. Jester laid a ridge of flames along the floor at the front of the platform and it stopped the arthropod advance. She could see them scuttling backward and forward on the other side and noticed big chippings of concrete falling down the length of the hall. The crack above them thickened and then the big hologlobe flickered and went out.

Jester tried to replenish the line of fire but the flamethrower stuttered and the fuel ran out. He hurled it at the nearest creature and they stood and watched the spray from the sprinklers thin the flames to hissing tongues.

When their defensive barrier was nothing more than a blackened trail, a gap appeared in the middle of the line and the adult pushed through.

They went to the short staircase and blocked its advance with staggered bursts of bullets. As the creature flinched and shuddered just a few yards away, Jodie felt her mind drift, part of her observing the young girl fight so resolutely and efficiently while the rest coldly pondered the futility of their situation. They needed to get out. Jester would have to drag Curtis, but if they could get to the door they stood a chance of escape.

She took a step back and was ramming her last ammunition into her gun when a noise behind her made her spin.

Curtis had fallen to his knees and vomited. His eyes were closed and his skin was wet with sweat. She quickly turned away, but out of the corner of her eye she saw him keel over and heard his head hit the platform with a thud that shook the boards. *Oh man. He's totally gone. This isn't looking good.*

In front of her the smaller arthropods had moved to the base of the stage and were starting to stretch themselves upward.

Leaping forward, she blasted them with tight bunches of shot. When she reached the end of the line, the reality of what they were facing sent a surge of panic through her body. *Seven. Fuck. Way too many.* She started firing again, knocking the climbing creatures back onto the floor until the trigger clicked empty and a terrible hollowness gripped her insides. *Shit! Nothing left.*

She swiveled the gun and was tightening her grip on the hot barrel when the entire line jerked onto their rear legs and a row of pincer-tipped arms grasped the platform. Her body leaped into action, her feet stamping on the claws and the butt of her weapon smashing at the rising heads, but they kept coming. In seconds they'd pulled themselves over the edge and were swarming toward her.

They moved fast. Giant scorpion bodies were all around her clicking their jaws together. Raw panic drove her and she swung in furious defensive circles.

Her palms were sore and her arms aching when an attacker slipped under one of her protective swipes. A long boney limb whistled toward her cheek and she blocked it with the shotgun. A second hit her wrist and sent her weapon spinning into the shadows. She covered her face and something hit the side of her head with the force of a speeding truck. Fireworks exploded in her skull and suddenly she was floating, looking back at the stage as she flew through a curtain of hot fumes. She caught a glimpse of the creatures swarming toward Jester and then smashed into the wall. Pain jolted up her spine. Silver stars fizzed in her vision and for a moment all she could do was blink and struggle to get herself upright.

"Tis a naughty night!"

Everything was blurred, someone was shouting, and the taste of blood was strong in her mouth. The hall was dark and water was falling in fat droplets. At first she thought that a pipe had burst or that the drilling had hit some plumbing, but after squinting at the ceiling she realized that it was rain. Real rain from the outside.

Ignoring the screams of pain, she pushed herself up onto her elbows and focused on the stage. Jester was swinging the hammer and shouting from behind a wall of the creatures.

"Tis a naughty night!"

Metal cracked off bone and bits of shell flew into the spotlight beam. He was moving fast, lunging left and right as he pushed back the limbs with the edge of the heavy weapon.

After a few seconds there was a lull. He'd cleared enough space to rest, and while the arthropods twitched in a loose circle around him he sucked in needy gulps of air.

Jodie found the curve of a revolver handle and starting to reload it, her fingers working quickly and mechanically while her eyes stayed glued to the front of the room.

She'd slotted in the first couple of bullets when the young surged forward again. As the ragged line started to close, Jester kicked up the head of the hammer. She could see the strain showing on his bloodstained face as he steered the whirling metal backward and forward in aggressive thrusts and charges. The juvenile creatures soon gave way, but as they scurried back, the adult pushed through the line and reared up. Her big teammate knocked away its snapping pincers and staggered backward.

For a few eerie moments there was a standoff, each combatant seeming to evaluate the other while Jester's chest swelled and contracted in a series of desperate breaths.

The big creature leaped forward and swiped, but Jester fell back out of reach, jerking up the heavy mallet and smashing the arm out of the way. Before the weapon fell, he grasped it in both hands and thrust it into his attacker's thorax. The giant insect skidded backward and Jester leaned on the shaft and studied it with a cocked head. "Dost thou know the difference, oh freak, between a bitter fool and a sweet fool?" he asked.

The creature drew itself up onto two legs and charged.

"No?" Jester met the attack with a powerful swing. "Then let me show you, fucker!" His swipe caught an arm and knocked off a chunk of shell, but a second appendage caught him on the side of the face and knocked him to his knees.

The young swarmed forward and he vanished behind a wall of shiny segmented bodies. Jodie caught a glimpse of the top of his coxcomb as he pushed himself up, then saw flashes of the spinning hammer. The sound of sharp smacks reached her again, and for a moment she thought he was going to fight his way out. Then she saw the adult push through the circle and her insides turned to ice.

The final stages were difficult to make out. She caught glimpses of Jester's suit and saw flashes of spinning metal, but more and more frequently she heard the whiplash crack of bone hitting bone.

A small gap appeared and she saw her teammate jabbing at his attackers. Whenever he faced one section of the group he took blows from the other. His head was lolling back and forward, sprays of blood flicking into the headlight beam with each impact.

The elder creature made a sudden jump and hit him with three of its upper limbs. Jester left the stage. With the hammer tight in his hands he flew a short distance and landed headfirst with a thud.

Jodie studied his crumpled body for signs of life and then flicked her eyes back up to the platform where the creatures had turned and were scrambling toward her unconscious companion. They had only moved a few yards when they stopped. Their screeching and chattering choked to nothing and the hall fell silent.

She pushed herself higher and strained her eyes. There were a couple of short pillars standing at the back of the stage. Something moved behind them and she realized she was looking at Curtis. His legs were bent backward at the knees and his upper body was rising slowly and smoothly as if he were lying on a hydraulic platform. He tilted mechanically until he was standing broad with his arms out wide and a steel pole in each hand.

Jodie flushed with fear and excitement. It was him but not him. There was a hideous pride and arrogance to his stance and his head was tilted at a strange angle.

She was staring in disbelief when his mouth snapped opened and a roar cut the air. His cry resonated with the power of a massive siren and the hairs bristled to attention on the back of her neck. With his face stretched up at the crack in the ceiling and the muscles and tendons in his arms stretched to breaking point, he let out a second cry. The sound was answered with a violent crash and the walls shook.

She slapped her hands over her ears. *That felt like a bomb. Is that the secret plan? An air-strike? Why not? They're going to nuke the creatures with us inside. I don't blame them. At least they've finally found the guts to take this seriously.*

But no wreckage struck her. She became aware that the air was cold and tasted of aluminum foil and risked a peek. *It wasn't a bomb. There's no flames. No shock wave.*

Another crack was accompanied by a flash of pure blue-white light and suddenly she knew. *It's lightning. Somehow there's lightning down here.*

Curtis's head snapped down and she caught sight of his eyes. They were sunset-red and bleeding from the tear ducts.

He let out the roar again; the sound of a hundred apes compressed into a note so loud and so complete it sent waves buzzing thru her clothes.

The platform erupted into a riot of movement. The young scampered away and the adult charged at him with arms flailing. In a blur of steel he knocked away the pincers and ducked and thrust a metal spear into its abdomen. It swiped but he blocked and replied, striking the side of the boned head with the back of his fist. The creature fell and skidded across the stage and he followed its path and spat a jet of blood onto its head.

The juveniles were fleeing; some had reached the floor and others were crawling off the stage.

Curtis leaped to the front of the platform and glared down at them. He shouted something she didn't understand and started to move with a speed and grace almost beyond human sight. There was suddenly another metal spear in his hand, and with a whiplash flick it appeared quivering in the chest of the leading creature.

He dipped and slung, dipped and slung, and soon every one of the giant insects was pinned to the ground with a steel rod through the chest. When he'd finished he threw open his arms and laughed, a long thunder that rolled along the walls and shook her bones. He aimed a command at the ceiling and it was answered with a flash and a bang. Lightning broke over his head and split into forks. The points of electricity found the metal spears and the room throbbed with a blue pulse. Glass shattered all around her and then the room went dark.

There should have been calm and quiet but as she squinted into the darkness she became aware of an urgent whining nearby. The tone was shooting up in pitch with the ominous electrical strain of a motor ready to burst. *The robot,* she thought, and was turning to look at the machine when there was a bang and something like a hot oven door smashed her into the wall. A prickle behind the eyes and she was gone.

Chapter 60

Cryboy

As soon as it had been clear that his rigs were going to get through the concrete, he'd persuaded Maddie that he needed to be up in the control ship. There was no need for him to risk himself if there were plenty of machines on the ground. Besides, whatever the outcome, it would be better to be in the air. He could move everything and everyone much quicker with the cranes.

The cloudbuster had done its job to perfection, and although its role was over, he'd decided to keep it in position high above them. He was still monitoring its feed, which meant that while he waited for the winch motors to warm up he was watching his own blimp from above, enjoying the way its sleek curved shape contrasted so perfectly with the sharp lines and right angles of the West Wing beneath it.

He tapped to one of the gondola cams and caught sight of the fist-sized sensor as it emerged from the bay door. The tiny machine swung a little then its internal jets brought it steady and he was able to push the joystick hard, zooming it toward a slot in the roof far below. It moved fast and in less than a minute was passing through the laser-cut edges and disappearing inside.

He flicked to the machine's cameras. They showed him a series of empty rooms sandwiched between a strata of stone and wood then he came to the hole in the bunker's reinforced concrete. In seconds he'd dropped into the presentation hall and the plan-view was showing the edge of the stage and a scattering of rubble.

The thermal scanner blinked into life with three gradients of color rising out of the cold background blue. Orange specks and tubes showed where some things were still hot. He recognized the scatterings of glowing pellets as shell casings, the thin blushing sticks as the cooling barrels of discarded weapons, but for a few moments he was confused by the four scarlet ovals near the north wall. The answer came with a pulse of frustration. He was looking at the remains of AGV-26, a robot that he'd painstakingly selected and kitted out and was now junk.

Just as he was beginning to stiffen with anger, his attention was drawn to the three yellow body shapes. Their cores were blushing bright, revealing that they were not cooling and were therefore alive. He absorbed the fact dispassionately, vaguely searching for some kind of appropriate emotional reaction but finding none. *So they're all there. They all survived.*

A flick of a switch broadened the scan range. Further out and arranged in a rough semicircle were eight light-blue ovals, living entities with a temperature just a couple of degrees above ambient. *The arthropods.* His eyes flicked to the scanners and his deduction was confirmed. *Unmoving and neutralized. They've done it. They're ready for boxing.*

A spike popped up on the sound monitor and he reached for his headphones. As he was pushing them over his ears a ring of light pulsed on the motion sensor and his eyes were drawn to the human in the middle of the room. *One of them's conscious and making some noise down there.*

"Poor Tom's a-cold."

It was a strained voice, high and squeaky. Cryboy frowned and started to dab at the controller, pumping up the light absorption to sharpen the image. A motley suit came into view and then, after a few twitches of auto-frame, his teammate appeared sharp and vivid in the center of his screen.

Jester was sitting cross-legged on the floor in the gentle drizzle, his cheeks streaked pink with diluted blood. He was holding a fool's head on a stick. Every few seconds he swiveled it in his hand and the bells on the hat swung and lifted. A happy smiling face moved into view—then a sad one. Happy then sad. Happy then sad. "His name's poor Tom." Jester was staring at the doll with empty eyes and his own face showed nothing; his features were perfectly blank and expressionless. He kept spinning, apparently mesmerized by the alternating expressions on the doll's tiny head. A happy face then a sad one. Happy then sad.

Cryboy tapped out clearance for the reconnaissance team and was just pulling the cans from his head when he heard another utterance.

"Poor Tom's a-cold."

He ran through a final set of scans then rose from his seat. *Weirdo.* Once out into the aisle, he moved toward the cockpit with his fists clenched tight at his side. *Let's hope he gets locked up after all this.*

Chapter 61

Jodie

There was something soft on her face and neck. *That Mom shaking me awake? I can't be late for school. It's too soft and too caring. I must be sick. There's a bowl of soup and a plate of toasty soldiers waiting on a tray.* A firmer force pressed under her elbows. *Someone's lifting me. It's Daddy!* Her heart swelled. *I've fallen off my bike and he's picking me up. I can feel his strong arms under mine.* She felt her head lolling against a broad chest then her body erupted with complaints. Spikes of pain shot down her spine and an ache grew in her skull. *The handlebars had just twisted, locked sideways and I was down. He'd come running. Rubbed it better. He could always make things better.*

Something squeezed her shoulders and a sound hummed near her ears. It was a familiar voice, someone new in her life, someone she liked. She got her eyes open and saw Jester with brown camouflage on his face.

"Can you open your hand for me, Jodie?" he said, squeezing her elbow. "Open and close."

Next he was moving her leg and she was wriggling her toes for him. *What crummy yoga. He must know some better moves than these. Weren't we doing something important?*

Gentle hands leaned her forward and fingers walked up and down her spine. Behind him there was a line of Cryboy's load shifters and the whole space was radiant with light. Ropes were swinging and people were attaching and lifting things. Everybody was focused. The organizer woman and the big Russian lady were there and they were studying her, observing what Jester was doing with affection. There was something else in their expressions too: admiration, pride.

"You can lie back for a bit," Jester told her, and she settled against the wall and let her eyelids drop.

"How are you now?" Jester's voice again.

She opened her eyes and saw he had deep gashes across his temple and his cheeks were crusted with dried blood. "Okay … I think," she told him, and her gaze came to rest on a square of metal by her hip. *Strange thing to find here: a cake tin without a bottom.* She reached out and discovered it was warm to the touch. "What's this?" she asked.

He glanced down and then indicated towards a rectangle of blackened-steel that was lying a few yards away. "Piece of R2-D2."

She nodded and then used the wall and his arm to get herself to her feet. The carpet was spongy wet but the air was clear and sharp and smelled of bonfires. The room was empty. All that was left of the clean-up operation was a single ladder hanging through the crack in the ceiling.

We did it and I survived. She tried to force the fact to lodge inside her, repeating the phrase again and again until she felt the first warm pulses of relief and satisfaction grow in her chest. *We did it and I survived.* She was still trying to get the message to sink in when he slung her arm over his shoulder and started moving her toward the middle of the hall.

Above them a long stretch of metal struts was flashing in the beams of multiple spotlights. She stepped onto a rung and Jester made sure her arms were wrapped around the rope before climbing on beneath her. He made a thumbs-up gesture to the sky and they started to move. As they rose they started to spin, and she saw a figure sitting on the stage watching them through bloodshot eyes. "Curtis," she said, a swell of affection almost choking the word in her throat. She watched him for a while and then turned back to Jester. "Is he okay?"

"Yep," he told her. "I'll come back and get him in a sec. He just wanted to be left alone for a bit."

As they neared the ceiling, she noticed her companion staring at the hall below them with a distant contemplative expression on his bloodstained face. When they'd moved into the big fissure in the concrete, he turned to her and spoke softly with a sense of undisguised wonder. "It was lightning wasn't it?" He shifted his gaze back to Curtis. "He did it with lightning. Got it in here and controlled it somehow."

She waited for him to turn back to her and then nodded.

He shook his head, a mixture of sadness, pride and admiration all glazing his eyes.

They rose through a gaping hole that bristled with shorn steel poles, and then through an elegant lobby lined with ornate marble columns. Looking down, she saw the presidential seal glistening under a thin sheet of water. The gold of the eagle's wings sparkled in the searchlight beams and the sight gave her a pulse of joy and optimism. It went dark for a second and they were lifted silently through a large office where rain-drenched documents lay plastered to a leather-topped desk. She noticed a mug full of rainwater slopping onto the papers and then the air freshened and they were through a narrow roof space and out into the night.

Sudden gusts of clean air set the ladder swaying, and Jester tightened his grip on her. Looking out along the driveway below, she saw the three big Foehammer trucks waiting at the perimeter fence, their red taillights twinkling rubies in the wet tarmac.

Their ascent got faster. Glancing up, she was dazzled for a moment in bright spotlights and caught a glimpse of the long envelope of a vast golden airship filling the space above their heads. The whine of a motor became audible and then they were inside the cage-like frame and stepping onto a mesh floor.

"Well done. Well done. You were fantastic." Maddie's face was close to hers. She felt her arm being patted and then allowed herself to be pulled into an embrace. There was the rasp of nylon as their vests rubbed together then the other woman gently touched her forehead. "You okay?" she asked with concern. "You got some cuts here."

Jodie was nodding and searching for words when she became aware of Helga's bulky silhouette in her field of vision. Her two female companions swapped places and she found herself enclosed in a pair of giant arms, her head pressed against the soft swell of a breast. The strength of the hug, the warmth rising from another human body and the sense of overwhelming security broke something that had been set solid inside her and she found herself weeping. Jerky sobs shook her whole body and she gasped for air. Helga gave her an extra squeeze and suddenly Jodie found herself laughing and crying at the same time, shaking her head and dabbing at her face.

Soon she felt strong arms guide her to a spiral staircase, and allowed herself to be moved up the metal steps toward a rectangle of light. As she neared the top she felt warmth on her cheeks, caught glimpses of light dancing in crystal, and then stepped into a large thickly carpeted lounge. A giant aquarium was magnetically suspended in the center of the cabin and the handrails and window frames were all plated with highly polished gold. "Oh my," she commented, noticing the bottles of champagne in ice buckets on the coffee tables. "A floating whorehouse."

"It is a bit exuberant, yes." Maddie was at her side steering her to one of the low divans. "We're hiring it from a gentleman in the music business."

Seconds later, Jodie was flopping back onto a long fur-lined sofa and allowing her aching body to sink into the cushioning while Maddie stood over her.

"So," their organizer asked. "Anything at all I can get you?"

"Do you know what would be great?" Jodie replied. "A cup of coffee. Just a big milky coffee."

"No problem." Maddie turned on her heels with a hostess's flourish. "Coming right up."

A mumble of low voices stirred her and she turned to see Curtis grasp the rail and pull himself up into the cabin. He paused to scan the room, and then his gaze met hers and a bolt of shock ran though her. His eyes were screaming death. The bright clean white she was so used to had gone and his pupils were surrounded by an ugly purple stain. Time seemed to freeze and she shivered. Memories of the horrors they'd fought in the bunkers were just flooding back when the corners of his mouth crept upward and the familiar warmth of his smile melted her fear.

He made his way toward her in slow painful shuffles, and as he approached she noticed blood crusted under his nose and dried vomit on his chest. He bent and touched his lips gently to her forehead and then lowered himself into the seat opposite and let his head fall back.

"You okay?" she asked.

The same soft smile rose on his lips and he gave a nod. "You?"

"Yeah," she replied. "Tired. Some cuts and bruises." She felt her chin lifting, pride strengthening her voice as she leaned forward. "That was quite something you did down there," she told him.

He nodded again, his body staying quite still while his hand twisted into a thumbs-up gesture.

The jangling of bells from the staircase warned them of Jester's arrival. When he'd hauled himself up, he stood grinning at them with his arms locked on the rails. "Hiya, kids," he said cheerfully, before swinging himself onto the carpet and sauntering toward her. "Great job, Jodie." He dropped heavily to his knees and planted a kiss on her knuckles. "You are a superstar. One in a million."

He dropped back onto his haunches and fixed Curtis with a stare. "And you! You were quite something."

The shaman slowly raised his hand into the thumbs-up sign again and Jester shook his head. "I really don't know what got into you down there," he said with a wink.

He dropped himself next to her on the sofa and started to survey the cabin. "Well, well," he commented after a while. "So we finally get upgraded to business class. Or … perhaps I should say pimp class." After a few moments sitting restlessly, he slid down then crawled toward Curtis's divan and started tapping the base. "Bound to be a stash or two hidden away in a place like this," he said. "There'll be cubby holes. Secret little drawers in the furnishing."

The cuts on her cheeks stung as she smiled and laid back her head.

In time her body sank deeper, her arms became heavier and she drifted in a doze. She was aware of Curtis slumped across from her and the faint tapping as Jester crawled around the cabin, but little else. Her sense of dreamy floating gradually increased, and when she opened her eyes she saw thin ribbons of cloud streaming past the porthole and realized that they'd set sail. A string of pleasant thoughts formed in her mind. She would never have to go down into one of those holes again. Never have to face those things again or shoot people or cut things up. It was over and they were going to get paid. Paid a lot.

Jester's lighter clicked. Then there was a crackling sound and she smelled tobacco smoke mixed with something sweet. Opening her eyes, she saw Maddie coming toward her with a mug of coffee and propped herself up. She was cradling the hot ceramic in her sore hands when she was handed a couple of pills.

"Pain killers," their organizer said kindly.

"Thanks," Jodie replied. "You read my mind."

As she tipped back her head, she caught sight of Jester lying on a velvet chaise longue on the other side of the aisle. The tips of his cigarettes were burning blue embers and when she met his gaze he gave her a Cheshire Cat grin, his pupils giant black moons swimming in his face. She smiled and then let her eyes close and tightened her grip on the mug. *Looks like he found something to keep himself happy*

A little while later Maddie stirred her with some gentle taps on the shoulder. "Do you want to come out onto the gallery?" she asked. "There's something you might like to see."

Jodie nodded and pushed herself to her feet.

Jester was lying with his hands across his chest and his eyes fixed on the chandelier above him. Curtis was slumped asleep, his arms spread out wide, his bare chest slowly rising and falling with soft slow breaths. She stood for a moment watching each of her companions affectionately then followed Maddie down the spiral staircase and out into the crisp cool air.

The night was quiet and still. The vast dirigible had stopped and was being held over a brightly lit mine shaft. Next to the huge pit she could see their trucks: three matt rectangles parked on a patch of waste ground.

Maddie put a hand on the balustrade and leaned close. "Final burial," she said softly. "Thought you might want to see it."

Jodie nodded and they stood and watched the distant vehicles reversing into the pool of harsh light and disgorging a spew of concrete. After a few minutes the surface began to lighten and glisten, and she realized that the hole was nearly full. She let her eyelids close and fell back on her heels until her arms were holding her weight.

"So that's it," she said, a sense of completion welling up in her chest and warming her like a hot drink. "We've done it."

"You've done it, yes." Maddie's voice was soft and sincere. "And you were outstanding Jodie. Amazing."

She tried to let the compliment sink in then found her mind drifting to her remaining concerns. "And the vote?" she asked. "Canmore was going to try and take over."

Maddie shook her head. "Already cancelled. The president and vice president were confirmed dead about an hour ago. There'll be a proper election in a few weeks."

Jodie allowed the information to sink in and then voiced her final doubt. "And we're going to get paid?" she asked. "The money's there?"

"Yes," Maddie told her. "Just as Weaver said. The money was the easy part. You guys did the hard bit."

While she absorbed the news, the pitch of the vessels motors suddenly rose and the ground started to slip away.

She glanced up behind them and saw the captain and a second tall figure sitting next to him in the cockpit, their faces lit in the faint orange glow of the ship's controls. *Ah. So there's Cryboy,* she thought. *I was wondering where he was.*

They watched the land roll beneath them in contemplative silence, and in time the sky on their right began to lighten. White crests became visible on the waves below, then they passed high above an empty beach and drifted back over land.

When the horizon had brightened to a deep blue, Maddie reached over and touched her hand.

"Jodie, I wanted to ask you something. Will you tell me honestly? Girl to girl? Did I do okay?" She held up her palms. "What I mean is. I didn't start too good. We thought it was going to be much easier. We only half-believed what was going to be down there, and I didn't have any real combat experience. I thought I knew a lot but—"

"Heh!" Jodie tried to sound jolly and upbeat. "We're all here, aren't we?" She put her hand on her teammate's and gave it a squeeze. "Maddie, you did okay. We all did okay."

Chapter 62

Weaver

It was all fairly wonderful. The colors around him were bright and sharp and he finally understood how well-designed the building's roof terrace was. In fact, he'd decided that everything that Sophos and his chums did was pretty damn cool. That was why they had so much cash. It was because they knew how to get stuff done and they had exacting standards. The world of academia could learn a lot from those guys, and maybe he was the one to start showing them the way.

He carefully balanced his glass next to him and gazed back up at the late afternoon sky. Just visible on the horizon was the shrinking oval of a vast intercontinental speeding its way to Switzerland. The last of his temporary employees was making her way home and there was no doubt they'd done a brilliant job.

He watched until the blimp had faded to a distant dot then picked up his wine, drained his glass and let out a loud belch. He heard the slosh of water and the crack of ice cubes nearby and turned to see Maddie dabbing the base of a bottle with a napkin. He yawned as she walked over, a long-drawn-out stretch that was only just closing when she reached him and held out her arm.

"More champagne?" she asked politely.

He peered at the bottom of his empty glass, nodded and held it out.

She poured slowly, carefully flicking her eyes between his face and the rising foam. "So," she said when she'd finished. "You happy?"

He looked up and found himself stifling a second yawn. "Yes. Very happy. Amazed. Delighted … shattered. Can't believe it really. We did it. Well, they did it. That Curtis kid is definitely …" He stared into his glass for a while and then took a sip. "He really is … I don't know the details of the plan with Cryboy and the drilling and all that … but it worked. I mean, you went down there … you saw … he stunned them with lightning. That was it, wasn't it?"

"Yep. Pretty incredible when you think about it." Maddie took a mouthful of drink. "I was getting more and more worried about Curtis, to be honest. Cryboy was in my ear stressing about the fact that his powers were going to run out. He'd heard that he was negotiating for cash and was absolutely certain that a shaman can't take payment. Said all the protection would fade away."

"You should've said. I could have told you."

"Told me what?"

"About the negotiations. He wasn't getting money for himself. It all went abroad." When he saw her frown he started to nod. "Yeah, rainforest foundations in South America. Some African terraforming funds, but that was it."

"Nothing for him?"

"Not a cent."

She snorted and tossed her head. "I wish I'd known. I thought the negotiations were confidential."

"They had the choice, but they all left it open." He waved an arm toward the meeting room. "You can see for yourself if you want."

"Really? So what about Jester? What did he want?"

"Him! He bartered like a madman. Seventy-five million to veteran's funds."

"Wow! And anything for himself?"

"Yeah." The roof seemed to wobble for a second and he swayed a little before placing his left hand on the plant holder and balancing himself. "He wanted twenty bucks in cash." He tapped his right hip. "I gave it to him myself."

"Twenty bucks?"

He gave her a slow exaggerated nod. Some wine sloshed onto the terrace but she got the point. The guy really was unhinged. He'd done all that and hadn't even taken any payment. But then she knew what he was like. She'd had to work with him and that can't have been easy.

Maddie puffed out her cheeks then put her hand to her mouth to cover a small release of gas. "We know about Cryboy," she continued, sticking out an arm to lean on the side of the big box. "But what about Helga?"

"Well. She took some money at least. A million for her. Fifty million for a children's charity in Russia."

"And Jodie?"

"Modest sums. Twenty million to a care home in Texas and ten million into her own account."

"Well, fair enough." Maddie nodded and started to smile. "She earned it."

He nodded and let his gaze drift back up into the clouds again. It seemed everybody had got what they wanted and he was now the richest academic in the city. And why not? Sophos had been right to choose him. Some of the other junior lecturers could be a bit wimpy but he'd always known he had the edge. He had a military mind and the solid nerves needed to see a difficult mission through to the end. He wasn't just Dr. Julian Weaver, he was *the man*.

Chapter 63

Cryboy

It was the first time he'd chatted to someone he knew. Sure, he'd communicated with his fellow hackers for years, but he'd never actually met any of them. They all had tags and avatars, but Helga just had a simple picture of herself, and when she sent a message she used her normal way of speaking. He could almost hear her talking to him and that was cool. She was alright. Her English was patchy but she was genuinely funny.

He couldn't do what she said though. She wanted him to promise that he would go out and get a hot meal. She was trying to bully him into eating borscht soup and pelmini dumplings, but there was no way he could leave his machines. He was finally making some progress on the broken missile platform mystery and he had to stay and see it through.

Trawling through the reports from the early robot investigations of the West Wing had yielded an interesting result. The broken hardware wasn't the only thing they'd found up there, there'd also been a body. Some low-level military technician by the name of Private Wilson. The soldier's hemorrhaged eyes suggested he'd been attacked by an arthropod, but those creatures liked to bury downward, so finding him on top of the building was pretty strange.

He had the very best data retrieval bots, and even though they had to break into encrypted military files, the results were slowly compiling in front of him.

A timer popped up on one of his screens and told him that the next update wouldn't be ready for four minutes. That was enough time to put in an order so Cryboy decided to make his new Russian friend happy. The details of a local restaurant were already open on one of his smaller micros so he started to make his selections.

There, he'd done it: soup, dumplings, bread, salad, the lot. He told her straight away. Strumming the message with a few flicks of his fingers, then sitting waiting for the reply. She was somewhere out over the Atlantic and struggling to get to sleep so might be slow to respond. No problem, he had plenty to do.

The results of his supply chain search on the missile system started coming in. The unit had been procured from an aerospace firm called Soljet. It had been tested and passed at their factory in Jefferson Missouri then signed over to a transportation company.

Except that something wasn't quite right. He ran benchmarked timing assessments and everything came back highly suspicious. The item should have arrived in Washington within forty-eight hours but it hadn't, it had taken over a week to turn up. So what had happened to it in the meantime?

He didn't need to put the question into his systems, his AI was smart enough to set off on its own and they'd already hacked the local logistics networks and tracked the big piece of hardware north to Wisconsin. Here, his automated detective got stuck at a dead end and he had to intervene. It took him just a couple of minutes to get into a warehouse file and start reading through the scanned dispatch dockets.

There it was. For no apparent reason the missile array was signed over to a company called Nightingale Expert Systems. Wow. None of this made any sense, but it was all so irregular it would definitely yield results. He just had to find out who owned this company and where they took it.

There was a buzz on the intercom but he ignored it. Probably a mistake or some bible bashers.

He worked on both lines of enquiry simultaneously. He started running traces on Nightingale and managed to find out that the hardware was put on a blimp and sent even further north. The route came to him city by city and ended at a depot in Alaska. Alaska! This was gold dust.

His ears filled with more buzzing and then a ping. Finally a result on the dead soldier. He'd also been based in Alaska at Fort Wainwright. Fascinating.

The intercom buzzed again.

A theory had formed in his mind but he needed to check it. He could get all the data. The relevant numbers were just sitting on the transfer slips. The machines couldn't read them because they got stuck on slang and bad handwriting. He could though. No problem. It was the weights. The answers were in the weights.

A messenger notification. Helga had sent the phrases *Bon appetit* and *Priyatnogo appetita.* Strange. She must be half-asleep.

The paperwork showed the air defense system weighing three thousand nine hundred pounds when it left Missouri. It was two thousand seven hundred when it landed in Alaska. This was so easy. The manual gave the weight of the motors and ammunition trays as about twelve hundred. Bingo! He'd been right. When it had arrived at Fort Wainwright it had been hollow.

Now to check the soldier's file. He weighed one hundred sixty-eight pounds. And the weight of the creature when they lifted it out of the West Wing? Easy. The airship's winch computer had that on record so it was a straight job of subtracting the mass of the lead box. There it was, two hundred and seventy pounds.

Pins and needles tingled up his arms and legs. This was just too good. He just knew the numbers were going to match and held his breath while he waited for the final figure. There it was. On arrival at the West Wing the missile array weighed three thousand one hundred and thirty-seven pounds. A fit to within one pound.

So why was the private first class put in the big hollow space inside the machine? Bait. Simple as that. He was probably unconscious and used to lure a hungry creature inside. This was so wonderfully planned and executed that the result of the final search came as no surprise. Nightingale Expert Systems was registered in a secretive offshore territory, but he'd managed to crack the share documentation. It was actually majority owned by Brutetek. By Canmore.

Epilogue

Close to the edges of Chicago's eighteenth gate there was a ribbon of shacks and shops that ran along the old highway. Here, small market stalls nestled under flapping polyethylene awnings and family dwellings were strung up inside the shells of old trucks. Here, untagged immigrants lived happily on a rich life of barter and scavenging. They sold reclaimed tools and clothing on their front steps and roasted an array of subprime foodstuffs on smoky oil drum fires. It was an area that struck terror into the protected citizens of the gated zone, representing all their worst fears concentrated in one location: foreigners, crime and disease.

This particular evening was, much as it always was, warm, windy and wet. Gusts were tugging at the strips of makeshift roofing and sending metallic-tasting drizzle into the faces of the shopkeepers when a familiar figure appeared in the distance. He wore no coat or cape against the elements, only a suit of red and black motley and a three-pronged coxcomb. As he plodded heavy-footed past the first of the stands, he raised his hand to the owners. The locals acknowledged him with a range of shouts and waves which he dutifully returned. When he encountered a large pothole or section of rusting automobile, he skipped or danced across it with startling dexterity, more ballet dancer than wrestler, and then returned to his heavy, exaggerated trudge. Jester was back.

He made his way directly to a hostelry inside an abandoned tanker and greeted the affable Cambodian barman with an ironic military salute.

Jack smiled at him as he walked toward his place at the end of the counter.

"Hi Mr. Jester, Where you been?" he asked, before frowning and peering closely at his best customer's face. "You okay?"

His visitor stopped and looked puzzled before lifting his hand to his neck. "Oh, these? Love bites. Ran into an old flame. Know what I mean? Some of those girls can't control themselves."

Jack nodded sagely, his face almost registering comprehension before he jerked up his chin. "No see you for a week."

Jester blew out a puff of air and dropped himself onto his stool. "Yeah, I had to go on some trips."

Jack turned to the refrigerator and started pulling out bottles. "What you been doing?" he asked.

“Oh, you know, the usual … bit of this … bit of that … bit of saving the world.”

An array of liquors were methodically laid out on the bar.

“Saving the world, heh?” Jack filled the shots and then popped the top on a beer. “That good?”

Jester handed over a crisp twenty dollar note then knocked back his first guaro and pressed a couple of cigarettes to his mouth. “Savin’ the world?” he reflected with his eyes closed. “Not bad. Long hours, but the pay’s excellent.” He lit his Marlboros and watched the smoke drift up to the manhole. “And I made some new friends.”

“New friends? Friends good,” Jack confirmed.

“Yeah. You’re right. Friends good.”

“I see them.” The young barman waved his hand down the counter. “You bring them for drink.”

“Yeah, maybe I will …” Jester gazed up at the blank TV screens hanging on the back wall and his eyes went watery and distant. “Yeah, maybe I will. They’re an interesting bunch, Jack. I think you’d like them.” As he finished speaking there was a faint crack and the ice in his glass split open. He looked down, grinning, and watched a tiny bubble drift toward the surface of his liquor and release itself into the air with a gentle pop.

—End—

Coming soon:

Foehammer Strikes

Foehammer Falls

Acknowledgments:

My gratitude, of course, to Killing Joke for providing the inspiration. Many thanks also to the great Mike Coles for the artwork. Rory, you were there with support and enthusiasm through some of the darkest times - I am grateful. Most of all though, to Polly, for putting up with me.

Thoughts and comments to;
duncancampbellwriter@gmail.com

9410863R00165

Printed in Great Britain
by Amazon.co.uk, Ltd.,
Marston Gate.